CITY OF ICE AND DREAMS

CITY OF ICE AND DREAMS

◆ ◆ ◆

A novel

J. G. Follansbee

Print ISBN-13: 9780984905461
Ebook ISBN-13: 978-0-9849054-7-8
ISBN: 0984905464
Library of Congress Control Number: 2017918301
Fyddeye, Seattle, WA

Seattle, Wash., USA
Cover art by Christian Bentulan
http://coversbychristian.com/
Edited by John Paine
http://www.johnpaine.com/
Proofread by Edith Follansbee

For Mom and Dad

CHAPTER 1

THE REPETITIVE SHRIEK OF THE ferry's klaxon drowned out Sento's pounding on the cabin doors. She hammered three or four times on each before switching.

"Everybody out! You have to get to the beach. The ship is sinking."

Frightened *inmigrantes* crowded the passageway. Hundreds of desperate black, brown, and white faces searched the armed woman's face for reassurance. She feigned a smile.

I'm scared I won't make it either. I'm more scared I won't get answers.

Sento urged them toward the stairs and doors onto the deck. A freezing Antarctic wind tinged with spray greeted them.

There weren't enough life vests.

"The AI is still in control. Wait for the crew's instructions. They'll tell you what to do."

Finished with the staterooms, she checked other spaces where she'd seen the group of pilgrims headed to Isorropia. They hoped to find a new start. They packed themselves into closets, heads, corners under stairways. The ferry from Punta Arenas was overcrowded, but that was standard for smugglers of human beings, the coyotes. She sought out an old woman.

Stray tawny hairs drifted in front of her eyes. She flicked the hairs behind her right ear. Someone once said she had the face of Aphrodite but the jaw of Hercules. *Who said that to me? I wish I could remember.*

The shipowner admired her buff upper arms and shoulders. He hired her as security for the trip from Chile to Nordenskjöld. He gave her a flak jacket. He compared the trip to rowing across a pond. She bought a pistol to protect herself.

The engine room was flooding.

Sento found the woman. She was a disidentified. Like ghosts, the disidentified inhabited a place between society's light and dark. They were living husks, legal non-entities, socially dead, without names, with all data about their existence expunged from every database and document that might have stored facts and figures about their lives.

"We have to go. We're taking on water."

"Go away." The voice was muffled behind a gauzy cloth.

Sento's eyes lingered on the tulip-shaped welt on the woman's forehead. The flower signaled an environmental crime of the worst kind. The bony growth warned the public to ignore the marked woman or face sanction. As if absently attacking an itch, Sento raised her fingers to her hairline, expecting to find a similar welt of disidentification.

Nothing was on Sento's brow, but the younger woman thought there should be. Instinct as vague as the sun dogs on the Antarctic sun suggested something similar had happened to her. In her case, the procedure was a failure, or botched. She couldn't nail down her feeling. She removed a food pack from her pocket and lay it near the woman's bare, calloused foot.

The ragged woman's shiny eyes stared at the meal. "They'll report you. They'll put you in jail."

The Bureau of Environmental Security didn't always ignore illegal acts of compassion, but Sento wasn't worried. "I don't think there's any bessies on this rust bucket. Come on, we have to leave."

"You have a beautiful heart. A little water, maybe?"

Sento handed the woman a sealed bulb of fresh water. When they first met, Sento wanted to ask about the crime, but the woman wouldn't know. Dissing—invented a century ago as a response to public outcries against capital punishment—not only erased all official traces of life, but the latest practices permanently damaged parts of the brain that held memory important to identity.

The woman probably didn't know her real name. Her memory was an empty shell, excised like a painting from its frame. Sento's memory was a frame with only a few flakes on the canvas, frustrating in its fragmentation.

Twenty-three months, one week, five days ago since I last knew my name or where I'm from. Was I dissed? Was I hurt? Or have I always been this way?

She had two facts: The date she woke up in an operating room and a certainty as solid as the spine of the Andes that the answers to her identity were at the bottom of the world. If she did not find the answers, she was condemned to a life like the damaged creature on the *Kildare*'s deck.

The dissed woman tore open the water pouch with hands that belonged to a skeleton. "Do you know why the ship has stopped?"

"Engine failure. We're running out of time." Sento hadn't seen any crew since the order to abandon ship. They were frightened too. They paid her to keep the *inmigrantes* away from them. That didn't mean let them die. as far as Sento was concerned. "Please. You'll drown."

She reached out to the woman's greasy clothes, but the elder shrank away.

Immigrants peered out a nearby porthole, terror in their faces. One screamed. A motorboat sped away from the ferry toward the beach below the hamlet of Nordenskjöld, a kilometer or two away. Sento recognized the captain and cursed him.

She protected the old woman from the building chaos. "We have to go. Now."

"Iso." Koi Nahim, one of the pilgrims, 11 or 12 years old, dropped to his haunches near Sento and the woman, his mop of black, curly hair in need in a comb. "Come to Isorropia, both of you."

Sento first heard the name spoken by the pilgrims on the road south. It represented salvation. The word meant something different to Sento.

"At least he pronounces it correctly," the woman said. Sento wondered if she was once a teacher. "Idiots say 'I so.'" The elder dropped the gauze cloth, which hid sores on her lips, to bite into the food pack. "Isn't that right, boy? It's the way moronic dreamers talk about Isorropia." She said the first syllable like the "e" in "equal."

"Iso." The youth nodded to add emphasis.

"It doesn't exist." The woman relished the chewy food. She ignored the pandemonium. "Think El Dorado or Eden or similar nonsense." The woman addressed Koi. "Child, Isorropia is about as real as the million euros in my hip pocket." She rasped and dismissed Koi. "Go back to your rat hole and dream your dreams."

Sento dreamed of a city as well, like an heirloom diamond, mysterious and captivating.

The youth lifted his head in defiance and marched off.

"Harmless little son." The dissed woman sighed. "Everyone wants a new life, sooner or later. That's Antarctica's promise, now that the West Antarctica Ice Sheet is practically gone."

"We'll both be gone if we don't get away." Sento lifted the old woman to her feet.

The klaxon stopped and the interior lights dimmed.

A tall, dark-skinned man in a tattered parka came up to Sento. "The batteries are failing. So are the pumps." Hosea was the pilgrims' leader. They'd talked a little.

"What about the lifeboats?" Sento said. "Have you lowered them?"

"They're gone. They're weren't enough."

"There's hundreds of people still here." Sento suppressed her shock. The rising panic was infectious. "Fucking coyotes."

"What do we do?"

Sento mind raced. She'd seen another boat on board, wrapped in plastic in the cargo hold.

"How do we get it out?" Hosea said.

When they boarded at Punta Arenas, the *Kildare*'s captain showed Sento a printout of all the passwords and DNA identification override codes to the ferry's com network. She needed them to access restricted spaces. Her minds-eye com network implants hadn't worked since she woke up in Valparaiso two years ago, but she knew of a console in a utility room.

As *Kildare* wallowed in the swell, Sento led Hosea to the console. Her hands trembling from fear and cold, she tapped in the pass codes and accessed the ship's AI. "All we have to do is tell the cargo bot to bring the boat to the deck."

Sento and Hosea stepped outside. A cranky, demanding *Arf! Arf!* reached her. Sea lions had gathered on nearby rocks, below a sheer cliff that knifed into the Weddell Sea. Behind the cliff rose mountains crowned with glaciers. The pinnipeds' yap sent a spike of anxiety up her spine, signaling another unpleasant crumb of memory. Like a submarine's periscope, the feeling meant something dreadful lay below the surface of her consciousness. As always, though, the substance was out of reach. One thread tied everything together: home.

Hosea tapped her shoulder and indicated *Kildare*'s cargo deck. A six-meter bot crawled out of a hatch carrying a bundle wrapped in milk-white plastic. The bot and its bundle resembled a spider carrying an egg sac. Sento cut off the plastic, which revealed an inflatable boat about five meters long, complete with electric outboard motor. It was already inflated. Overhead, a derrick slewed into place, guided by the ship's AI. A hook lowered, and *inmigrantes* attached it to the boat. On cue, the ship's AI lifted the boat and lowered it to the icy water.

A Jacob's ladder draped over the ship's side. The ladder handled only one person at a time, or a parent holding a small child. Sento stifled her impatience. It would take hours to offload the ferry. The navigation AI kept the ship's head into the breeze, but the sea boiled. Immigrants puked or lay on the deck, seasick. The frenzy magnified Sento's own terror, but the act of guiding pilgrims to places on the boat kept her focused and calm.

The boat settled low in the water, overloaded. The beach was only 250 meters away, though the immigrants would have to push through breaking surf. Most people were soaked to the skin and hypothermic by the time they collapsed on the dry land.

Sento marveled at the determination of the immigrants, a laser-like focus on survival at all costs, of striving toward an abstraction of hope in a land none of them had seen, except in holo-pics or vids. Poets and promoters called Antarctica "The Last Frontier." After the Warming, Antarctica was the only continent not conquered by humanity *en masse*. That was changing.

Her place was on shore as well, though not with the pilgrims. She followed the feeling like a migrating bird, driven on and on southward. Only a sense of duty, of doing a job until it was done, kept her on *Kildare* until everyone was off.

Hosea fought to bring the boat back to *Kildare* for another load. The remaining passengers on deck urged him on as twilight approached for the four-hour night. Darkness was as deadly as the freezing sea.

Sento felt *Kildare* rock sharply to port. The roll surprised her. *Is the AI trying to compensate?* Instinctively, Sento donned one of the remaining life vests.

Kildare rolled further to port, making the climb down the flapping Jacob's ladder nearly impossible. Arms and hands reached down to loved ones who had made it to the boat, but the foaming sea between them was a chasm akin to a castle's moat. Sento winced when a child's arm was crushed between the boat and the hull.

The ship drifted against the background of the ramshackle town.

The cargo bot knocked—*pushed?*—an immigrant into the water. The others stampeded in the narrow space. The *Kildare* pitched forward, then rolled 45 degrees to port, then back to starboard, the ship lumbering as if drunk. Immigrants dropped into the frigid sea, belongings falling after them as if trying to catch up.

The bot appeared unaware that it tread on humans like an angry bull. Sento remembered something about semi-autonomous industrial bots, about an emergency shutdown lever or switch. Another roll of *Kildare* dropped her to the deck as old men and toddlers tripped over each other. She crawled toward the bot, and she spied a bright yellow patch on the side of its body. A round red button poked out from a box. Sento reached out, and pain stiffened her entire body.

The water was so cold that her muscles seized, and she took huge, panting breaths. She'd fallen into the sea. *The bot pushed me.* Something splashed beside her, and she snagged loose clothing floating in the chop. The attempted rescue was irrational, but instinctive. She couldn't help herself.

A baritone voice deep within her mind yelled "Kick! Kick!" and she kicked her feet. The movement turned her body toward the shore, and though the salt water stung her eyes, she saw the surf crashing on the pebbly beach. The cold sucked the heat out of her body like a vampire. In pain, she kicked again and pulled with her free arm, dragging the immigrant. She echoed the voice: "Kick! Kick!"

In her half-conscious state, the voice was accompanied by a shrouded face that shined like a new silver coin. The water's chill brought to mind the emotion of a woman, older by a few years, diffuse, jealous, a loving rival.

Sento touched bottom. After another kick, she had enough purchase to stand up, but no energy to reflect on her phantoms. She collapsed prone on the beach, coughing. She vomited sea water and the remains of her dinner. Her body vibrated with cold.

Her shivering kept her from standing, but the tide was ebbing, leaving flotsam from *Kildare* among the detritus of past tides. Bodies punctuated the mounds of driftwood, seaweed, and barnacle-encrusted garbage. The woman Sento had dragged ashore lay an arm's length away, her skin blue, her sore-encrusted lips white, her eyes already milking over. The bone welt on her forehead was like a stone on the grave she would never lay in.

I've survived.

Sento's ears popped and water drained away. Men, women, and children keened over dead loved ones. If she put her arms out for balance, she could stand, and her eyes focused on Koi, who stared at her as if she were an apparition. She fell to her knees, gravity overcoming her weakened muscles.

A silver thermal blanket adorned his shoulders, and he handed one to Sento. Donning it, her trembling eased, and her mind regained awareness of what had happened. The bot had knocked her over the side when she tried to shut it down. Deliberately or by accident, she couldn't say. She wiped salt from her eyes and searched the horizon.

"Where is it?" Sento raised her voice at Koi. She couldn't hear herself for the roaring in her ears. "Where's the ferry?"

He shook his head, mute, as if stunned. He knelt in front of Sento and cupped her face in his hands. Her body was so numb from the cold that her emotions slowed to a crawl, but she heard Koi say with the certainty of the saved, "Boat is gone." He gazed over the bay, the horizon empty, the sun already below it, resting from its low-energy journey. "We go to Iso now."

Isorropia. A city of ice and dreams.

CHAPTER 2

SENTO WAS DIRTY, HUNGRY AND tired, but relatively unscathed. She was angry as well. The coyotes had abandoned her and the pilgrims. The survivors stood like zombies, blank-faced and lost. She had little in common with the pilgrims, beyond the betrayal. While they were searching for a new beginning, she was on a hunt for herself.

Nordenskjöld was on her right. A camp, probably full of refugees, was on her left. She took tentative steps.

"Sento!" Hosea hobbled up. "Where are you going?"

Sento barely had the energy to speak. "The town."

"But that's where they went."

"Who?"

"The captain. The crew."

Sento stopped. The town was a collection of shacks. A whirring wind generator stood over it. "I'll take my chances."

"Sento, wait. We need your help."

She bit her lip. She tried to help on *Kildare*. What good did it do?

"Stay with us for a few minutes. We need to find shelter. Can you help?"

A few camp dwellers approached, bringing food and UN blankets. No one came from the town.

Sento sighed. "Just until you're settled."

The refugee camp had a rough street grid and makeshift signs in Spanish, Portuguese, and English. As she stared at them, a bearded man brushed against her. She put her hand on her pistol. He grinned, his teeth stained and his beard matted, more kin to the dogs that darted in front of her than the humans. He had an aura of familiarity, not unlike the old woman, but without the welt. It was another of Sento's foggy recollections. He gestured to follow, then disappeared down a narrow alley.

Compelled to follow, Sento turned the corner, but he had vanished. She found herself surrounded by metal. Hands on hips, she examined one machine with the scrutiny of potential ownership. She already knew a fragment of its history. She touched the chrome arm, which needed polish. She thought of the silvery man.

"Be careful," said a doughy man at a table. "It bites."

"I know," Sento said. An identification number and a stenciled KILDARE marked its flank. "It nearly killed me."

The man lifted a soldering iron from a circuit board. "I brought it here this morning from the beach. You must be one of the survivors of that shipwreck. How did it try to kill you?" He folded his arms, mirroring Sento's thoughtfulness.

"Pushed me overboard."

"Doesn't surprise me." A line of smoke wafted up from the board. "Worst AI programming south of the equator." He scratched the wispy whiskers on his double-chin. "Poor quality catches up to the maker eventually."

The man called himself Bruce Nay. He had acquired three large shipping containers, creating a home, a workshop, and a warehouse packed with tens of thousands of parts from bits of wire to generators the size of a man's head. His energy impressed Sento. *Kildare*'s cargo manipulation bot was parked outside among larger pieces, including a modified ground car with caterpillar tracks. Sento eyed the nooks and crannies of the salvage yard.

Nay said, "Most people called me Bruce."

"The survivors need a place to stay, just for the night, so they can regroup. Is anyone in charge here?"

Bruce laughed. "It's a refugee camp, not a military base. Are you proposing to squat, or forcibly take over?" He indicated Sento's gun.

"They're peaceable. They've had their fill of violence." Sento imagined breaking the *Kildare* captain's arm. "The survivors'll pay somehow, I think."

"This isn't a hotel. Don't expect room service." Bruce spoke as if shipwrecks and drownings happened every day.

Sento heard a northern European accent to his English. "I suppose you'll offer a discount due to the lack of towels."

Bruce frowned, then smiled. "I appreciate sarcasm. It so happens I'm cash short at the moment. Anything, euros, renminbi, even US dollars would be good. What about you? Are you with them?"

"I'm making my own way."

Sento brought Hosea, his wife Awilda, Koi, and the others to the yard. Bruce scratched his beard as he watched the decrepit group trudge in. He admitted that he was a squatter, the same as everyone in the camp. "The Chileans and Argentinians have been fighting over the Antarctic Peninsula for centuries. Even the Brits had a claim once, though they can hardly keep their country together these days, so I hear." He lunged at a young woman fingering a scratched box alone on a shelf. "Don't touch that. That's the only one I have."

The woman, Gwen by name, moved her hand away. Her eyes met Bruce's.

Though his mouth opened, no sound emerged for a second or two. "I mean," he said, quietly, "be careful, please." He lowered his eyes, then glanced back at her.

Hosea handed Bruce a few coins and a small tablet computer. The squatter picked up his soldering iron. "You're leaving tomorrow, right?"

"If you want us to," Hosea said.

Gwen examined another piece of broken electronics.

"Maybe two nights," Bruce said, a sour, pained looked on his face, "if you pay."

The junk yard was like a hedgerow, or a forest with a thick understory. Enterprising pilgrims discovered tarps or blankets which they draped over the junk as if it was ready-made frames. It was soon a camp within a camp. Sento kept an eye out for the feral-looking man who had led her here, but he did not reappear. One pilgrim started a fire in a tiny, but cozy open area.

As the flame flared, Sento remembered a moment in her childhood. She was five or six, in a shelter near the ocean. The sand was soft, the artificial light low, and the adult sleeping next to her breathed deeply. *Father?* The adult's arm, a man's arm, was draped over her. *"Snug as a bug."* The warmth of his words and his strong arm nearly overwhelmed her. She searched the pilgrims' faces, as if expecting to find him.

Disappointed, she extended a hand to Hosea. "Well, Mr Taft, I wish you luck."

Hosea took her hand, reluctantly. "Please, it's Hosea. You're not staying with us?"

The childhood memory faded. It was another fragment, like the dusty piece of a jigsaw puzzle found under the living room sofa, disconnected from everything.

"Where will you go?"

Sento didn't know the answer.

Koi stood a short distance away, eyes pleading for Sento to stay. "We won't be here long. Iso is near."

How is he so certain? "Your people will be fine, Hosea. They trust you." Sento laid her hand on his shoulder. She brushed her finger on Koi's cheek. She liked the immigrants, especially Hosea's pilgrims. They were undaunted, even bound, by the misfortunes they shared. Awilda worried Sento the most. Even as the others recovered a little from the disaster, her condition had deteriorated. She constantly held her belly as if trying to sooth herself and the unborn child. Older women around the fire whispered in pity.

Sento wasn't an *inmigrante*, however. She wasn't running away, escaping a bad situation, or looking for a new start. She was running toward something, though she couldn't say exactly what, except that it was south. It was probably called Isorropia.

"At least rest a while with us," Hosea said. "You're part of our family now."

Hosea's claim struck Sento as odd, but she admired him for his strength and compassion. She was certain she had true family, at least a father. She felt less certain about a mother, but there was a strong hint of a sibling, probably a sister. Persuaded by Hosea's offer of tea, she took a seat in the huddled gathering. She didn't have to leave immediately.

Hosea rested on a barnacle-encrusted box with his elbows on his knees, his arms around Awilda, protectively, like a cocoon. His face worked as if he was trying to solve a vexing problem. The woman's face was blank, as if an organ in her body had been removed before she realized what had happened.

"Excuse me, but where are your children?" She recalled seeing the couple with a boy and a girl.

Awilda's eyes snapped on Sento, first angry, then they watered, and her hand went to her mouth, as if to stifle a scream. Hosea tightened his grip on his wife.

Koi's whispered, as if he were an apparition. "*Eles se foram.*"

They are gone. Sento heard plenty of Brazilian Portuguese on the walk from Valparaiso. *Gone.* On the beach, Hosea and Awilda kneeled over bundles of fabric, arms, and legs at odd angles, like rejected dolls, and the cries of grief. Alive, aboard the ship, the girl was about four, with intelligent eyes. The boy was two or three, constantly crying, from hunger or anger, Sento didn't know. Both were now silent.

"I'm sorry," Sento said.

"They were beautiful," Hosea said. "Good and kind. Never any trouble. Always obedient."

Sento gestured to Awilda's swollen belly, hoping to make up for her social blunder. "Your baby is safe."

"I don't feel safe." Awilda wiped her eyes. "What do we do now?"

"We came her hoping to find Iso," Hosea said. "We've lost everything, though. All our belongings were on the ferry."

"I don't want to stop," Koi said. "Iso wants us there."

"Your name. Sento." Hosea was eager to change the subject. "Is it Japanese?"

Is it? I don't know. It's all I remember. Sento asked herself occasionally if her name was Japanese, or perhaps Korean, but an inner voice said No. It felt like a partial name, a half-forgotten name, or a name made up of pieces of a true name, like an ancient piece of pottery with chunks missing.

When she had money for a net account, she searched "Sento" and found thousands of hits, but nothing felt familiar or correct. She wasn't even sure of her age. Maybe 28 or 29. She paid a street vendor in Santiago to sequence her DNA, but there were no hits on the births or deaths databases. She spoke near-perfect Spanish, but the vendor asked if she was American. Sento didn't know, but didn't say so. The vendor remarked on the quality of her clothes. Too good for the slums of Valparaíso.

"I'm sorry if I offended," Hosea said. "It's been hard, you see—"

"No, it's alright. We're all hurting." Despite his unease, Sento sensed a quiet confidence, a natural calm that kept him balanced in difficult moments. It also suggested a distance from others, even his wife, as armor against a painful world.

"Back aboard the ship—" Hosea bit his lip, holding back emotion. "We were a little afraid of you."

"Afraid?" Sento wasn't sure what Hosea meant.

"You always had a scowl on your face, as if you were permanently angry." Hosea grinned. "I stayed out of your way, but I saw you with the dissed woman. You were kind to her."

The ulcerated face of the disidentified woman came back to Sento. "She was alone."

"Are you alone? I mean, are you traveling alone?"

Of the few facts Sento was certain, her solitude was one. "Yes, I'm on my own."

"Are you heading for any place in particular?"

The only other certain fact about herself was her compelling need to find Isorropia and her identity. Watching Koi, though, dance around in the sun like a crazed rodent, she kept the name to herself. *Am I as touched as he is?* Even so, the craving to find Iso was her best companion, always with her, never faltering, never doubting. "Just moving south."

"South eventually ends, you know."

"I've been sick, and, well..."

"I'm sorry. Awilda always says I ask too many questions."

Sento didn't mind the questions, but she had no answers. One thing encouraged her: the memories. With each kilometer, the memories of what she supposed was her former life became more frequent and stronger, as if she was getting nearer a kind of transmitter, allowing her to home in to her self. The disquieting sound of the sea lions in the bay. The silver man. *I saw him again yesterday, when I was in the water.* The voice urging her to kick was male. That was new. The menacing older woman always nearby was not. Sento feared her.

Hours later, as she lay in a nook in Bruce's workshop, Sento's consciousness hovered at that place where people met deceased relatives or mythic creatures from other worlds. Her heart jumped, and she raced through a maze, gun in hand, shouting an order to halt. She chased a person, hooded, all in black, visible only in its outline in the intense moonlight. A bullet whizzed by, and she fired her pistol, a different weapon than the one she bought in Punta Arenas. The figure disappeared, and she awoke with a start at Koi's jostling.

"They've come! They've come!"

Terrified voices and orange flickers blew away the fuzz of her dream.

Koi pushed her blanket away. "Please help us. They're burning everything."

Sento's boots tightened around her feet. Out in the street, parents carried babies and crying children and half-packed knapsacks while smoke hung heavy over the shanties and tents. Her mind flashed to the sinking's horror, but she was on dry land.

Two single shots from a handgun were succeeded by the *tat-tat-tat* of automatic weapons. Sento retrieved her pistol and realized she hadn't cleaned it since its immersion in the bay. Worried it might misfire, she buckled and zipped her flak jacket.

Two more shots popped in the cold air and she ran to the pilgrim's camp. She heard shouts and found two men beating a figure huddled on the ground. The figure whimpered, protecting his head with his arms.

"Hey! Stop!" She pulled her gun, a nine-millimeter. The assailants, both teenage boys, broke and ran.

Sento gave chase to the nearest. They weaved into and out of the warren of tents and lean-tos, resembling dancers, pushing off jerry-built walls and jumping over skittering bots. Sento yelled at the boy to stop as if the words had special power, but he stayed one step ahead.

Unbidden, the still fresh image of her dream overlay her consciousness like a double-exposure. The fleeing hooligan pushed a barrel in front of Sento and she dodged it like a slalom skier. In tandem, the dream-image sped through the squalor like a fox in a forest. The boy nearly lost Sento when he made a 90-degree turn, but she made the turn. The alley where he hid was pitch dark and she held out her weapon. He was invisible in the darkness.

She called on him to surrender, but a glint of metal made her flinch, and an aluminum pipe caught her head in a glancing blow, not even hard enough to break her skin. The surprise magnified the large creature in the corner of her eye. It was the wild-looking man who led her to the salvage yard. He stepped in and shoved the attacker off-balance. He fell to the mud and sewage-soaked ground.

Ignoring the wild man, Sento held her gun at the boy's head, cocked. She was ready to kill him; he had tried to kill her. *It would be so easy.* The boy's face was a blur, same as the hermit-like creature. In the dream, she fired on her quarry. *Did he die? Yes.* In the fetid alley of the refugee camp, however, she did nothing. Her trigger finger would not move, as if paralyzed.

The boy on the muddy path saw her hesitation, scrambled backwards a meter or two, and ran off. Sento lowered her weapon, wondering what had held her back. *I couldn't do it again.*

Sometime before Valparaíso, she had killed a man. She knew its truth as sure as she knew that she had let her attacker go. In the same way she knew nothing about the boy, she remembered nothing about the man she had killed, and it ate at her soul like acid.

Sento loosened her grip on her gun, and she stared at it as if it were a cancerous tumor that could not be removed. She flicked on the safety and holstered it. As before, the creature disappeared.

The smoke and flickers of orange flame brought her back to the moment, and she raced back to the *Kildare* camp. Gwen tended to the unmoving figure on the ground. A mob surrounded a large, bearded man—called Ox—his blood-matted hair draped over a dirty, frightened face. He screamed as the mob looped a line around his neck and tied his hands behind his back. They were going to kill him in revenge.

He doesn't deserve to die.

Sento pushed her way through the mob to Ox. They let her pass without objection. Sweat from the chase ran down her temples.

Ox spat in her face as Sento took his arm. "Filthy *inmigrante*."

Sento summoned all her strength not to twist Ox's arm and tear his ligaments. "I'm trying to help you."

"Fuck you, and fuck all your kind." The rage in his face was magnified by his dread.

Sento said, "Do you want to live? Or do you want to die?"

Ox bared his teeth, but said nothing.

Sento lifted the loop of rope from Ox's neck, ignoring the protests of the mob. Hosea appeared beside her, but he was placid, if pale. She handed the rope to the farmer, and led Ox roughly to the edge of the camp. He came from Nordenskjöld.

"Why?" Sento said.

"Why what?" Ox spat out a tooth.

"Why attack these defenseless people?"

"Because you're killing us! My people came here a dozen years ago to start a new life. Things were going fine until *inmigrantes* showed up. Every one of you is fouling our world, just like people have done for a hundred-thousand years. Everywhere, humanity has done nothing but corrupt and pollute the land. Now it's happening to Antarctica, and there's nowhere else to go."

Ox limped toward the town, and Sento watched the back of his parka, illuminated by the conflagration of the camp. *The world has gone mad.* Ox had lumped her with the pilgrims, which she couldn't accept. Instead, she was overcome with the sense that she was on home turf she had sworn to protect, and failed. It was another vaporous memory.

A film of gray ash settled on the remnants of the refugee camp, reminding Sento of a dusting of snow. The *Kildare* survivors gathered in the tiny square of Bruce's yard, the aluminum shells of robots and vehicles like hovering skeletons. Next to the smoky fire, he huddled under a blanket with Gwen, his pinched face searching in the fire for answers, or deliverance. *Is he comforting her, or she him?*

Sento suppressed a twinge of jealousy and despair. The angry townspeople had sentenced the refugees to death. They didn't need to kill them outright. Antarctica would do it for them. News chan images would distribute the true message: *Inmigrantes* were not welcome in the unpromising land of the Great Southern Continent.

What next? Bury the dead? Hadn't these people just buried the dead? First the drowned, now the burned. How will the third group die?

Hosea came up beside Sento. The fire's destruction revealed the graceful curve of the beach. He squinted, as if trying to see something in the distance. "It's time to move on," he said.

Glancing at Hosea's face in profile, with its Roman nose and strong jaw line, Sento rejected the possibility that the shipwreck and the fire had enmeshed her future with the survivors'. But her resolve to continue by herself was wearing thin.

"Iso." Koi stood behind Sento and Hosea.

"Koi, even if you knew where it was, these people are in no condition for a cross-country journey."

"It's south."

"South to where?" Unlike the journey through the Andes, she had no trail to follow, or border guards to bribe, or relief agencies to pester. Like the pilgrims, she wasn't sure of next steps.

"I've heard rumors of inland settlements since the day I got here," Bruce bit into a UN ration pack. "There's always been a trickle of people heading south from here. None of them come back."

Sento blinked away an image of frozen or decayed corpses stretching for a hundred kilometers. *They didn't wait for permission or a threat to move on.*

"Perhaps they don't come back because they found what they're looking for," Hosea said, thoughtful, as if considering an irrigation problem.

Awilda emerged from a catatonic funk. "What are we supposed to do? Stay here?"

The circles under Awilda's eyes were dark. Her skin was dry and cracked. Sento read increasing instability in her manner, which might prove dangerous to the refugees or herself.

Awilda's green eyes settled on each pilgrim in turn. "I'm going to have a baby. I can't have it here, but I can't go back." She glanced at the bay. South America was as distant to the refugees as the moon. "If we stay here, we'll die. Why not die looking for something better?"

"Iso," Koi repeated.

"You say the word like it's Heaven." Bruce sipped a liquid ration.

"Oh, it is!" Koi brightened, as if asked a question he loved to answer over and over. "It's like Heaven. Warm, bright, with all the food you can eat. It's safe and everyone loves each other. No hate, no sickness, no problems."

"A dream," Hosea said, laying a hand on Awilda's belly.

"A mirage," Bruce said. "The rumors are consistent, though. Sometimes that means there's a nut of truth to them. I suppose it's possible someone tried to settle Antarctica's interior, but failed." As if debating it in his mind, Bruce shook his head. "No one has ever found Iso or put it on a map. It doesn't exist."

"Like El Dorado," the dissed woman said.

"Antarctica is a big place," Hosea said. "It's bigger than America north to south, east to west."

What if the people want it kept a secret?

The woody fumes and thoughts of secrets triggered another of Sento's memories, shrouded by a shamanic gauze of colors, shapes, echoes of voices, and emotion. The strongest sensation was a fragrance, thick, pleasant, erotic, and forbidden. The scent hinted at the beeswax candles of the Cathedral of Saint James in Santiago, or the outdoor grills of street food vendors. It was sweet, cloying, sensual, and … a*garwood.* The word startled Sento like an unexpected bell. With its recognition, her faced flushed. Her hands shook. The thing or person she feared had no name in her recollection, but the curtain over her past had a new pinhole.

"Sento, what is it?"

Hosea's voice penetrated her internal fog, clarifying her thoughts, like focusing a lens. *Someone did this to me, took away my memory, my identity, when I threatened him… or her.* Sento had lost her memory shortly before arriving at the hospital in Valparaiso. Whatever the cause, it was unconnected to anything, until now. *Agarwood. Incense.*

"Sento, you look pale. Are you sick?"

"I'm fine."

Hosea shoved his hands into his pockets. "I heard the stories too after we left Panama. I never spoke to someone who lived there, but it sounded so real, that it had to be true. About ten of us banded together to try and find it. We were all aboard the ferry. Gwen was one."

"They all drowned, except you, Awilda, and Gwen," Sento said.

"I believe in it more than I ever did before," Hosea said. "What choice do I have?"

Bruce scoffed. "You people are insane. We need to rebuild the camp. Start over here."

"And get attacked again by the town?" Sento's hand went to her holstered gun. "They burned the camp last time. They might do worse next time."

Bruce sneered at Sento. "Iso doesn't exist. You people need to get used to it."

"Why do you want to stay, robot man?" Awilda scoffed. "You live in the middle of a pile of scrap, and all your customers are dead."

Bruce held his hands to the fire, unresponsive. Sento wondered how he did the delicate work of electronics repair with his stubby fingers. *He's afraid, like all of us.*

"Sento, you haven't told us what you think," Hosea said.

"If I say Isorropia exists, what then? Are you going to pack up your wife and walk there? Are any of you going to believe a lunatic child or a crazy woman who doesn't even know her real name?" Sento meant herself, bouncing her fist off her chest for emphasis. Her throat closed as the loneliness of the past months and years squeezed her heart.

"It's the only hope Awilda and I have. Gwen, too."

It's my last hope to know who I am.

Bruce mocked the refugees. "If you head south, you'll walk into the most dangerous, hostile land on the planet. There's nothing there. It makes the deserts of the world look like tropical jungles. If you don't freeze in the six-month night, you'll die of starvation."

Hosea took the hand of Awilda. "My wife is right. We die here, or we die trying to find something better. That's all we've been doing for a year."

Bruce stared at Gwen, pain on his face. "Iso is a dream. You'll die chasing a dream."

Gwen shrugged. "What else can I do?"

Bruce whispered. "You can stay here with me."

Gwen squeezed his hand.

Hosea raised his head, preparing to speak to the listening *inmigrantes*. "I'm leaving with Awilda. I'd be obliged if you all came with us. We have a better chance as a group, like those old wagon trains back in America, where I grew up. They helped each other when things broke down, or people got sick. We probably won't find Isorropia, but we might, after all." He lowered his head and closed his eyes.

Without hesitating, Koi said, "I'll go with you."

Gwen followed suit, though Bruce shook his head, resisting the tide. When eyes turned to Sento, she looked at each pilgrim. Upon reaching Antarctica, all of her thoughts and emotions were imbued with the word *home*, and her universe had changed. She was the native, they were strangers, and she couldn't stiff-arm these people who asked for her companionship. She would still follow her own way, though it would run on the same trail as the pilgrims.

Word spread quickly through the camp that the *Kildare* refugees were leaving the bay and going south into the wilderness. Like a chorus, all the *inmigrantes* in the camp joined the decision. The fire had destroyed their lives as well. At that moment, all the refugees became pilgrims, not just Hosea and his group. The morale of the camp turned from despair into hope, even high spirits. Children played in the devastation. Adults found boxes or fashioned bags out of shredded tarps and began to pack their belongings.

Bruce returned to his workshop and closed the steel door to the recycled shipping container.

Hosea said to Sento, "Are we insane?"

"We're desperate. It's a kind of insanity."

Sento watched the activity. They'd forgotten—or forced themselves to forget—the hopelessness of their situation. It was the only way to face the unknown.

CHAPTER 3

From the diary of Artemis Macedon

I stalk her on behalf of the man who keeps me alive. I observe and scrutinize her every move because he demands it. I send reports to him, but keep my private thoughts in this diary. He says he'll tell me when to act, when he's ready. "In the meantime, be invisible, but keep her from harm." A hard thing to do, but not impossible for a feral. I care about her too. I pointed her toward the salvage yard, because Bruce Nay is a good man, but it was pure chance when I encountered her during the chase. I had seconds to take out the militiaman. Saving her saved me, because if she had died, my patron would've abandoned me, and life out here is fucking tough.

When I found her by accident, I nearly screamed in shock. I thought my patron was crazy to think she might turn up. He wasn't.

Let me back up. I spend a lot of time scrounging in garbage dumps. It's sickening what people throw out, even in a remote station where resupply might be days or weeks away. Sickening, but good for me. The rubbish tip between Nordenskjöld and the refugee camp is a gold mine for single worn-out socks or scraps of food left in a tin can. As I was foraging, I spotted her in the group of survivors. I saw that ship go down and all those people drowned. I was horrified, but they had taken the chance and Antarctica is never kind and only occasionally tolerant. After seeing her, I couldn't keep myself from sneaking up on the group. It was easy to hide myself from the slovenly vigilantes that call themselves an "indigenous defense force." They're ignorant and dangerous. I got close enough to hear the survivors talking. She called herself "Sento," but that didn't compute. It must be a cover, or a *nom de guerre,* or possibly a fragment.

Her swimmer's shoulders and upper arms were as muscular as I remembered. Her manner was confident. Her mind was sharp. In many ways, she was the same woman who'd worked for me. She had changed, though. She looked cautious, skeptical, diffident toward others. Whatever she'd experienced had worn on her. There I go, pretending I'm a cop again, pulling psych profiles out of my ass, but it was impossible for me not to think something was very wrong. I'd seen people months after they'd been disidentified, and it's as if they'd shrank, like the way an iceberg melts into the sea. She hadn't.

I reported what I saw to my patron. I'm not a real feral, not one of those lunatics who believe the only way to human salvation is rejection of every technology after the invention of agriculture. I look like a feral, all wild-eyed and wild-haired. I probably smell like a feral. I've seen them, and I've been downwind. Phew! At first, I thought my patron was one of those people who secretly help the ferals, but don't want to live that way, something like giving money to contemplative nuns. Hedging their bets, or assuaging their guilt, or thinking that symbolism is the same as acting out your beliefs. But my patron's requirement that I keep an eye out for Sento was different.

Is it really her?

I had to be sure. Always check your facts. Double-check. Use your own eyes. I followed her into the camp, staying just close enough to hear the survivors talk. They needed shelter. I thought of Nay. I'd brought him stuff—broken bots, discarded tools, an actual paper book once—from the rubbish tip over the months, and he was good to me.

Now I can watch and wait. Bait and wait. Like fishing. Only I don't want to hook her. Not yet.

Maybe she doesn't remember her real name, or only a part of it, and enough remains of her identity to keep her almost, but not quite whole. It must be a weird thing to experience. Most importantly, why is she here? You'd think she'd want to put as many kilometers as possible between herself and Antarctica. It doesn't make sense, except to my patron, I suppose, though he doesn't explain himself to me.

Why protect Sento? If the man who exiled me—not my patron—finds out she's here, she's dead. The attack on the camp proves it. Someone down south is watching them, advising them, prodding them. There's a common interest between the two. He was involved. I'm still afraid of him, in spite of two years out here alone and out of sight. I see the signs: new uniforms, new com gear, the guns. If they intended to drive off the migrants, the plan worked. Most importantly for me, and my patron, Sento survived, like I have. She's going with them, which means I'll follow, at a distance, stalking.

It's my chance to set things right, but my patron has to let me go, like a hunter letting loose a hound.

He has to do it before I go insane.

CHAPTER 4

Elita Soares loved First Harvest ceremonies, though this was the first since her election as First Citizen. The events encompassed everything she cherished about her Isorropia. More importantly, she banked their success as political capital against future elections. She needed every ounce of goodwill they generated if she were to win reelection by more than the tenths of percent margin of her unexpected victory. She lived on a political razor's edge. A few swing votes going the wrong way, and she was out on her ear. Most of her predecessors had left the ceremonies to staff, but she took charge of them on her first day in office and for this ceremony, she ordered her minions about in the farm's concourse like a field marshal, approving every detail down to the fragrances. *The scent of agarwood is perfect for a sweet day celebrating balance.*

In a few minutes, she would lay a diminutive porcelain plate of fresh broccoli, red lettuce, and a single slice of wheat bread in front of the guests at the high table. With the gesture, she symbolically delivered on her promise as Isorropia's leader: to preserve, protect, and sustain her people and its way of life. Elita's breast swelled with pride.

"You seem thoughtful today, my dear." Benjamin Soares was Elita's father.

"I'm thinking about miracles." Over a half-century, extending the pioneering work for the northern hemisphere's Mars programs, Isorropian horticulturalists in City Farm 14A had turned the ice and rock deserts of Antarctica into a bread-basket more productive per hectare than North American farms at the height of the Carbon Age. All with selective breeding and without man-made fertilizers and other banned technologies. As 24-hour winter sunlight streamed into the cantilevered roof of the largest conservatory ever constructed, Elita reflected on the triumph of Isorropia over the cause of so much environmental destruction: wastefulness. "It's our city, right here, in this food we're about to eat. Every calorie and molecule grown with an absolute balance of inputs to outputs, Father. *Ισορροπία*. Balance. It's an old, old dream. We've done everything right."

Other miracles came to mind, such as her come-from-behind win. *Taking in the Australians was too much. It upset the balance we love. Voters said no more.*

"You've done well with the farm project, Lita." Ben's eyes twinkled. "You deserve the compliments I saw on the com boards."

At least I've pleased him on something, for once. Elita touched her father's cold, metallic arm in thanks. As the heir to the Soares political dynasty, the public expected her to follow her father's old-fashioned, open-handed politics, but she saw the writing on the wall, and broke away, winning on her own. It hurt him, and inviting him to these ceremonies was a way of mending fences.

Ben winked. "I wouldn't agree we've fixed everything. We still make mistakes. We're still imperfect examples of *homo sapiens*."

Mistakes? She'd called out the government when the previous leadership decided to welcome hundreds of refugees in the ragtag flotilla that had made the sea voyage from the Great Australian Bight to Casey Station. It was an amazing feat, but the com net social tribes were full of angry posts and comments against welcoming more refugees. Isorropia was a small city and her resources were strained to the limit from previous migrations, and each new group threatened a carefully crafted image of reticence, privacy, and her namesake *ισορροπία*. Her father had supported that government from the sidelines, but his faction had lost when it came time to confirm the *status quo* or change course. *I made no mistakes.*

I'm too sensitive. It's an innocent remark. Her father's wink was the last nonverbal way he could express irony. When she was a child, before his atrophy appeared, his whole face had the plasticity of an actor. She missed that face. "You used to be so optimistic, Father. We may not be perfect, but we're closer than any community since—"

"When you get older, you'll understand that chasing perfection is like caging a phantom, impossible."

Ben Soares was Elita's hero, and she would not be First Citizen without him, but he was out of sorts, and it worried her. The doctors and roboticists warned of periods of depression, despite the benefits of the exo. She leaned close to him as she poured wine in his glass. "Father, are you alright?"

"I'm fine, Lita."

"You're keeping something from me."

"I'm surprised you don't know."

Elita shook her head, uncertain at his meaning and ashamed of her ignorance. *I can never fathom his expectations.*

"Two years ago, we lost Marissa." Ben's eyes were sad, not just at the memory, but at Elita's forgetfulness. "The last time she was seen was two years ago today."

Elita took a breath and sighed. "I'm sorry, Father. I should've remembered." *I'm probably working too hard.*

"I always wanted you and Marissa to be closer." Ben's artificial voice had a subtle reproach. "I can't let go of my hope that we'll be a family again, that maybe she's..." His voice trailed off.

Family? We were never a family.

"We were too far apart in age and temperament, Father." Marissa was ten years younger and the daughter of a different mother. "I tried to reach out, but nothing sparked." *I loved her once, and I tried to love her later, but Ben always loved her more than life.* Elita needed to reassure her father that her jealousy of his closeness to her was unimportant and in the past, now that she was gone. "I'll check if there's any news about the investigation."

"No need to do that, my dear. I check myself every few days. There's never any news. The police are almost certain she's dead, but without a body, they can't be 100 percent sure."

"I have more resources than you."

"I doubt that, Lita, but I appreciate the thought." Ben gestured at the gathering. "The celebration is more important right now. You need to give it your full attention."

You gave Marissa your full attention until the day she vanished. If I had given her more of mine, would things be better between us?

Elita and her father took places at the high table, decorated with flowers, a modest tea service, and elegantly decorated mist sticks. Gliding among the VIPs with her dancer's body, she served a portion of the First Harvest food to every guest on the dais. At the tables in front of the dais, the enameled bots serving the guests were slaved to Elita's movements, laying down the final ritual plates as she finished with the VIPs. Elita stood in her modest, business-like clothes behind her chair on the platform, the fourth from the right, if you were counting. The number of guests on the high table—eight—was significant. In the ancient world, "8" was the number that stood for material and spiritual balance. In Isorropia, it referred to ecological symmetry as well.

The final step in the meal ritual expressed her status as one of equals, deserving no more or less than any other citizen of Isorropia. Speaking with a melodic voice, she spread her hands as a supplicant might.

"Please, ladies and gentlemen, don't wait for me."

Stainless steel forks and spoons clinked on plates as Elita took her seat. Apart from the harvest food, her mouth watered at the feast before her: quinoa salad, steamed yams, and medallion of cultured beef. The wine came from her own special reserve. Her father sat on her right, the place reserved to honor previous First Citizens. Ben's active career had ended many years before, due to his ataxia, but there were rumors he plucked strings behind the scenes.

"I envy your ease, Lita," Ben said. "I feel silly sitting here, as if I'm a manikin." His synthetic voice captured his irritation and self-consciousness. "I can't even take a single bite."

"No one faults you for your disability, Father. The people love you, and they need to see you still giving service to our beautiful city." Elita lifted a few grams of salad to her mouth. Her upper lip was fuller than the lower. "Being here helps me, too."

"You're torturing me by making me watch everyone else eat."

Elita laughed. "You used to torture me by making me eat peas."

He leaned closer, an intimate gesture for him. "You learned to eat them eventually, didn't you?"

Decades in the past, Ben might have been bedridden. Elita was grateful for the advances in assistive robotics that made his disability irrelevant. She needed her father's mind and charisma, even if it was encased in a titanium-collagen composite, but he was moping about the loss of her half-sister. She imagined him at his apartment, staring at his holo-pics of the girl in a pinafore dress or the high-school graduation gown or the official portrait of the fresh-minted BES officer. *Would he pine for me, if our fates were swapped?*

"You mentioned *homo sapiens*, sir," said a bearded man at Elita's immediate left. "Some of us believe we've evolved to a higher level. Antarctica has transformed us into *homo austri*."

"Are you a member of this new species, Galla?"

Please, Father, no more arguments about refugees. It's settled.

"I can't say, sir, but some of our people seem to believe that we have a duty to help the failed members of our genus."

"Some of our people forget that we've learned from those failures. We owe them a debt, don't you think, Galla?"

"Allowing them to collect on that debt will impoverish us, wouldn't you agree?"

Elita tutted. "Lucius and Father, you're embarrassing me. Can't we set aside our differences for an hour?"

"Of course, Lita."

"I agree. We'll spit at each other later." Laughing, Galla leaned over to whisper in Elita's ear. "Doesn't he have an 'off' switch?"

Elita choked back a teen-like giggle, noticing her father's glare.

Galla lingered by her shoulder. "By the way, did I ever tell you that you have the most delicious-looking ears in the city?"

Elita texted him via her minds-eye rather than speak. She saw and heard the conversation with Lucius in her minds-eye, which manifested itself in her visual and aural cortex, as private as anything in a hyper-networked culture. Eat your lunch, Lucius.

You know what I'd rather eat.

Elita kicked him under the table. Her lover's broad shoulders and confident strut made her palms sweat, but she was careful not to yield to sentimentality. She had never married nor officially partnered, and didn't plan to. The desire of most women for children mystified her. Work was her partner, and Lucius, for the moment, satisfied her base needs. First Citizens in office could not afford the distractions of romance. The advantage tipped the power scales viz Lucius in her favor. She was comfortable with nothing less. "Dessert is here, Lucius Galla."

As guests finished their entrees, the bots served a teacup pudding flavored with passion fruit. Elita met Lucius at a dinner party shortly after her inauguration. Ambitious underlings fought over invitations in a bid to make impressions on incoming FCs. Already known city-wide as a rake, Lucius had slept his way into counter-intelligence at the Bureau of Environmental Security, or so the rumor-mongers claimed. One side of his mouth was higher than the other, which gave the impression he knew more than he was telling, even if he didn't. People were afraid of him, or hated him, or both, but Elita found his aura of danger attractive. He had a reputation for getting things done, one way or another, and Elita thought it smarter to have him near. She appointed him her Special Adviser on Environmental Security.

The meal concluded, wine glass in hand, Elita mingled with guests handpicked for his or her connections in the city, and in a few cases, the world outside Antarctica.

"Are you avoiding me?" Lucius sidled up to Elita and he swallowed more wine.

"Of course not. I'm the official host. I have to press the flesh."

Lucius chewed on a mist stick and he glanced at Ben. "Why are you so anxious to please him?"

"He's my father. What daughter doesn't want to please her father?" Elita lifted her glass in greeting to the man, who returned it with a pleasant smile.

"I mean politically. It's been years since he's really helped—" Lucius cut himself off, thinking better of finishing the thought.

"I know you have a low opinion of my father, Lucius, but he's not my enemy. He's my flesh and blood." *So was Marissa, but her flesh and blood was more precious to him.*

"Elita, for a smart woman, you can be incredibly naive. Haven't you read your Shakespeare or the Greek plays? Relatives will stab you in the back with relish, if it's in their interest. Blood may be thicker than water, but the blood of family flows just as readily."

Elita would not accept that Ben Soares had anything less than her best interests at heart. She eyed Ben, chatting impassively with a minor guest, and suppressed a doubt. "Thank you for your concern, Lucius."

Lucius eyed her, puzzled. "Apparently, you haven't heard."

"About what?" Elita rolled her eyes, exasperated.

"Today's *boule* committee action."

"Yes?" Elita put her skepticism on display. The standing ad hoc committee of the city legislature had been behaving lately, but it was unpredictable.

"It passed the Refugee Relief Act out of committee and on to the full Ecclesia."

Elita gaped. "You're serious." She'd been so distracted by preparations for the ceremony, she'd neglected to follow the goings-on at Government House.

"It seems your father had an ally in the *pro tem* chair while the appointed chair was in the bathroom. A quorum appeared out of nowhere, including a proxy for your father. Made some speech about how 'our beautiful city must open its arms to this new wave of our brothers and sisters fleeing the depredations of climate change.'" Lucius' sarcasm bit hard. "The motion carried by one vote."

Stunned, Elita struggled to comprehend the development's meaning. She'd won her office on a promise to roll back support for refugee resettlement, but the legislation boosted funding and manpower. *Father, what have you done?* She'd have to confront him.

"Uncomfortable?"

"What?"

"To have a knife in your back?"

Lucius grabbed another full glass of wine from a buffet table as bots and technicians cleared tables and prepared for an athletic demonstration by the city's premier high school. He would soon cross the boundary between tipsy and drunk. "I have more news."

Elita huffed. "More bad news? Can't it wait until the morning?"

"Another group of refugees has landed on the Peninsula at Nordenskjöld."

Not again. The simmering refugee crisis was flaring, and one of Lucius' top priorities was to nip it at its source. *Is he failing me?* Elita took his arm, smiling at nearby guests to put off suspicion, and ironically, to confirm it. It was part of the thrill. Her personal relationship to Lucius was an open secret. No one thought twice of their retreat to a semi-private corner.

Except her father.

"How does this keep happening, Lucius?"

"I'm doing all I can—"

"No, you're not." *Scold, but not too much.* "These landings are out of control. I was elected to stop them. Your people are supposed to be discouraging them."

"This one's different." Lucius related the story of an overloaded ferry and the drowning of hundreds, maybe a thousand people, including infants. He shared a vid over the network with her.

"Mother of Heaven," she said, as she watched the vid in her minds-eye. "Where did you get this?"

"You know better than to ask," Lucius said smugly. "Other vids from the accident are already circulating. They're bound to strengthen sympathetic factions in the Ecclesia."

He means my father. "They're too busy squabbling with each other to make trouble." *Wishful thinking, after what happened in the committee?* "Taking in refugees upsets the city's balance. Sensible voters finally understand that." Privately, Elita understood that videos of dead children's bodies washing up on a beach, even if it was a thousand kilometers away, encouraged common cause among her enemies. She would have to act. "You have contacts among the townspeople there. They resent these invaders."

"We have informers, yes. They keep us apprised of what's happening."

"Isorropia has been generous to them. I think we need to call in the debt."

"We have options, but you won't like them."

A chime sounded, calling guests to chairs set around an open area of the floor.

"I don't have time to tell you how to do your job. Three generations have overcome the harshest climate on earth to build Isorropia. Science and a will to treat the earth as an equal partner, not a resource, have made our city as close to a utopia as humanity's ever seen. I'll protect that with my last breath. Do what you need to do."

"No."

Elita swung around on Lucius. The day had started out so well, and it was falling apart in front of her. She was on the edge of losing her temper. Lover or not, she expected obedience from everyone who worked for her. "Do what I tell you."

"Not unless you approve specifically of my plans. Things are reaching a critical point. I'll not be hung out to dry when you claim ignorance."

"What plans—" Elita thought better of her hands-off attitude, but another chime interrupted her. She strolled with calculated nonchalance back to the crowd, leaving Lucius behind. "Just fix it," she hissed over her shoulder. Immigrants had to prove how their output, from work to waste, kept the community in balance with the earth. Very few could, and she had tightened the controls her first day in office. Her poll numbers soared. *I won't let just anyone in my world.*

"No, wait, Lucius." Today was a day for appreciating the perfection of her home and way of life. "You're liable to swing a sledgehammer to kill a gnat. Don't do anything until I tell you. Now, sit down and enjoy the demonstration."

Lucius huffed, but stayed quiet.

Elita took a seat in the front row next to her father. Despite the egalitarian pretense, the seating arrangements signaled a pecking order with Elita at the apex. Her father was technically with the mass of people who formed the wide base of the social hierarchy; He was a simple citizen with no power other than the franchise. The reality, however, shown by his proximity to his daughter, was his ability to work the levers of power behind the scenes. *I'm not as naive as Lucius thinks.*

"What were you and Galla discussing?" Ben said.

"What do you think? City business, of course."

Sotto voce, Ben said, "Lita, I really wish you were more discrete with him. You let your feelings toward him show too much."

"I do not." Elita realized too late that the retort came too fast.

"Do you love him?"

"That's none of your business." Elita was content to keep others guessing about her true feelings toward Lucius, even her father. *He's my lover, not my love.*

"I'll warn you again. Your entanglement with Galla is bound to hurt you." Ben twisted his composite-encased body toward her, reminding her of—she thought sadly—a manikin. "I'm hearing from several people. It's almost daily. They don't trust Galla."

"I didn't hire Galla to be popular."

"It's affecting their trust in you."

Elita pricked up her ears, listening for an unwanted subtext. "Do you still trust me?"

"Of course I do."

The trouble with Ben's exo was the ease at which he could hide what he really felt. Elita prided herself at her ability to read his emotions despite the silver mask and synth-voice. His eyes gave everything away. Almost everything.

Elita dismissed her doubts. *Everyone wants to give me bad news on such a perfect day.* She was one of the few in Isorropia who could silence her father and get away with it. They respected each other, and every father bowed to the power of his daughter sooner or later.

The power of daughters. Parental love isn't boundless, Elita reflected. Mothers and fathers don't conjure love out of nothing when a new child is born. Elita experienced a more common truth, that a parent's love waxes and wanes, and that one child receives more attention and gifts for reasons a sister or brother can't understand. She thought of the first time her father held Marissa as an infant. *The light in his eyes!* Elita was his only child for ten years, then his mistress gave him a gift of joy. *I tried to love her so he would love me, but—*

Recorded music with a driving beat filled the room, and a dozen of the best gymnasts in Isorropia tumbled and jumped into the center of the floor. They moved with the grace of birds, delighting the audience with intricate moves as they wove in and around each other. The First Harvest ceremony was reaching its climax, echoing the celebratory games of the classical world. Instead of honoring gods, this performance honored the accomplishments of Isorropia's people, no less amazing than the act of a god.

A girl, about seven or eight, flew in on slippered feet and gave Elita a bouquet. As the child backed away, Elita blew her a kiss.

The performance came to a head with a human pyramid. The powerful bodies of young men formed the base, with smaller, but no less powerful young women forming the next levels. Children as young as five poured into the space, climbing the arms and legs of older brothers and sisters. The little girl made the final climb, and as Elita took in the sight, she noticed a young man at the base of the pyramid. He tried to hide it, but he was in pain. *His knee?* Elita's experience as a dancer and gymnast herself told her than he was hurting. Perhaps he'd injured himself during the performance, and he was too embarrassed to admit it, but his pride was threatening everyone in the human structure he supported. Elita almost felt his pain, in her heart, and in her bone. He shifted his hand a millimeter, and his right leg trembled with the pressure. Beads of sweat collected at his temples. Three seconds more, Elita thought, and he would collapse. The girl at the apex was high enough from the floor that a fall at just the right angle would kill her. The child kept her face forward, the trained smile brilliant as the Antarctic sun. She was unaware of the danger.

A clap sounded, and within those three seconds, and one more, the pyramid collapsed, but in an orderly manner, with every gymnast beaming as they took a bow. Elita let out her breath. The crowd broke into loud applause. Even the injured young man forced a grin, but Elita knew her First Harvest ritual had missed a disaster by a stretched ligament or a torn muscle.

Is Iso as fragile?

The ceremony was over. Elita shook the hands and kissed the cheeks of her guests. She kissed her father's metallic cheek, lingering for a moment over the man she loved more than anything in the world. Lucius, on the other side of the room, leered at her. *Which one of these, or which of all others in Isorropia, threaten us?* Elita tossed her head, as if throwing off the thought, and drank the last of her wine. *Which one of them threatens me?*

"You orchestrated the committee vote and you didn't tell me." With the ceremony over, and the guests long gone, Elita stood over her father in the conference room with hands on her hips.

Ben Soares sat on the mobile recharger, reclining as if royalty. It was a trick of the exo-skeleton and the design of the device.

"In fact, I think it was all your idea," Elita added.

"You should've been more careful."

He's lecturing me as if I was one of his poly-sci students. "You betrayed me."

"For Christ's sake, Lita, you love to overreact, don't you? It's your biggest weakness."

"And you're a calculating, conniving..."

"Enemy?" Ben laughed. "I love you, Lita. I can't be anything but your friend in the Ecclesia, but that doesn't mean I always agree with you."

Elita took a deep breath and brushed a mote of dust off her knee-length skirt. "Alright, tell me how you did it."

"It was pretty simple. We applied what we knew about the committee chair and took a chance."

"What you knew?"

"What everyone knows. He has a bowel problem and he always visits the men's room right before an afternoon session starts. The rules say the sessions must start on time, so he appoints a *pro tem* to get things started in case he had—trouble. We risked that he might take some extra time and it paid off. We packed the room with supporters during the lunch break and moved to reconsider as soon as our man banged the gavel. It took three minutes."

"You didn't, uh, use poison, did you?"

"Don't be ridiculous."

"Your tactics are dirty." *I would've done the same thing, but I'm his daughter, for God's sake.*

Ben shrugged in his mechanical manner, the servos of his exo hissing. "How many times have I told you to count your friends and enemies in all things? You forgot to count this time."

"What happened to working together? What happened to our partnership? I'm starting to think you're turning against me."

"In this one thing, I'm not in agreement with you, sweetheart. It's just politics."

Why is he doing this to me? Elita would've thrown something at her father, if the conference room had any throw-able objects. Instead, she went to him on one knee and clasped his hand. "Father, I don't like it when you work against me. It hurts. I need you by my side all the time." Elita was aware that she appeared over-dramatic, but her father's behind-the-scenes maneuvering scared her. "Next time, tell me what's going on. Don't keep things from me. I won't interfere."

Every child lies to her parent.

Ben patted her hand with his exo-assisted limb, an unkind smile playing in his eyes. "We were only taking advantage of the rules, Lita. All is not lost."

"Father, I'm your daughter, your friend, in everything. Not just politics, but everything. What can I do to make you my ally again?"

Ben's eyes softened. "Remember that time when your arm got caught in the spokes of your bicycle wheel?"

Elita rubbed her elbow, remembered the pain and the fright. "I was about eight or so."

"And there was that time when I got you that robotic pony?"

"I had to have one because my friends all had one or I was going to die." Elita laughed. "That must have cost you a fortune."

"I wanted to be a good father, your friend, your protector. The trouble is—" Ben's gaze became distant. "—I don't remember if you said, 'Thank you, Daddy.'"

Ben's face could not frown, or express sadness, or loss, but his silvery hands were limp in his lap. Elita was sure she had expressed gratitude, but what nine or ten-year-old understands the social niceties? "I'm sorry, Father. I didn't know."

And then Marissa was born.

His synth-voice strengthened. "I want to be partners, Lita. I really do. Isorropia's architects would've have found a way to share our bounty, rather than bar the doors. 'Share and share alike' was their mantra in the early days."

"That precept was applied to their community, not to anyone who happened to waltz by," Elita replied. "'Outputs equal inputs, with no waste' was another mantra. Accepting refugees makes that impossible."

"In the short term, Lita." Ben turned his head away from this daughter, as if knowing his words would fall on dear ears. "We would adjust. At the end of the day, we'd be proud of caring for hurting people and maintaining our environmental values. It's not a zero-sum game."

Elita wanted to argue that the required re-balancing of all the carefully managed inputs and outputs might take years, or it might never happen, but she said nothing. Resources were scarce in Antarctica. Even water was scarce, despite the billions of tons of ice. It took energy to melt the ice into potable and irrigation water, and building new solar and wind farms took time and money. She wanted to bring these points up, but she stayed silent, disappointed in her father's attitude.

Up to this point, Elita counted on Ben's support in virtually everything she did on behalf of Isorropia. When they disagreed, it was usually on details that had no major consequence. His was a vote she automatically put in her column. Something had changed. Perhaps he was simply getting older and softer. Maybe the anniversary of Marissa's disappearance had affected him more than Elita thought.

Or maybe Elita was wrong about the growing refugee crisis. Was it arrogant or unfair for Isorropia to keep its hard-earned success to itself? Was it morally necessary to welcome desperate people sailing to a land that was their last chance at survival while the rest of the planet succumbed to the Warming? She kissed her father on his bare cheek and smiled. "Let's make peace before there's war, Father. Let's find a way to compromise. I want you to be happy."

I'll welcome the refugees when Hell freezes over.

CHAPTER 5

From the diary of Artemis Macedon

THEY'VE DECIDED TO LEAVE. AND she's going with them. No surprise, not after what happened. I went down to the camp from my shelter, stalking Sento to protect her. I hadn't quite figured out how, because I'm supposed to stay in the shadows. It was pure chance that I pushed that child thug off balance when I saw him raise the club. If Sento survives, I survive. Did I do the right thing, my secret friend?

I didn't see the demon among the dogs, which made sense. He likes the shadows too. Perhaps he was observing from the Nordenskjöld garbage heap, where I saw him within hours of hiking down from the mountains to browse the aisles of my feral man's supermarket. I joined the rats grubbing for rotted fruit, remnants of canned meat, and moldy bread heels. With no warning, ricocheting bullets plinked at my feet. Shocked, I thought I was the target. Nordenskjöld's people aren't friendly. I ducked behind a large rock. When I saw one rat explode and then another, I figured out the truth. They were the targets. The shooter either didn't see me, or avoided me. How kind of him.

I eased myself to another spot where I could see the shooter, the demon from my past. He was unmistakable, tall and angular with close-cropped hair and a face that would freeze the bowels of perdition. That crooked smile. He promised to kill me if he ever saw me again. God help me, even disidentification would be a mercy compared to facing him.

The demon handed the military-style rifle to a man in a line of three townspeople. One was a bull of a man, perhaps a wrestler in some other life. My nemesis was by far the best dressed of the four in his plain forest green uniform of the Bureau of Environmental Security, the tulip insignia on his collar glinting in the sunlight. He was leading or training for a covert action. I'd participated in my share, so I knew the attitude. Nearby was a staser in its distinctive case. Small arms with a big punch. I've seen those take out chunks of flesh like a great white shark.

It didn't take long to find out why he was here. The tiny driftwood fire I'd built in my cave kept me warm, but the smell was wrong, a mixture of plastic and seared meat. The scent didn't come from my fire. My cave was a few hundred meters from the refugee camp, but shouts drifted up the shallow valley leading to my shelter, along with the smoke. Flickers of light drew me closer, and the *pop-pop-pop* of automatic weapons fire made me think of the target practice. Figures moved about in the pre-dawn. A few carried guns. No doubt the staser was in someone's hands.

Others did his dirty work. What's more, the demon did nothing on his own. He was told to come here and wreak havoc. I knew this by instinct, but I couldn't say by whom, except that it was someone high up in the Isorropian government. I know that cesspit. I used to work in it. And I screwed up too. Trying to keep Sento in sight, I ran right into one of the demon's curs, a special, loathsome breed. I didn't recognize him at first, but he recognized me. For a millisecond, we stared at each, gaped-mouth, but he reacted faster. He shoved me against something hard and bared his teeth. "What are you doing here?"

I licked my lips. "Just trying to survive, like everyone else."

"Who are you working for?"

"I don't know." It was the truth. I couldn't name my controller.

"You're lying, but I don't have time to deal with you." His mouth was so close to my nose that I could see his fillings. "If you say one word about me to anyone, I'll disembowel you. Got it?"

I thought my bowels would let go there and then. They didn't. I nodded.

A name came to me. Half a name. Italian, maybe. "Tea"-something. "Titch"-something. I couldn't remember.

After that, I retreated to my cave, and I cried. I felt so helpless. I'm nothing but a wraith living in the cracks of the world. I shouldn't have cried, though. There was beauty outside my door. The white and blue of Antarctica is giving way to green. A tuft of hair grass had taken root in the gravel by the door of my rocky shelter out of Nordenskjöld's sight. The colors of the two-centimeter patch ranged from a yellowish green to a deep forest green. Every schoolchild in Isorropia knows about *Deschamsia antarctica*, one of only two flowering plants native to the continent. The other is *Colobanthus quitensis*, the Antarctic pearlwort. A little garden had grown on my doorstep since my last visit. It's disturbing and soothing in the same instant. The Warming molds my home into an inscrutable future shape, but the green puts me at ease.

I've seen *Deschamsia* practically every place I've been, especially near the coasts. Tufts are popping up like green moles on the continent's skin. Outside my cave, the grasses took root in the gravel underneath the lichen-encrusted, slate-gray rock. Maybe a seed stuck to my boot on my last trip and dropped into the coarse soil. Maybe a gull ate a few seed heads and pooped here. At least the plant is native, unlike the invaders brought by the refugees, or the Nordenskjöld colonists, probably without knowing it. I've seen invasive tussock grass from South Georgia Island and the South Orkney Islands marching up a rising plain above the town.

I suppose it's only a matter of time before the beech trees come back. They were here a hundred million years ago, and there's a few of them left in Australia. If Antarctica ever warmed up enough, maybe they'd grow again below the Antarctic Circle. It's happened before. One-hundred-thousand millennia in the past, they grew during the six-month day and consumed their internal food reserves in the six-month night. There's fossils to prove it. Forests at the South Pole. Crazy.

Green is an amazing color. Back home, people spend as much time as they can in the parks and gardens. Half the land reclaimed by the environmental engineers is dedicated to parks. People go outdoors when the sun is up, hiking and skiing, but the temperature never rises more than a few degrees above freezing. We're a long way from lounging under beech trees, and so the doctors tell us to spend time in the parks, soaking in the green, reminding the ancient parts of our brains that grew up in the forests of Africa that we're still human. My tuft of grass in front of the cave was my own little garden, soothing me as I cried for myself, and grieving for the refugees whom the demon had killed, and fearing again for the safety of the woman who calls herself "Sento." Time again to haunt the edges of her life.

CHAPTER 6

SENTO REPORTED THE REFUGEES READY. "Let's get this done."

Hosea kissed his wife and looked over the throng behind him. He took the first steps on a barely readable trail that led down the beach. A cheer went up from the pilgrims, more powerful than their rags and affect suggested. Within a few minutes, a narrow column formed behind Hosea, stretching back a kilometer.

An *ad hoc* council had formed among the pilgrims. Apart from Sento and Hosea, regulars included Gwen and Bruce, who'd overcome his skepticism at Gwen's urging. Another regular was a man who lived in the camp before the *Kildare* disaster. He called himself Enzo Ticino. He was a few years younger than Hosea, and he had a following among the refugees. He claimed to be a former city planner from a suburb of Caracas. To Sento, he had the look of a bureaucrat: ordinary, nonthreatening, noncommittal. He asked questions, and never offered answers or suggestions.

"Have we decided on a route?"

Hosea said, "We've scoured the camp and we've found several maps of Antarctica. If you'll browse the 'map' folder on Bruce's private com network, you can see the best ones. Unfortunately, none show a straightforward route into the interior. Some are quite old and probably don't show bare ground where the ice has retreated. But we've come up with a proposed route and methodology." Hosea explained how to access the planned route. The council agreed all information should be shared with the entire community, a decision that made Sento nervous, though she couldn't explain why.

Hosea continued, "We have to get to our destination—"

"Whatever that is," Bruce interjected.

"Hush," Gwen chided.

"—by the solstice, when we lose our daylight."

"That's also about the time Awilda is due," Gwen said. "Four weeks, maybe five."

"What happens if we don't find Isorropia by the solstice?" Enzo said.

"We die of hunger and cold." Hosea was matter-of-fact. "The baby too."

"No one is going to die," Gwen said.

"We saw so many graves on the journey down the Chilean coast. Unburied bodies, too." Hosea said.

Sento thought of the bodies on the beach at Nordenskjöld. "Where did you come from?"

"We're originally from California."

"You mean America?" Sento was surprised. Few of the immigrants she had met were from the Northern Hemisphere.

"The rain stopped." His face was wistful as he spoke. "Maybe five centimeters in five years. Whole forests turned dry and dead as matchsticks. The fires burned in the mountains for months. The bugs killed what was left. Dunes marched across our valley like an invading army. One gigantic dune buried a whole town. Summer water was as scarce as an honest banker."

Sento grinned at the humor. As the water dried up, so did the population, except in a few areas. Desalination kept the big coastal cities alive.

"When we lost our farm, we went to friends in Mexico," Hosea continued. "The jobs dried up there and recrossing the border into the U.S. was difficult even for citizens. I heard about work in Panama, and my Spanish was good, but the work was only a rumor. We kept going."

"Then I heard about Isorropia." Hosea's eyes a brightened. "A new city in a new land."

"Isorropia is about as real as the million euros in my pocket." That's what the dissed woman said.

"All I'm hoping for," Hosea said, "is a job and place to raise my family. Is it so much to ask?"

Humanity was living in the "end times." Soapbox preachers proclaimed it everywhere. The Warming was proof. Didn't the Year of Storms destroy a dozen coastal cities a hundred years ago? Aren't all but a handful of mountain glaciers gone? Aren't tropical diseases rampaging across the planet? Maybe the earth has finally had enough. On the other hand, Sento had seen many large cities—Valparaiso, Santiago, Buenos Aires—and all seemed healthy, if poor, except for enclaves of the wealthy. The scale of the difference struck Sento as deeply unfair, though she had no power to change things.

She was following another dream, or perhaps an obsession. The answers to her own questions were near the ends of the earth. "We're feeling more confident about the location of the city. We've gone through all the resources we could find—maps, references, recollections among older people who've been to Antarctica before—and the consensus is that a large settlement is between here and the pole."

"But you have nothing definite?" Enzo's habit of question after question had a way of keeping the conversation going. It could also be irritating. "What if we find Isorropia and they lock us out?"

Hosea and others discussed this possibility. If they found a settlement, what if the people were like those in the town, hostile and belligerent, perhaps worse? Or what if rumors and stories had magnified a few ragged buildings into a paradise? The refugees risked their lives against a hope that fellow human beings would take pity on them.

"The reward is at least equal to the risk," Hosea said.

"Vague maps and prayers? Is that all you have?"

How Hosea maintained his patience with Enzo mystified Sento. "Sento has volunteered to scout ahead a few kilometers, and look for the easiest route. We think it's best to stick to a route that takes us directly to the pole, and hope to see signs that might show us the way to Isorropia."

Enzo furrowed his brows. "You mean road signs?"

Hosea chuckled. "Of course not."

"I just want the route to be safe." Awilda's exhaustion was constant.

"The most likely signs are outposts, weather stations, communications gear, maybe vehicle tracks," Bruce said.

Like a sheep dog guiding a flock, the tracked vehicle and its small trailer flanked the chaotic column on its right near the head. Extra tent poles and spare fabric became human-drawn travois or home-made backpacks. On the left further back trod the *Kildare*'s cargo bot, which caused a sensation when Bruce and Gwen showed up with it not a half-hour before the column departed. The bot, scratched and rust-stained, but deft and steady, looked like a spider with a net slung underneath.

"The bot can handle a full, 12-meter steel container on a pitching deck," Bruce said, making the case for bringing it along. "We can put heavy stuff in the net."

"Or injured people." Gwen explained that she was a trained nurse who worked two years at a trauma center in Lima.

Bruce patted one of the bot's legs. "I've welded some extensions to its arms to act like pads or feet. It'll take a day or two, but the AI will learn how to walk on solid ground."

"Like a sailor getting his sea legs." Sento was amazed.

"Isn't he clever?" Gwen was proud of Bruce's ingenuity. "It needs a name."

"Already thought of that," Bruce said. "'Kanthaka,' after a mythological horse."

'Kan,' for short," Gwen said brightly.

Sento ran her hand along the bot's flank. The kill-switch button was still in its place. She hoped it wouldn't be needed. "Who's going to run the bot?"

"Bruce is a trained engineer," Gwen offered. "He worked on the Ceres mining projects."

"You mean the asteroid?" Sento was impressed. "How did you wind up here?"

Bruce shrugged as he toyed with Kan's controller. "I get restless."

"A woman broke his heart," Gwen said.

Bruce scoffed and pretended to examine a joint on one of the bot's legs.

"A string of women, actually." Gwen leaned in conspiratorially to Sento. "He hasn't told me all the details, but the last one promised to marry him, and then she ran off with an astronaut."

Bruce coughed.

Sento stifled a laugh, because his reaction was so juvenile. Plainly, his social skills didn't match his intellect. He was lonely, and Gwen had managed to earn his trust. Love emerges in the strangest places.

As the column found a rhythm, the cargo bot, towering over the humans, moved with a grace and gentleness that surprised Sento.

"Sen, have you seen Koi?" Gwen called out to Sento from a place near Hosea.

"Not since we left camp."

"I'm worried he's been left behind. There's a few other people missing, too."

"Alright. I'll take a look around." Sento walked down the column, asking if anyone had seen Koi. No one had. She reached the end of the column, and Koi was not among the stragglers. Climbing a rise, she scanned the area. She shaded her face from the sharp sun, and she spotted a huddled group atop another hill a hundred meters inland. She found Koi at a horizontal driftwood log worn flat on one side. A plastic cup with water and a saucer lay on the log. A half-dozen pilgrims knelt behind him. "Koi, we're leaving. People are worried."

"Shush," one of the pilgrims said. "Mass is almost over."

Sento was taken aback. "Mass? Koi, what are you doing?"

"Shush!" the pilgrim insisted.

"Lord, we ask your protection on this dangerous journey." Koi turned around and blessed the congregation. "Be grateful to God and go in peace."

The congregants crossed themselves and gathered their belongings.

"Go that way." Sento pointed south toward the column. "You'll catch up if you hurry."

Koi shoved his cup and saucer into his homemade satchel. "You didn't need to interrupt the ceremony, Sen."

"What are you talking about?"

"I told you. I'm going to be a priest when we get to Isorropia. People heard me, and they asked me to say Mass to ask for God's protection and blessing."

"You're not a priest. You can't be one for years." Sento knew a little about Catholicism. Becoming a priest took years of study. "What you're doing is illegal."

"I don't think so."

"It's breaking some rule or something."

"Jesus wasn't a priest and he said the first Mass."

Sento had exhausted her knowledge of the subject. "Still, you're misleading those people."

Koi left Sento on the hill by the pretend altar. "What was I supposed to do? Say No?"

Sento understood she was beaten. "I suppose not." *No harm done.* "Why do you believe so much in Iso?"

"Because of the priest."

"What priest?"

"The police came one day, and told us we had to leave. There were too many people in our *favela*, and not enough food or water. They told us to go south."

"How old were you?"

"I was eight. My mother gave me a present, even though we had no money." Koi pulled out a silver-plated crucifix from beneath his tattered parka. "Our family walked for days. My father disappeared, but my mother and I stayed together. We came to a camp." Koi wrinkled his nose, struggling to remember. "There were lots of people there, maybe thousands. It was raining. It smelled like pee. The priest found her, and he took her to the hospital. Her skin was all gray."

Cholera.

"The doctors tried to help, but there were hundreds of people in the hospital, lying on the floor, in the hallways. The priest stayed with her. He gave her the Last Rites when she died." Koi clutched the crucifix. "He told me Iso was a beautiful city, a perfect place, and I thought it must be like Heaven. He died the next day of the gray sickness." Koi's visage became calm and accepting, almost angelic. "Iso is Heaven, and I want to see my mother there."

Koi's certainty gave the pilgrims courage, even faith. Koi had confused the myth of an afterlife with a place described by a priest, if that's what the man really was. Koi touched his forehead at the hairline. "He was marked."

Disidentified. Sento's forehead tingled, but she resisted an impulse to touch it.

Returning to the head of the column, and reporting Koi found, Sento cut across a plain until she reached a watercourse and a prospective campsite. Hosea and the council agreed the first day or two of travel ought to be relatively short to build up the pilgrims' stamina and set good traveling habits. The column caught up with her and the pilgrims spread out to make camp. Soon, small fires were burning.

A child screamed.

Adults rushed to the noise. When Sento and Hosea arrived, the child's father was comforting her. He pointed to a mound below a boulder. Snow melt had eroded the mound, revealing a tuft of hair and a bloated face. Birds and rats had eaten out its eyes.

"Does anyone know her?"

No one said a word.

Koi stepped toward the corpse and knelt.

Sento pulled at his shoulder. "What are you doing now?" *Why am I so concerned about his behavior?*

The youth shrugged off Sento's hand. "Fixing this woman's grave. Can someone help me?"

The pilgrims glanced at each other, waiting for someone to move. Calmed by Koi's quiet contemplation of the dead woman, the frightened child who screamed picked up a stone and added it to the pile over the corpse.

As others joined the repair detail, Sento and Hosea walked back to the camp. "Where did you find Koi?" Hosea said.

"Pretending to be a Catholic priest. It didn't seem right. But—" Sento shrugged.

"Prayer is about all these people have."

"I think they've found a saint."

The camp took a while to settle down. Kanthaka carried extra clothes, food, and medical supplies. Bruce struggled maneuvering the bot into a convenient position.

Sento said, "Your controller is kind of old-fashioned, isn't it?"

"It's a backup." Bruce dropped it into his coat pocket. "I'm controlling the bot via the local com." His face scrunched like a dessicated orange.

"Oh."

"Don't you see the network, Sento?" Gwen said.

Virtually everyone was looped into the global com system from age two or three, but Sento's com connection hadn't worked since Valparaíso. "Um, it's been broken for a while." She tapped the side of her head behind her right ear. "Maybe the cold water did something to the wetware when the bot pushed me off the *Kildare*." A non-working com was a social misstep in some circles.

"I can fix it, I'll bet." Bruce's eyes lit up with the challenge.

"He's very good," Gwen confirmed.

The last time Sento was on the com network, she guessed, was prior to her memory loss. "Ok. It'll be good to share again."

Locking down Kan for the curious children to admire, Bruce sat Sento next to a portable workbench, stained by machine oil and dark dots that might have been dried blood. *Watch for sharp objects.* He placed a standard, if worn, diagnostic cap over her head. It covered roughly the same area as her hair, including the area behind her ears where batteries and the main processor were installed. Sento heard a tiny click, like a switch. She swallowed, ignoring the butterflies. "That tingles," she said. "Static electricity?"

"No," Bruce said, distracted. "Normal feedback."

"How long has it been since you had a checkup?" Gwen said, in nurse mode.

Sento was unsure how much to say. She had no memory of what com diagnostics felt like. She wasn't up to explaining that her memory went back only a couple of years. She had to fake her way through it. *Maybe getting back on the network is a bad idea.* "Since before Point Arenas." The walk from Valparaiso had taken three months. She spent another three in the port city before signing on with the refugee ship. "I never had time to get my com fixed."

Gwen's face was a mixture of curiosity and skepticism. "It takes five minutes."

"Well, I—"

Bruce interrupted. "The circuits look fine. The leads into the visual and aural cortex are solid. What are you seeing, Sento?"

Stars, like the ones after a punch, floated in front of Sento's eyes. Random tones sounded in her ears. The visual and aural signals were part of the diagnostics, Sento supposed. The brain was perceiving without input from her eyes or ears. *I don't know what's normal or not.* "The usual stuff. I'm not in any pain."

"That's an odd thing to say." Bruce shrugged. "I'll assume that means you're not seeing or hearing anything bad." A keyboard clicked. "Language center interface is strong. This is high-quality work, very high end. You invested quite a lot of money into this installation. Seems strange that you wouldn't take care of it."

"Bruce!"

"I'm just saying. I wish my install was this good."

"You'd void the warranty by hacking it," Gwen said.

"Warranties are for corporations scared of their own customers. Hang on a sec, I want to check the manufacturer ID and the serial number." Bruce tapped. "Well, then. The query for the maker info returns 'no data.' Never seen that before."

Sento shifted in her seat. *He's going to find something I won't like.*

"Just fix the problem so she can get on the net." Gwen's tone was protective.

She knows something's not right. If she asks about it, I'd have to lie.

"Fine," Bruce said. "The batteries are completely dead, even the one that keeps the clock alive. Maybe that's the problem. I'm going to reboot the system with outside power. Sen, let me know if you see anything weird."

I have no idea what "weird" might look like. "Okay."

A saturated white gleam filled her visual field and faded, and a dull Middle C tone sounded in her ear. Then, as if floating in the air 20 centimeters in front of her face, a sequence of commands and readouts flashed by. She recognized the general pattern of diagnostic probes from devices, such as Bruce's bot controller, but the specifics meant little. Computers and software weren't her strong suit.

"Crazy, crazy, crazy," Bruce said.

Sento couldn't help squirming as her anxiety rose.

"Hold still."

"Bruce, you'd make a terrible doctor," Gwen said.

He'd make a fine master of torture.

"The file system is completely blank. There's just nothing in ROM, not even an operating system." He turned to Gwen. "That never happens."

Sento felt as if layers of clothing were being peeled from her body, leaving her vulnerable, but she was trapped. *I don't know why I'm scared.*

Gwen sensed her patient's fear. "Bruce, just help her. We don't have time for geeky detective work." She put a hand on Sento's arm. "Be patient with him, dear."

Sento held still, trusting that these people she'd known only a few days wouldn't harm her.

"Sen, I'm going to load a generic com OS into your install. The software's rudimentary and meant for testing circuitry, but you'll have all the basic functions. Thing is—"

"Yes?"

"It won't restore any files. The headers, the bits, everything is wiped. Sorry."

Disappointed, Sento realized the files could've told her everything she wanted to know about herself. "Don't worry. It was just a few pictures." In truth, she had no idea if they were pictures, documents, vids, saved engrams, or if the bio-logic memory had always been blank.

"Good," Bruce said. "Here goes."

Sento's visual field flashed again, and after a second or two, she saw the login prompt. With no memory of ever using a com, she wasn't sure what to do. She recognized the pattern from advertisements and vid shows she watched on monitors in bus and train stations. The poorest people, derelicts, and, of course, the dissed, were frequently off the net. A cyber-detective show had hooked her, and she remembered how the characters accessed the com. A sense of competence returned. "I've got a prompt, but I don't remember my user name."

Bruce sniffed. "It doesn't matter at this point. The public com network is unreliable around here. For the time being, you'll just be on my network. Enter something in the login. It'll prompt you to create credentials when it doesn't recognize you."

Sento stared at the prompt and the word "Isorropia" popped into her consciousness. It also appeared in the prompt. *I just have to imagine what I want to do.* She thought "Go," and the security prompts appeared.

"You're slow," Bruce said.

"I'm out of practice."

"Give her some time, Bruce," Gwen chided.

After a few misfires, Sento found herself on the network. It was a strange feeling, uncertainty overlaid with a sense of mastery, as if a lifelong skill lurked beneath her consciousness. She saw two avatars, which she guessed were Bruce and Gwen. Bruce's was a dragon, Gwen's an asklepian. A burst of excitement and wonder nearly overcome Sento. She had entered a new virtual world, and she wanted to explore it.

Bruce tapped the keyboard again. "Gwen, send Sento a text or a photo. Put an emo-sig on it."

Sento, we're so glad you're here with us.

Sento blinked, then stared at Gwen. The woman's statement was loving, almost intimate. The emo-sig radiated an emotion that relaxed the younger woman.

Thank you, Gwen.

"Everything good? The privacy settings mean I can't see the content, only the fact it was sent," Bruce said.

"All good," Sento said, echoing Gwen.

"Cool. The battery recharge will take about an hour, so we'll sit tight until then," Bruce said. "The persistent inductive recharging from your install's mitochondrial generators will take over from there."

Sento breathed out, and let herself drift into Bruce's network, which was named "Valinor." She recalled a saying that a person never forgets how to ride a bicycle, and she felt as if she hadn't ridden for decades as she stumbled through Bruce's virtual world. At the same time, however, her sense of comfort, that traversing a virtual world was as normal as the physical world, grew quickly, faster, she guessed, than if she had never traveled in cyberspace. It was as familiar in that way you speak to an old friend not seen for decades.

"More weirdness," Bruce said.

"Baby, can you try to be a bit more gentle? Sen hasn't had com for a long time."

"I'm just saying that I found another odd thing. It's not like cancer or anything."

"What is it?" Sento said, more irritated than she'd like to be.

"It's a signal, near your optic nerve. Are you seeing anything out of the ordinary?"

Sento shook her head.

"It's definitely not part of your com. And it's inside your head."

A sense of alarm grew. *Is something wrong with me I don't know about?* "What do we do?"

"I've got a portable MRI I traded from one of the UN ships. It might show something."

Sento nodded.

Don't worry. It's just an MRI. The text came from Gwen.

"I have to put this mesh over your head. It won't interfere with the com recharge." The mesh was gauzy enough that Sento could see through it, but it was solid, like a helmet. Sento was not prone to claustrophobia, but she couldn't escape a feeling that she might choke.

Tools and equipment clanked as Bruce pushed them aside to make a space on his workbench for the MRI equipment. "Okay, getting data. Looks good. Hey. Whoa. Gwen, check this out."

Sento lost her patience. "What the hell? What's inside my head?"

"Sorry. Take a look. I'll ship the live image to your com."

A second later, Sento opened the video image. She recognized the cross-section of her head, with the bones of her face and skull, as well as the musculature, and the outline of her eyeballs.

"Zoom in. Look behind your left eye. See that bright spot next to the optic nerve?"

The spot was solid, about two millimeters long and a half-millimeter wide. "What the fuck? What is that? Can you take it out? Am I sick or something?" Sento never got sick, not even colds. Medical devices that released drugs and bots that attacked cancer cells were common, but she'd never heard of anything deliberately placed in someone's eye. *Someone wanted to hide it or make it hard to remove.*

Sento wheeled to face Bruce. Gwen huddled next to him, fearful in a way Sento hadn't seen before. "What is going on? What is it for, the thing in my head?"

Bruce swallowed. "I've only seen pictures. I've read about them, too."

"What the fuck is it? Tell me now!" Terrified, Sento grabbed Bruce's sweater and shirt in her powerful hands. Gwen blanched.

"You won't like it," Bruce said.

"Fuck you!" Sento's heart raced, as if her body knew the answer. "I'll break your neck if you don't tell me now." An idea surfaced, and she shook her head, trying to drive it out, because it was too horrifying to contemplate. It was like discovering that someone in your family was a mass murderer, or a victim of a mass murderer.

"It's a disidentification chip," Bruce gulped, his voice a whisper.

Sento's jaw dropped and she hissed. "You're wrong! How can that be?" If it was true, then her life made sense, but the wrong kind of sense, the opposite of the sense it *should* make, the sense that most people want and hope for. She wanted to learn the opposite of what it meant.

"I don't know how it happened, but you've been dissed, Sen."

Sento let go of Bruce, who lost his balance and tripped over a disassembled bot at his feet. Sento was too wrapped up in her horror to apologize.

"Sen, I'm so sorry." Gwen reached out to Sento, but the nurse didn't touch her.

I've been disidentified. I've been dead for two years.

The discovery of the disidentification chip cleared up a piece of Sento's story, and her initial revulsion dulled into disbelief. She'd suspected it all along, while hoping it was just a horrible fantasy. With no facts, she had no way to judge if her punishment was deserved. Only the worst criminals were dissed, just as corporeal execution was reserved for mass murderers prior to the adoption of disidentification. Bruce ran more tests and confirmed with 98 percent certainty that object behind her eye was a disidentification chip, intended to block or wipe memories associated with identity. It was standard punishment for the most heinous crimes, along with the legal destruction of all external memory of a person's existence, and the demand that society treat the dissed as non-existent. *Shunning. Social death.* The techie guessed the chip had malfunctioned.

Bruce and Gwen speculated she'd received a last-minute reprieve or authorities realized she was not guilty, but it was too late to stop the procedure. The chip did its work, despite her dreams and memory fragments, but the executioners didn't touch her skeleton's DNA to grow the tulip brand on her forehead. To avoid embarrassment, they dumped her on the street. No other plausible scenario occurred to Sento.

Another dream, or memory, it was hard to tell which, came to her that night. She was in a small dark room, swaying and pitching, and the nausea was so palpable that she woke up with vomit in her mouth. The motion was much like that of *Kildare* on the trip from Punta Arenas to Nordenskjöld, so much so that Sento was certain that the vaguely remembered journey was also an extended run at sea. The destination was veiled, but the anxiety was as vivid as she experienced during the death throes of the ferry. She feared for her life, but the voyage itself did not account for all her terror. Another person—not the silver-faced man nor the man she remembered chasing during the camp fire—was the cause. As she thought it through, the idea came that the boat carried her north, away from all she knew, including family and friends. *Is this why I want so badly to go south, even if I don't know exactly where? Who sent me away from Antarctica in the first place?* She had been kidnapped. She believed that's how she wound up in Valparaíso. The black curtain over her past was an intense as ever, but it was fraying and lifting.

In the morning, she watched the camp come to life. The pilgrims' origins were as diaphanous as her own. Their faces were light, dark, and in-between. Most spoke the main languages of the Western Hemisphere. She heard a smattering of sounds she didn't recognize, though the people who made them had the features of Africans, Indians, and East Asians. The whole world had sent representatives. *Did they dream as I did?*

She was an outcast among the exiled, but a sense of kinship grew as she circled the company, her pistol on her hip, loaded, with the safety on. She slipped into the role of guardian/protector/peacemaker, though the usual reasons for fighting were missing: religions were tolerated, political persuasions were irrelevant, and virtually everyone was a have-not. All shared the solidarity of poverty, persecution, and irrational hope. Many of the refugees had fled government maltreatment, or religious intolerance, or they had violated environmental regulations. On the Old Continents, huckster politicians enacted environmental restoration laws as an excuse to run poor farmers off their land or push low-wage workers out of the cities to protect their rich constituents' jobs.

Sento paid extra attention to how the throng handled its trash and waste. Ninety-nine percent of Antarctica was still pristine, and a distinct voice in Sento's heart urged her to protect even the smallest patch of hair grass. She suspected the impetus came from her previous life, but she had no way to know.

Why aren't I like the old woman on the ship, a husk of a person? Sento touched her forehead, just below the hairline, where the tulip welt had been on the dissed woman who drowned, and where it should've been on Sento's forehead if she were dissed. *What was my crime?* A broken dis-chip. A failed welting. The dead com was part of the pattern as well, else why wipe everything from ROM or storage? Sento compared herself to a soul in Purgatory, between acceptance in human society and a tortured exile.

Sento rested on a flat stone on low rise that allowed her to watch the camp. Hosea dropped to his haunches beside her. "People are asking about you. I know you're a loner, but they think of you as part of the group."

"You should talk to Bruce. Or Gwen. They'll tell you a different story."

"They're worried about you." He pushed around a stone. "Nobody cares about the dissing."

"You're sure about that?" Everyone was trained to consider the dissed as unworthy of a thought or glance.

"Very sure," Hosea said. "We're all drifters now, all criminals in someone's eyes, all invaders, all dispossessed savages with nothing to lose. It's ironic that those who claim the mantle of civilization are the ones inflicting the violence."

Sento couldn't disagree, but she was not in the mood to discuss the world's inconsistencies and contradictions.

A crunch of gravel announced Koi's arrival. "We've saved some breakfast for you, Sen."

Shame did not make room for an appetite. *What was my crime?*

"What's wrong with her, Hosea?"

"I don't know. Feeling guilt for sins she can't remember?" The question was directed to Sento.

"You don't know anything about me." *That's because I know so little about myself, except for the memories. The man with the silver face. The shooting. The kidnapping. The emotions without substance.*

"Wait, I can help." Koi took a place directly in front of Sento, went to his knees, and put his hands together, palms and fingers of each hand flat against the other. He closed his eyes and moved his right hand in the pattern of a cross. *"Deus, Pater misericordiárum, qui per mortem et resurrectiónem Fílii sui mundum sibi reconciliávit et Spíritum Sanctum effúdit in remissiónem peccatórum, per ministérium Ecclésiæ indulgéntiam tibi tríbuat et pacem. Et ego te absolvo a peccatis tuis in nomine Patris, et Filii,+ et Spiritus Sancti."*

Sento huffed. "What the hell?" The gesture and incantation were unnerving.

"I think he just forgave you all your sins." Hosea chuckled.

"It's not funny." Koi remained on his knees. "It's what the priest said to my mother before she died."

"That's supposed to wipe the slate clean?" The gravel was rough, and Sento imagined it cutting into Koi's thin trousers.

"It cleansed my mother's soul, leaving it pure and white as a linen sheet. I can do it for you, when I take Holy Orders."

Sento laughed, then stopped when she saw Koi's frown. "Sorry."

"Nobody believes in anything. But I believe in something. I'm going to be a priest and help people. We're going to live in Isorropia and be happy. All of us. I might see my mother. It's going to happen."

Sento admired the child's faith, but she could not match it. She glanced at Hosea, who rested his big hand on Koi's shoulder. An incipient longing for Hosea's blessing irked her. *He has a pregnant wife.* She respected Hosea's more mature faith. He understood the odds, and she decided to let fate take its course.

She got to her feet and brushed off the dust. "I'm hungry. We've got a long day ahead."

CHAPTER 7

ELITA SOARES TRACED HER FASHIONABLE fingernail from the back of her lover's neck down his spine to the small of his back, letting her journey rise to his buttocks. She detoured her finger over his hip, resting her hand on his erection, discerning his skipped breath. His testicles were drawn up against the base of his phallus like loaded weapons. The corner of her mouth curved into a smirk. Lifting her finger over his right ball, she jabbed it hard with her nail.

"Owww!" Lucius Galla sprang out of Elita's bed, protecting his anatomy from further attack. Sunlight draped his face, highlighting the rage of a child whose best friend had betrayed him. For a man of violence, Lucius had few scars on his body, at least none that she'd ever found. His wounds, however, were hidden, according to his personnel record, which she had studied before taking him to her bed. A classic case of borderline personality disorder: unstable, impulsive, and an intense fear of abandonment. Perfect for manipulation.

Elita rested her finger on her tooth, testing the sharpness of the nail with her tongue. "That is your punishment." She rolled onto her back, redolent on the tightly woven, hand-sewn futon.

"That hurt." Lucius' hard-on flagged.

"I meant it to hurt." Elita replaced her finger with a mist stick, sucking it while keeping her focus on Lucius.

"I explained what happened." Lucius parted the drapes. The window of Elita's bedroom looked down on a square surrounded by the best addresses in Isorropia. "I had no idea the idiots in Nordenskjöld would burn the camp. They were supposed to push the *inmigrantes* around, fire a few shots in the air, scare them shitless."

Lucius was a brilliant security chief, and Elita relied on him to keep tabs on enemies internal and external, but his unpredictability was as annoying as it was useful. He carried out his orders like an automaton. Subtlety and interpretation were alien to him, and his thoroughness led him to extremes. He may not have told the town militia to burn the town, but he likely left no doubt that the camp was a threat to be eliminated. On the other hand, Elita consistently forgot to instruct Lucius with a precision that might keep him—and her—out of trouble.

"I'm still angry at you and your stupid BES goons. The idea was to contain the camp and discourage more refugees from coming."

"I can't control everything. You said, 'Do something about that camp,' and I did."

"How many people did the militia kill?"

"How should I know? I didn't ask for a body count."

The news chans distributed the story within hours of the fire, showing charred bodies and weeping children. The city's chattering class went ape. Snap polls showed public sympathy for the refugees rising, which was bad for Elita and her policy of keeping climate exiles at arm's length. *At least the Old Continents prefer ignorance. They never send journos south.*

"If your militia morons are linked to you, they'll be linked to me, and then my career is over." Elita snapped her fingers. "That means your career is over. Not even the Argus Dome weather station would hire you." The Dome on the East Antarctica Ice Sheet was possibly the remotest place on the continent, which made it the remotest place on the planet.

Elita needed to punish someone, and Lucius was deserving. She put on a show of enjoying her torments of Lucius, but in her heart of hearts, she didn't relish her cruelty to him. She liked him, but they were one of those couples whose conflict was part and parcel of their bond. Her father told her the fire would burn out eventually, or his flame would threaten her, and she'd have to let him go. It was a variation on the conversation she and Ben had every few years about her preferences in men. Her mother—divorced from Ben shortly after Elita's tenth birthday—was a liberal woman who let a teenaged Elita welcome young mens' attentions under a watchful eye. Elita was anxious to please her father, and she picked boys from prominent families, each with a clear path to power or professional success. *Even in a society with egalitarian pretensions, blood and connections matter.*

After a time, however, she despised them. Every male with fuzz on his chin knew Elita as the popular, sharp and beautiful daughter of the metaphorical king. Most followed the public proprieties, even if they pressed her for sex like rutting stags. She allowed herself the trophy role in school rituals, and she praised them when their marks were high at semester's end, like the supportive girlfriend should. When she shared photos with her father, he related his knowledge of the fellow's family and background. One suitor, however, asked once too often when he would meet her father, and the revelation was swift and painful: Elita was only a means to inclusion in her father's circle.

Though her father had never put her up to be a dynastic pawn, she lashed out at him anyway. The opportunity came on her secondary school graduation night, the same night, by coincidence, for a ceremony "graduating" eight-year-old Marissa from second grade to third. Ben promised to be at both events, but he showed up so late to Elita's ceremony that he missed seeing her receive her diploma. He apologized, but Elita was unmoved. That night, at an after-the-reception bacchanalia, Elita found a young man with a record as an under-the-table mist dealer and slept with him. When Ben found out via an explicit photo posted on a public c-tribe, he lost his temper, threatening to "cut her off," whatever that meant. It was an empty threat. Nonetheless, she begged forgiveness, but crossed her fingers behind her back. Elita knew exactly what she was doing; she had posted the photo. On top of this, the hoodlum, understanding his incredible luck, obeyed her slightest command. By accident, she discovered that her name and sexual powers were like puppet strings. Lucius was only the latest conquest, though he was more useful and intelligent than most.

Now Lucius has screwed up. Was Father right all along? The Nordenskjöld disaster had all the hallmarks of an unfolding crisis, and Elita needed to yank Lucius' chain. "Your mistake, lover boy, plays right into the hands of my enemies."

"Stop lecturing me. How many times do I have to tell you that it wasn't my fault?" Lucius' attitude was high-handed. "Besides, you know I don't care about politics. You're the brains of our partnership."

Good. Let him continue to believe we are partners. The only political partner Elita allowed in her life was her father, though she feared even he was becoming unreliable. She was undecided on whether Lucius could be anything other than a subordinate or a bed partner. *Love takes energy I don't have. Someday, maybe...* Elita rose from the bed and donned her dressing gown, letting the satin drape over her open legs.

Staring at her flexed calf, Lucius licked his lips, like a starving dog, then frowned. "Have I told you how much I hate your enslavement of me?"

Isorropia's First Citizen laughed. She ordered the kitchen bot to make coffee. "Lucius, the coffee pot is the closest thing I have to a slave. You and every other citizen of Isorropia are 'free and independent souls.'" Elita quoted one of the most famous phrases of the Isorropian constitution.

"Not this citizen." Lucius pouted. "I can't take a piss without your approval. And when I do what you want, you're never happy."

"So? Leave me. Find some other woman to fuck. It's not that hard."

Lucius faced flushed. Elita knew the look. He was hurt again, and this time in a place far more sensitive that his right ball. He approached her, his body as taut as a bowstring. "Leaving you is impossible." He lowered himself to the carpeted floor, sitting on his heels, like an acolyte at a teacher's feet. Elita wasn't sure she liked it.

"I can't stop thinking about you," Lucius confessed. "I'm in love with you. I'm obsessed with you. Every time you touch me, my whole body turns to fire. If you told me to jump into the Southern Ocean naked or the walk across one of the New Deserts barefoot, I would do it."

He's sweet, and sad, at the same time. Elita cupped his cheek in her hand. "You're such a romantic, Lucius."

"You're the cruelest woman that has ever lived."

Did he mean as a lover, or as a political leader? Elita enjoyed the exercise of power, even in an office as proscribed as First Citizen. If a major crisis was coming—and she believed it to be true—she was ready to revel in it, like the first taste of a rare, expensive food. She'd watched her father lead the city through numerous political crises, and his advisers hovered around him like workers around a queen bee. She was now the queen bee, though she'd yet to have a real crisis test her. *Bring it on, and I'll show him what I'm made of.* Unlike her father, whose inner circle was little more than a mob, as far as she was concerned, she relied on a few people she could control, such as Lucius. The fact that Lucius was a skilled and devoted lover was icing on the cake. "I'm only hard on you when you deserve it, Lucius. Don't screw up, and you can continue to screw me."

Lucius jaw dropped. "What's that supposed to mean?"

"Do what I tell you, but don't go too far." The kitchen bot set down the espresso cups, but Lucius did not take his. Elita watched him close the bathroom door, a twinge of guilt tempering her admiration of his powerful body. She sighed and scrolled through her daily intelligence briefing via her mindseye. The military sent more recent high-resolution images of the burned-out camp. The random devastation immediately after the militia's attack was replaced by pockets of cleaned areas and stockpiled goods.

Back to business. "Lucius, your spooks say the refugees have broken camp."

The BES chief emerged from the bathroom in a t-shirt and briefs. "Interesting. Where are they going?"

"You tell me."

"I haven't a clue."

"Good God, Lucius, you can be exasperating. Find out!"

"Calm down. I only meant that there's no information either way."

"You'll let me know, first thing? Right? If they're a threat, we'll need to stop them."

"I don't know what you're worried about. They've got no supplies for an overland journey. No warm clothing, no vehicles, no food. Certainly no weapons outside of a rusty pistol or two. I doubt they know any more about us that our propagandists have told them or the rest of the planet. We're at best a myth to them. It would be suicidal to look for us, even if they knew where to look." He sat at the table, sipped the lukewarm latte, and scowled. "Eighty percent of Isorropia is underground. We're shielded from virtually every kind of electronic surveillance. We've set electronic decoys to confuse unwanted visitors. They couldn't find us." Isorropia's main defense strategy was concealment and misdirection, beefed up once the city understood that the Southern Ocean no longer served as a moat.

"All the same, Lucius, we may need to take preemptive action," Elita said.

"Such as?"

"It will depend on the circumstances, but I won't just hand over our beautiful city to primitives."

"They're human beings."

"You sound like the humanitarians in the Ecclesia."

"Just sayin'."

Is he sympathetic? No, just petulant. "That reminds me. My father asked me about any developments on the investigation."

"Which one?"

"My sister's disappearance."

Lucius groaned. "That again. No, there's nothing new. There hasn't been anything new for a year and a half. Tell His Honor that the trail is as cold as permafrost."

Elita took a sharp breath and let it out quickly. *Father knows this, so why does he keep asking?* The last time Elita saw Marissa was on the final night of the Summer Solstice celebrations two years prior. All Isorropia reveled annually at the reappearance of the sun and the six-month day. As a functionary in the BES' investigative division, Marissa was invited to one of the dozens of *de rigueur* events for government workers. The older half-sister carried a mental image of a modest woman wearing ordinary street clothes that showed off her fit physique. "She was intense, but attractive."

"Like you?"

"Do you think so?"

Lucius shrugged. "That describes you, but I barely knew Sentillius. She was too far down the chain of command."

Another memory surfaced. Elita's jealousy of her half-sister surged that night when she saw her on the arm of Ben Soares. He made no secret of his relationship to his illegitimate daughter, and Elita felt snubbed. *Shit, it's happening again.* Ben was rebuffing Elita politically by supporting the humanitarians. After Marissa's disappearance, Elita had her father to herself again. Now her enemies were getting his love, in a manner of speaking. *Can I win him back?*

"What do you think happened to her, Lucius?"

"Hmm?" He pulled his attention away from a tablet.

"What's your hypothesis on the disappearance of Marissa Sentillius?"

"I have no opinion." He sipped his coffee, eyes locked on the device.

"I don't believe you. It's one of the most notorious unsolved crimes of the past dozen years."

"You're assuming a crime was committed," Lucius said.

"You mean one wasn't?"

"I mean, what if she ran away?"

"That's never been floated as a possible explanation."

"It would be embarrassing, don't you think?"

Lucius was right. Apart from her culpability, Marissa's involvement in a criminal enterprise would embarrass her father. "You're talking about the shooting of the seal poacher?"

"Not exactly. I'm talking about self-preservation."

"I don't understand."

"The BES investigation of the shooting of the poacher during the raid showed that it was her weapon that killed him. Internal Affairs recommended sanctions, but the disciplinary board declined to act."

"That always mystified me," Elita said. "You guys are a tough bunch, but you take extra-judicial activities seriously."

"Her father is a powerful man."

Elita was shocked at the implication. Ben Soares followed the rules, though he was not above using the rules to his advantage. "That's pure speculation."

"Indeed." Lucius drained his cup. "There's no 'smoking gun,' so to speak. Whatever happened to Marissa two years ago could've been simple revenge."

"By whom?"

Lucius sighed, as if explaining something obvious to a dense student. "Despite Isorropia's self-image as a society in perfect balance, environmental and otherwise, we have an underworld. The seal poaching was part of an organized crime ring. The mob might've have wanted Marissa dead as retaliation. The ring originated in Argentina, a country with a long tradition of 'disappearing' enemies."

Lucius' own family comes from Buenos Aires, a sewer of crime if there ever was one. His hypothesis had the ring of truth, but it was only speculation. The evidence was scanty. If her father asked again, she'd say that the case was still open. Gathering her dressing gown around her, Elita's eye caught the koto on the woven bamboo pad next to the window. Ever since her election as First Citizen, she had no time to practice the instrument with the koto master.

"Play something," Lucius said.

"I haven't in months."

"You're not performing at the All City Music Festival," Lucius said. "It's just me."

Elita couldn't resist a chance to show off, and she loved the koto. Ben introduced her to the instrument when she was ten—around the time Marissa was born, it occurred to Elita—and she fell in love with the koto's sharp power. Playing it pleased her father. She kneeled before the polished kiri wood and put the three plectra on the fingers of her right hand. She tested the silk strings and tuned the instrument. Despite her rustiness, the classical music flowed through her like a quiet stream. She had forgotten how playing brought her to an intense state not far from orgasm. Working another part of her mind released blocks on her consciousness. Doubts about Lucius' theory on her sister's disappearance surfaced again. She finished the tune, and leaned back on her calves. "Lucius, are you sure about Marissa?"

"In what respect, my love?" He rested his chin on his hand.

"You have two theories: running from a prosecution or revenge by a criminal gang. Both have overtones of a conspiracy." She was tempted to pluck a koto string to make her point, but she would not show disrespect to the instrument.

"Your point is..."

"Conspiracies are very hard to hide."

Lucius tapped his empty espresso cup. The *clink-clink-clink* irritated Elita after the melodic tones of the koto.

"Occam's razor." The pitch of Lucius' voice was high, a sign of stress. "The simplest solution is usually the correct one."

"Usually," Elita echoed. Life was infinitely more complicated than most people believed, and throughout her career in politics, she had learned to expect the unexpected, though her instincts sometimes failed her, as with Ben's subterfuge in the *boule* committee. She sighed. *Lucius knows more than he's telling.*

"In any case, there's not enough evidence to support any theory," Lucius said. "Martians could've plucked her off the ice, for all I know."

Lucius' blithe dismissal raised Elita's hackles. She made a note in her minds-eye notepad to review the case file, though she hardly had time to read the daily department reports. She had more important things on her priority list, such as the refugees and the humanitarians in the Ecclesia, but Lucius worried her sometimes.

Elita checked her minds-eye calendar, which updated to show an early meeting moved earlier. She glanced in her closet and decided to wear the robin's egg blue suit. The color matched her favorite hue of Antarctica's dozen colors of ice. She slipped off her dressing gown, in full view of Lucius, opened the shower's faucet, and stepped in. Through the translucent curtain, she noticed Lucius come in and lean against the vanity.

"You're asking a lot of questions this morning," Lucius said.

"It's my job." Elita let the warm water wash over her.

Lucius pushed the curtain aside. It made an unpleasant scraping sound.

"What are you doing?" The act surprised Elita, but it didn't scare her.

"I'm not used to interrogations."

"Don't be stupid. You know that I—"

Lucius snatched her wrist and twisted it toward him. "I conduct interrogations, not suffer them." He squeezed Elita's wrist, and the pressure made Elita wince. "You're hurting me."

Her lover released the pressure, but not his grip. Nude, he stepped into the shower and pulled her close. He was a head taller than her with shoulders almost too wide to fit into the shower stall. The water flowed over his pectorals. His erection pressed against her hip.

What is he doing? He gets rough, but this is different. "You're crossing a line, Lucius. Be careful."

"We have unfinished business." He kissed the nape of her neck, mouthing it with his teeth, and he licked the skin behind her left ear. She shuddered, the water turning cold as her body's temperature rose. His hand still held her wrist, and he forced her to face the wall.

Dominance. It's all about who's in charge with him.

Elita lifted her right foot and brought her heel down on his right instep. The stomp hurt her but he yelped in pain and lost purchase on the slippery surface, and he fell. "Do that again, and I'll have you thrown naked on the ice when the sky is clear and the night is darkest."

CHAPTER 8

Elita's schedule marked the gallery opening as optional, but she needed a distraction from her worry about her father's loyalty. The appearance of the Refugee Relief Act on the Ecclesia's agenda buzzed in the city media, along with speculation about Ben's involvement. An incipient sense of disaster weighed on Elita, like a dull headache. Her disciplining of Lucius didn't help her mood, though he returned to his old self after Elita pledged forgiveness for his attempted assault.

"Your artist friend should do very well in the auction, lover." Lucius stepped back from the monumental painting, twice as tall as the viewer and five paces wide. He exhibited a measured, appreciative look Elita had never seen before. "She's taken New Representationism in an interesting direction, in my opinion. I might bid on this one."

"What do you know of fine art?"

"Nobody ever asks me about my interests other than work. You never have."

Elita admitted the truth of it, but the thought of Lucius as an art lover, much less a collector, was far-fetched. She'd purchased a few inexpensive pieces over the years, mostly from friends to keep them in paints or clay. When Marissa was about five, and Elita was sixteen, she and her father toured the city's art museum. Ben doted on Marissa, endlessly picking her up when she complained of all the walking, praising her when she pointed at any old picture and commented, and buying her an ice cream afterward that was bound to give her a bellyache. Elita, fresh from a basic art appreciation course in high school, also expressed her opinions, slipping her arm underneath her father's to bring him close and discussing the merits and style of each artist. Then Marissa would whine, and he'd shift his attention, abandoning Elita in the middle of a sentence. Elita pouted, but Ben explained that Marissa needed his care more than his nearly adult daughter. Elita fumed, arguing that she had as much right to her father's attention, but Ben ignored her.

Lucius shifted his viewing angle on the mixed-media work, and the expression on his face changed from casual interest to studied contemplation. For Elita's part, the painting stirred unexpected emotions. The image portrayed the nation's Founder as a powerfully built man in body as well as spirit. The wind-blown fur on the hood of his parka framed his face, reminding Elita of Renaissance paintings of the Catholic saints. The figure's cobalt blue eyes exuded the confidence that goes with certitude.

"Do you think he looks like your father?" Lucius said.

The recognition startled Elita. The set of the eyes and mouth were as familiar as her own but the artist was far too romantic. The Founder stretched out his hand, pointing south across the Ross Sea to the Transantarctic Mountains and the Pole beyond. Below his outstretched arm, men, women, and children begged his protection as a storm from the Warming-ravaged temperate zone threatened in the distance.

"Your friend knows how to suck up to wealth, doesn't she?" Lucius chuckled.

The comment had no effect on Elita. Sitting on a bench, she followed the composition to the figure's lower body, where the artist had placed scenes of the Founder's life, as if composing a biography. One of the groupings included two women. Back in school, her old art teacher droned about the viewer bringing as much to a painting as the artist, and as Elita looked at the figures, she swore she perceived herself and Marissa, though without the age difference. A pain in her chest interrupted her breathing. *He embraces her, while his back is turned on me. Was he so transparent with his feelings to the outside world?*

Ben and Elita's mother divorced when she was ten, and he took full advantage of his freedom as the most eligible man on the continent. Marissa was his by a socialite and former Defense Minister who later died in a helicopter crash. However, his ataxia was taking its toll, and he wore one of the early versions of his custom-made exoskeleton. *Was this the same man I watched in my pinafore and saddle shoes? He was invincible then. What is he now?*

At sixteen, Elita was lovely, bright, and popular, all that many expected of the eldest daughter of a First Citizen in his second term. Though they weren't living in the same household, they spent most weekends together. Marissa's arrival did not interfere with the routine, but the elder half-sister made no effort to include Marissa in her time with Ben. The visit to the museum was Ben's idea. Despite Elita's habit of cutting remarks against peers and the occasional vicious bout of revenge for a real or imagined slight, she kept her jealousies about Marissa to herself for fear of hurting her father's feelings. She gave Marissa a gift every Winter Solstice, usually a version of the year's trendy toy or, later on, tween fashion obsession. Her feeling, however, was one of family obligation, rather than affection.

In the gallery, Elita's teenage resentment of her father and jealousy of Marissa flooded back along with the same bewilderment at her father's favoritism. *Marissa was the baby, and the baby needed care. That was his excuse.* As Elita matured, her covetousness faded. Whatever remained of it disappeared with Marissa's death, or what everyone imagined was her death. The painting opened the old wounds.

"Compelling, isn't it?"

"Father! I should've thought you'd be here." The synthetic voice over Elita's shoulder sounded too much like her father's smooth baritone as a young man, despite a mechanical growl, as if he was almost recovered from a deep chest cold.

"Do you remember the times we visited the art museum together?"

"Of course." *I wish I could forget.* "Like it was yesterday."

Lucius sidled up to listen. Ben noticed, but didn't react. *Father must think we're joined at the hip.*

"Memory is such a tricky thing." Ben's actuators hissed. "Take this painting, for example. The story is almost a lie. A myth for sure."

Lucius sighed. "Here comes the lecture."

"Like all cultural origin stories, it's a fantasy." Ben parked in front of the main figure. "The Founder led a group of Chilean refugees to Antarctica, but after a winter that killed four out of five, the survivors returned to Chile. It was a second wave ten years later that founded Isorropia, but the original immigrant story became the source of the city's moral identity."

"I met an American once." Lucius smacked his lips. "He talked about a holiday called 'Thanksgiving,' based on a story about English colonists helped by the indigenous people during a difficult winter. What no one remembered was a war a generation later by the colonists on the indigenous people that nearly wiped them out."

"Father, are you trying to draw a lesson from this?" Elita gestured at the work. "It's only a painting."

"Not really." Ben shifted. "Don't you think it's funny, though, how it's the lies we remember about our country, more than the truths?"

And ourselves, and our families, such as how Marissa was this fragile doll that needed extra protection.

"Could it be that the artist found an opportunity to mix lovely colors together, not make a grand moral statement?" Lucius said.

"You may have a point there, Galla," Ben said. "But you wouldn't recognize a moral statement if it punched you in the face."

Lucius turned as if to confront Ben, but Elita brought her lover to heel with a glare.

"Are you going to bid on it, 'Lita?" Ben's eyes were curious.

"Bid?"

"That's what everyone's here for, to bid on the artists' work. They have to make a living, you know."

A trickle of collectors and aficionados strolled from painting to painting, wine glasses in hand. Though many glanced in her direction, no one interrupted to press the flesh with their elected leader. Perhaps they were intimidated by the sight of the silver-clad icon instructing the daughter and her frightening paramour. "I may offer a few euros, Father."

"And you, Galla? Collecting fine art is your only redeeming quality."

Lucius had cooled. "At least someone appreciates my good side. I may bid on it."

Elita found the gallery on the city com net and registered for the auction. She'd make a show of bidding to encourage others, as well as demonstrate her support for the arts. In truth, her bank account couldn't handle a large, frivolous purchase; First Citizens' pay kept them in noodles, not fine art. Power and influence were the main compensation. *And maybe a consultant job afterward.*

The painting was the last item on the auction list, and as the auctioneer worked through it, Elita tuned herself out of the action, while Lucius and Ben gathered with the other buyers. *Even enemies have things in common.* Elita remembered a promise to Ben and called up the file on Marissa's disappearance via the com net. She went first to the update log, kept by a functionary in Lucius' office. The last entry was dated three days previous, and it echoed most of the weekly entries for the past year: "No new leads." Elita pulled out the case summary, and re-read the narrative. Marissa Sentillius, three years in the Bureau of Environmental Security's enforcement arm, already with a distinguished record, was promoted to the investigative unit. She was looking into the illegal importation of agarwood when she disappeared without a trace. The last entry in her case file log was "informant meeting" and a time, late in the evening, but no location. *Lured into a trap.*

Reaching the end of the document manifest, she selected the last item, and it failed to open. It was password-protected and encrypted. *Odd. I thought my credentials opened everything.*

She texted: Lucius, what's your password for secure documents? Mine's not working.

Lucius was hidden in the crowd of bidders. Should I contact IT?

Just give me your password. You can change it later.

But... Okay, fine. He sent the code that mapped to a specific DNA sequence in his genome. He also sent the override code that would let Elita use his password.

The authentication worked, and the file opened. Labeled simply "Follow up," the document was about a half-dozen references to other documents with a few links. One of them was marked "LRG" and highlighted in red, as if warning away a reader. Elita clicked the link, and a prompt appeared about privacy of personnel documents. At the prompt, Elita entered her credentials, and the server, never fast, cranked away. The shock of the result blocked Elita's awareness of everything around her. The name and the photo at the top of the personnel file belonged to Lucius Ram Galla. Aware of eyes on her, she refocused her gaze. Lucius, successful at a purchase, winked at Elita. A chill went up her spine.

She closed the file, fearful that Lucius was monitoring accesses. *Is Lucius connected to Marissa's disappearance?* She blinked, as if she could erase what she'd read via her minds-eye, or turn back the clock. "Trust" was not a word she used to describe her feelings toward the man, but his predictability helped her feel comfortable. She didn't expect to discover a link between him and her own family that implied murder. *I'm jumping to conclusions. Calm down.*

"Your father's in a buying mood." Lucius returned to her side. "Feeling good about himself, I'd say."

"What now?"

"You read the report in the *Essayist* today about the persistent rumors of private aid on its way to the refugees, didn't you?"

If I had a penny for every article I'm supposed to read, I'd be richer than Father. "I skimmed it. As usual, pundits are passing rumors off as facts."

"Maybe, but you should look at the comments. They're often instructive."

Elita sighed and brought up the article in her minds-eye.

He's right, but who cares?...I don't want any of those people on my street...We need to help them...Can't we build a settlement for them away from the city?..What about our values, our ethics?

The bulk of public sentiment was still with Elita, but it was slipping. People were forgetting how a wave of migrants had nearly swamped Isorropia. The fear of losing the unique Isorropian identity was one of the things that swept her into power, though it took two recounts to confirm her election.

Lucius folded his arms. "My people hear the same thing reported in the article, but they're having trouble nailing down anything concrete."

"It's not illegal to collect donations and buy goods to relieve suffering," Elita said. Finger to the wind, she flirted with taking her father's side. *I must be crazy.*

"Your father's name has come up a couple of times."

Elita spun on Lucius. "That wasn't in the *Essayist*."

"It's in my reports. See for yourself."

Elita didn't need to. Ben Soares had made his sympathies known—albeit discreetly—and his manipulation of the *boule* committee on the Refugee Relief Act was clear enough. It grated on Elita that her father would undermine her policy objectives, even if his behavior was perfectly acceptable. *He might have been the source of the article. It would be like him to pull the media's strings for his own purposes.*

"What if..." A thought had been brewing in Elita's mind, and now it was ready.

"What if what?" Lucius tilted his head to hang on Elita's next word.

"What if we stopped fighting the Relief Act. What if we accepted it in principle?"

Lucius stepped back, as if Elita had a contagious disease. "Are you kidding? We'd be overrun with undesirables."

"No, Lucius, you have it wrong." Elita's voice turned oily. "We need to help those poor people. It's the right thing to do."

"You've been sniffing bad mist."

Elita grinned as a plan formed in her mind. "Not to worry, my dear. My head is as clear as an Antarctic summer's day."

Her grin didn't last long. A wave of loneliness hollowed her out, like a parasitic insect chewing at her insides. The potential for Lucius' involvement in Marissa's disappearance, and her father's underhanded actions in the Legislature, left Elita feeling isolated. The person most important to her—Ben—was not as unconditionally supportive as she always imagined, and Lucius was acting in character. She felt as if she'd been fooled by a practical joke, and it embarrassed her.

The auction halted for a five-minute break. Lucius headed off to relieve himself. Ben replaced him at Elita's side. She wrapped her arms around herself, as if the Antarctic cold had seeped into the gallery.

"Lita, I need to talk to you." Ben's voice was soft, or as much as it could be, with its artificial tone. "I know you're angry with me."

Elita could not hold back her sarcasm. "Why would I be angry? You're practically leading the charge against me."

"I believe it's best for our beautiful city. It's not that I don't love you."

A notification in Elita's minds-eye signaled the start of the bidding for the mural. She entered the fray with a few euros above the reserve price. "What you believe is best? Who elected you First Citizen? No one, but you're behaving as if you were."

"I've always acted in your interest, but I believe you're making a mistake, by standing in the way of suffering people. Just like your mistaken belief that I've favored Marissa over you."

Elita clenched her fists, her rage barely in check. "I've never said that. Never."

Another notification: A bid by Lucius. Other bids followed, then one by her father, a trigger bid once the bids reached a certain level.

"You've never said it," Ben continued, "but I've seen it in your eyes and the way you carry yourself whenever we talk about Marissa."

"Father, you're..." *Crazy?* "I'm worried about you. You're not yourself."

"You have to understand, Lita. Marissa was very young. I felt responsible. I made a mistake with her mother, and your mother, but I couldn't abandon Marissa."

Is he asking forgiveness? Elita placed another bid, throwing caution to the wind.

Ben's eyes were puzzled. "Lita, are you sure about that bid?"

"Yes, I'm sure. I'm damned sure. I'm sure as hell you're lying to me or manipulating me to support you in the Ecclesia, but it's not going to work." She narrowed her eyes. "This is what I'm going to do. I'm going to accept the Refugee Act, and then I'll gut it, either in the Ecclesia or by fiat in the bureaucracy. You think you're going to win, like you always do. Not this time."

Ben stepped back, either in fear of his daughter, or because she had won the auction. While she argued with her father, she automatically bid up every other participant, until the auctioneer declared, "Sold!" When she looked at the total, she froze. *Father let me win.* She had no choice but to pay, or cause herself serious political damage. She had already wiped out her bank account, and then some.

Bidders approached her, congratulating her for the purchase. The artist was practically in tears. The amount of the sale was more than she had earned the entire previous year. Lucius was gape-mouthed. "I didn't think you had it in you. I've never seen you behave that way, with money, anyhow."

Elita's own shock was as powerful, but she smoothed out her jacket and acknowledged everyone's praise. She pulled Lucius aside for a private word. "Do me a favor?"

"Of course."

"Take delivery of the painting for me."

"Okay, I suppose. Then bring it to your apartment?"

"Hell, no. As soon as they give it to you, burn it."

CHAPTER 9

From the diary of Artemis Macedon

THE YOUNG MAN, THE ONE named Koi Nahim, is fascinating. I observed him performing what appeared to be a religious service. He and a few others were at the top of a hill, the classic location for getting physically closer to a deity. It made me wonder: Why did God make Antarctica? What lesson did He mean to teach?

I have a hypothesis. Genesis says God created the earth in six days, and He rested on the seventh. Genesis does not say *where* He rested. The Lord worked hard those six days, and He needed a pause for a project review, and like the humans He created in his own image, He wanted to get away. Impervious to cold, and anxious for a change of scenery, He escaped to Antarctica, the last place any of His pesky new worshippers would look for Him. It's not hard to hide here, especially for an immaterial spirit. He could blend in to the white of the mountain snow, the blue of the bergs floating in the Weddell Sea, the breath of the desiccating katabatic winds flowing down Dome Argus and Dome Circe of the great East Antarctic Ice Sheet. Somehow, I don't think He's been back since that first visit. The climate is terrible for a God used to a temperate-zone desert.

I'm laughing as I record this in my minds-eye diary. My personal diary, not my report to my patron. Of course, the ideas are silly. I don't believe in a God that shapes continents or universes. No Isorropian takes seriously the notion of an all-powerful, all-knowing perfect Being. Our city was built by engineers and scientists who practiced the scientific method, and the empirical evidence for a God of the type popular in the monotheistic religions is scant. That said, if God were a poet, and he needed a symbol for the isolation and loneliness of individual humans, Antarctica works. A feral man living alone on its 14 million square kilometers knows the meaning of "godforsaken."

God might not have the power to help the refugees filing past my hiding place. They've set out for Isorropia, an impossible, if understandable goal from their perspective. Unwelcome anywhere, they're heading to the smallest hope of welcome. I need my patron more than I'm scared of Ticino (I remembered his name), but I stay as far away from him as possible. On the other hand, I stay as close to Sento as I can, without being caught. She's a fascinating woman, almost charismatic. Even though the migrants have made Hosea their leader, she leads in her own way with confidence and single-mindedness. She's almost Hosea's alter ego. I think I'd follow her, if she asked. I might even fall in love with her. Good thing I have to keep my distance. It's like insulation for my emotions, viz a viz Sento.

Even so, I wish I could approach her and the other leaders and tell them that the city will never let them in voluntarily. It might be even resist them with violence on a scale orders of magnitude greater than the ignorant fools of Nordenskjöld. The migrants don't even have a guide, beyond some old, useless maps. I've seen them. I tapped into their crude local network. I hid my snooping using the old BES security masks still in my minds-eye database.

I could guide them. If I did, and the man who exiled me found out, he'd kill me socially, maybe physically. I prefer to stay alive. Yes, I'm still afraid of him, two years after my exile, and I hate him for exiling me. I'd go back for revenge, if I weren't so scared.

I'm scared of a lot of people, apparently.

Maybe my best revenge is in that column of refugees. Perhaps I can show the way without guiding them, give them a fighting chance. Listening to the leaders talk, watching their network traffic, I have a general idea of the route they plan, at least in the early going. It's one I would follow, and I know what they're likely to encounter in the way of physical barriers and human-laid traps. It's more a matter of supplies and logistics than pluck. People have walked around the world with enough food, fuel, a place to sleep, and some serendipity.

The man who helps me stay alive, the one who gives me hope that I can return to society someday, might do the same for these refugees. Trouble is, I have no idea who he is, and I can't risk trying to contact him. It would expose both of us. But I know he knows where I am, because just when I'm at the edge of starvation or freezing to death, he (I assume it's a he; English is a crappy language when it comes to gender) rescues me with a meal or a blanket, so to speak.

It occurs to me that my protector is like a god, veiled and magical, at least in my life, and I'm now playing the role of his messenger, or spy, hugging the edges of the column of pilgrims, reporting back what I see, even if I don't know for certain how I'm telling him. Are you reading my diary, omniscient one? Fucking hell, that's an embarrassing thought. Some of the things I've written down I wouldn't tell my mother or my wife, if I had one. Too late now. Oh secret patron, hear my plea! If it comes time to help these people, let me help them, let me show them the way to survival, but protect me from my enemies in the BES.

CHAPTER 10

SENTO'S MILD INSOMNIA EVOLVED INTO a habit of ranging the camp at all hours. After a few days, it was easy to pick out families and clannish groups camped together, their banks of solar cells like flags announcing allegiance. Bruce and Gwen settled underneath Kanthaka, the cargo bot, which protected them like an oversized pet. Hosea and Awilda slept nearby, though Awilda got little rest. Gwen worried aloud about the pregnancy, and she tended to Awilda two or three times a day. As the days settled into a routine, a thief turned up.

On one morning, the day after the pilgrims lost sight of the sea behind them, Sento came across a sunburned woman frantically searching through a tattered bag repaired many times over. She complained of missing UN food packs, which the pilgrims had carefully conserved in preparation for the trip inland. The woman scolded two children inside her shelter for eating their reserves of food, but no matter how hard their mother accused them, they protested their innocence, and after a prolonged argument, she relented. Sento approached the family, and reassured the perplexed and beleaguered woman that the community would help her.

"Who would steal food from us?" the woman said. "What have we done to deserve such a thing?"

Sento thought the packs were simply misplaced, or lost, but the woman stood firm on her claim they were stolen. Sento attributed her insistence to anxiety, until she found empty UN packages a dozen meters from the shelters behind some rocks, away from the designated trash area.

Sento showed the empty packs to the woman, who recognized them, and when Sento checked the ID numbers against the camp database of food supplies, they were listed in her family's meager inventory. Given the thin rations in the camp, Sento thought it unlikely that the woman would make up such a story, and she judged the shivering children unlikely suspects for serious crimes: stealing food, hiding the empty packages, and worst of all in Sento's mind, violating the camp rules against polluting the landscape. In short, the family's story checked out, which meant someone in the camp was not only stealing food, but willfully damaging Antarctica's pristine environment. The latter angered Sento almost as much as the former. She reported to the morning meeting of the camp leaders.

"Any other theft reports?" Hosea rubbed his chin in thought.

"I've heard none."

Bruce, Enzo, and the others all shook their heads.

"Could be just hungry children. A crime of opportunity," Gwen said.

Koi sniffed. "Adults always assume it's the kids who break the rules." The leaders let him participate in the meetings, though not the decisions.

"Our food will run out soon enough," Sento said. "There's none to forage. It doesn't make sense to steal. It hurts everyone."

"I disagree." Enzo said. "Isn't it true that if someone thinks they can survive one more day by stealing, they will?"

The man's non-threatening manner masked an aggressiveness Sento didn't like. "Maybe in a few weeks, but not now. And why eat the food, instead of keeping it for later?"

"Perhaps it was done to distract us from something else?"

"What could that be?" Sento said. *What do you know?*

Bruce and the others shifted uneasily in the rising tension. Thrown together by circumstance and a common desire for a better life, they had known each other only a short time. The strain of taking a wild chance at finding Isorropia might bring out the best in some, the worst in others.

"There's no reason to be suspicious of each other," Hosea said. "We have more to gain by helping each other than mistrusting one another."

"Until the food starts to run out," Enzo said. "Agree?"

Enzo was not a man Sento wanted to travel with, but she was stuck with him, the same as every other pilgrim in the train.

"Enough before this descends into bickering." Hosea slung a backpack with his and Awilda's belongings over his shoulder. "Awilda's feeling a little stronger today. Let's see if we can make 10 kilometers."

Sento was packed within two minutes, and she stayed on the flanks of the column as it snaked up a broad valley. In the mornings, she watched the clumps of pilgrims trudge up the thin trail on the right bank of a shallow stream. The trail led across rushing creeks that flowed down from mountains slowly losing their glacier shrouds. Pregnant Awilda still rode in the tracked vehicle, wan as ever to Sento. Pilgrims besides Bruce had salvaged small robots repurposed from serving carts, landscaping buggies, and bot-drawn trailers. In another century, horses and oxen might've provided the motive power. The 24-hour sun provided all the power needed by these machines.

Thumb-sized clumps of hair grass hugged the stream, and Sento wondered what animal might have beaten the barely visible trail. The only other explanation was human, and in the afternoons, when she picked up her pace to scout ahead for the next camp site, she came across faded food packaging, bits of oxidized metal, old latrines. The signs thinned as the kilometers ticked off, and her compelling, maddening urge to move south was a strong as ever. Accompanying the urge was a foggy sense of familiarity, like the clouds that hugged the peaks guarding the valley's flanks. She knew this land, even as she could not nail down how she knew.

Koi fell in beside Sento. "I've been thinking," the boy said. "When we get to Isorropia, I will visit the archbishop and ask to be admitted to the seminary."

Sento stifled a laugh to keep from discouraging Koi. Dreams were a part of hope. "What if the city doesn't have a seminary?"

Koi thought hard. "Then I will ask to be apprenticed to a parish priest."

"Interesting idea."

"After I am ordained, I will serve my parishioners with the sacraments, and I will ask them to set up services to help integrate refugees into the community."

"You've got this all planned out."

"I will also need a wife."

Sento picked up Koi's furtive glances.

"Are you married, Sento?"

How do I answer? "Not that I know of?" "I'm a loner by nature."

"You're a strong, attractive woman. You need the best kind of man." Koi was referring to himself, though he was modest enough not to broadcast the point.

A few times since Valparaiso, once in Santiago, and once in Punta Arenas, when she felt a hole of loneliness in her chest the size of an iceberg, Sento accepted a man's attentions, if he was kind and gentle, and he had clean sheets. She didn't care that much about whether he was married or not, and not at all if he was white, brown or black, or some religion she didn't understand. She even let the man in PA say he loved her, though it was a lie. She wasn't sure if she could love anyone. How can you understand love when you don't know the first thing about yourself?

She balked at her feelings of pity for Koi, the worst kind of condescension. "Koi, you're a child."

"Now, but not forever."

Sento bounced between enjoying Koi's flattery and sadness at his puppy love. Before she could reply, Koi ran ahead to help a family pull its travois over a small rise. Bruce maneuvered Kan the cargo bot through the gap in a pair of hills that separated one part of the valley from another.

"That boy puts us all to shame with his helpfulness." Bruce reset Kan's AI to autonomous mode.

"He wants to minister to Iso's people."

"Good luck with that, kid." Koi was far ahead of Sento and Bruce, and he couldn't hear Bruce's sarcasm. "I've been finding more bits and pieces about this mythical city. It's famously secular."

"You mean religion isn't allowed?"

"Freedom of religion is one of its cherished values." Bruce sniffed in the chill air and adjusted his parka. "But no one practices any religion, at least in the same way in other places. It's just not popular or seen as a necessity. Science is the closest thing to religion Isorropians have."

"This worries you," Sento said.

"Not at all. I'm not religious, and I'm a trained engineer. If something can't be measured, or shown to exist with objective proof, I don't waste my time with it."

Though she wasn't religious herself, Sento found Bruce's strict rationalism depressing. "How do you measure your feelings for Gwen, or hers for you?"

"Don't be an ass, Sen." Bruce swiped the tab and put it in a pocket. "You're smarter than that."

"Sorry." Sento didn't usually pry into people's personal affairs. *Maybe I care about these people more than I'm willing to admit.*

Bruce punched Sento's arm in forgiveness. "Don't worry. It'll all be moot after we starve to death."

"No one is going to starve." Gwen took Bruce's hand to balance herself as they stepped over a jumble of rocks. "There's no reason to be so pessimistic, Bruce."

"It's not pessimism. It's realism."

"At least Koi has a dream," Gwen said. "What are you going to do when we get to Iso, my realist companion?"

Bruce's eyes fell to his feet. "Assuming we make it, I thought I'd start an electronics shop, maybe do some custom robot construction." He pointed at the cargo handling bot as it made its way over one of the perpendicular rivulets. "Kan has worked out pretty well."

"When I get to Iso," Gwen said, "I'm going to find a job in a hospital, maybe a maternity ward. That's the thing about babies. No matter how hopeless things are, children remind us that a good future is always possible." Gwen squeezed Bruce's arm, and he blushed.

Sento smiled at the pair. They weren't quite a couple, at least not yet, but Sento thought they complemented one another: the cautious realist and the optimistic healer.

"What about you, Sen?" Gwen said. "What are you going to do when we get to Iso?"

Sento did not know the answer to Gwen's questions. Sento wasn't even sure she believed in Isorropia, though she believed the magnetic pull south was connected to whatever habitation had given rise to the myths. The closest thing she had to an aspiration—apart from understanding her drive to move south—was deciphering her nighttime dreams: the silver-faced man, the ghost she chased at the fire, and the boat journey. As the column progressed, the images, sounds, even tactile sensations that appeared to her during sleep grew sharper, but not enough to resolve into anything she could name. The experience was a constant source of frustration, like a pebble in a shoe she could not shake off.

"What do you think, Sen?" Gwen voice was excited. "Bruce could use your help."

"What?" Sento had no idea what Bruce was talking about. She realized they'd been talking about her. "I'm sorry. I was just thinking about my own future."

"And?"

"I'm not sure I have a future." The words tumbled out of Sento. *Without knowing my past, how can my future mean anything?* "I mean, I haven't decided what I'm going to do yet."

Bruce said, "When my shop is open, come and see me, Sen, if you need anything."

A moment later, word passed down the column that the head had reached the next camp site. After an hour, the stragglers came in, and the clumps of families and clans were soon eating supper. They heated the rations on solar-powered stoves. Kids collected ice from nearby ice fields for drinking and washing water. After the evening meal, only a few children had the energy to play amongst the tents. Most of the column settled down for the night after the meal, though the sun still shone strong. An unwritten rule developed about privacy. A flick of a switch turned the fabric of the UN tents opaque, which blocked light and created the darkness most people needed for restful sleep. Pilgrims without a UN tent found ways to darken their shelters to create at least a twilight that satisfied their biological need for darkness. Once opaque, the inhabitants expected to be left alone.

The theft of the previous day signaled the need for a sentry while the camp slept. Sento volunteered, but Hosea persuaded her that another pilgrim could do the job just as well. A young man in Enzo's group raised his hand, and he was given strict instructions to wake one of the leaders if he spotted anything unusual.

When Sento rose the next day at her usual time, she found the young man asleep in the pilgrim city's temporary square. A scream startled both of them, and she sprinted through the maze of shelters past the quiet cargo bot, where Bruce had poked his head out from underneath a low canopy. She stopped at a boulder where a woman bent over a motionless figure, keening. Her tattered haven was in the boulder's lee, protecting it from the light winds flowing down the valley. The figure was male, his eyes open and lifeless. A jagged, bloody rock lay by his ear, along with torn packaging from a UN ration. *The killer is near.* "Did you see who did this?"

The woman clung to the dead man, rocking over him.

"Tell me what you saw. We need to find whoever did this."

The woman sobbed. "My husband, he stepped out to use the latrine. He shouted, 'Stop!' and I heard them fighting. I came out and I found him." She stroked the man's hair, caked with blood.

Gwen arrived with Hosea. The nurse took one look at the bloody head of the dead man and raced away.

"Can you describe who you saw?" Sento scanned the immediate area. She called up the camp map which showed all the pilgrims' avatars, but nothing appeared amiss.

"I didn't see who it was. I only saw my husband." The woman cried again and shook the corpse as if trying to revive it. Gwen returned and touched the man's carotid artery to confirm what everyone knew.

Sento turned to Hosea, anxious to offer an explanation, despite the lack of information. "The victim probably surprised the thief. The thief panicked and killed him."

"Why do this?" Hosea was perplexed. "We all need each other."

"Apparently, one of us disagrees." Sento unholstered her pistol and slid a round into the chamber. "I'm going to look around. The killer will be easy to spot. He's probably got blood spattered on him."

Alert for anything, Sento followed the periphery of the camp, keeping her eyes on the rising slopes of the valley on either side of the site. She guessed the man she chased—she assumed it was a man; a woman was less likely to attack a male victim in the head with a heavy rock—had run into the jumble of ice falls above the camp. Hiding would be easy among them, but he wouldn't last long, especially if he were injured in the fight. She searched for blood drops, a thrown-away coat, or a body, in case the killer was himself mortally wounded in the fight and died later.

A grunt made her flinch enough for the attack to miss her head. She spun and fell, rolling away. She dropped her gun. Sharp stones dug into her shoulder, but she saw the second swing of a long arm, and she ducked. It missed again, leaving his flank open, and she punched her attacker in the kidney. She was angry and surprised, but she felt in control. The thick parka absorbed much of the punch's energy, but the attacker lost his balance and fell face first into the dust. He reached for her gun, but she tumbled onto his back and brought his right arm behind him, nearing tearing it out of its socket. He barked in pain.

"Who are you?" Sento demanded, holstering up her weapon.

"No one." His head hung down, greasy hair draped over his face.

"I need a name."

He grunted, and Sento tightened her grip.

"People call me Vel."

"Where's your partner?" Sento thought a stab in the dark might answer Enzo's question about causing a distraction.

"What? I'm alone."

Was Enzo blowing smoke? "Did you kill that man?"

Vel shook his head, but Sento didn't interpret the gesture as a denial. Breathing hard from the fight, she pulled him to his feet and pushed him down the slope toward the center of camp. She asked for twine and tied Vel's hands and feet. He lay prone, like a captured goblin. A crowd gathered, and the newly widowed pilgrim was brought forward. "I never saw him before."

As Sento's head cleared of the adrenaline and the excitement of the attempt on her life, she saw a man in his 30s, with a crust of dirt and sores on his hands and face. His boots barely covered his feet.

"Does anyone know this man?" Hosea said.

Individuals in the crowd looked at each other and said nothing.

"Are you in a group? Do you have family here?"

Vel shook his head again. "I'm alone. I am dead." He started to sob. "I'm hungry."

Dead?

"Yes, well, I don't think you'll be getting any meals from us for a while," Bruce said.

"Quiet," Hosea said, surprising Sento with the force of the order. "Awilda, please get one of our meal packs."

"What? No! That's all we have. You're not going to give it to this murderer, are you?"

Hosea stood up. "We know nothing about him. We don't know if he's a thief, a murderer, or just someone who thought he was defending himself. I don't know about you, but I happen to believe in innocence before guilt is proven." Hosea stared at his wife, who sighed and returned with a package of crackers. Hosea dropped it at Vel's feet. He stared at it ravenously. "You'll eat as soon as we're sure you're not going to harm us. Sen, you have a police officer's instincts. See what you can find out."

Hosea's statement fit Sento's feeling, that she was a protector for the column, but she hadn't thought of it as police work until Hosea said as much. It confirmed an idea that her past life had something to do with security or the military. The defensive moves against the suspect in the fight were pure instinct, but they were purposeful, like training remembered as reflexes.

Rifling through Vel's pockets, she found crumbs that might be from a UN ration pack, and she found a sliver of a package with an ID number. Droplets of dried blood covered the upper portion of his coat, and splotches were collecting in the cracked skin of his hands. She'd seen hands like this before on the dissed woman who drowned when the *Kildare* sank. Vel did not have the characteristic welt of a dissed man.

To satisfy Hosea that the killer was found, Sento had to connect the evidence to the murdered man. She looked up the ID number on the food pack in the camp database. Eager to redeem himself, the young volunteer from Enzo's group was dispatched to the listed owner. He came back with a teenage girl, who confirmed that the pack, along with a few others, were missing, their absence undiscovered until just this moment.

Gwen tended to the suspect's fresh wounds, mostly cuts and scratches on his face. Her work reminded Sento of a tool in the first aid kit. "Is the victim's medical history in the camp database?"

"Yes, as far as we know them. It's all self-reported. We don't have access to any external medical databases."

"What does our record say about him?"

Gwen stopped applying a bandage and took on the mildly dazed visage of someone reviewing a network document in her minds-eye. "Only one thing out of the ordinary. He has a rare genetic disorder of the colon. It's manageable with diet and medications, though the camp has none."

"Can you sequence a genome from dried blood with the first aid kit?"

Gwen nodded. "I see what you're asking." The nurse rummaged in her bag and gave Sento a few swabs. Sento touched one to the blood spot on the back of the suspect's hand and one to a fresh stain on his jacket. She gave the swabs to Gwen. Vel remained passive and silent through the procedure.

"Not exactly a sterile environment," Gwen said. "But the sequencer was built for field work, so let's hope we get some good information." A timer counted down to zero, and Gwen studied the readout. She looked at the almost catatonic suspect, and then Sento. "A match."

Sento sighed. She had met killers in the two years since Valparaíso, but this one was different. He had killed someone who might've been her friend, had she got to know him better. She had to be right to satisfy Hosea. "Assuming we can discount the frequency of false positives, what are the chances that this genetic disease would show up twice in this population?"

"It would take an epidemiologist to know for sure, but I can't believe that it's likely."

Sento studied the torn package from Vel's pocket. "His DNA is probably on this. Maybe the victim's DNA is on it."

"Or his wife's."

Sento's hypothesis identified Vel as the murderer. She assessed the strengths and weaknesses of her case: Packaging from a stolen pack, but not stolen from the victim's cache. A dead man, a bloody rock a few centimeters from the victim's body, blood on the suspect that matched the victim, a witness that heard a scuffle, but could not identify the suspect as the killer. The suspect's behavior pointed to his state of mind, but it wasn't proof of murder. She discarded Enzo's idea of an accomplice; nothing supported it. *What would an investigator do now?*

"On your feet!" Sento lifted the suspect by his uninjured arm and put him on a camp chair so that he faced the sun. Gawkers gave Sento and the suspect a wide berth. "I'm asking you again: Who are you? Vel's not your real name, I'm betting."

Gwen listened to Sento's interrogation.

"I told you, no one." The suspect squinted in the sunlight.

Sento scanned the local network. "You don't have an avatar on the network."

"My minds-eye hasn't worked for years."

A broken com terminal allowed you to hide in plain sight, which is why Sento couldn't see Vel before he attacked her.

"What happened back there?"

"You mean with you?"

"I mean at the tent by the boulder."

Vel shook his head.

Sento recounted the evidence to him. She gambled. "The blood is enough to connect you to the murder."

"And what are you going to do? Take me to court?" The man laughed, a raspy sound. "What are they going to do, execute me again?"

Sento and Gwen looked at each other. "I don't understand," Sento said.

"Wait a minute, Sen." Gwen touched the suspect's forehead near the hairline. "Check this out."

Gwen's hand cast a shadow on the suspect's forehead, and Sento saw the lighter skin, the size and shape of an old coin, round, but irregular around the edges. "What's this?" Sento asked Vel.

"A failure," he said weakly.

"I've seen this once before," Gwen said to Vel. "You're dissed, and you tried to have your welt removed, didn't you?"

At Gwen's mention of disidentification, Sento touched Vel's scar. The texture was smooth with tiny hints of ridges in the bone. As if she had stepped into a strange time and space machine, her mind flashed to a room. Men and women in sterile smocks stood around her. Beeps and hisses filled Sento's ears. Her mind was fuzzy, as if drugged, and she could make out only a few words of the conversation. She wasn't sick, or injured, but the people in the smocks were working quickly. A sharp, but transitory pain burned her eye, and one of the ghost-like figures who stood over her said, "Nominal function." A distant voice said, "Memory centers located." A tray clanked as it was moved into position. One of the men touched her forehead. Her entire head had been shaved. "Just now marking the area for the welt. Is the DNA transequencer ready?" "Yes, doctor," someone said.

"...Sen, Sen! Are you alright?" Gwen squeezed Sento's arm. Sento blinked. "I'm fine. I was remembering something."

Vel watched the women.

Gwen whispered, "Something about the dissing? Tell me."

The word sent her back into her reverie, but something was wrong, as she told Gwen the story. She recalled a rumble. The lights in the operating theatre dimmed, and the doctors and nurses scrambled. Sento was strapped to a table, and it shook like a carnival ride. The lamp above her dimmed again and wobbled. *Earthquake!* One of the nurses had unstrapped Sento's right arm, and she was working on the left. She whimpered as she gave up on her act of compassion and ran out. Every cell in Sento's body screamed *Run!* The shaking continued, but Sento was awake enough to let her finish unstrapping her left arm. The shaking stopped and she bent up to get off the table. Undoing the last straps, she fell to the floor. The room was pitch dark, but after a few seconds, red emergency lights came on. Her head cleared a little, and she saw the swinging doors ajar. The rolling started again, weaker this time, and it propelled her into the corridor. With tubes and bandages dangling from her arms, Sento stumbled towards sunlight, as if drunk, and she found herself in a parking lot. Sirens sounded, and she feared the police or... *Who?* ... was after her again.

Sento smelled incense, a sweet *non sequitur* of a scent in a parking lot.

"Sen!" Gwen cupped Sento's face in her hands. "You know what happened now, don't you?"

Vel laughed, the kind with pain the majority part. "I'll tell you what happened. She was getting the procedure." He moved his tied hands toward his forehead. "You got the chip, but not the welt. A fucking earthquake. Unbelievable. I got my welt removed alright, but the fuckers botched the chip job. It didn't help a bit. I don't know who the hell I am, what I did, and I never will. But you--" he pointed at Sento's forehead "--were saved by an Act of God. Bloody fucking hell. And the chip's probably not working either, or you'd never remember anything. Not the smallest thing. Thank God in Heaven for incompetents! Your tax dollars at work!" Vel's laugh edged toward insanity. "How does it feel to be so lucky, Sento? Wait a minute, you can tell us your real fucking name. What is it?" Sento ignored his mocking.

The new revelation, as all her revelations had been, was fragmentary. Sento did not recall her true name, nor the crime for which she was partially dissed. *What about that smell? It's important, but how?* "Gwen, there was something else about the operation I remember."

"Yes?"

"I've been in operating theatres. This one was wrong. It wasn't a hospital, not even a clinic. When I ran away, I was in an industrial park, surrounded by warehouses."

"What do you think it means?"

"I don't know."

Vel coughed.

Sento addressed him. "I'm going to untie your hands enough so that you can eat the packet Hosea gave you. If you attempt to hurt me or Gwen, you'll answer for it."

"I've already answered for everything. I have nothing to lose." Vel sighed. "I won't run. Where would I go in this wasteland?"

A few hours later, Sento and Gwen presented their findings to Hosea and the other leaders. After discussion, Hosea pronounced the sentence: exile. It was really a death sentence, but Hosea and the others could not bring themselves to break the century-old prohibition against physical execution. "Humanity may be in trouble," he said. "but at least we're no longer savages."

The next morning, after burying the murdered man, the pilgrim train departed, leaving Vel tied to the boulder where he had killed the man. Hosea put one food packet in Vel's pocket. The dissed man could not eat it until he had freed himself from his bonds. If he was careful, the food would last two or three days. Sento guessed he would break the loosely tied knots in a day or so. By then, the train would be ten kilometers away. Hosea told Vel if he was seen within five kilometers of the camp, he would be killed on the spot like a rabid dog.

For the first time in the journey, the trailing edge of the column was as orderly as the lead. No one wanted to be near Vel as he screamed invective at the pilgrims. He predicted death and destruction to all. "And you, Sento, will suffer the worst, because you'll live to learn who you are."

Unimpressed by Vel's warning, Sento compared her suffering to that of the refugees, and found it wanting. She had another life, perhaps one privileged, and someone had taken most of it away. Or tried to. Fate had intervened, but it had made recovery of her identity a trek with no end in sight. Memories were returning, but none fell into a place that made sense as a whole. However, she had learned how she had lost her sense of self, and it wasn't through the usual legal means of disidentification. Someone wanted to keep her quiet, though the reasons and her powerful or threatening knowledge were still a secret. Turning from Vel as he slumped in despair, she wondered if she wanted to know the truth.

CHAPTER 11

As Elita's masseuse worked out the kinks in her muscles, she sucked on her favorite flavor of mist, Blue Heaven, to smooth out the kinks in her mind. Each variation of mist peeled back emotional and cognitive layers to reveal core thoughts and feelings to a greater or lesser degree. The package label crumpled in the recycle bin also warned of side effects, including vivid waking dreams. Elita opened her eyes, and the bland studio sculpture in the corner was Marissa in her seventh-grade school uniform.

"Why do you hate me?"

Elita licked her lips. "I love you."

Marissa was Ben, a young man without his exo, who said. "Why do you hate me?"

Elita opened her mouth to inhale. "I love you."

Ben was Lucius. "Why don't you love me?"

Elita wished the masseuse didn't press so hard. "I love you."

Lucius shrank into Marissa. "Why did you kill me?"

Elita flushed. "I didn't kill you. I love you."

"You have a fine way of showing it. You let a snake bite me, and there aren't even any snakes in Antarctica."

"There are in the zoo."

"Zoos are immoral. I'm going to kill your snake." Marissa, eight years old and wearing a dancer's tights and tutu, stomped her foot. The head of a writhing viper was under the heel of her slipper.

"Who is it?" Elita demanded. "Who did you kill?"

Marissa was encased in an exo-skeleton exactly like her father's."I'm not telling."

"Tell me."

Marissa was four, playing with a doll. "No."

"Tell me!"

Marissa was two, holding a limp reptile, head a mush of green and red. "Someone you hate."

"You stole him from me!"

Marissa was a newborn, blue as death.

Elita took a sharp breath. She awakened from her dream. Marissa was gone. The young Ben was gone. Lucius was gone. The sculpture was the sculpture. A burning rage resisted the persistent attempts by the masseuse to rub out the emotion. *Do I hate her that much?*

Her father was on the next table over. He was at his most vulnerable, at least physically. For his massage, a technician removed his motorized exo-skeleton, including the delicate connections to his central nervous system. *I could order the technician away, and the masseuses out, put my hand over his nose and mouth. It would be easy*— Ashamed of her thoughts, she gulped.

Ben didn't notice her discomfort. Disconnected from his speech synthesizer, he texted his daughter via his implanted minds-eye, which was independent of his exo-skeletal system. We live in a beautiful city, don't we, Lita?

The question caught her off guard, unrelated as it was from her unwelcome desire to commit patricide. *It's only the mist. I love him and couldn't hurt him.*

"In what way, Father?" Elita spoke, rather than using her minds-eye, which required more concentration and effort than speech. Her father's hearing was perfect. She hoped he didn't hear her quaver.

Our founders thought three hundred years of networked communication had cut people off from one another, rather than bring them together. Individuals segregated themselves based on their worldviews. People still talk about the "echo chamber." The Greeks and Romans had the solution: bathe together.

"I still have a private shower in my home. Most people do."

That's for hygiene. The baths combine the ideals of privacy for our bodies and intimacy of the mind and heart.

"I've always thought the isolation problem with the com system was overblown. Emotional self-sufficiency is the real problem." The conversation helped Elita regain a feeling of control over her own mind. "Still, I can hardly imagine the isolation from the community. The com system is literally the tie that binds us."

The real ties that bind are our values.

"Such as?"

Concern for the earth above all things. Sharing our knowledge with others. Acknowledging the essential unity of the human species. Striving for beauty and perfection in design and art.

What about marital fidelity?

Her father's head was turned slightly toward her. His eyes moved, but nothing else. His lips parted in slack grimace. A towel was draped over his hips, heightening his attenuated body. The masseuse gently, but firmly stroked his arms, legs, and chest. As a younger man, Ben was vigorous and athletic and he spent several hours a week in the gymnasium next to the baths. *The Ben I saw in my hallucination.* These days, he spent time in the pool with a robot attendant bearing him. Elita tried attending to him herself once, but the experience was too emotional for her.

He lay there, almost nude, ribs showing through pallid skin, and she had a fleeting thought about his emotional health. He had no female admirers she knew of. Did he seek out the services of a licensed cyprian? There was no shame in it for a widower, if kept discreet. *It's none of my business, but I'm my father's daughter, and I need erotic release. Does he as well, as his body fades?*

A silence hung over the pair while the masseuses worked. As his disease progressed, Ben became harder to read, though Elita was still adept at interpreting his mood. He had something on his mind, perhaps the same thing he wanted to discuss at the auction, but didn't get the chance. She winced at borrowing the money against her apartment to pay the sale price and the auctioneer's fees.

Lita, how much do you remember of the scandal?

He can only mean one thing. "I was only 11 when it came out."

I know, but tell me what you remember.

More than 30 years later, the details were fuzzy for Elita. Her parents' marriage was on the rocks, but they maintained the public image of a loving family, a necessary fiction central to the success of an up-and-coming political figure in a democracy. Elita's mother, a rising attorney, had almost as much to lose as Ben. The news stripped away the facade. The wife of a department head had gone through a messy, public divorce, and in the court records, she named Ben Soares as the father of her daughter, Marissa. The cuckolded husband, Sentillius by name, refused to support the child, and under Isorropian law, he could not be forced to pay child support as part of the divorce settlement. Confronted by the media and pressured by his political allies, Ben acknowledged the child as his own. Within a few weeks, Elita's mother divorced Ben.

"What I remember most is bewilderment." Elita sighed. "My parents split up, and I suddenly had a sister whose mother was not my mother."

Your mother took you to live with her in Amundsen Town. It hurt me terribly, but it was the right thing to do. I couldn't raise you in the way you deserved, but you might as well have moved to the North Pole.

Ben attached an emotional signal to his text: regret. He rarely used emosigs, preferring to keep his emotions to himself. *It's a little late to feel sorry, Father.* "I was angry, too. I couldn't understand why you accepted Marissa as your own. It seemed too easy for you. You didn't put up a fight. I wondered sometimes if I was really somebody else's child, not yours or Mother's."

A long fight would've made things worse. Besides, it was the truth. I was Marissa's father. Lying about it would've wrecked everyone's life, maybe even yours. He paused. Lita, I'm sorry.

"No need to apologize again, Father. I'm over it."

I always felt that I never said...

"I said I'm over it." *He can can so irritating. Am I still angry after three decades?*

That's not what I mean. He sighed, one of the few sounds he could make with his body. I never said 'I love you' enough.

Elita could not remember one time in those days or in the aftermath when Ben said *I love you*. He stayed in touch, insofar as her mother would allow. He made the required appearances at dance recitals, gave birthday gifts, gave solstice gifts, and so on, but he was distant, physically, and emotionally, for many years. "Did you say it to Marissa?"

I—I don't remember. I'm sure I did.

"You said it to her mother, didn't you?" Elita lifted her head, and the human masseuse, trained to ignore conversation among clients, even if it was one-sided, worked her shoulder muscles harder, as if counteracting the new tension.

As usual, Ben was completely passive, except for his eyes, which looked away. I loved Marissa's mother until the day she died.

"And her daughter became the center of your life."

That's not fair.

"It is. You doted on her. The news chans would show pictures of you together, and the social media gossips wondered if you had forgotten that you had *two* daughters."

Those gossips deserve dissing.

"Did you forget?" Elita raised herself on her elbows, but not so much that she violated modesty. For an instant, she thought she was back in the Ecclesia, confronting her father again.

Of course not. For one thing, your mother wouldn't let me near you. She had a right to be angry, but I didn't push back. I couldn't take the risk you might be hurt.

"Thank you for your generosity, but I didn't need it. I needed a father who doted on me once in a while." Elita lowered herself.

Watch the snippiness. The text came with a laughter emo-sig. You get that way when you're peeved.

Ben's humor broke the tension. *He's right. It was so long ago, and Marissa is dead.* "Why are you telling me this now, Father?"

Because I regret what happened, and I don't want to repeat my mistakes.

"You have another child on the way?" Elita's sarcasm got the better of her.

Because I don't want another rift to open up between us. It was painful enough last time, and I'm not sure I could survive another one.

"Father, you're making a mountain out of a mole hill."

You don't understand. I'm giving you a warning.

"About what?"

I can't say anything more. You'll have to trust me.

Despite her anger, Elita's trust in her father was absolute. *What could worry him so much?* "Now it's your turn to be unfair. Trust has to be shared. Tell me what's on your mind."

Ben was silent. In his case, his reserve was far more frustrating version of the dearth of emotional communication so many women complained about in their men. If it were possible for Ben Soares' face to lose more expressiveness than it already lacked, he achieved it. The last clues, the set of his eyes, told Elita nothing.

"I'll have to guess what you're thinking. I know you, Ben Soares, First Citizen, so it's a well-educated guess." Elita realized she was goading him. *So be it.* "You're angry about your loss in the Ecclesia, hence the banalities about values that bind the nation. You don't have the time to try the same strategy again, but you have a big enough constituency to pursue a different tack. Maybe some sort of big charity push? Save the Refugees, or something? Put me down for fifty." She let her barbed analysis sink in.

Even if I could raise the millions needed, how would I get relief to those people? You twisted the intent and letter of the law to prevent any real help from reaching them. I'd be wasting my time.

"You know that it had to be done. The *inmigrantes* are a threat to the city."

I'm not interested in debating the question with you again. You won in the Ecclesia, and as far as I'm concerned, you've condemned those people.

Elita sniggered. "Spare me the bleeding-heart humanitarianism. 'Those people.' Your patronizing shows your true feelings about the refugees. They're 'poor things,' not human beings in your world."

Ben's eyes were open and staring at Elita. His fury was unmistakable. *Still passionate underneath the dead muscle. What would a cyprian do with that?* "All right, that went too far, Father. You are genuinely concerned about their well-being. I apologize."

Ben's masseuse finished and the technician brought back the exo-skeleton, cleaned of sweat and grime. It sparkled with new polish.

Lita, I've enjoyed our time together, even our disagreement. It reminds me of the dinners we shared when you were just starting out in politics. We were close then.

And Marissa was closer. "I feel the same way, Father." Saddened by the new distance between them, she almost reached for another mist stick. She hesitated. *What would I see this time?* Instead, she watched the technician plug the exo-skeleton into the leads on the back of her father's skull and along his spine. She had almost forgotten about how the device transformed her father from a wasted husk to a cyborg with the charisma of the man at 40. *He ought to have a dozen women admirers. If only his batteries would last longer.* What few saw—though Elita did—was the hybrid's fragility. A bump, a fall, a forgetful technician, a million things could go wrong, forced or unforced, and he would die within hours.

With his exo operating, his synthesized voice filled the closed room. "Your analysis is wrong."

"In what way?"

"You assumed my warning had something to do with the refugees. While it's true that I haven't given up on helping them, that's not what I had in mind."

Ben settled into his powered chair. He could walk, if he wanted to, but he preferred to conserve his power for moments when he needed to make an impression. *A talk with his daughter doesn't qualify.*

"You said you wouldn't tell me what was worrying you."

"I'll say this: The people closest to you are keeping secrets that could destroy you. I don't mean just professionally."

"This is about Lucius."

"Indeed. And your sister."

Marissa again. Her father's tone suggested business, not family drama, and Elita's mind flashed to the file on Marissa's disappearance, the note about "LRG," and the link to Lucius' personnel file. "What exactly are you getting at?"

"You're my only daughter now, and I can't help but try to protect you. That is what you've always wanted, true?"

When I was ten, but now? Elita did a double-take. When Ben said, "only daughter," he looked away for a millisecond. *He's holding back the real secret.* "I accepted Marissa eventually. You know that, Father. I even helped her career get started."

"For which I'm eternally grateful."

"What do you want from me, then?"

"Lucius Galla is a dangerous man, a criminal, in my view. I know about his provocation of the Nordenskjöld militia. It was unnecessary and it backfired."

Elita's father was still a powerful, if unelected, political figure in the government. Hundreds of bureaucrats and functionaries owed their careers to him. If he wanted something done, he could get it done. The sense that he was changing into an adversary, if not an enemy, disturbed her. *Can you love a man determined to stand in your way? Does Ben know that I'm the one who turned Lucius loose on the refugees? All leaders need their hatchet men. Who was his?* "'Criminal' is a strong word, Father. Perhaps he did it as a way to serve our city."

"People died. That makes him an accessory to murder."

And that makes me—what? "Don't moralize. You cheated on my mother."

An acknowledging sigh escaped Ben. "Your mother got rid of me. You should get rid of Lucius."

"The two things are not equivalent." As Elita stood to leave, the masseuse draped a plush white robe on her shoulders. "I will do what I need to do to protect Isorropia."

"Can I count on you to do the right thing? Can I trust you to act in our city's best interests? I'm no longer sure."

And so it comes out. Have I banked too much on him all this time? Whom else would he trust with all his heart and soul? Marissa is gone.

"Lita, I—" Ben's tone, insofar as Elita could hear it in his synthesized voice, turned conciliatory. "I have no proof, but Lucius is a bomb waiting to go off. If he were gone, maybe things between us would be better."

Elita saw the thread of her relationship to her parent fraying. Like him, she was not ready for it to break. "I'll speak to him about Nordenskjöld. He and his minions are overzealous sometimes." *And relentless as a, well, a snake.*

CHAPTER 12

From the diary of Artemis Macedon

I'm depressed after what I've seen the last few days. I'm amazed that the pilgrims have made it this far, but it doesn't alleviate my sadness. Their steady progress south should have ended in disaster hundreds of kilometers back, but Antarctica is exacting her price. She is like a mob boss who took a little time off to rest and recharge, and returned to her territory surprised to find a competitor. What would Al Capone, or a Chinese triad do? The deaths of the pilgrims, one by one, are the evidence of Antarctica's wrath.

One could interpret the discovery of the thief Vel as a windfall. I'm embarrassed to say that his appearance was as much a surprise to me as the pilgrims. He was almost as good at hiding from civilization as the true ferals. I agreed with the pilgrims' decision to exile and expose the dissed man to Antarctica's jaws. He'd committed a horrible crime, evidenced by his welt, tried to escape his punishment, and committed further crimes against innocents. When I approached him, a day after the refugees had departed, he was hours, perhaps minutes from his end. Too weak to break his bonds, he must have thought I was a fiend sent to claim his soul. I had no pity for him, and offered only indifference. Antarctica accepted the pilgrims' gift.

The continent was not appeased for long. The long valley rose to a plateau, which transmuted to a patchwork of ice fields, bare ground, and dust. A steady wind lifted the particles a half-meter off the surface into a streaming fog of grime. The slow encroachment of plant life from the coasts had not yet reached the plain, and apart from low, rolling hills, nothing broke the landscape's monotony. I kept to the horizon to maintain my distance. I feared the pilgrims might discover an important cache of my food and supplies, and they nearly did, if it weren't for the unsteady, but human wailing. I was downwind of the chilling sound, which allowed me to camouflage my goods before the immigrants were upon me. I frantically dug a foxhole in a remnant of an ice field carved into the shape of a gauzy, flowing wedding dress.

They stopped about 30 meters from my hiding place. There were eight pilgrims, including Sento, who stood apart, at once a guardian and an observer. Koi accompanied the group, which was too far away for me to pick up com signals. As the wailing continued, three of the pilgrims began to dig with shovels, and after an hour, they lowered a canvas-wrapped bundle into the pit. A low-slung tracked robot acted as a hearse. Why they had chosen a place so far from the refugee camp mystified me. No animal scavengers were poised to defile the corpse, nor rainfall to wash away the soil above it. Some religious or cultural reason alien to Antarctica's world drove the decision. The grave was filled in, and after some words by one of the pilgrims, the funeral party left.

After the distance had turned them into specks, I approached the grave, already disappearing in the blowing dust. They left no marker. An anonymous burial, appropriate in an anonymous land. It was the first of many, and the number mounted as the days wore on. Disease was the most likely cause of the deaths, but the pilgrims were careful about hygiene and waste management. I ruled out thirst; Antarctica's ironic plenitude of water in the form of ice probably saved them from the disaster of a similar journey across a temperate zone desert. That said, they had reached some kind of limit. I gathered that the elderly and physically weak were dying from malnutrition, preexisting diseases that defeated their weakened systems rather than cholera or typhoid, simple age, and abandoned hope. I wondered if an Isorropian coroner had the power to list despair as a cause of death.

The slow dirge of pilgrim grave-digging brought me down to an emotional low point matched only by an awful day a few months after my exile. Truth be told, my two-year-old banishment started joyously. I had avoided the dissing reserved for the investigator who worked for me. My identity was intact. LRG's restraint showed he had a modicum of humanity left in his heart. Joy, though, turned to fear as my initial supplies of food ran out, and hunger drove me to do unspeakable things at tiny human outposts. I stayed in the west; nothing lived long on the domes of ice still thousands of meters thick on the hellish eastern two-thirds of the continent. Garbage was my salvation, but the crusts of stale bread and moldy fruit didn't forestall my own despair. After I got lost near a settlement below the Vinson Massif, I found myself at the edge of a cliff, with a pounding sea a hundred meters below. Starving, freezing, and lonely, I was within seconds of stepping off when I spotted birds' nests below. One had an egg, which I stole, and ate raw, the chick half-formed. The embryo gave me enough strength to live a little longer.

Two days later, I found the first cache left to me by my benefactor. All he wanted in exchange was regular reports on what I'd seen. I charged my minds-eye, composed my observations, and uploaded them to the network chip stashed with the survival supplies. I don't know how he received the reports, but the next cache included an acknowledgment. At first, I thought it was LRG returned to torment me, but that didn't add up. My benefactor made no threats or promises, as my executioner loved to do. The supplies were laughably limited; I starved a month for every day of feasting. I concluded that someone outside the Bureau of Environmental Security discovered what happened to me. He decided not to rescue me, a torment in itself, but I wasn't in a position to argue my case. Perhaps if I pleased him enough, he would find a way to bring me home.

To myself, I denied the guilt of having plenty, in a relative sense, as the refugees slowly starved. My tiny hoard, all of which fit into my tattered backpack with room to spare, would do nothing to help the pilgrims, and I was following my benefactor's instructions to stay out of sight. I sensed he was waiting for a trigger of some kind. To him, I described each of the leaders' personalities and explained decisions when I could hear them via their local network. I paid close attention to Sento, partly at my benefactor's request, and partly because I knew who she was, even if she didn't. I studied her so closely that I thought of her as a relative, maybe a daughter, though I had no children. When the time comes for an ultimate decision, she will be at the center of it, the target of my pounce.

CHAPTER 13

THE LAST-SEEN EVIDENCE OF HUMAN activity was 10 days previous. Koi found a meter-long piece of a single fiberglass ski, perhaps a castoff from an early exploratory expedition, or a relic of one of the record-making stunts people in the 20th century were so fond of attempting. The eerie discovery caused a stir in the camp. Some took it as evidence that Isorropia was near. Enzo pointed out that the ice might have carried it hundreds of kilometers before Koi spotted one end of it sticking out of a snowbank. For a moment, Sento thought it might have been a jury-rigged marker for a food or equipment cache, or a grave. After a frustrating hour of searching, she found nothing. No other artifact or hint of habitation came to light, but Bruce picked up almost imperceptible signals from a live com system not his own. He could never connect, and he cursed electronic ghosts for teasing him.

The weather was remarkably benign, apart from the freezing cold. Fortunately, the UN had provided plenty of thermal underwear as part of its relief deliveries back at Nordenskjöld. The days, however, blended into one another. The featureless ground, the constant wind and dust, and the endless daylight broken only by passing clouds did little to vary the monotony. The trail itself was nothing but a straight line on a virtual map that followed no curve of a river or climb a hill, because the pilgrims had no information about the terrain ahead. Boredom was catching up to the cold as an enemy. *The tedious landscape drains hope, the only thing that keeps these people alive.*

The first pilgrim died of malnutrition on the fifth day traversing the plain. On the sixth day, a premature baby died. Bruce had a chisel and hammer to fashion a marker, but Hosea forbade wasting time carving a stone. For the third death—a mother of three children—someone produced a pen with permanent ink, and the family wrote the mother's name on a rock placed atop the grave. Sento sympathized with the need for the family to say the woman was not forgotten, but she imagined the words fading to nothing within weeks or days. After the first deaths, Hosea made the macabre comment that the food would last longer now. Sento was not one to make such a heartless calculation, which was why Hosea was a better leader, in her view.

The sense of getting near to *something important* was never as powerful for Sento as it was on the plain. It kept her head up, while the minds of others, namely Awilda, spiraled downward. The deaths sent the pregnant woman into a depression as deep as the horizon was unbroken. She had long, flowing, black hair, and for as long as Sento had known her, she never missed combing it before bed. On the plain, she stopped her ritual. Within a day or two, her hair was a clumped, tangled mess.

"Awilda, let me help you with your beautiful hair," Sento said one evening after Gwen completed an exam.

"I've admired it for a long time," Gwen said. "Sen helped me with my braids."

Like Sento, the nurse wanted to encourage Awilda, whose advanced pregnancy made her appear ready to explode. Sento's own hair was fine and difficult to manage. Awilda lolled on the worn sleeping bag. She shook her head in the dim light, her eyes vacant.

"Tell us what's wrong, Awilda." Gwen touched her shoulder.

"You're very close to your time." Sento echoed the nurse's assessment, which rarely changed these days.

"It's normal to be anxious, especially out here in the middle of nowhere," Gwen said.

Awilda draped her arm over her head, as if hiding.

Sento's could no longer hold back her irritation. "We can't help you if you keep your back turned to us."

Gwen gave Sento a sharp look, not liking her tone.

"You'll slow down the whole train," Sento added. "Is that what you want?"

In an instant, despite her bulk, Awilda turned and faced Sento. "Maybe it is. Maybe that's what should happen. Maybe we should just stop and face the inevitable."

Gwen soothed Awilda. She reached for the woman's hair, comb in hand, but Awilda slapped the comb away. "Don't touch my hair. I'll tear it out before I let you touch it again." Awilda yanked at her long locks, taking out handfuls.

Sento grabbed her wrists. "Stop, Awilda. You're hurting yourself."

"Why not? I'm going to die anyway. You're going to die. My baby..." Awilda's face transformed from fury to fear. "My baby will die too."

"That's impossible, Awilda," Gwen said. "You're as healthy as can be. We've all made sure of that." Sento and the others had given Awilda some of their rations when Gwen began to worry about the amount of nutrition Hosea's wife was getting. She was eating for two.

"You're keeping me alive for no reason." Her eyes flashed. "Maybe I'm just a baby-making machine to you, to keep humanity from going extinct."

The unexpected and nonsensical vitriol bewildered Sento. Awilda had never said anything so paranoiac.

"Listen to me." Gwen's voice was quiet, but firm, a nurse's voice of reason and calm. It calmed Sento as well. "We're going to find Iso. Bruce keeps picking up sophisticated radio signals." In truth, Bruce had not reported a signal for days.

"You're all lying to protect me." Awilda's eyes closed tight, like a castle lowering its portcullis. "There's nothing but ice and stone for ten thousand kilometers. Every one of us is going to end up in one of those graves, except you, Sento. You will have no one to bury you."

Sento was taken aback.

Awilda cupped Sento's cheek with her hand. "You're the best of us, the strongest of us. Everyone sees that. You have a real reason for going south. Something happened to you, and you want to know what it is." Awilda swept her hand across the scene outside the tent. "The rest of us are just stumbling forward on nothing but a wish for salvation."

Sento had never explained to Awilda her obsession to head south, but the woman was sensitive enough to put the clues together. *I've probably let on more than I ought.* Like Gwen, though, Sento was more concerned about keeping Awilda from falling into an emotional pit from which she might not climb out. It would harm her, and drag down the train. "I know it's hard, but think of Hosea. He needs you." The man had aged as he and everyone else in the train lost weight and fell ill. "He's a hero to everyone. He's always at the front of the train, always the first person to say hello to people and smile. He needs you by his side."

"He's a liar," Awilda's voice fell to a whisper. "You don't know what he says when we're alone. He says we'll be fine, but I know him. I hear the words, but I know what he's really thinking. Starvation, sickness, accident. Something will kill us, and it won't take long."

After the burial of the young mother, Awilda watched the family and when the two oldest children, a boy and a girl, wandered close, she called them over. However, she never used their real names, assigning them the names of her drowned children: Juan and Rosie. No matter how the children protested, or how often their father reminded Awilda, she called the children Juan and Rosie. She ignored the third child, a babe in arms. To the boy and girl, Awilda smiled and cooed, finding bits of food to share, and once braided the little girl's long hair. She reached deep into a pocket and removed two palm-sized dolls. "You can play with these, children, but remember to put your toys away after playing with them. The neighbor kids can't be trusted." Sento had no idea whom she meant. After the gift, the children accepted Awilda's names as if they were nicknames, though the father sometimes pulled them away, suspicious of Awilda's instability. Hosea watched the scenes play out, but he did not correct his wife, or remind her that Juan and Rosie were dead.

Awilda gasped. Gwen felt her belly and ordered Awilda to lie down as she wailed like a child.

Alarmed, Sento said, "Is it time now? Should I tell Hosea?"

Ignoring Sento, Gwen examined Awilda's cervix as the pregnant woman cried out. "Don't worry. I think it might be a false labor. Did it happen with your other babies, Awilda?"

The woman winced and nodded.

Gwen felt Awilda's belly again. "There's no show and I can feel the baby moving. It's not your time."

"Not yet?"

"No, my dear, it's not your time."

"Not my time to die. Not yet."

Awilda's descent got under Sento's skin. Leaving the tent, she found Hosea at the flap, as if debating whether to go inside. "How is she?" he said.

"Fine." Sento thought better of her automatic response. "No, Hosea, I won't lie to you. She's upset and anxious. We're worried about her. Gwen is doing all she can. The baby seems fine."

Hosea gripped the tent pole, examining it as if it had a secret code he couldn't decipher. "She was a dreamer when we met at school. She loved art and poetry, and I fell in love with her habit of seeing beauty in everything. She was so beautiful herself. Tall and graceful, like a dancer. I couldn't believe she fell for me. Maybe it was an attraction of the opposites. I was the practical, get-it-done farmer. She was the optimistic artist."

"Two sides of a coin."

"Yes. She made a wonderful mother. She pinned every drawing or painting by the kids on every wall in the house, even the inside of the tool shed. We had started home-schooling our children when another crop failure forced us south. It seemed that each kilometer chipped off a piece of her heart. Caring for our boy and girl kept her going. That was taken away when the *Kildare* sank."

Despite the story's sadness, Sento envied Hosea, because he had a story to tell. She knew hers only in fragments, though the pieces, especially the failed dissing, were adding up. "Awilda will be fine." Sento believed it for Hosea's sake. "Caring for the new baby will give her something to live for."

"Now you're the one wearing rose-colored glasses."

"I'm sorry?"

"Imagining the world to be something it's not. You're talking like Awilda used to."

Have I lost my cynicism? Or am I covering it up to encourage Hosea? He must be lonely. An unexpected urge to kiss Hosea's grizzled face startled Sento, and she shrank away. She felt as if she was betraying the woman in pain only a meter away. *For God's sake, she's about to give birth to his child.*

"Something wrong?" Hosea said. "I didn't mean to offend—"

"No, you didn't. It's just that, I mean, I'm tired. We have a long day tomorrow." Sento turned to her own tent on the edge of camp. Uncomfortable near Hosea, she walked quicker than necessary.

Sento slept little. Worry about Awilda kept her awake, as well as guilt over her unexpected and unwanted feelings about Hosea. Sento blamed them on the strain of living up to her self-appointed role as the camp's police officer, but she admitted to herself that wariness toward others contributed. *I'm terrified of finding someone. What would I tell them about who I am?*

Sento's declining physical strength dragged her down. Only a few weeks ago, she could walk all day without a rest. These days, she rested every couple of hours. The dull, colorless landscape didn't help, but after a week of almost no variation in the topography, she discovered a gentle downward slope. Five hundred meters later, she descended into a ravine carved by a narrow creek. The ravine emerged onto an ice canyon with a broad stream racing through the center. Beyond the translucent river, blue ice coulees rose again to the plain. Sento found an easy route to the stream bed and a place where the river was broad and shallow, though the water was swift.

"Will we be able to get everyone across on foot?" Enzo said.

"Not the sick or injured," Bruce said. "They'll have to ride the vehicles."

"Are the vehicles big enough to cross? Not all of them are built for crossing swift water, correct?"

"I don't know about this, Hosea," Bruce said. "Kanthaka can make it, and the tracked vehicles, but some of the smaller bots carrying belongings..." He shook his pudgy head.

"We might be able to carry a few of the smaller carts, but I'm more worried about the people. Some of them don't have boots that will survive immersion. At least we can put the small children on our backs."

Enzo broke in. "If anyone slips and gets carried away, can we rescue them?"

"This is impossible," Awilda said. She waddled up with Gwen supporting her.

"Darling, you should rest." Hosea's spoke with a gentleness reserved only for his wife.

"We should never have left Nordenskjöld."

"It's too late to go back," Hosea said. "We can't stay here and starve. We have to go on and maybe find Isorropia."

Sento agreed, but she kept her opinion to herself, afraid she might appear too supportive of Hosea with his wife so near. Inexplicably, Awilda sobbed and Gwen led her away.

Bruce snickered. "What a debbie-downer. She really gives me confidence in the future."

"Shut up," Hosea snapped. "Focus on the problem. Can the cargo bot ferry people across?"

Scolded like a pre-schooler, Bruce cast down his eyes to the ice. "I suppose. Yes."

"Let's get this done."

As she always did, Sento broke the trail, Koi close behind as they walked through the swift water. Her boots and outer clothes were in relatively good condition, but she was shivering within a few meters of leaving the bank. Crossing back to the north bank of the stream, she steeled herself for more cold as she led parties of ten. Water swirled in maelstroms, threatening to take everyone's feet out from under them. Koi organized them on the far bank. To prevent frostbite, he urged everyone to light camp stoves to dry their clothes and feet. With salvaged line, Bruce rigged a system of securing vehicles to Kanthaka. He supervised unloading part of her cargo to make room for people who could not cross the stream on their own. By mid-afternoon, most of the pilgrims and vehicles were across without a major loss.

Then Kanthaka went berserk. One of its feet slipped on a smooth patch of ice, and as it fought to regain balance, the three passengers panicked. A woman jumped off the bot and landed in the water, which carried her away. The bot jerked like a crazed horse, only five times bigger and heavier. It bolted and ran towards the far bank of the stream, the two remaining passengers, an elderly man and child, screaming and holding on to netting that kept the cargo in place. Bruce frantically sent commands to the bot via the tab.

"Send a kill command," Hosea barked.

"It's not obeying." Bruce ran after the bot down the near side of the river as the machine lurched into the ice canyon's walls.

The other vehicles acted strange as well. The tracked car that carried Awilda stopped and started, as if it couldn't decide what to do or where to go. Manual commands failed with it as well, but it stopped long enough for Awilda and the others to scramble off. Other vehicles queued on the near bank took off in all directions. One spun in place like a top. As carts and gigs bounced like uncoordinated clowns, bundles, tents, and boxes scattered on the ice. Some fell into the river, which tossed the packages like toys.

"Bruce! What the hell are you doing?" Hosea was near panic.

"I'm not doing anything. They've all gone crazy!"

Upstream, halfway across with another group, Sento watched in horror as one vehicle after another went insane. People chased the vehicles hoping to find an off switch or a kill switch. One finally succeeded, but only after the cart ran him down at full speed. Finally able to break away, Sento took off for the cargo bot, remembering her last dangerous encounter with it on the *Kildare. It tried to kill me, but I can stop it, if I can get near it.* It thrashed against a ice wall, as if trying to climb it. Chunks of ice crashed down from above. The passengers were both on the ground, injured, bleeding, and crying. Sento dragged them away from the raining ice, and she approached the deranged machine, but its movements were so uneven and unpredictable, she couldn't reach the red, palm-sized switch.

Bruce appeared next to her, soaking and shivering after fording the stream, looking like an under-inflated beach ball. "I don't know what's wrong. No command is working. The network is fine."

Sento saw the bot's avatar in her minds-eye, but the error icon appeared over it, blandly announcing a problem. "I can't get near enough to shut it down."

"Its legs are flailing. You'll break an arm or worse."

Sento noticed that the netting holding the cargo on the bot was loose. Boxes of tools and tents had already fallen off. "What else is on there?"

"Our food."

God help us if we lose the food. Sento noticed a ledge above the flailing bot. Determined to save the pilgrims' supplies, she climbed up to the ledge, took her field knife out of its sheath on her leg, and leaped onto the chrome and steel beast. It threw her off immediately, but not before she managed to slice one of the lines. A few packages fell off, one into her ribs. A crunching pain forced a yelp.

"Look out, Sen!"

Sento opened her eyes and skittered away as one of the bot's feet landed where her head had been. It gamboled off, its addled AI adjusting to the new imbalance of its cargo. Sento raced after it, Bruce behind her. As it ran, it lost its footing again and vanished.

Sento stopped in time before she followed the bot over the cliff. The stream had carved a falls and dropped 10 meters to a new level. The bot stumbled off a ledge above the falls. Peering nervously over the edge, Sento saw the bot on its side, half-submerged in water, one of its legs sheared off, still jerking as if trying to run away. As unexpectedly as it began, the bot's movements stopped. It was as still as death.

"There," Bruce said, satisfaction in his voice.

"What did you do?"

"Nothing worked, so I disappeared the AI. Just deleted it and dumped it from memory."

Sento didn't want to think about what that might mean for the bot or the train.

"I did the same for the other bots. It's the only thing that works."

"I wish our troubles were limited to that." Sento indicated the stream below. The swift water was carrying away supplies.

Sen! Bruce! The texts from Hosea appeared in Sento's minds-eye. She could almost see his fear in the messages, though the primitive network didn't support emotional signals. Get down to the bot. Salvage as much of the food stores as you can. Sento acknowledged, and she saw Hosea, Enzo and others from the train going after the floating food packets.

Hours later, the pilgrims had salvaged a little more than half the food and other supplies that Kanthaka cast off during its frenzy. The rest was lost downriver. The packets were waterproof, but that didn't keep some of them from tearing open and spoiling. As for Kan, Bruce and three others managed to drag the bot and its torn-off leg out onto the bank.

"Can you fix it?" Hosea said.

"I can fix anything." Bruce made the statement often, but to Sento's mind, he sounded doubtful. "These bots are pretty tough. Some of the metal bolts sheered off, but I can salvage parts from the other bots."

"You mean some of the vehicles are permanently broken?"

"I didn't have space for a ton of spare parts. We'll end up leaving one or two behind."

"Shit." Hosea rubbed his face.

"We should take a break," Sento suggested. "Bruce needs time to repair the beasts."

Hosea announced that the train would rest for a day or two while the pilgrims regrouped. Bruce cannibalized the other bots and set to work on Kanthaka. The refugees avoided him, except for Gwen. She dismissed his growling as hot air, and brought him tools, water, and meals. Sento was allowed to watch his attempts to reprogram the bot's AI.

On the third day, Hosea could not contain his impatience to get moving. "How much longer?"

"Not long." It was Bruce's standard answer.

Hosea huffed. "Can you at least tell me what happened to Kan?"

Bruce glanced at Sento, as if expecting her to know what was in his mind. "You won't like it, for a bunch of reasons."

"Such as?"

Bruce threw a screwdriver and wrench onto a blanket scattered with other tools. "It's pretty clear that a virus made Kan, um, sick." He pointed to his head.

"A virus?"

"Its storage and memory were clean as new when I repaired it back at Nordenskjöld. Same goes with the other bots. So the virus wasn't resident in our AIs when we started out. I've kept a pretty solid firewall up on our network since then. I didn't download anything accidentally."

"You're sure about that?"

"Do you doubt me?" Bruce's irritation had more to do with his own sense of failing the train than anger at Hosea's implied accusation.

Sento rescued Bruce from an argument. "Somebody inserted it," she said. "Someone got past the firewall."

Bruce was predictably defensive. "No security is perfect, but mine's fairly sophisticated. Anyway, someone put the virus there, and it activated in every machine at once. It was a well-thought out attack, meant to do maximum damage."

Sento said, "Those network pings you kept seeing, that's when the virus was inserted."

"Probably."

"Do you realize what you're saying?" Hosea paced, then looked up at the canyon's rim. "Someone is watching us, maybe following us."

"And they don't like us," Sento had come to the same conclusion. "They want us to go away, maybe turn back."

"Or just die," Bruce said. "That would be the most convenient. That way, we don't carry back their secret."

"What do you mean?" Hosea crossed his arms.

"Think about it. The virus was sophisticated, and it got through my firewall. That means really solid technological know-how. Who could do that? Those militia idiots? Hell, no. The UN? Maybe, but why would they? No, it's someone much smarter."

Hosea was thoughtful. "That leaves Isorropia." He paused, working the problem. "It really exists."

"That's the only thing I can think of," Bruce said. "Question is, why attack us? We're harmless as babies. And why not just shoot us or something, if we're so bad?"

Sento leveled a finger at Bruce. "To make it look like we failed on our own. To make it look like Antarctica killed us." She saw into the plan as if it were laid out to her in the Antarctica summer sunlight. With that thought came another revelation. She remembered the face of the man who tried to silence her, and her palms sweat in the near-freezing temperatures, because he was a predator who cared nothing for a few men, women, and children alone on the world's last continent.

CHAPTER 14

Elita exited one of Government House's side doors, hoping to avoid the crush of reporters, but they caught up with her like a pack of wild dogs. Enemies had attacked her again in the Pynx—the chamber housing the Ecclesia—after the story broke about the pilgrims' disaster at the river. Lucius had briefed her on the malware attack, but only after he'd launched it. The humanitarians made the most of the consequences by calling on Elita to resign, blaming her for the deaths of three migrants. No First Citizen had ever resigned before the end of his or her term. *I won't be the first.* The public challenge confirmed the growing gap between herself and her father, and the potential consequences alarmed her. *Who holds the real power, him or me?* The uncertainty turned her stomach. She waved off the reporters and headed down the street, her entourage in tow, Lucius among them.

He elbowed his way to her side. "You're upset."

"What makes you think I'm upset?"

"You're walking like you're being chased."

"Bullshit."

"The pitch in your voice could cut glass."

"Careful. I'll use it to cut you."

"What the hell did I do?"

"You're such an idiot."

"At least tell me what those fools were up to. Where in hell did that 'crisis' shit come from?"

"Grandstanding. Father sees that the public is softening on the refugees and he's trying to win more support. Sow doubt, and reap the doubters."

"For what? The Ecclesia has already said it's not interested in aid. You beat him there."

Lucius climbed into a pod car with Elita, whose breath came hard from her exertion and her agitation. Lucius brushed Elita's cheek with the back of his hand. The stroke gentled her as if she were one of the Patagonian horses she read about as a child. Isorropia had no animals as pets, but her father bought her a membership in a riding club that used robotic horses almost indistinguishable from the flesh and blood creatures. At eight years old, she didn't grasp the difference between an anxious animal and a robot programmed to behave anxiously, though they responded to the same gentling touch. Elita leaned into Lucius' hand, but she didn't want to risk being seen kissing him.

"My father is cooking up something, but I don't know what it is," Elita said.

"I could find out."

Should I send Lucius to spy on my father? How do I know he isn't already? And what of Marissa? Elita didn't want to return to her office just yet. "Car, take us to the Agora."

The pod acknowledged with a signal to Elita's minds-eye. The trip would take fifteen minutes. *Time enough to search for truth.* "Lucius, say that you love me."

"I love you with all my heart and soul."

Elita was pleased with his lack of hesitation, as near as she could tell.

"What about you, Lita?"

"I think I could be in love with you." She glanced at him. *A half-truth.*

Lucius snickered. "Always the chess master, aren't you?"

"What do you mean?"

"Playing games. Thinking three, no, ten moves ahead. You always have some strategy in mind that no one can fathom, least of all me."

"You make it sound like a weakness."

"It's the way of politicians. I've never understood it. There's no problem that can't be solved with a sword stroke."

That's why I keep him close. He's incredibly exciting to have near. "I don't mean to play games with you, Lucius. You don't deserve it. I guess I'm not sure about my feelings for you."

Lucius softened. "What can I do to help?"

"Tell me the truth about something."

"Anything, my love."

"What do you know about agarwood?"

Lucius shrugged and frowned, as if digging deep into memory. "Um, south Asia wood, used for its fragrance, valuable even before it was declared more or less extinct. Why do you ask?" His face was empty, if not quite innocent.

"I was going through some old files, nothing important, from a previous administration." It was Elita's turn to shrug. "One of them was about an investigation into illegal wood imports, including agarwood."

"Your point is?"

"I was wondering if you knew anything about it."

"Why would I know anything about it?" Lucius grinned in the way a merchant in the Agora knows he's about to fleece you.

Elita maintained a chess master's face. "The investigation happened while you were head of investigations at BES, before I elevated you. It seemed interesting to me, and I was curious if you knew more."

Lucius sighed. "We had dozens of investigations going at the same time, everything from recycling fraud to illegal petroleum extraction. I didn't track every time an inspector wiped his nose in my section."

"Including Marissa Sentillius?" That got a reaction from Lucius. Elita was unsure if it was discomfort, or anger.

"What's she got to do with this, Lita?"

"Marissa was following a lead on the night she disappeared."

"On the agarwood case. So?"

"There's a note in the case file pointing to someone with the initials 'LRG.' Do you know who that might be?"

Lucius obfuscated the obvious answer with sarcasm. "It's a big city, Elita. Lots of people might have those initials, assuming the note is accurate, and meaningful."

Points well taken, Lucius, but Marissa wasn't a sloppy woman. We're daughters of my father. "Here's the Agora. Let's do a little walkabout."

The Agora was Isorropia's original commercial district, though it had gone through several iterations since the city's founding. It started as a combination government and commercial area, but Isorropia's government buildings, such as the Pynx, were now in a separate part of the city. The main street of the Agora, along with a few side streets, was lined with shops, restaurants, and storefronts for professionals. Most were open-air, reflecting the founder's aspirations to recreate the culture that supported Athenian-style direct democracy. Later generations were more circumspect. They appreciated the irony of an open-air market at the coldest place on earth.

Elita quit her interrogation of Lucius, for the moment. Instead, she strolled from shop to shop and stall to stall. She chatted with the shopkeepers, most of whom recognized her. Isorropia was big enough for mobs to form, and Lucius kept one eye on the surroundings and one eye on his boss/lover. Apart from his obsession with Elita, he was not much different than the security bots discreetly stationed in alcoves in the building walls. On the other hand, Isorropia was small enough that people afforded their elected leader the appearance of anonymity.

"What do you think of this sari, Lucius?" Elita draped the red and gold cloth over her breast and modeled it for Lucius.

"Lovely," he said, "but nothing does justice to your beauty."

Elita was not taken in by his flattery. She saw nervousness, and not because of the danger of crowds. The First Citizen asked for the merchant's business card, which contained her license confirming local manufacture of all her products, and moved on. She stepped into a parfumerie, its doorbell jingling as if transported from the 19th century. The air was a riot of smells. A corner of the shop was given over to incense, and an older gentleman in a traditional, but dapper suit used a special burner to let Elita sample the wares. Every few minutes, she whiffed coffee beans to clear her olfactory sense.

Lucius had stayed outside, rather than follow her into the shop. She left the perfumier and opened the shop door. "Lucius, come inside. I want you to smell this."

"I'd rather not."

"Why not?"

"I'm not interested."

"Don't be stupid. Come in." Elita grabbed a fold of his shirt and dragged him inside. He did not resist her.

When the perfumier spotted Lucius, his face fell. Even in the low light, Elita saw him blanch. Lucius was steely. Elita wondered if he was sending private texts to the merchant, instructing him to stay quiet, or simply frightening him with a stare. "Now, Lucius, tell me what you think of this." Elita held up the censer to Lucius' face, and though he did not move a muscle, she felt as if he was ready to knock it out of her hand. "Lucius, is something wrong?" All the while, he kept his eyes locked on the perfumier, who trembled. The door bell jingled, and the merchant excused himself, relieved at the interruption. Lucius' eyes followed the man mechanically.

"Well, that was strange," Elita said. "Anyhow, what do you think of the scent?"

"I wouldn't know," the BES official said coolly.

"It's agarwood," Elita said. "Artificial, of course. If the shopkeeper were selling the real thing, he'd be a candidate for disidentification under the environmental security laws."

"Indeed."

"Still, the temptation is there when the price of authentic agarwood is several hundred thousand an ounce. Marissa was very close to identifying a key player in an agarwood black market, someone who was covering the ring's tracks in return for a substantial cut of the profits."

"Mmm."

"In fact, she visited this shop two days before her disappearance." Elita nodded to the perfumier. "She spoke to that man, but he was tight-lipped, and she didn't have enough evidence to arrest him. Marissa said he was, how did she put it, 'a bit player.'"

"And did she say who the kingpin was?" Lucius' hooded expression concealed the intent of his question.

"I was hoping you knew." Marissa's investigation notes weren't clear, but as Elita read them, the person with the initials "LRG" was her prime target. *I've checked the population database. Only one Isorropian has those initials.*

Lucius suddenly turned to Elita. "And who in their right mind would risk dissing by purchasing a product banned because the plant was near extinction?" His eyes were icy.

His bluster was childish. He needed her far more than she needed him. "Marissa's notes aren't clear on that either, though there's something about high-priced cyprians buying it for well-heeled clients, or off-regulation mist-makers producing it on the side. In any case, she was interested in the suppliers, not the buyers."

Lucius relaxed slightly. "You're jumping to conclusions, Lita." The use of Elita's diminutive was not a signal of warmth. "You're reading too much into fragments, a common mistake among amateur sleuths." He brushed her cheek again with his fingers. It felt like a blade about to slice her. "I'd leave crime-fighting to the professionals, if I were you."

With that, Lucius left the shop. The perfumier cringed as the taller man opened the door. Lucius' attitude convinced Elita that he was the "LRG" in Marissa's report, and she had—to her horror—inadvertently revealed what she knew. *The truth can kill you.*

CHAPTER 15

THE REPAIRS TO KANTHAKA TOOK far longer than Bruce predicted. The bot's carbo-metal snapped his tools and his temper. The second time a team of pilgrims lifted the 250-kilo bot for fitting the leg, and it didn't fit, Bruce and Sento argued over his competence as a mechanic. She sprained her ankle when they tried a third time, which was successful. After the fix, the mechanical beast, walked with a limp and it couldn't take a full load of gear or people. Sento limped around the camp as well, cursing under her breath. As the repair team's frustration boiled over, the train's grumbling reached a fever pitch. On the fourth morning in the ice canyon, a delegation led by Enzo demanded the attention of Hosea and the other leaders.

"How much longer?" Enzo's snarl was backed by a half-dozen pilgrims, mostly his group from Caracas.

Hosea deferred to Bruce.

"A day or two." The techie's face was masked by a virtual reality microscope as he fussed with a circuit board. "Some of the configurations—"

"That's too long." Shaking his head, Enzo lost his habit of speaking in questions. "Our food is running low. There's fights breaking out in camp."

"Bruce is working as hard as he can." Hosea stood from his camp chair. His tall frame filled the space around him, simultaneously giving Sento confidence and intimidating the scowling challenger. As the camp's mood deteriorated, he remained upbeat, without being sappy. "It'll get done. We have to be patient."

"We're hungry." Enzo raised himself to his full height, attempting, and failing, to match Hosea. "We don't have time for patience."

"You don't have a choice."

"Are you sure, Hosea?" Enzo slipped back in his questioning ways. "What if we turn back?"

Almost from the day they departed Nordenskjöld, pilgrims wondered aloud about turning back, but the complaint had become as expected as grit in the meltwater. The persistence of the idea got under Sento's skin, though she was careful to hide her annoyance, at least until this point. Returning north made as much sense to her as a sunset during the Antarctic summer. "Are you crazy? After we've come this far?"

"Success seemed possible a few weeks ago, don't you agree?" Enzo glanced at his supporters, who nodded gravely. Among the group was the father with the children Awilda called "Juan" and "Rosie." "We've lost relatives and friends since then, and now failure seems more likely," Enzo added. "It's a question of survival."

"Survival?" Sento scoffed. "How do you think you'll survive?"

Enzo's tone became bureaucratic. "We've inventoried the food and supplies among us. We think there's just enough to get us back to Nordenskjöld."

"Who's 'us'?" Hosea didn't like the turn of events.

All told, the group accounted for about half the pilgrims. Sento kicked herself for not seeing the factions develop into a dangerous split in the train and reporting her fears to Hosea.

The leader sighed. "I don't suppose a speech about how we're stronger as a larger group will persuade you to stay."

Overhearing the argument, Awilda waddled to Hosea's side.

Sento approached the agitator. The delegation, except Enzo, shuffled their feet, doubting their resolve. "If you take half the food, you'll cut the odds of survival to less than half for each group. We'll break down further and start fighting for scraps. You'll never make it to Nordenskjöld."

"What about the UN relief?" Enzo was defiant. "That's what will save us. The UN delivers supplies every few weeks. There's a feast waiting for us back there." He nodded, as if indicating the old camp on the beach.

"We'll end up like animals, snapping at each other," Gwen said, holding Bruce's hand.

"Why don't you just shoot us and take all the food, you selfish bastard." Sento was exasperated.

Hosea touched her arm. "Sen—"

"Don't take the children," Awilda whispered, but no one paid attention.

"We're so close to Isorropia, I can smell it." The halt at the canyon had become physically painful for Sento, beyond her ankle. Names, sites, faces from deep within her memory were coming into focus. The oddest memory was a scent, smoky and sweet. Enzo's threat to take half the train back to Nordenskjöld meant she might never learn her identity in full.

Enzo scoffed. "Isorropia is nothing but a ridiculous hope for people who have nothing."

Koi, listening to the debate, shook his head. "No, Sen is right. It's real."

"Are we going to stake our lives on the word of a child and a woman who was supposed to be dissed?"

Sento wanted to be angry, but she was ashamed, instead. Enzo reminded everyone that she might be a criminal of the worst kind, and she wasn't sure herself of the truth. *Everyone says it doesn't matter, but it's like a gun in a drawer, put away, but available when needed.*

"Insulting people doesn't help, Enzo," Hosea said. "The facts support the city's existence. Only Isorropia would have a reason for inserting malware into the bots' computers."

Bruce chose the moment to back up Hosea. "The virus was sophisticated."

"And his network was as porous as an old fishing net," Enzo retorted. "The virus could've come from anywhere. How do we know that another one isn't lying dormant in the bots' bio-processors?" He pointed at the inert Kan.

"I've scrubbed every circuit clean." Bruce was indignant.

"Enzo," Hosea interrupted, "I can't force you or anyone to stay with the train. You can make your own choices. You'll have to live with them, or die with them."

"So you're saying our choice is to die with you or die trying to get back to the beach camp, which we know for certain exists?" Enzo pointed to each one of his delegation. "We're not stupid, Hosea. You're going to freeze or starve in this wasteland. If anyone is threatening to kill us, it's you. You're crazy. You're willing to risk your wife and baby on a phantom."

The mention of Awilda and the unborn child broke through Hosea's reserve. He snatched the rags that were once Enzo's parka and pulled the shorter man close. "You little shit, I've had enough of your criticism and complaining. How about I lose my mind now and snap your neck and take your share of the food and supplies." Enzo's eyes widened with surprise and fear. Sento didn't see murder in Hosea's face, but he was dead serious when he addressed the others. "If you people want to follow this fool to your destruction, that's your business. At least I'm trying to find something better. Enzo wants to go back to a world where he's failed." Hosea let him go with a shove. The rebel stumbled back to his delegation. They spoke in whispers. As one, they returned to the train, though one or two cast unsure glances at Hosea, Sento, Gwen, and the other leaders who wanted to go on.

"I don't understand," Koi said. "Iso is a beautiful place. Who wouldn't want to go there?"

Sento rested her hands on her hips. "They're more afraid of what's ahead than what's behind."

"Maybe they'll stay with us," Gwen said.

"No, they won't," Sento said.

Awilda's face was stricken. "Hosea, what are you doing?"

"I'm not doing anything. They're leaving. It's their choice."

"They're taking our babies." The woman's voice rose like a geyser. She pointed to the father who'd lost his wife. "That man is taking our babies. Why are you letting him do that?"

Gwen put her arm around Awilda's shoulders, but she pulled away from the nurse. "Get away from me. Stop those people. They're taking my babies from me. Hosea, stop them."

"Darling, they're not our children. Juan and Rosie are dead."

"You're a fucking murderer." She glanced around at the other leaders, hands out in a plea for sympathy. "Why aren't you stopping him? Why aren't you helping me?"

"Awilda!" Hosea hissed through is teeth. "Get hold of yourself. Juan and Rosie are dead." Sento saw tears well up in his eyes. "Our children died weeks ago." He took her by the shoulders. "Look to our future. Care for our new child. It's all we have."

The pregnant woman's eyes drilled into her husband's, then flicked to the retreating group led by Enzo. She spat on the ice.

Sento was torn between helping the woman and keeping her distance. *What do you say to a woman or man who's lost touch with reality?* She paused when she couldn't decide for sure whether Enzo was the crazy one, or Hosea and her other companions.

Despite these doubts, her prediction proved correct. Within hours, almost half the train trudged up the coulee that had brought them to the ice river, the father and his three children were among them. Enzo's group left behind only their vehicles, which the virus had disabled. They weren't willing to wait for Bruce's fix, or they didn't trust him.

"Good riddance," Sento said, not believing her own sentiment.

"We'll never see them again." Hosea lowered himself into his camp chair. Disappointed in his failure, he stared into the artificial fire. Sento combated an impulse to comfort him with a touch. Before departing, the girl Awilda named "Rosie" gave Hosea the two dolls that had once belonged to his children. He stuffed them into his pockets, but didn't remove his hands, as if he wanted to hold them, but keep his grief private.

Another day passed before Bruce decided Kan and the other vehicles were safe enough to run autonomously alongside the remaining pilgrims. They didn't have enough controllers to manage all the vehicles manually. Satisfied, Hosea declared the journey would resume the following morning. With Koi as her companion, Sento wrapped her sore ankle in a strip of cloth and scouted a few kilometers to the south. Standing atop a low rise on the ice plateau, they saw dark peaks of a mountain range on the horizon. The new goal lifted their spirits.

On the way back, Sento lost sight of Koi. His avatar disappeared from her minds-eye, and after an hour of calling and searching, she was frightened enough to totter back to camp and raise the alarm. However, as a search party collected itself, he appeared out of nowhere, thoughtful, but none the worse for wear. She scolded him, but he only smiled in a way that suggested compassion, rather than understanding.

Sento spent the evening working with Gwen to update the camp inventory of food and supplies, mostly to see if Enzo had taken more than his share. He hadn't, but the tiny supply of antivirals had gone bad, and the remaining supply of antibiotics was too meager to fight off a serious infection. The refugees at highest risk were Awilda and her baby.

"I think she may be overdue." A worried Gwen dabbed petroleum jelly on Sento's cracked lips. "I can't be sure, but the baby is the right size to be at term."

Awilda rested in Hosea's tent a few steps away.

"Will we have to, um, what's the word?"

"Induce." Gwen inhaled and exhaled. "I hope not. We don't have the drugs or the equipment, anyway."

"No, I meant—"

"A caesarian? The nearest bot surgeon is a million miles away, and I've never seen one done outside a hospital." Gwen looked in the direction of Awilda's tent. "It would probably kill her."

"Is there anything else we can do?"

"Have patience."

Despite Enzo's stupidity, he was correct that people in the column were losing patience. Squabbles broke out over the smallest problems, and Sento broke up one fistfight, taking a punch in her temple. The woman who hit her apologized and begged forgiveness, but the hit left Sento with a blinding headache, as well as flecks of light in the eye that hid the inert disidentification chip. She held an ice pack to her head, wondering if she would have a black eye in a few hours. "I'm not as strong as I was when we left the beach camp, Gwen. I don't like it."

"No one is, but things could be far worse." Gwen's face had a faraway look.

Sento lowered her ice pack. "You know how much worse it could be, don't you?"

Gwen wrapped a thin blanket around herself. The nurse was fastidious, sponging herself with a cloth soaked in warm water every morning. The camp stank like a cesspool, but the pilgrims, including herself, had lost the ability to perceive it.

"After the hospital closed in Lima, I had no job." Gwen brushed a curly hair from her eyes. "My husband lost his job at the university, and we were running out of food. Everyone was leaving. The drought had lasted ten years, and no one believed the winter rains would return. Lima had no water. People gave up. We had no choice but to head south."

Sento listened, silently urging Gwen to tell her story.

"We hired a coyote to get us to Santiago. That was as far as our money would take us. We loaded a bus along with six or seven other families. I supposed I should've seen something was wrong when the coyote said he would not ride with us, but I'd taken a lot of bus rides on the international autonomous system, so it didn't seem odd at the time. No one objected. We hated ourselves for needing him."

Gwen placed a tea pot on the solar-powered stove, but didn't switch it on, her recollections distracting her. "We were exhausted from the long trip. Sleep was impossible. The bus came to a cutoff I'd seen a dozen times. It veered into the wrong road, but I didn't think much of it. Washouts and closures were common, and the government was slow about repairs. The AI took us into the mountains. After a couple of hours, it made another turn onto a gravel road. By this time, other riders saw the danger, but no one could access the AI on the local network."

The terror of the moment came alive in Gwen's eyes. "It was a nightmare, Sen. I can't describe it to you without reliving it."

Sento touched Gwen's arm. "Please tell me. I want to know." Sento was unsure why she was willing to listen to a horrific story, except that it felt right to share among friends who had suffered much and would suffer more.

"Men with automatic weapons came out from the woods and ordered everyone off the bus. One man had a staser. I had seen the kind of terrible wounds they inflict. At first, I thought the men might be police or even BES officers in plain clothes, but they were bandits, and they were drunk." Gwen shuddered. "They made us unload our luggage and open everything. It was cold in the mountains, but they made us strip to our underwear. They found everyone's money and valuables and made us give up our minds-eye pass codes. They laughed every time they found something they liked. They chewed mist sticks like they were candy. Eventually, they ordered everyone to strip off their underwear, even the children. They were taking no chances at missing anything."

Tears filled Gwen's eyes. "One of the bandits had a bad case of folliculitis on his face. He came up to me and I could see each infected hair follicle. He smelled like a wet dog. He looked through my clothes and pawed at my brassiere as I shivered in the shadow of the bus. He looked at me like an animal he wanted to buy. He reached a dirty hand to my breast, and my husband"--Gwen closed her eyes--"said 'No!' and grabbed the bandit's hand. Not a second passed before he shot my husband. Everyone screamed and scattered and gunfire erupted.

Bullets flew everywhere and bodies dropped against the bus, which was sprayed in blood. My son ran to me, but before he reached me, the ugly bandit dragged him off. He hit him, and my son slumped down in front of a group of children that had been separated. Every one of them was screaming or crying for parents or grandparents they had just seen murdered."

Sento had heard the stories, but she had never witnessed a slave-taking. Gwen continued speaking, describing the truck that arrived, and how the bandits and slavers forced the children, some still naked, into the back. Gwen's son, a boy of eight, was unconscious as the truck drove away. "What happened, Gwen? Tell me, please." Sento was alternately fascinated and repulsed.

Gwen wiped her face. "It's been three years since that day. I've told what happened to many people, including Bruce. He's such a kind and smart man, a lot like my husband." Her face darkened again. "My husband's body was at my feet. Other people were wounded and bleeding, and I started helping the wounded. Maybe it was a way of avoiding the truth of what just happened, but I couldn't help myself. The survivors threw clothes on and we moved the bodies away from the bus and bandaged the wounded. Several died. The bus was the only place warm nearby, and the survivors, about ten or so, climbed in. Something triggered the AI, and it closed the door, and drove away, leaving the bodies by the side of the road. We screamed and pounded on the windows and pounded on the access panel to the bio-processor, but the bus wouldn't stop. It returned to the main highway and it didn't stop until it got to Santiago."

Sento imagined a blood-stained bus pulling into the Santiago station like Charon's ferry. "What about the police?"

Gwen wiped her eyes again and smiled at Sento. "You know better, Sen. We were nothing but another unfortunate group of climate refugees whose family and friends disappeared at the hands of mountain bandits and slavers. What could they do?" She shrugged, mocking the indifference of the law. "I never saw my son again. I managed to walk and hitch rides to Punta Arenas. My nursing skills brought me a little money, and I bought a place on *Kildare*. Now I am here, maybe walking to my death. I have nothing to return to, so I will follow a dream. I have nothing to lose but my life."

A scratch on the tent called Gwen away to another pilgrim's shelter, and Sento tried to process what she'd heard. Everyone in the column had a horror story to tell. A disaster had driven them from their land or their city. The journey to Antarctica had nearly killed them, in the case of the *Kildare* survivors, or they had lost everything between.

Sento felt as if she had lost the least. She may have had money at one time. She certainly had parents and probably family before her failed dissing. The lack of memory and identity protected her emotions like an invisible armor. *How do I mourn the nothingness of my past?* Every person in the column sought to fill a hole in their lives caused by suffering that was little more than an abstraction in Sento's life. The only thing that substituted for their loss was her drive to move south.

That night, though, brought a change. Sento's dreams were never more vivid. Colors, sounds, and smells fleshed out the visual images, which were far sharper than before and solid as the stone and ice of the continent. She still wasn't able to name all the people she saw, but it was as if she had put her hand on the handle of an immense door, and a pull would open it to all the answers she sought. Usually, she awoke frustrated. On this morning, she awoke with a religious certainty that she was on the threshold of realizing her goal. *The only thing I need is patience.*

The column formed as usual after breakfast. Habits reasserted themselves after days of idleness. Sento led the way with Koi again at her side, eager, but serene. Two teenage girls walked with them. The three young people said little for an hour or more, which should've been a sign of something amiss, Sento reflected later. Around mid-morning, Koi and the two girls were gone. Her thoughts flashed to Gwen's story, but there were no bandits in Antarctica's wastes to kidnap unwary children. Worried nonetheless, she trotted down the column, calling Koi's name, and when the girls' parents asked Sento if she'd seen their children, Sento feared trouble.

As it had yesterday, Koi's avatar vanished, along with the two girls'. Hosea halted the column while Bruce conducted a thorough search for the digital signals. Sento took off for the area where she had last seen Koi the day before. She found footprints in the snow, three sets over an older set going to and from the camp. *Probably Koi's.* After a dozen meters, the prints dropped into an ample, shallow crevasse. Nothing indicated the trio had fallen. Sento called down into the ice fissure, and heard only echoes. Sitting silently for a moment, she grew aware of a constant *swooshing* sound, not too much different from the water flowing in the ice river. Torn between going back for help and imagining her friends' lives slipping away, she followed the trail a few meters. It dropped quickly into a narrow tunnel just tall enough for Sento to stand.

In an instant, the universe changed. The cave's ambient temperature was colder than the outside temperature, but the air was still and Sento's active thermals and outerwear kept the chill away. The walls of the cave glistened with a layer of clear ice. Answering her hesitation, the ice on the descending path crunched underfoot as she followed the footprints of the unseen youth and girls. Despite the downward pitch of the trail, she perceived a lifting in the atmosphere, as if rays of light were bouncing among individual water molecules suspended in the air. The *swoosh*'s volume increased to a low roar. She stopped.

Koi and the two girls knelt in front of a pinnacle of ice and rock. They murmured, as if in prayer.

The children perched on a shelf looking over a chasm 30 meters deep. A void separated them from a spire of dark rock rising from the floor of a cavern at least 100 meters in height and 50 meters wide. Except for a portion of the spire near the top, the entire object was covered in blue ice. It was the deep blue of an Antarctic sky, a luminous turquoise and ultramarine of glacial ice made of frozen water devoid of air bubbles. The shape of the spire reminded Sento of the belfry of an ancient European cathedral, with the ice flowing over it much like a draped cloth. A hole in the roof of the cavern let in natural light.

Sento gasped. As she gazed upward, she saw a oval-shaped crag below a small outcrop at the peak, hooded by ice.

"Isn't she beautiful?" Koi whispered reverently on seeing Sento. "It's a miracle." His companions kept their heads bowed. "Pray with us, Sen. We're giving thanks to God for making it this far to Iso, despite our troubles and fights." He glanced upward.

Sento wasn't sure how to respond as she stepped back, mentally. The human instinct to impose familiar patterns on the randomness in nature had fooled her eye, but she didn't have the heart to explain the cold logic to a believer. There was nothing supernatural about what she observed.

"Don't you see her, Sen?"

"I see ice and a shape like a face."

"You're not seeing her, then." Koi's disappointment was pointed. "She's come to care for us and show us the way to Iso. Come closer and she'll speak to you."

The boy's hand in hers, Sento edged closer to the precipice, though the footing was as solid as concrete. She leaned against the wall of the cave, her breath forming a fog in front of her, as if her soul were attempting a sojourn into a place between reality and unreality. The shoulders of the girls shook in sobs, but the tears were of happiness, even ecstasy, and they stared upward. Sento lifted her gaze again, and she saw what they saw, the face of a young woman, so benevolent and loving that Sento's throat caught. She did not recall her own mother, but in an instant she recognized the form. The image was exactly as she had imagined her parent in dreams.

"Do you see her now, Sen?" Koi whispered. "It's Mary, don't you see?"

Sento did not take her eyes off the ice face until a tiny clicking sound caught her attention. All three children whispered to themselves, holding blue-beaded rosaries, mouthing a prayer Sento remembered old women reciting in the cathedral in Santiago. "Hail Mary, full of grace..." That was all Sento recalled, but the children knew the prayer by heart. A secular woman by temperament, or by an unremembered training, she was nonetheless moved by the childrens' devotion and the natural wonder of the ice and rock sculpture.

Koi still held her hand, and a new wave of sadness overcame her. The reality of the world intruded, knocking down the random beauty of what Koi and his followers had found. *The Warming created this place, and the Warming will destroy it.*

Behind the perch, a narrow ledge of rock formed a natural bench. Koi returned to his prayers, and Sento rested in the humidity, which seemed ready to freeze into a sarcophagus around her. The urgency of the rescue faded into a quiet contemplation of the patterns of blue, gray, and clarity of the ice. Again, the instinct to find patterns took over, and her eye fell on a jumble of shapes in the ice wall. Rising, she reached out to a dull red triangle, which she recognized as a flag frozen in mid-flap.

Excited, she found a rock and chipped at the ice until she exposed the flag. Pulling away chunks of the ice, she found boxes with markings in English that read "tomatoes," "carrots," "freeze-dried," "keep chilled," and "National Science Foundation." Chinese characters paralleled the Latin letters, as if whoever was meant to read them might be fluent in either language, or both. Sento whooped for joy as she tore into one of the foil-covered packs labeled "MRE" and chewed on something that tasted like chocolate, though she hadn't tasted anything close to it since Punta Arenas.

The noise in the cavern abruptly increased as Hosea and others poured through the entrance to the cavern. When she had failed to answer pings, they sought her out, and Bruce heard her automated signals. Sento dragged Hosea to paw through the ancient supply cache, a remnant of a scientific expedition preserved in Antarctica's formerly eternal deep-freeze. Human thoughtlessness, caution, and sheer luck had given the pilgrims a second chance. Koi called it another "miracle." Sento did not accept the word, but her resistance was nothing compared to the gratitude she felt and the tears streaming down her cheeks to express it. Koi wiped them away, and she leaned her cheek against his palm.

CHAPTER 16

THE MOUNTAINS SENTO AND KOI spotted from the ice river resolved into a horizon-spanning cordillera with no obvious break hinting at a pass. *Beautiful, but dispiriting.* Before Antarctica, she had followed old, well-worn Inca roads along the spine of the Andes, but no human had ever crossed the mountains ahead, and the pilgrims weren't in a condition to pioneer a route. The number of edible food packages from the cache at Virgin's Cave—as Koi called it—disappointed the train, but Hosea, ever optimistic, thought it gave them a few more days of travel, perhaps enough to find Isorropia.

"Once they understand our condition, they'll change their attitude toward us," Hosea declared. "We're good people, ordinary people, like them, I'm sure."

Sento held that the Isorropians were less sanguine about the pilgrims, or they would've helped already. It didn't matter. *We don' t have much choice, except to go on.* Sento spent more time walking with Hosea, and less time prowling the edges of the column like a guard animal. She noticed a growing distance between him and Awilda, whom Kanthaka carried in state, bedraggled and infirm as she was. Hosea was preparing himself for a dark moment with his wife, but Sento kept her silence on a subject that was none of her business.

The benign weather was changing. The pilgrims knew Antarctica's reputation, and thus they knew their luck with the climate would run out. Since Nordenskjöld, storms lasted a few hours at most, and the cold was tolerable in their thermals and cold weather gear, but as they approached the cordillera, the wind rose, the temperature fell, and the eternal sun was always veiled by high clouds. The relatively flat ground gave way to foothills and the base of sheer cliffs that thrust upward a thousand meters through the ice cap. After two days of scouting the base of the mountains, Sento sniffed sea air, and she hoped open water might offer a way through or around the mountains. Rolling sea fogs, penetrating as they were, encouraged the pilgrims.

An unmistakable barking caused a frenzy in the group. The fog carried the sound like a phantom up a gorge that led to a wide beach at the end of an inlet. Dozens of fur seals lolled above the surf, their bawling muffled by the fog as they crawled on the slurry of gravel.

"Unbelievable." Hosea's jaw dropped in amazement.

"I thought they were extinct," Gwen said.

Bruce disagreed. "Some populations are holding out in the most remote areas. We're pretty far inland. This must be one of the new fjords that's opened up as the ice has disappeared."

"It's a haven for them." Sento shivered, but not from the cold.

Koi crossed himself. "It's a godsend."

That's when the shooting started. A group of pilgrims broke off from the train and charged down the gully. One of the refugees fired indiscriminately at the herd with a pistol. The seals panicked and bolted to the surf, which boiled as hundreds of animals plunged into the sea. Bullets flew like angry bees, but none struck.

"What the fuck? NO!" Something snapped in Sento, and she raced after the cruel pilgrims. *They're killing the seals. I have to protect them.* Stumbling on the loose soil, she reached for her nine millimeter. She hadn't fired it or even cleaned it in weeks.

A big male halted and stood its ground, challenging the refugees to pursue the rest of the herd pouring into the fjord. The inexperienced hunters pulled up, unsure how to counter the male's objection, despite their weaponry. Their confusion gave Sento a chance to close in.

"Stop! Stop now!" Sento brandished her pistol. "These are protected animals. You have no right—"

"Sen, put away the gun." Hosea caught up with Sento and the group.

The male seal roared, angry, terrified, and defiant. Pilgrims surrounded it to prevent its escape.

"It's wrong to harm these animals," Sento pleaded. "There's only a few left anywhere. This might be the only population left on the planet."

"I don't fucking care," one of the pilgrims shouted. "I'm hungry. My family's hungry." The pilgrim pointed an old rifle at the bull, which threatened with blubbery growls. Behind him, hundreds of pointed, black-eyed heads bobbed in the inlet's water, watching the drama unfold.

Defending the seal as if it were an injured child unable to protect itself, Sento pointed her gun at the pilgrim's head. "You shoot the seal, I shoot you."

"Sen, wait."

It was the rifle man's turn to plead. "You're completely crazy. We've got a right to survive!" He lifted the rifle to his cheek, but glanced at Hosea, hoping for support, or an escape from his dilemma.

Sento cocked her pistol. "Last warning." An inner voice warned her to stay calm, even as a competing voice urged her to take whatever action was necessary to protect the seal.

"Sen, back off!" Hosea stepped forward, the gravel crunching under his feet.

Sento swung her pistol around at Hosea. "It's a capital crime to kill the seal. My job's to protect it. It's what I've sworn to do." The words surprised her, as if she were playing an unfamiliar recording. *Sworn? What in hell does that mean?* The desire to protect and enforce some rule or law was overpowering. She held the pistol at her friend, but the bitter argument in her heart was as real as the plaintive pinniped calls that bounced among the walls of the fjord.

Hosea held out his hands. "Sen, these animals are protected, but we're starving. We need food. Why are you threatening us? Put down your gun."

The male seal howled, unable to get past the cordon of determined pilgrims to the surf and safety. *Trapped!* Of Sento's swirling, confusing emotions, the sense of being cornered by an unexpected enemy stood out. Sento knew what it was like to be ambushed, in danger of death, and then dying. The raw fear in the bull seal's roiling muscles, tensed and ready to run, but with no place for refuge, was as real as the ever-present Antarctic cold.

"If anyone shoots this animal, I'll kill him."

The pilgrim with the rifle pointed it at Sento. "If you don't let me shoot it, I'll kill you first, then shoot it."

Hosea spoke quietly. "Sen, put down the gun. Let's talk about this."

That's a death sentence for the seal. Sento swung her automatic between the pilgrim leader and the man with the rifle. She was outnumbered by the hungry travelers. She faced the choice of shooting a friend or someone she had watched over for weeks.

Desperation forced the issue. When Sento looked away from the armed pilgrim, he fired at the bull, which dropped to the gravel. The report echoed in the fjord, startling an army of seagulls into flight. Sento aimed at the rifle man, ready to carry out her threat, but Hosea grabbed her wrist, lifting it high. She pulled the trigger, and the gun fired harmlessly, its report chasing the rifle's.

Weeks ago, ages ago, she might have resisted Hosea, but she was as tired, weak, and hungry as all the other pilgrims. Failure, guilt, frustration, and loneliness forced tears from her as Gwen embraced her and Hosea took away her pistol. The dead seal quivered on the beach. Starving men, women, and children attacked the carcass with axes and knives.

Koi stood tall, holding a strip of meat that streamed blood with the same hand that had cupped Sento's cheek in the cave. The memory of his touch and the vision of his gore-soaked hand sickened Sento.

Within minutes, makeshift spits held chunks of the seal near the flames of a driftwood fire. Fat dripped and spattered on the coals as the pilgrims anticipated the feast. Adults sliced off barely roasted meat and give it to their children. A woman chewed a chunk of flesh, spat it out, and offered it to a toothless elder. Koi chewed a bone like a dog to get the last bit of gristle.

Sento's vision of chasing a hooded man through the beach camp now clicked into place. Her declaration about protecting the animals made sense more and more as she turned it over in her mind, because it was linked to the hooded man and a vague sense of guilt that infused her mood.

Hosea offered Sento a roasted strip of seal, but she refused.

"Don't be foolish, Sen. You need to eat something."

Sento shook her head.

Hosea placed the meat on a flat rock near Sento's foot. "Eat when you're ready. I've had my fill."

Sento pushed hair from her face, but didn't reach for the flesh.

"What happened today, Sen? I've never seen you like that. You're always so calm and methodical. But you went crazy. That's the only word I can think of. Your eyes were as wild as the seal's. I really thought you were going to hurt somebody."

As each moment passed, Sento understood better her blurted words and their meaning. A corner of the puzzle of her identity was complete enough to see the pattern. "I was a police officer."

Hosea inhaled and nodded, as if expecting the new information. "That would explain a lot about you. Your demeanor is always..." He thought for a moment. "I always thought you behaved like someone with authority or a mission. You're the most vigilant person I've ever met."

"Actually, I think I was more than an ordinary cop."

"How so?"

"I mean I wasn't an officer walking the streets, preventing burglaries and such." Sento gazed at the feasting pilgrims. "You know about environmental security?"

Hosea's gaze turned judicious, as if doubting that he should speak. "Environmental security agencies are everywhere, not that they've done much to fix the planet. They just harass people trying to make a living."

Sento was not in a place to argue the best ways to balance human activity against the needs of the planet. "I was in one of those agencies, here in Antarctica."

A puzzled look infused Hosea's face. "How is that possible? Antarctica is the one place where the agencies don't reach, at least regularly. That's what I always thought."

"I'd heard that too, but I'm certain it was here, which leaves one possibility."

Hosea drew the same conclusion. "You worked for the Isorropian version."

"I remember wearing a uniform and I remember going on some sort of raid. The mission had to do with illegal harvesting of seal meat." She picked at a stone with her finger. "On this raid, I shot someone. I think I killed him." *Was I was punished for it? I'm not sure.*

"Was he shooting at you?"

"I don't know. All I'm sure about is that he and the other poachers were running. We caught them red-handed, literally." Sento thought of blood-spattered clothing on the hooded man. "I saw the man again when I was chasing the boy back at Nordenskjöld. I almost shot him, but the memory got in the way."

Hosea was thoughtful. "If I'm not mistaken, poaching an endangered species is punishable by disidentification."

The pilgrim leader was correct, though Sento did not express her agreement immediately. *Was I somehow connected to the poaching gang?* A quiet voice inside her said No, but she had lost some trust in her powers of self-reflection, particularly as she was ready to pounce like a cat on the forbidden food at her feet. *That's making me feel as guilty as shooting the hooded man.*

Hosea chewed slowly on a strip of meat. Neither he nor Sento said a word for several minutes, until he saw the balance of the train picking its way down the gully. He carried meat strips to Awilda, who lay in the sling underneath Kanthaka. Sated by the feast, the pilgrims pitched camp above the high-tide line. The camp resembled the old camp at Nordenskjöld, though smaller, dirtier, and skeletal. After weeks and weeks of mildness reminiscent of the serene, if chill atmosphere of the Virgin's Cave, the weather closed in. Birds picked clean the ribs and long bones of the seal as the incoming tide claimed the bloody remains.

As always, Sento struggled to place the new bit of information among her collection, as well as disentangle contradictory emotions. Perhaps her training had led her to identify strongly with the animal, but the feeling of being trapped was visceral, as if she was inside the animal's head. Her pragmatic nature wouldn't allow her any kind of mystical interpretation, but it was an experience she'd known before. She'd been trapped once, her life threatened, and the thing in common with the killing at the gully, apart from the terror, was the seal himself, or a representation. In that instant, a new image formed in her memory, one that made no sense by any standard. The snarling, bobbing head of the seal glowed a bright shade of aquamarine.

As a gull eyed the untouched strip of meat at her feet, Sento toyed with the idea that she was losing her mind. *My empty stomach will drive me mad first.* The memory of the raid elicited more than images of chasing and shooting a criminal. Hurting a magnificent wild creature revolted her. The earth and its creatures were sacred, but not in a conventional religious sense. They, like humans, were the universe manifesting itself in its own kind of miracle. Eating this animal was not far from cannibalism. It deserved as much respect and space on the planet as humans. The taking of the seal's life was akin to murder, which justified the sentence of disidentification. *Is this what living in Isorropia meant for me?* For the first time since leaving Nordenskjöld, she wondered if she belonged with the pilgrims.

She replayed the seal incident in her imagination. The death of the animal lifted a veil, and her terror for the creature brought forgotten principles and standards into focus. Values by which she lived her former life reasserted themselves. It turned her inside out. The seal was a masterpiece of nature, a rival to the lion as king among beasts. The fire in its desire to protect its herd made its loss all the more tragic. Sento nearly cried at the seal's death, as if it had been a loved one. Like she had done in whatever previous life she had led, she was ready to kill the man who shot the seal. The hooded man had motives less desperate than the refugees, but his demise was an outcome of a noble code that protected the natural world. *He died violating a higher law I believed in.* Like the bull seal tried to do for its herd, she had once tried to protect a herd of endangered animals, perhaps seals, and the hooded man was sacrificed for her zeal. It was her job, and she was good at it, and she was proud of her service.

However, she had failed at the fjord. The circumstances were wholly different, to be sure, but she still felt she had let the seal, and its herd, and all of the natural world, down after promising to protect and to serve it, guarding the rights guaranteed it by… what? She didn't remember the details of the code itself, but it didn't matter. The sense of failure arose as strong as the urge to move south.

Sento imagined what she might have done to the seal-killer in her other life. *Arrested and charged him with all manner of crimes against non-human species.* In the context of the moment, however, his act was rational, even justifiable. He was defending himself and his family against starvation. Protecting a species against extinction was a luxury he couldn't afford. While she did not know the man in any detail, he was a member of her community that had formed around a dream to find a better life.

Early on, she joined the train for convenience sake. Contributing to its success was in her self-interest. Her memory was returning, piece by frustrating piece, but at an unknown point since the *Kildare* disaster, she had crossed over a threshold into a different, adopted society. Her old values were absurd compared to the needs of the malnourished bodies sleeping in the tents on the beach. In the end, survival was the only value, and it was a monumental tragedy that humans were unsurpassed at surviving at the expense of every other sentient creature on the earth.

The best way, the proper way, to reconcile an individual human's survival with that of other creatures was thoughtful consideration of the options and proper policies providing for living and breeding space for all concerned. Sento snorted to herself, wanting to flip the bird at the arrogance of such a thought. She had read it on the plinth in a memorial park for some environmentalist hero who never had to worry about where his next meal was coming from. *Tell that to the mother of a child with a swollen belly.* Sento lifted the strip of cooked seal meat to her mouth, tore off a piece with her teeth, chewed, and swallowed.

"How is it?" Hosea returned from Awilda's side.

"A five-star chef could not have cooked it better."

CHAPTER 17

An excerpt from the diary of Artemis Macedon

I followed Ticino's group for a couple of days, just to make sure he didn't have some other idea than taking people back to Nordenskjöld. Once they were away from Bruce's network, I couldn't eavesdrop, because they didn't have the wherewithal to set up their own network. Ticino, however, called a halt after a day, and he appeared to wait for something, glancing up at the sky now and then. I took a risk and presented myself, despite his warning to stay away given back at the refugee camp. I was thinking of the other poor people whom he'd managed to drag with him. There were kids in that group. He wasn't interested in my offer to tell my benefactor, saying he had more resources backing him up than anything I could bring to bear. He had to mean Isorropian resources, and Galla came to mind.

Ticino's behavior made sense if Galla had put him up to it, but I could only speculate. Maybe Ticino is in the same mold as Galla, who takes psychopathology and recklessness to a new level. After all, he exiled me out here. In any case, Ticino threatened to kill me if I showed my face again. I believed him and retreated. He'd shoot his own mother. I made my way back to Sento and her group. I don't know what happened to him and his group, but my level of confidence in his success is low.

I didn't sign up to be a spy. I didn't imagine spending all my time surveilling a gaggle of vagrants chasing a mirage. I once led a team of warriors protecting our beautiful city and Antarctica from base behavior rooted in the tragedies of the industrial age. I can't help but laugh now when I write "our beautiful city." My enemies in Isoroppia tossed me onto the ice like so much garbage when I got too close to their hypocrisies. Honestly, I'm as much a failure as they are. For example, I was as surprised as the pilgrims at the appearance of the herd of seals. Like them, I thought the species was extinct. It's Isorropian orthodoxy that humans are the root of all environmental evil. We've made a religion of our own style of mastery over the environment, veiled in humble rhetoric about living in harmony with it, and when it shocks us with the unexpected, we don't know what to make of it. I suspect that's how Isorropia is dealing with these refugees and their march to its gates. It's watching this drama, I know. I see the drones at a hundred meters, feeding video while the pundits congratulate themselves at the city's perfection even as the barbarians approach. Pride goes before the fall, someone once said.

Disillusionment won't feed me, though. My benefactor has kept me alive, but I'm a convenience for him, eyes on a prize. The object of the spy's desire changes, though. He despises his quarry at first, which keeps him wary and alert. I'm not a spy by training, and I suppose the trainers would tell him how to keep his distance as he grows familiar with the objects. Take the pilgrims. I've come to know these people, if not as friends, then as individual people, like getting to know characters in a net drama. There's Hosea the calm and sturdy leader, unperturbed, but worn down by the drip-drip of the day-to-day struggle. Awilda, his wife, is on the edge of lunacy, but carrying on for the child she carries. Gwen has wounds deeper than a glacier's crevasse, but she's the epitome of compassion and patience. Bruce is the secret optimist kept going by Gwen's love. Everyone is slowly pulling Sento, the outsider, toward the refugees' fate, like a black hole. How will she react when she learns that her true role may be that of enemy?

I'm doing a job. Maybe it'll mean I can return to Isorropia. Do I really want to? I have my doubts. Out here on the ice, causes and ideologies, even saving the planet, are an incredible waste of time. The ferals have it right; an always-full stomach is not a human being's normal or proper state. A surplus of calories causes nothing but trouble. All humans need are each other and a purpose. Until my benefactor approached me, I was lonely for companionship and desperate for an aim in my life. Is spy the best I can hope for? I hope not. It makes me want to melt into the continent. Disappear. Thing is, it would be slow suicide, and I'm not that depressed, not yet.

I envy Koi, up to a point. He is the angelic caretaker of the spiritual fire that keeps the pilgrims going, but I can't fathom his addiction to a religion that gets him to worship a hunk of rock and ice, no matter how fetching. The fact that others are willing to agree with his interpretation is beyond me. Some of the pilgrims were so convinced of the miraculous nature of the Ice Virgin, they had to be dragged out of the cave. Where does that faith come from? They're just as devoted to the idea of Isorropia's existence. That's a far more rational belief from their perspective, given all that's happened to them, though the city might as well be at the bottom of the Arctic Ocean than just over the mountain range that has blocked their progress.

I've been tempted to disobey my benefactor's orders and reach out to Sento. I was once her boss, maybe a friend, after a fashion. I was close to panic when she and the others disappeared into a fog coming up from the ocean. Antarctica's weather does funny things to wireless signals and equipment. One minute my minds-eye captured the net carrier, and the next minute it was gone. The panic was as much about fear for her safety as it was about pleasing my patron. I wandered around the ice for a whole day chasing digital ghosts as if I they were playing an exasperating game. And then Sento and I nearly crashed into one another. Like a burrowing creature, I covered myself with snow and ice to hide, hoping she wouldn't pick up my masked com carrier signal. It worked, but only just.

Would she recognize me if I showed myself? After a failed dissing, it's hard to tell. My appearance might shock her or anger her, or it might hurt her, which I couldn't bear at this point. When she's scouting, she looks into the distance as if hoping the sky and clouds and horizon will tell her something more than how far she has to travel. It won't be long before she gets her wish and puts together all she's learned. I'd like to be there when it happens.

My role as fly on the wall might be ending. I'll soon have to make a recommendation. The affair with the bull seal clinched it, and not just because Sento nearly killed one of the pilgrims. The devouring of the entire animal by the group in one gulp, figuratively speaking, shows how desperate they are. As individuals, many of the pilgrims are smart, but they've stored or preserved nothing of the bull's flesh. Except for a full belly, they are in the same situation they were before they found the herd. Do these people deserve to be saved?

By my reckoning, the pilgrims have barely enough food to reach the outer edges of Isorropia's defensive ring, which serves as its border, for lack of a better marker. If I recommend against help, I'll condemn them, including Sento, to death by starvation. If I recommend help for them, I can't say their fate will be any better. I know my home, and it's not known for opening its doors to strangers. Will the pilgrims open their door to me?

CHAPTER 18

ELITA HAD JUST PUT THE thin-sliced potatoes with herbs and olive oil in the oven when she heard a room-shaking crash and a curse foul enough to make a sailor's hair curl. She rushed into the living room of her apartment and found her dog-sized disinfecting bot in pieces. The wall had a gouge in it where the bot had hit. "What in the Mother's name is wrong with you? I'm still making payments on that thing, not to mention the monthly subscription fees."

"It got in my way." Lucius breathed hard, as if he'd come in from a run.

Elita was frightened by her lover's increasingly unpredictable moods, especially after the encounter in the parfumerie. He was scared as well, though he wouldn't talk to her about his apprehensions. It went back to her discovery of the connection, albeit tenuous, between him and Marissa's disappearance.

Elita picked up the fragments of the bot and her chest ached when she noticed shards of glass. Her lover had also broken an art vase given her by Marissa on her 30th birthday. Marissa's presents tended toward the practical, but she had taken care with this one, probably with Ben's help. Elita received it a few weeks after Marissa was accepted into the BES Academy, a position she got with Elita's back-channel help. *It was a beautiful piece. My jealousy gets the better of me sometimes.*

She nearly called for the sweeper bot, but thought better of it for fear of provoking Lucius. *Why am I so worried about his reaction all of a sudden?* After a ten-minute search through the apartment for the old brush and dustpan, the security chief cursed again. She rushed down the hall and found him pacing in front of her picture window. *At least nothing's broken this time.* He ran his hands through his hair like an anxious teenager. She thought about challenging him a second time, but her anxiety prevented her.

"Dinner's almost ready. Can you keep from breaking anything until then?" It dawned on Elita that something on the screen upset him before he turned it off. There was a news report playing when she found the broken bot. She didn't have time, however, to figure it all out. She disposed of the sad fragments of the vase in the recycler as the oven signaled that the potatoes were ready. As she arranged the baked chickpea burgers, sliced tomatoes, and potatoes on plates, her hands trembled. Lucius' temper unnerved her, and she hated the feeling. She practiced the Relaxing Breath Exercise from her yoga class, but the tension hung on.

At the table, Lucius gulped a glass of merlot. He shared a bottle with Elita during most of their meals, and he often took a glass of whiskey at a social function. She had never seen him roaring drunk. "Something's really rattled you, hasn't it?"

"Why do you keeping pushing me on this?"

Elita remained silent, preferring to let the sparks between them dissipate. *Have I done something to upset him?* Perhaps her recent coolness toward him had contributed to his mood, but she wouldn't blame herself for tonight's troubles. They ate in silence, sipping the wine. She brought out two servings of chocolate pudding made from soaked chia seeds.

Lucius took another sip of wine and drummed the table with his fingers. "Thank you for the meal."

"I'm glad you liked it." *He's being sincere.* However, he was debating something internally. He stretched out both hands and laid the palms flat on the table, as if to steady himself.

"I'm sorry I broke your bot. And the vase. I'll pay for it. For both." The promise came through clenched teeth, as if he didn't want to declare his responsibility.

"Apology accepted." *That came out rather* pro forma. *Am I sincere?* "It's too bad about the vase. It was an Arneson, a very limited edition."

"Like I said, I'll replace it."

"I'm not sure it's replaceable. My sister gave it to me. Only a few—"

"I said I'd replace it." The tension in his neck was visible, but he breathed in and out, similar to Elita's exhalations. His hooded eyes focused on a wall sculpture titled *False Truths #4*, a housewarming gift from Ben.

"Suppose I told you I saw a ghost," Lucius said.

"A ghost?" The retort betrayed Elita's skepticism of the supernatural.

"A specter."

"A scary ghost."

"An image of someone you know." Lucius folded his hands in his lap. "No, not a ghost. A living human being."

"You're not usually one to tell riddles. What are you getting at?"

"I saw her tonight."

Elita was losing patience. "Get to the point, Lucius. What's upsetting you?"

Lucius sighed. "Marissa."

The way he said the name cut into Elita's marrow like a shard from the shattered vase. "I don't understand. How did you see her?"

"I'll send you a link."

A second later, a video appeared in Elita's minds-eye. It was one of the daily reports on the refugees. The news chans' shameless exploitation of their slow destruction disgusted everyone, even as the entire city was obsessed by their journey. Most of the article's video was taken from a height, then it zoomed to a set of faces the report said belonged to the train's unidentified leaders.

"Look for her about halfway into the report."

Elita heart skipped. The young woman was filthy, with clothes so ragged Elita wondered how they stayed on her body. Oddly, everyone else's clothing in the group was in far worse shape, as if the woman had been outfitted with the best of whatever the group had salvaged. *Or what she'd salvaged on her own.* Her face was thinner and grayer than Elita remembered, perhaps from the lack of bathing, or makeup, or malnutrition. She conferred with a tall, dignified man, who stood next to a red-haired fellow holding a tablet with a cracked screen.

The report's narrator was incensed over the killing of a wild seal in a herd unknown to Isorropia's biologists until the chan discovered it. Elita, however, barely heard the baritone voice. She was transfixed by the image of Marissa, who resembled a fiend more than a human being.

"You see, a ghost," Lucius said, noting the look on Elita's face.

"Everyone thought she was dead."

"No corpse was ever found. Everyone *assumed* she was dead."

"Then how?" *How did she survive?*

"I haven't a clue."

"Did you know about this before?"

Lucius looked in Elita's eyes. "I swear I did not."

"Even with all your—"

"Even with all our signals intelligence, and gadgets, and a fucking army of analysts, I had no idea. At least no one told me or noticed."

Elita believed him. He was as shocked as she. *Marissa barely resembles the woman I knew.*

"Does my father know?"

"I don't know. Honestly."

Elita's mind raced. *What do I do now?* She rewound and watched the video again, trying to work out its underlying meaning. Bewilderment, suspicion, and relief were her chief emotions. Everyone—except her Father—accepted that she was dead, but here she was. *How do you react to a resurrection?* Despite Marissa's reedy thinness, she appeared healthy. Elita believed Lucius' assertion that he had not known Marissa was with the refugees, but that's not why he was upset. She remembered her sister's investigation notes on "LRG" and Lucius' behavior at the parfumerie. After seeing her alive, Elita expected him to be relieved on her behalf, if not his own, and suggest that she contact her father to tell him the good news. Instead, he was afraid. *Lucius sees Marissa as an unexpected threat. Why?*

Elita rolled the video image back and forth, as if the repetition made her sister's appearance a solid event, instead of a weird, unwelcome illusion. Marissa's resemblance to Ben was unmistakable. *Our mothers' genes must be pretty weak. We look like we have the same mother, instead of different ones.* Once Elita let her rational mind evaluate the new situation, the shock faded, replaced by curiosity and a desire to talk to her and hear her story. So much didn't add up. Where had she been? *You'd think if she had somehow become lost away from the city that she would make her way back as soon as possible, but she's been gone more than two years.* A lost person wants to be found. Why is she with the refugees? Does she understand the danger they represent to Isorropia? Is she leading them here? Elita did not want to entertain the possibility that the answer to the last question was Yes.

"Do you think we should contact her?" Elita said.

"And expose the city to these migrants? Absolutely not."

Lucius' words were standard policy, but his tone was harsher than usual.

"You're sure my father doesn't know?"

"I have no idea. I certainly haven't told him."

Elita's instinct for calculation reasserted itself. "Father has invited me over to his apartment for a house concert tonight. He asked me to come. He's trying to mend fences. I can tell him about Marissa then, assuming he doesn't already know."

"What about me?"

"Spouses and partners are invited. You can deliver the good news yourself, if you like."

"Are you sure telling him is the right thing to do?"

It was the reaction Elita expected, and it disappointed her. Although Lucius was as Machiavellian as she, his question confirmed unspoken motives. Lucius' mood was the weak point. Elita was willing to gamble that his volatility might get the better of him, as it did with the disinfecting bot. She wanted to know what he knew about Marissa's disappearance, down to the last detail, but she wasn't ready to ask him directly. The pressure cooker of an encounter with Marissa's father might reveal something. "Why wouldn't we want to tell him?"

Lucius paced again. "I don't think I should go."

"I don't think you have a choice. This is work as much as it's pleasure. I need my security adviser by my side. I expect powerful Ecclesia members will ask questions about the refugees and other matters. I need you there."

Lucius tensed again, as if ready to punch the wall, but he checked himself.

Ben Soares' apartment suite was far too big for one man, but he was more than one man, Elita reflected, in a sense. As the city's leading elder statesman, he had an obligation to entertain the city's leading political leaders, businessmen and women, artists and writers, and ordinary citizens, when the moment demanded it. In fact, he enjoyed showing it off. His address was in Isorropia's toniest neighborhood, and although the décor was modest in line with the city's Scandinavian-derived values of elegant richness, three families could easily share the amount of space his home occupied. Though Isorropia's First Citizens had nothing like Brazil's Palácio da Alvorada, or even the American White House, Ben's apartment was closest to it, though he owned it, unlike the other nations' public homes. Elita wondered if she might occupy it one day, instead of living in an ordinary apartment. *If he should die prematurely, does this place come to me?* She had never talked to him about his will.

Elita dismissed her cheap envy and gave her father the benefit of the doubt. He loved entertaining. The hint of incense, a necessity in a city which re-filtered and recycled its air, sparked her earliest memories of dinner parties and late night meetings in the apartment where she spent her childhood, before the divorce which separated her from her father. In her penguin pajamas, she listened at the door as her father argued with his cronies about things that were meaningless to an eight-year-old. Instead, she absorbed the passion behind the words into her DNA.

Even as his ataxia destroyed his body, Ben's exo allowed him to maintain a vigorous public schedule, including regular soirees at his place. Officially, tonight's party was intended to honor the 30th anniversary of the guest of honor's first solo appearance at Isoroppia's main concert hall, which Ben had built in his first term as First Citizen. Unofficially, it was an opportunity to strengthen the bonds within Isorropia's governing elite, a class of citizens polite Iso society did not like to acknowledge. The founders wanted government power to flow directly from the governed, and they built processes and institutions to discourage the rise of a governing class. They failed, though Isorropian manners required public rhetoric to maintain the fiction. *Some would say our manners perpetuate a hypocrisy. Maybe, but reformers always forget that governance takes time, effort, and special skills only a few people can master.* Elita was welcomed into that elite like a princess royal.

Ben's gleaming exo made him look like Apollo descended to earth to meet his mortal worshipers. As the soloist and the chamber quartet belted out the sweeping second movement of the Explorer's Concerto, the eyes of most of the men and all of the women lingered on Ben for at least a few minutes of the performance. He sat modestly in the second row, publicly eschewing his status, reserving the first row for the families or friends of the special guest.

The last few pages of the concerto's third movement always brought tears to Elita's eyes. Even as it mourned the end of the heroic age of Antarctic exploration in 1917, it celebrated the anticipation of a new era for humanity. It made Elita think of the risks taken in the late 21st century by the founders—some were her ancestors—to create a truly sustainable society in which ecological balance was at the center of everyday life. Over decades, the founders secretly gathered the resources, the know-how, and the human capital to reach a critical mass ready to survive and thrive while the rest of human society crumbled under the pressures of global climate change. Unlike their attempts at creating a classless society, they had succeeded with sustainability, and Elita would not allow a group of people living no better than rats threaten their achievement. After past disasters with admitting refugees, the citizenry had placed a burden of faith on her, and she wouldn't let them down.

Marissa must be helping them, else why would she be with them? Will I have to sacrifice her to keep them away? How would Father take this?

She and Lucius had arrived late, and their seats were in the last row near the buffet table. Elita grinned inwardly. *An appropriately humble place.*

Lucius growled. He'd swallowed two cups of the vodka punch, but it was sometimes difficult to tell if he was drunk or not. He liked to keep people guessing, but Elita worried he might be that worst species of guest, a drunken sulk. "Have you noticed them, Lita?"

The audience applauded enthusiastically as Ben presented a commemorative medal to the soloist. Ben's synthetic voice dominated the room. Elita clapped with the *gravitas* required of an elected official, despite her admiration for the music and the players. "Shall I give you a list?"

"You can start with your enemies. They're all here." Lucius sipped more punch.

"All three or four thousand of them?" Elita laughed. The main room, decked out for the performance, seated fifty or sixty at most.

His speech too sharp, despite his buzz, Lucius itemized name after name, and the reasons Elita should distrust or hate each one, an inventory she stopped after a dozen. "You've made your point. It's not as though I didn't notice a pattern, but sometimes a party is just a party."

"I don't believe you actually said that, you calculating bi—"

"Watch yourself." *He is drunk.*

Lucius laughed into his sleeve, then folded his arms, thoughtfully. "There's more going on here than a recital."

The security chief's paranoia was too much for Elita. "Intrigue is a politician's stock in trade. Scheming is work for them." A human server offered champagne. "Have a drink and enjoy the company."

Lucius swallowed a glass in one gulp. As most of the guests departed, he watched Ben and a knot of close supporters gather in a corner, then move toward the dining room.

Elita said, "We'd better tell Father our news before he gets sucked into a conspiracy."

The group with Ben turned to Elita and Lucius when they approached. Elita kissed her father lightly on the cheek not covered by the exo brace that held his head erect. His skin was warm, if loose, with a hint of stubble. He smelled of incense. "Father, that was a brilliant performance."

"By me, or by the artist?"

"You know what I mean."

"I'm glad you could come." His eyes grinned, while the rest of his face was slack.

Elita pulled at her father's arm. "Could I have a word in private?"

Lucius hung back until Elita used her eyes to call him into her conversation. "Father, have you seen the latest reports from the refugee column?"

Ben contemplated an answer. "I avoid most of the press reports on the issue. The media panders to people's fears when it's not feeding them destructive gossip."

The statement surprised Elita. "You're keeping up with the news, though."

"In my own way."

Lucius' eyes narrowed. "How?"

Ben ignored the security chief's accusatory tone and focused on Elita. "What can I help you with, my dear?"

Elita second-guessed her decision to tell Ben what she and Lucius knew, but she pressed forward. "We've seen Marissa, Father."

Ben breathed sharply. He wobbled, despite his exo's AI efforts to keep him erect, and he reached for a chair. He sat heavily, the servo motors hissing in counterpoint to his breath. "That's not possible."

"I've seen the video." Elita related the details and shared the video with Ben.

If Ben felt shock, joy, or some other emotion, he didn't show it. His avatar on the com network was as blank as his face. He rarely used emo-sigs. *He was that way before the ataxia took away his muscles.* Ben swiveled his head to Lucius. "Is this verified? Did you know about this?"

"I did not."

"That seems unlikely." To herself, Elita translated: *You're lying.* Instead, Ben grunted, a hollow sound that was more derisive than the same sound made by a healthy man.

"The Bureau of Environmental Security is not omnipotent, sir," Lucius said.

"No, only reckless and ruthless."

When Marissa was declared missing, Ben pined for her like any father would for his lost child, calling Elita daily for updates and sitting in on press conferences, despite his misgivings about the media. Gradually, as leads dried up, he withdrew to mourn what appeared to be her death. The investigators said no other explanation fit the evidence, though they were hard-pressed to explain the coincidence of her supervisor's disappearance. Six months ago, Ben's questions ceased, which Elita chalked up to an acceptance of her passing. There was doubt in Ben's reaction tonight, but not about the fact of Marissa's survival. It recalled Elita's suspicions about Lucius' connection.

"Does this change anything, Elita?" Ben said.

"In what respect?"

"Your attitude toward the refugees. Does it change your policy?"

"Why would it?" The question came from Lucius.

"I didn't ask you, Galla."

"Stop it." Elita saw the beginnings of a quarrel. She doubted her decision to bring Lucius to the party. She couldn't afford a tantrum like his attack on the cleaning bot. "I came to give you happy news, Father, but Marissa's appearance does not change my policy."

"She and the refugees are a threat to Isorropia," Lucius said.

Christ, he shouldn't have said that.

Recovering control of his exo-supported frame, Ben stood and faced Lucius. "Are you saying my daughter is a threat to our city?"

Lucius assumed the character of the fearless souse. "If she has thrown her lot in with the migrants, yes."

Again, the exo masked his inner reaction. "And what do you say, Elita? Is your sister a traitor to Isorropia?"

Elita did not agree with Lucius in whole, but she could not publicly disagree with her subordinate. "Of course she's not a traitor. Other than her presence, there's no evidence that she's actively assisting the refugees. She may even be their prisoner." *If I'm going to take a leap, it might as well be a big one.*

"And how do *you* know she isn't a turncoat?" Lucius said.

Ben turned again to Lucius. Even though he lacked the musculature to signal it, Elita felt his growing rage. She knew her father like no one. Lucius was treading on thin ice.

"You're beneath contempt, Galla. I know your—" Ben stopped himself. "I know my child. If anyone is a traitor to our values, it's you."

"No more than you, half-man."

Before Elita realized what was happening, Ben reached out with his exo-bound hand and arm and closed it around Lucius' throat. His servos hissing, Ben pushed Elita's lover backwards. Lucius stumbled to maintain his balance. Ben's hand, like a noose, was the only thing holding him up. They crashed against a wall of the apartment, and Ben lifted Lucius off the floor. Lucius grabbed the exo-hand, its grip as tight as a vise. Lucius' hand flailed, brushing against Ben's cheek where Elita had kissed it. The attack happened so fast that no one reacted. As Lucius' face purpled, Ben leaned in. He was saying something Elita could not hear, but Lucius blanched, despite dangling in the air by his neck. Ben dropped him, and Lucius coughed and choked. Ben returned to Elita. Party guests rushed over.

Ben stepped away from Lucius. "Get out, both of you."

"What did you say to Lucius?" Elita demanded.

Ben's breathing was heavy from the exertion. Elita had never seen him paler. He opened his mouth to speak to Elita, but said nothing. He turned to his guests instead, his exo-covered feet pounding on the woolen carpet.

"Father, wait. Tell me what you said to him."

"You already know. If you don't, you are not a child of Ben Soares."

Elita raced after him, but he closed the door to the dining room before she reached him. She had no idea what he meant.

The pod car proceeded on the quickest route to Elita's apartment, the couple arguing all the way. "Why won't you tell me what he said to you?" The First Citizen was stung by her father's anger and her own confusion about his attack on Lucius and her lover's recalcitrant silence. Everything was so tangled, and the worst of it was Lucius' giggling. He licked his fingers as if he'd eaten greasy fried chicken. "What is wrong with you?"

He winked at her. "I have to kill them. Saliva does the job. They only survive on the skin."

Elita wondered if he'd gone round the bend. "What are you talking about?" The redness around his neck took the shape of her father's exo-hand.

"The bacillus. They'll die in a few hours, even on his skin."

Fantasy images flashed in Elita's mind from old stories about assassination attempts using secret technology. "What have you done? If you've harmed him in any way, I'll have you dissed faster than—"

"Put your drama queen costume away and listen." Lucius sent her a link to an audio signal. The voice of her father and others she recognized from the concert came through muffled, but understandable.

"Your father thinks he's so smart, so in control, like an Olympian god." Lucius hissed. "He's as stupid as anyone."

"Wha—" Elita was non-plussed.

"While your hero daddy was trying to kill me, I smeared the bacillus on his face. The bacteria is an artificial life form and it's sending us the audio."

"You provoked him."

"It was the only way to get close. I'd got wind of an important meeting tonight, and when I saw all the principles in the same room, I knew it was on. My little friends here—" He raised a small vial of clear liquid to show Elita. "—will tell us all we need to know."

"You're diabolical."

"Just good at what I do."

"You're sure it won't hurt him?"

"Harmless as the algae in the ag tanks."

"If he so much as sniffles—"

"You can have me marooned on an iceberg."

Unsure if he could say anything to reassure her, Elita set aside her fears and focused on the conversation in the audio signal. Even in an age of genetic engineering that produced most of the food, fiber, and medicines that kept Isorropia going, Elita was impressed with the living eavesdropping devices, bugs of microscopic size, invisible to the naked eye, but powerful enough to upload an encrypted signal into the com network for her to hear. As she listened, her amazement at Isorropia's intellectual prowess turned to dismay and frustration. With every word her father spoke, and the agreement of all in the dining room, the shape of the conspiracy against Isorropia was clear. Her father was ready to betray everything he had taught her.

CHAPTER 19

THE TRAC BROKE DOWN ON Sento's third day out. Hosea had handed her the key, thinking it was a better way to search for a pass through the mountains than wandering. Now she was trapped in a jumble of ice hills and crevasses, waiting for the weather to clear. The wind shook the tracked vehicle randomly, keeping her awake, and she missed the blackout feature of her tent, which created the illusion of night and maintained her circadian rhythm.

She also missed Hosea. She could've managed by herself, as she had for two years, but his strength and encouragement was as important to her now as her own inner resources. Sento marveled at how he supported his wife, as well as the other pilgrims, though the toll on him was mounting. His patchy beard no longer hid his dry skin, a sign of malnutrition, but he managed a smile as she said goodbye.

Once out of the arroyo that led to the fjord and its beach, the blue funk that lurked in her subconscious emerged like one of the skin boils that plagued the refugees. She'd experienced depressions after she woke up in Valparaíso and on the road to Punta Arenas. They'd last a day or two, but the urge to move south and find Isorropia overcame the energy-sapping gloom, or distracted her from it.

She never imagined choosing between a new community—a new identity—and an old one. Her old principles had re-emerged, but it was impossible for her to judge the seal-killer by a value system as alien to her now as an extragalactic civilization. Sento believed once that she would take up her old identity once she found it, as if donning a comfortable old coat. However, the pilgrims were her people now. She wondered if the city was watching the refugees. *I would, if I were them. They must see our suffering. Why don't they help us?*

She thanked the heavens or luck that the Trac kept her warm. In the wee hours, however, she wondered if she was seeing things. Twice she saw a shape through the near whiteout, bouncing across her field of vision like a child's toy. The tight insulation of the Trac's cab allowed no sound from the outside, except for the tinkle of ice crystals as they slammed against the windows. As she peered out the front window, wiping off the condensation with her sleeve, the hallucination dissipated.

The surprise appearance of the man's face made her jump.

His equally abrupt disappearance steeled her. *There's someone out there. Another food thief?* She didn't recognize the man in the half-second of his manifestation. The face was camouflaged by a thick beard and hooded by an anorak. Her rational mind told her to stay in the cab and keep the doors locked. No attacker could get through the carbo-glass and steel without a cutting torch or a 10-kilo sledgehammer. However, she couldn't see underneath the Trac. An attacker hidden by the storm could do serious damage and she'd never know it. *Wouldn't I hear something? Maybe not.* Bowing to her instincts, she felt for her pistol, put a round in the chamber, switched her thermals on, and opened the door.

Sento saw nothing three meters in front of her. The whiteout created a wall as impenetrable as the cordillera above her. She remembered a two-meter gap in the pressure ridge to the Trac's left, and she moved ahead two steps. Glancing behind her, the Trac was almost invisible. Desperate, she yelled into the wind. "You! I know you're out there. Show yourself!" Sento barely heard her own voice. The wind drowned out every sound. Where another person might fall into paranoia, Sento saw the moment objectively. She chuckled at her own silliness. She shrugged and turned around in time to see a man bolt into the Trac's cab and close the door. *Fuck. I forgot to lock it.*

Via her minds-eye, she saw that whoever had jumped in had locked her out. She raced to the window and pounded on it. "Hey!"

A thick arm wiped at the inside of the window. The same face she saw outside the cab was now inside it.

"Open up!" she screamed, remembering the insulated quiet. Yelling satisfied her, even if it was pointless.

The door opened. "Get in, for Christ's sake."

Sento hesitated. Events were moving too quickly. She thought he had locked her out deliberately.

"I bumped against the manual lock switch. Didn't mean to." The man moved over to the passenger side door. "What are you waiting for?"

Sento climbed in, closed the door, but did not lock it.

"Do you always go for rides with strangers?" The man grinned. His teeth were stained, but intact. Sento remained silent, waiting for an assault. She had nowhere to run.

The man shrugged. "Sorry about the scare. I saw the network, but couldn't log in to tell you I was outside."

"So you broke in." Her nod indicated the cab.

"The door was open. And you were holding that thing." The man glanced at the pistol, which Sento was pointing at him. "Guns have volatile personalities."

"Do you have a weapon?"

The man cocked his head in derision. "What would I shoot out here?"

Sento flashed on the bull seal. "I don't know. Me?"

"You are the last person I would ever shoot."

The man's statement was firmer than you might expect from a perfect stranger, as if he— "What's your name?"

"Artemis Macedon." He flipped off his hood and extended his gloved hand, hastily removing the glove. "Pleased to make your acquaintance. You can call me Artie."

Ignoring his hand, Sento studied his face. His skin was filthy, his hair matted, and a stench rose from his clothes. Despite his savage look, he had an intelligence and purpose reminding Sento of a scientist gathering data from an experiment. He was familiar in a collegial way. Absently, she touched her forehead with her free hand.

"No, I'm not dissed, despite my appearance." He leaned in. "I'm a feral."

Sento caught a whiff of his breath and thought the word was inadequate. She crinkled her nose. "A feral what?"

"A feral." Macedon said it expecting Sento to immediately understand. "A feral human, technically. A feral wannabe, if you *really* want to be precise. I aspire to be feral."

"You mean like a domestic dog gone wild?"

"Something like that, except it's by choice." Macedon's eyes shifted to the blowing ice outside the cab. "We ferals eschew the civilization that has virtually destroyed the planet's biosphere." He made the statement as if speaking to a large room of people.

"We?" Sento wondered if he was waiting for compatriots. *I can't take on more than one attacker.*

"Well, there are groups of ferals, but I'm by myself."

"And you survive out here by yourself?"

"Mostly by foraging at settlements. It's amazing what people throw out. And I have a little help now and then."

Isorropia? "From whom?"

Macedon wet his lips. "I'd better not say for now."

Sento didn't trust this wild man. She had never heard of "ferals," and she suspected it was a cover of some kind. *Why was he really here?* "Get out."

"Wha—"

"I don't know who the hell you are or why you're stalking me. For all I know, there's an army of your friends ten meters away."

"But I'm cold."

Sento huffed. "A true feral wouldn't complain about the cold." It was a stab in the philosophical dark.

Macedon lifted his eyebrows. "A valid point, but I know you. You'd wouldn't turn someone out in a storm, even a feral. Even a dissed."

Throughout the conversation, she had kept the gun on Macedon, and lifted it by a centimeter to remind him. "I've never met you. How would you know?"

"It's a feeling I had. By the way, what's your name?"

Sento hesitated. Instinctively, she wanted to keep information about herself a secret as self-protection, but her true name was a secret even to herself. She was so accustomed to "Sento" that she might have signed it as her name if presented a contract or asked to confirm her identity. In spite of his resemblance to a half-starved squirrel, Macedon had done nothing and said nothing she interpreted as a threat. His presence, here and now, was still a mystery, however. *It's not a coincidence.* "People call me 'Sento.'"

"Sento. Sento." Macedon chewed over the word as if trying to fit it into a larger data set. "It's a fragment of reality."

Sento's heart quickened. Her life for the past two years was one of fragments, bits and pieces of memory that collected like dust on a shelf, random and shapeless. Macedon knew something about her he wasn't sharing, important information she'd been seeking ever since Valparaíso. *Perhaps he is stalking me. If that's true, how is it that I've never seen him near? It's his turf. He knows the ground.* "Get out."

"Not that again."

She reached over with her free hand and pushed open the passenger side door. He watched her gun hand, but didn't make a move to take the weapon. In an instant, the warmth of the cab escaped into the Antarctic atmosphere. "Get the fuck out. You're playing games with me. I don't have time for games." She pushed against him, but he braced himself in the frame.

"I know your real name."

What boiled up next in Sento was a seething rage, an anger that had simmered over the heat of months and months of uncertainty and ignorance, a fury at grasping at dreams and memories that never linked into an explanation for her sense of being lost in a personal wilderness. For all this time, she suppressed these feelings in order to function, to make a living, to sleep at night.

"It's Marissa Sentillius."

Other than the first syllable of the surname, she didn't recognize it. She shook her head slowly and released her grip on Macedon.

The feral closed the cab's door. The latch hesitated before clicking. "I wouldn't expect it to mean anything to you." His voice lowered to a calm and compassionate level. "That's one of the first things they destroy about you."

Sento's throat thickened to the point where she couldn't breathe. She struggled against the tears, desperate to maintain control in front of a stranger who said he knew her. She was near her goal of discovering her past and thus her true self, but as she stood on the threshold, a part of her didn't want to know, because she had constructed a new life, and the old one seemed less relevant, even extraneous. She didn't want to make a difficult shift again, but she wanted to fill the emptiness left when her rage ebbed. Her hand wavered, though she still pointed the gun at Macedon. He edged his open hand toward her and wrapped his fingers around the pistol barrel. When he gently tugged, she let go.

"'Sen' must be a fragment. The disidentification failed."

It's all true.

"You're still the Marissa I once knew, though you don't know it for yourself."

An explosion of questions filled Sento's mind, too many to articulate. She asked the only one that mattered. "Who am I?"

Macedon sighed. "Isn't that always the main question?"

Sento ground her teeth. "Stop fucking around. Tell me who I am."

The feral man reached out to touch her arm, but didn't make contact. "I know. I know. You'll have to trust me on this, Mar—. Well, I should call you Sento for now. There aren't a lot of cases of failed disidentification, but the literature is fairly clear. Telling you everything at once pretty much guarantees insanity. Let's take it slow."

Sento absorbed this advice, and decided he made sense. "Tell me what I did."

"Did?"

"Dissing. Social execution. It's for the worst criminals."

Macedon turned his shoulders to Sento, as if preparing to tell her a relative had died. "I'm going to tell you this once, my friend. You did nothing, nothing at all." He became thoughtful. "Neither of us did anything, except our jobs."

"But—" She touched her forehead again.

Gently, Macedon pulled her hand away. "Used to be that criminals simply killed their enemies. These days, our so-called civilization has found a worse way to take revenge or keep someone quiet: A living death, a signal for others to be afraid and to stay in line. Only you managed to beat social death somehow. Now you're in a place very few people have ever been. I get it after living two years out here. It's like you can breathe underwater, and you're wandering the bottom of the sea, completely alone, all for just doing your job."

The metaphor fit Sento's sensation of choking on her lack of knowledge, except for a unassailable obsession to move south, as if a sub-aural voice urged her along.

"Speaking of jobs, we need to finish up your task."

Macedon's change of tone snapped Sento out of her reverie. "The pilgrim train."

"The storm's done. I know the way across the mountains. I'll show you."

When Macedon suggested they switch places in the cab so he could drive, Sento didn't hesitate. As their conversation progressed, his manner and voice convinced her that she had known him in her previous life, and that he was a friend, perhaps a colleague. A well of trust already existed. She sent him the passcode into the Trac's AI, and after a couple of tries and a reset of the on-board computer, the vehicle came to life.

The feral scratched his beard. "It's been a while since I've driven anything."

"It's not as though there's any traffic."

Macedon laughed. "That's the spirit."

"The AI will keep us out of crevasses and such."

Macedon put the Trac into gear and it lurched forward. After ten minutes of driving and reviewing the radar images, he turned into a canyon.

"I've already been in here," Sento said. "There's no way up that slope."

"The route's easy to miss if you're not familiar with the area."

The weather had cleared, leaving fluffy clouds clinging to the peaks of the cordillera. The Trac stopped at the entrance to a short side canyon. "We have to go on foot now," Macedon said. "Do you have any food? It's not a long way, but the climb is steep."

Sento saw no trail to follow, but Macedon's goal was clear. The canyon was part of a surface fault, appearing as if a mythical giant had sliced the mountain range with a knife and slid the two pieces apart. They climbed up scree and across bare areas of rock. Other than patches of gray-green lichen, nothing lived in the area. The air was empty of birds. In Sento's weakened state, she had trouble keeping up with Macedon, despite his claim of living on refuse, and she wondered if he had found a supplement to keep him going. He was also accustomed to living out in the open.

"Almost there," he said after a couple of hours of consistent rise in elevation. "I've got two surprises for you."

He does love a game. "Two more?"

"Hah! You'll like them both."

After a final push up the slope, Macedon's path flattened into a narrow valley that opened into a plain in the middle distance. "Come on, Sento. We're almost there." Her companion bounded across the fresh layer of snow to the structure, which was his height plus another half. He zipped open the entrance and ducked inside. "Come on! What are you waiting for?"

Sento stepped in, and before her were boxes and bags of every kind of food and supplies imaginable. Macedon tore into one of the boxes and pulled out a package. Everything was unlabeled, but Macedon behaved as if he knew the contents.

"I'll give you access to the local network in a second and you'll see all the labels and contents. Let's eat first."

Sento opened her package and within seconds, it was a steaming hot toasted cheese sandwich.

"Eat slowly. You're not used to this kind of food."

Sento fantasized about fruit, soup, bagels, enchiladas, even meat in the cornucopia around her.

"There's fresh clothes and tents, and medicine and everything." Macedon spread his arms like a benevolent god. His mouth full, he held a finger in the air, begging Sento's attention. He rummaged around until he found a heavy canvas bag and unzipped it. "Look."

Sento stopped chewing. The bag contained handguns, extra clips, and a staser. Sento removed it. The power light was dark. Expensive weapons, she'd only seen them on the hips of BES agents in Santiago and Punta Arenas. She found a fresh power pack and shoved it into place. The power light came on. She switched the staser off, removed the pack, and returned the weapon to the bag.

"Where did all this come from?"

Macedon swallowed the last of his bran muffin. "Long story. I want to show you the second surprise now."

Sento didn't want to leave the dome, fearing it might disappear if she turned her back on it. Feeling woozy, she wished she'd heeded Macedon's advice to eat slowly. *He hasn't poisoned me, has he?* He handed her a plastic bottle. She couldn't keep herself from sipping it.

"It's just water with some supplements, but drink it slowly."

The feral wiped his mouth with his sleeve. "I can't wait any longer. You're going to love this." Macedon jumped to the dome flap and Sento scrambled to keep up. Her excitement rose, if only in sympathy with her companion's. She hung on his mention of two years, the same amount of time since Valparaíso. Perhaps for the same reasons, he'd suffered an exile as well, but not as harsh as hers. Their experiences made them two of a kind, and she wanted to know him better. On the other hand, his behavior and manner of speech reminded Sento of Awilda, who had a tenuous grasp on stability, in Sento's opinion. *Antarctica twists minds into pretzels.*

"You'll see it better from that ledge." He scrambled up the scree for fifty or sixty meters to a viewpoint. Sento was out of breath when she came up beside him. He gazed down through the opening of the valley. "Do you see it?"

Sento followed Macedon's eyes as closely as she could. His pride was leavened with sadness.

"It's what you've been looking for, my friend. Welcome to Isorropia."

Macedon's excitement left her confused. Stretched before her to the horizon was a blinding white, flat, empty plain, crossed only by snaking tendrils of ice crystals.

CHAPTER 20

"How do you know we can trust him?"

Hosea's question embarrassed Sento. She brought Artie to him, an excited lightness in her chest, but the conversation fell to pieces like a calving glacier. They arrived at the fjord to find the scene buried in fresh snow. New cases of frostbite kept Gwen busy, failing electronics and heating systems overwhelmed Bruce, and the pilgrims' leader looked as though he had aged years in the days since Sento last saw him. "He hasn't lied to me yet, Hosea."

"I think he's full of lies," Hosea said.

"Wait a minute, mister. I'm a lot of things, but not a liar," Artie said.

Koi pushed his way into the argument. "He's telling the truth. He's an angel sent by the Virgin to guide us to Isorropia."

"Bullshit. You declare everything that can't be immediately explained as divine intervention."

Sento had never heard the leader so impatient with Koi, but she chalked it up to the strain of the new losses. Another pilgrim had died during Sento's scouting mission.

"I don't understand why you don't believe him," Koi said, hurt by Hosea's observation.

"Let me tell you. We're a thousand kilometers from anywhere, and all of sudden, this creature turns up. He calls himself a, what?" Hosea waved his hand at Artie.

"Feral."

The leader snorted.

"More precisely, a technological culture rejectionist, or a practitioner of extreme re-wilding—"

He said "wannabe" back in the mountains.

Hosea's sarcasm was thick as the Eastern Ice Cap. "You and Koi are two of a kind."

That makes three of us. Sento felt the need to defend her new friend again. "What he's said makes sense. I believe him."

"Why now? It's very convenient for him. We're out of supplies. The only reason more people haven't died is the seal we killed. And now he turns up with armloads of bread." Hosea poked Macedon's chest with an accusing finger. The feral man endured it without complaint, as if Hosea's rudeness was a standard reaction to his self-identification.

Sento sympathized with Hosea's skepticism, but Artie's knowledge of her own background suppressed concerns about his veracity. "I admit it's hard to believe, but I saw the cache for myself. I brought back some of the supplies. How do you explain them?"

"We've seen caches before. Half the cache back at the Virgin Cave turned out to be spoiled. Maybe you got lucky with your cheese sandwich." Hosea went nose-to-nose with Artie, who didn't flinch. "But I still don't get the timing. You've been following us, haven't you?"

"Does it matter, Hosea?" Koi pulled at the leader's parka. "He knows where to find Iso. He can take us there."

Hosea ignored the child, focusing on Artie. "You're working for somebody. Maybe the same people who sabotaged our vehicles."

"Why would I do that," Artie said evenly, "and then show you enough food to last months?"

Sento followed Hosea's logic, and her doubts grew with his. *What if Artie's been sent to finish the job of silencing me?*

Hosea lifted a corner of his mouth. "And then there's your hallucination."

"My what?" Artie was confused.

"Sen says there was nothing on that ice plain, despite your declaration."

In her desire to tell the complete tale, Sento mentioned that she didn't see any buildings or other signs of a large settlement, though the lack of evidence didn't necessarily mean the city was a hallucination.

Artie spoke again, patient, but not condescending. "You don't understand, sir. It's hidden."

"Oh yeah, it's hidden." Hosea nearly laughed, but not at the humor of Artie's claim, as he saw it. "It's hidden up there." The leader poked at Artie's forehead at where a disidentification brand would go. "And just as real."

Hosea turned his back on the group.

"I don't think we have a choice but to believe him." Sento's frustration mounted. Hosea was behaving oddly, as if the last few days had taken something away from him that had kept him going through the journey. Awilda had not given birth, and her distress was as bad as ever. Prior to Sento's scouting mission, Gwen decided she had miscalculated conception, but not by much. Awilda was in a near constant state of babbling delirium, possibly from some kind of infection. The pregnant woman could not go on much longer before they'd be forced to take extreme action to save the child and Awilda. It could even come down to a choice of saving one or the other. "The baby will need that food and supplies."

Hosea glanced over his shoulder. "It's a lost cause."

Sento was uncertain what he meant. Was his wife lost? Was the journey a lost cause? *If he's past his breaking point, we're all dead.*

Sento went after him when she noticed a limp. "You're hurt."

"I'm tired is all." Hosea examined his patched and mended boots as they walked together, out of earshot of the others. "I'm tired of helplessness. The woman who died while you were gone, she was young, maybe 22. I remember her when we started. As strong as an ox. She was a skeleton when she died. Death was a mercy." He rubbed his face. His beard was matted and flecked with frozen spittle. "I'm tired of fighting everyone and everything. I'm tired of fighting Antarctica. I'm tired of dreaming." He glanced at Artie and Koi. "I'm tired of listening to dreamers."

"You can't give up, Hosea."

"Yes, I can. I've given up before. I gave up the ranch. I gave up looking for work in Mexico. I nearly gave up after I lost my boy and girl. My wife has pretty much lost her mind. I brought her here to save the baby. I threw the dice for the last time on this insane trip to a phantom city, and out of the blue comes a lunatic who claims to know how to make the phantom materialize. Why should I trust him?"

"I trust him."

"You keep saying that, but I don't understand why."

"There's something on that plain for me. I would've walked here by myself. That's how powerful the feeling is. The answers I want are so near I can taste them. Artie has already told me part of what I want to know."

"So leave, and go find Iso."

"I can't leave without you. It doesn't matter as much anymore what I've lost. I've found you." Sento realized she meant Hosea specifically, not just the pilgrims and her friends. "It's embarrassing to say it, but you're my family now and I don't want to lose a second family."

Hosea sniffed, and Sento was unsure whether he heard her.

"We have to survive just a few more days and reach the cache," Sento continued. "We can decide whether to press on from there."

Hosea sighed. "I still don't trust Artie." He grinned, which delighted Sento, despite his yellowed teeth. "I trust you, though. Maybe you're the one who's saved us."

The next day, as the clouds thickened and flurries punctuated the air, the pilgrims moved up through the arroyo from the bay, which they had named Slaughter Inlet. Artie had disappeared in the night, as Sento expected. He was not used to crowds, he complained, but he promised to stay nearby. *That's what he's been doing for weeks. Hosea is right. He's watching us, but why?* Sento stayed near the line's head, rather than ranging. Hosea had his place in front, Koi next to him. The Trac played its role as pack horse. Awilda rode with Gwen in Kan's sling, with Bruce walking close, nursing the cargo bot along. The machine clanked and wheezed, and its bent frame from the fall at the River Kanthaka gave it a lean that resembled an old man with a cane.

"Don't let the noise worry you," Bruce declared to the train. "She's as strong as she ever was."

Gwen patted one of the bot's steel struts. "We couldn't have made it this far without you, Kan."

"The AI doesn't understand your gratitude, Gwen."

"Maybe not, but I'll be grateful, just the same, for its hard work. I'm also thankful to its makers for making such a fine machine. I'm also thankful to you for keeping it healthy. You would have made a fine doctor, Bruce."

The technologist blushed. He had lost enough weight to transform from a pudgy, waddling tinkerer to the thinness of a welterweight wrestler, though he had none of an athlete's grace and subtlety. His red hair made him look like a matchstick. At nearly every one of the dozens of campsites, after everyone else had set up tents, eaten, and rested, Bruce worked far into the evening on the cargo bot, the Trac, and the other odd robots and electronics serving the train. More than once, Hosea or Gwen asked him to set down his tools and rest, and allow everyone else a break from his pounding and filing.

"You've got a bedside manner with Kan that I envy. I've seen you patting her and encouraging her."

"No, I couldn't be a doctor," Bruce said. "I can't stand the sight of blood. I can hardly stand the sight of hydraulic fluid."

"You love this old bot, don't you, Bruce?" Gwen teased him with a smile.

Bruce flushed again. "It's just a machine." His twinkling eyes, though, betrayed his true feelings.

The trip to the canyon and the trail over the cordillera took 18 hours, a third as long as Sento needed to find it the first time, but twice as long as a normal traveling day for the pilgrims. Sensing an approaching crisis, Hosea pushed the train like a cattle drover, not bothering to consult with the other leaders. No one argued with him. The refugees, already exhausted from lack of food and an intensifying battle with the cold and wind, collapsed into their shelters. Even Bruce skipped his daily maintenance routine. Instead of resting, however, Sento scouted ahead for the landmarks she stored in her minds-eye indicating the point where the climb began to the pass. She knew she'd never sleep until she had relocated it, if only to ensure the climb, the dome, and Artie Macedon's claim to have seen Isorropia weren't a fever dream. Sento found the trail head within ten minutes, and when she returned to her campsite, she found Artie sitting on a camp stool.

The feral chewed on a piece of dried seal meat. "You people could've taken it a little slower. The food cache isn't going anywhere."

Sento secretly agreed, but she also understood Hosea's reasoning. "If we don't reach that cache within the next day or so, we'll never reach it. That's what the boss thinks, anyway."

"What do you think?"

Sento thought a moment. She spoke quietly, so others in the train could not overhear. "Some people won't make it, that's for sure. Maybe most."

Artie spat out a bit of gristle. "I have to agree." He rose from the chair. "I'll be off now. It's been a long day."

"Wait."

Artie halted.

"I've been thinking about you all day." Throughout the day's walk, Artie had never left her mind. More specifically, what he knew, but hadn't yet shared, dogged her.

"All day? I'm flattered."

Sento failed to notice Artie's suggestive look. "I need to talk to you."

Artie's eyes shifted, and he whispered, "About what?"

"What you know." Sento hesitated, misgivings nagging her. "What you know about me."

Artie's shoulders drooped. "I see. Well," he said, raising the flap to Sento's tent. "Step into my office."

Sento's suspicions about Artie's motivations flared as he sat across from her. "I'm talking business here, nothing else."

Artie flicked a perfunctory hand at Sento. "I know. I'm just playing games with you. You're interested in someone else, anyway."

Sento was nonplussed. "What's that supposed to mean?"

"You mean you don't want… Never mind."

Who among these creatures would I want? Except maybe… Sento shook off the thought. "Just tell me who I am."

"I'll tell you some. Remember what I said about the risk to your mental state. Dissing screws up your brain chemistry. Too much information too quickly—"

"Talk to me. Now. Please." Sento didn't care about the potential consequences. "You said you knew me."

"Fine, then." He rested his hands on this knees. "I did indeed know you. I was your boss."

"My boss?" Sento was incredulous, but she realized that with every revelation, she might not believe it. She decided to accept Artie's statements at face value, at least for now. "I mean, you were my boss."

"You were Detective Sergeant Marissa Sentillius, seconded to the investigative branch of the Bureau of Environmental Security." Artie lets this sink in. For her part, the agency title brought to mind the uniformed and armed BES officers that were frequent, if not common sights everywhere in the world. The last time she saw one was in Punta Arenas. "I should add the Isorropian version of the BES is somewhat different than the global agency and the regional branches. For one thing—"

"You can give me the backstory later. I want to know about me."

Artie nodded. "I was Deputy Chief Inspector Artemis Macedon. I was in charge of your section, and you reported to me."

Sento understood the implication. She had been dissed, and Artie's exile was somehow related. "Were we kicked out of BES?" Sento remembered the hooded man and her near-execution of the boy at Nordenskjöld.

Artie pursued his lips. "In a manner of speaking, but not for anything against the law or BES policy."

Sento compared Artie's information with her experience. "I have these..." She had trouble finding the right word. *Dreams? Visions? Hallucinations?* She did not want to appear unbalanced to Artie, but she related the apparition of the hooded man and her feelings of guilt and remorse.

"It makes perfect sense to me," Artie said. "It was one of your first cases. There was a ring of bush meat smugglers killing fur seals in a remote area. We staged a surprise raid on their camp and you chased one of them down and shot him when he turned on you. He died later."

The story explained so much to Sento. "Did you see the fur seal we killed at Slaughter Inlet?"

"From a distance."

"People say I was a mad woman. All I wanted to do was protect that seal."

"Understandable. Isorropian society puts the highest value on protecting nature and her children, particularly animals and plants that are in danger of extinction. And that's most of Antarctica's native flora and fauna these days. As a BES officer, you had a sworn duty to defend the seal, but respecting the natural world is as ingrained in your personality as loving your father." Artie sucked a breath. "I shouldn't have said that last bit."

"Why not?"

"Too much too soon—" Artie rose to leave.

"No, not yet," Sento pleaded. "Listen, I won't ask about him." *I want to know everything!* "But you have to tell me. Was that why I was sentenced to disidentification? Because I shot that poacher?"

Artie laughed, but it was mixed with pain. "No, Sen. In fact, you were decorated. You became the star of my unit, not for the shooting, but for your, um," Artie paused thoughtfully, looking into the distance, "'meritorious valor conforming to the highest ideals of loyalty, service, and ισορροπί.'"

"You said that last word oddly."

"It's the classical Greek pronunciation of 'Isorropia.' It means 'balance.' A core cultural tenet."

Something about the story didn't work for Sento.

"Here, take a look at this." Artie shared a photograph over the local com network, which Bruce managed to keep alive. The photo showed Sento/Sentillius with a metal plaque standing next to Artie. Both were in uniform, shaking hands in that friendly, slightly awkward pose of people who prefer to stay out of the limelight. Sento's attention was wholly on herself in the photo. She saw a competent young woman on the rise.

"Like I said, you had a bright future."

"Had."

Artie lost his proud grin. "Both of us lost our futures."

"You have to explain why."

"I will, in time. Right now, you have a duty, really both of us, to get these people to the food cache."

Sento sighed, not wanting to accept Artie's insistence on sharing information in drips. "And then what?"

Artie didn't answer as he let the flap of Sento's tent close behind him. He had said enough for one evening. She rustled in her pack for one of the self-heating meals, and as she chewed, wondering if her loose teeth signaled the onset of scurvy, she understood the missing piece. The visions she had were rooted in sorrow for taking a man's life, even if he was a despicable poacher who's actions might end up destroying a species as noble as the seal's. Reopening the image file, she noticed the difference. Sentillius, young, strong, attractive, intelligent, accepted the accolades in an important Isorropian ritual, but she was not proud of what she did. The man she killed had a mother, a father, perhaps a wife, maybe children. He was a criminal, to be sure, but she had experienced most of what the worst criminals endure as punishment, and she would not wish the near total loss of all she knew on her worst enemy. Taking a life had gone too far, even if it was in the service of some glorious ideal. She lay on her pad, the wind lifting and lowering the darkened fabric of her tent, and she dreamed of the silver-faced man and the glowing blue seal, but not the hooded man.

"She's like a sister." The bitterness is Bruce's voice cut into everyone's soul. "I will not leave her behind."

Hosea accompanied Sento and Artie on a partial reconnoiter of the route to the cache, and they brought back a strategy for getting everyone and their belongings over the pass. Not everything would make it. The Trac was built for flat or gently sloping surfaces. The few pilgrims who'd managed to carry their possessions a thousand kilometers from the old beach camp would have to abandon them with the vehicle. The quarreling started after Artie argued Kanthaka was a burden to be shed. "The slope is 30 degrees in some places and loose gravel. This monster will never make it." Artie pointed at the impassive bot.

"Who are you calling a monster?" Bruce said. "You're barely more than an animal."

Bruce pushed Artie, who stumbled, then stalked back. "I don't have to take that from anyone."

"You'll do fine if we leave *you* behind. Kan will rust away into scrap."

Hosea put out his hand to stop the incipient fight. "Enough."

Sento was ready to enforce order, if necessary. *I was a cop once.* Bruce was a lynchpin to the group because of his technical skills, and they needed Artie for his knowledge of the area.

"It's not about what I want," Bruce said. "We might need her up there. I've seen Sen's recordings. It's nothing but another wide plain after we get over the pass. Kan'll carry our gear, like she always has."

"You don't understand," Artie said. "Isorropia is closer than you think."

"Shut up, Macedon." In addition to losing weight, Bruce had lost his reticence. "You're a stranger. You're spinning yarns. You're out for something. You've no right to tell us what can and can't be done."

Sento wished Gwen was near to calm Bruce, but she was tending to Awilda, as always.

Hosea addressed Sento. "What about the rest of the trail after what I saw?"

"It's nearly flat in places. There's a couple of hairpin turns. It's not easy, but Kan could get through those parts." Sento was reluctant to take Artie's side wholeheartedly after hearing Hosea's earlier skepticism.

"Not the steep part," Artie insisted.

Hosea paced, deep in thought. "I remember seeing or reading somewhere that the mid-19th century migrants who crossed North America got their wooden wagons over mountain passes twice as high this one. Seems we should be able to do the same thing with robots, line, and some elbow grease."

Koi and his clutch of believers crossed themselves. They prayed to their Savior, asking deliverance to the heaven of Isorropia, promising to sacrifice whatever was necessary.

"We have the line," Bruce said hopefully. "We used it to rescue Kan at the river."

"You people are crazy." Artie threw up his hands.

"You're not exactly sane yourself," Bruce countered.

"Quiet, both of you," Hosea ordered.

The leadership group decided on two projects. Artie would lead the pilgrims to the food cache. Sento, Hosea, Bruce and a few others would figure a way to get Kanthaka to the Isorropian plateau. Sento worried that Awilda would not make it even a few hundred meters up the trail, but she emerged from her tent with Gwen with a determination Sento had not seen since the beach at Nordenskjöld. Supported by other women in the group, she trudged up the path, putting all her concentration on the journey. For the first time in days, Sento thought both mother and child might survive the journey, though the destination was still unclear.

As the line of pilgrims snaked up the trail, Bruce removed the winch with its carbo-steel cable from the front of the Trac. Sento heaved nylon line on her back, while Hosea carried tools and other equipment. Bruce drove Kan as high up the trail as he could before the slope became too unstable for the bot to handle. Sento found an outcropping of rock for anchoring the electric winch, setting up a solar station to provide power. The weather was holding, but she smelled a thickness in the air that depressed her. A breeze rose and abated in the canyon with an irregular pattern, as if the wind was uncertain whether to attack the pilgrims or let them be.

Bruce worked with another pilgrim who was once a rigger for a solar power company to position the winch and hook the cable to lifting bolts on the bot. Sento and Hosea steadied the bot with the nylon line. The group would lift Kan in stages past the steepest part of the route to an area where Bruce thought it could manage on her own, that is, where he could guide each step. "Her AI is designed for a pitching deck, not a mountain path," he said. "If she stumbles, she won't recover."

The first stage, the shortest, went smoothly. After Kan was told to fold her legs into a parked position, the winch dragged her up the slope. Rocks and pebbles tumbled behind her. The pilgrims were a hundred meters or more away and safe from the rock fall. The winch strained. The monitoring software in Sento's minds-eye showed the solar power converter barely keeping the on-board super-capacitors charged. Normally, the winch drew off the Trac's capacitors, but the abandoned vehicle was silent in the canyon. It's avatar on the network was grayed out. The overcast skies were supposedly not a factor in the convertor's performance, but Sento wondered if they were worn out from age, cold or poor quality.

The second stage was about the same travel distance, but steeper. Bruce and the rigger repositioned the winch for each stage. Sento tried to keep her concentration on the monitor as she kept her line taut to keep the bot steady. Hosea did the same with his line. In an emergency, Hosea and Sento acted as a brake to keep Kan from tumbling back to the starting point, though Sento guessed that if Kan got loose, she'd never be able to stop it. Just as Kan's deadweight reached the end of the middle stage of her journey, the winch halted and set its brake automatically, saving the motor from burning out. "We'll have to heave her by hand," Bruce declared, and after a struggle finding purchase in the broken ground, and a strained muscle in Hosea's back, the team secured Kan.

"I hope this is all worth it," Sento told Bruce, agreeing silently with Artie that Kan wasn't worth the energy of men and women short on calories to maintain their health, much less drag a heavy machine over a mountain.

"It is. It is." Bruce's repetition was quiet and thoughtful, as if he tried to convince himself of its truth.

The third stage was the longest and the hardest. Not only did the team need to drag Kan up the slope, they needed to get her over a ledge and through a gap in a pair of house-sized boulders. Along with the winch, guide lines, and block and tackle, Bruce decided to enlist Kan's help. With careful positioning, he believed she could lift herself over the worst part of the pathway. After 10 hours of work, the team was exhausted. The last of the pilgrims had disappeared up the route to the pass, but Hosea argued the team had momentum behind it. Once over the final hump, Kan could take care of herself. All agreed, albeit reluctantly, and the winch was positioned while Bruce adjusted the bot's programming to handle the unfamiliar task.

With everything in place, the winch did its work, dragging Kan to a point below the ledge. After a short rest, Bruce gave the command, and the carbosteel cable lifted the bot into the air. The cable dragged over a notch in the rock, and Sento watched steam rise from the friction. Bruce ordered a halt, while he commanded Kan to lift a foreleg to a boulder to leverage herself forward and over the granite outcrop while the winch took in cable. Just as Kan's footpad anchored itself for the maneuver, the cable parted. Sento didn't see where the part occurred, but the flying ends whipped through the air, and Kan fell. Sento had dropped her guide line to rest her hands for a moment. If she had the line in her hands, her arms might have been yanked out of their sockets.

Even so, the end of her line sped past her, snapping back and forth like a snake. The end leaped and wrapped around the neck of the rigger, who flew off into the air like a bird. Sento was amazed his head hadn't been torn off. Bruce screamed from surprise and pain, and he dropped to the ground, tumbling down the slope until he slammed into a boulder. His left arm ended at his bloody wrist, which streamed blood as if he'd been shot with a staser at full power. The cable end had wrapped itself around his hand and sliced it off in a millisecond. Kan tumbled down the slope, pieces flying off as if it were a toy. It came to rest with a comical plop on its side, rocks and dust tumbling after it.

The next hours passed for Sento as if she was drugged. Bruce screamed incessantly from the pain of his injury and his failure, but also the loss of Kan, the closest thing he had to a friend besides Gwen. Sento rushed to the techie's side, ripping the waist belt from his tattered parka. She tied it around his upper arm as a tourniquet, and after a moment, blood dripped rather than poured from the stump. Hosea reported the rigger dead.

The remaining members of the team took turns carrying Bruce as Sento led them up the trail, leaving the rigger's body behind. No one had the strength to carry it. As the snowfall turned into a blinding blizzard, she feared fumbling the route to the dome, but her map was solid, and Artie had left behind marks for her to follow. They appeared as pins in her minds-eye display, arrows indicating the direction to the next waypoint, like following a trail of breadcrumbs. A virtual flag appeared over the welcoming shelter.

In the dome, Gwen had already dealt with one emergency. Awilda had given birth. Mother and child snuggled in a new thermal blanket, looking lovely to Sento as new mothers often did to her.

Koi knelt nearby, his eyes closed, his fingers interlaced in urgent prayer. "Dear Lord, thank you for this miracle in the wilderness, a gift to people who've lost so much, a gift to reward us for our faith and fortitude. We're almost home!"

On closer approach, however, Sento saw a listlessness in Awilda's gaze different than the normal exhaustion Sento observed in the train. For his part, Hosea was overcome with emotion, crying openly as he held the baby boy in his arms. Sento was happy for the family, and jealous, remembering her lack of knowledge about her own family. *I need to ask Artie about my parents.*

The feral appeared with an armload of weapons, including the staser with a power pack. The ready light glowed green. "Why do we need these?" Sento said.

"For protection," Artie said.

"From what?"

"From whom."

Unspoken was a threat from Isorropia. Only trusting herself with the powerful weapon, Sento shoved the staser in her coat pocket. Her pistol was snug in her holster. With Bruce sedated, and the baby sleeping, Sento lay her head down and was instantly unconscious.

An alarm woke her, a steady bleeping that penetrated her consciousness without deafening her. Smoke filled the inside of the dome, and as she roused, an incongruous scent of incense filled her nostrils. Flickering, however, indicated flame, and her eyes snapped open. *Fire!* Terrified that the pilgrim's salvation was turning to ash, she woke Gwen and grabbed the baby and yelled orders at the pilgrims who had taken shelter. Just as she pushed the last one out, the dome filled with a hissing sound, and a fog blanked her vision. The fire was out in seconds. Another rush of air and a sudden drop in temperature signaled an evacuation of the dome's atmosphere and whatever chemicals suppressed the fire.

Awilda's new baby in her arms, Sento found herself in the midst of the blizzard, which raged as hard as ever. Outside the tent, Hosea called Awilda's name like a madman. Sento saw a glow in the distance, and the snow cleared enough to reveal Awilda holding a magnesium flare, screaming incoherently about judgment and failure and lost children. Hosea appeared, calling out his wife's name, begging her to come back.

Artie raced by Sento. "Come on, we can't lose him."

Him? What about Awilda? Sento handed the baby to Gwen. She caught up with Artie as he dragged Hosea back to the dome. He fought like a dog. "Awilda's out there. Awilda! Awilda!"

Sento saw the new mother again, holding the red-hot flare, rags hanging off her naked body.

Artie tugged at Sento's coat as he struggled with Hosea. "Help me, Sen!"

The flare died, and Awilda disappeared.

In his hysterics, Hosea suffered from the accumulated loss of people whom he had agreed to lead to safety. They had all watched people die or get hurt. They had no idea if Enzo and his group had survived the journey back to Nordenskjöld. Awilda had gone insane. The group had a second chance now, if Artie was to be believed. The group might never recover if they lost Hosea. Sento grabbed the man's arm and pulled him back into the dome. It smelled faintly of burnt plastic, but the structure itself was undamaged. Hosea collapsed into a sob next to his cooing son.

The storm blew itself out within a few hours. Exhaustion overcame Sento as she agonized over Hosea's distress. *How do I comfort him?* Artie shook her from a doze, and she whimpered as she flashed on Bruce's torn arm and the dead rigger. "Sen, wake up. I found her. I found something you need to see."

Confused in her half-conscious state, Sento followed Artie into blinding sunlight, though the sun seemed lower than it should be. It was dipping little by little, day by day to the horizon for its six-month sojourn to the top of the world, while the bottom of the world was bathed in night. Humans had learned to survive in Antarctica during its summer, but its night was a different story. As Sento processed this, she followed Artie more than a kilometer into Isorropia Plain. He made for a dark spot that poked up from the ice crystals. The spot resolved into a human shape, and Sento recognized Awilda, her body frozen.

"Too bad for her." Artie's voice was unemotional. "Antarctica is hard on the weak."

Sento wanted to argue about the dead woman's perseverance through a difficult pregnancy in an alien land, but she said nothing. Instead, she noticed the odd position of her blue-tinged body, eyes wide in the illusion of surprise. She did not lay prone on the ground, like someone who had collapsed from hypothermia. She was propped up, as if sitting on the floor in the corner of a room.

"This is what I wanted you to see, my friend." Artie was nonchalant, even proud. He knocked on an object, and Sento half-expected a door to open.

The trouble was that Sento saw nothing but the endless plain in front of her. Her curiosity overcame her grief over Awilda's death. She reached out, and at the point where Artie rapped his knuckles, she felt it, a wall, transparent as air, which held up the body of Awilda. The crazed woman had inadvertently bumped into it in the final moments of her life.

"What do you think?" Artie said, toying with Sento.

"About what?"

Artie sighed. "You never play along, do you? I'm trying to tell you you're home."

Sento removed her hand from the invisible obstruction and examined it, as if it had also disappeared, like Bruce's. The appendage was still attached, however, and she touched the wall again. It was as cold as Awilda's corpse.

CHAPTER 21

From the diary of Artemis Macedon

Sento/Marissa probably thought I was as crazy as the dead woman at my feet. She's changed, recognizable, but different. I've changed, too. I've been out here so long that I can barely talk to people. I'm fine skirting the edge of the pilgrim train, like a scavenging fox, but when my boss—her father—told me to make contact with her, I couldn't just walk into the camp like I owned the place. A lot of people take me for a dissed, and they ignore me like they're supposed to, but I couldn't count on that. They might shoot at me or run me out, like I was a bandit. Catching up to her when she was alone was better, though I had my doubts when she pointed that pistol at me.

Ben Soares is the one who tracked me down, soon after Galla put me outside. I have no idea how. The supplies Soares set out for me were a hundred meters from the rock cave where I'd found shelter. There was a week's worth of food, fresh thermal clothes, a compact tent, and a solar-powered battery charger, thank God in heaven. It wasn't always enough, especially in winter. I once went ten days without eating more than a spoiled MRE from an old military site. I think I was delirious at one point, because I remember a dark man, face hooded, with his voice muffled by a balaclava. It might've been Soares himself. I don't know. Hands lifted me into a bed and I thought I had died. I woke up in my tent, snuggled in my sleeping bag, surrounded by fresh supplies. Nothing comes without a price, and Soares wanted practically the same thing Galla wanted: for me to disappear and watch the pilgrims. Soares saved my life. I owe him.

The feral idea was pretty good cover. Soares suggested it, in case I was challenged. At BES, we heard rumors about the ferals, but nobody knew much.

They avoided civilization as a matter of principle. They followed an old 20th century idea called "re-wilding." The early believers revived and practiced stone age skills, but they were hypocrites, because they always managed to fall back into modern habits. Turns out that hunting and gathering is harder than it looks. Civilization evolved for a reason.

I've seen the real ferals, though, especially near the coasts. They're either crazy or the toughest, wiliest people on earth. Can't be more than a few dozen, maybe a hundred. I couldn't believe it the first time I saw them. It was probably a family, two women, two men, and a child. Their faces were Caucasian, which gave them away as ferals. Re-wilding was strictly a North American and European thing. They trudged along the edge of an ice field, wearing seal skins, like Cro-Magnons transported to the 23rd century. One of the women had a basket slung over her back. They set up a shelter of whalebone and skins. I watched them from a rise about 500 meters away, and the wind was in my face. I couldn't hear anything, though I saw them speaking. I wondered if they could smell me, like those stupid old 2-D movies would say about indigenous hunters, but now I believed it, because I swear one of them spotted me. Spooked, I took off for fear of getting skewered by one of their stone points. When I crawled back a few hours later, they were gone.

I was born and raised in Antarctica, but it's still hard to believe that the climate has changed so much that humans can revert to a Stone Age culture and survive at the bottom of the world. I sometimes think the ferals are smarter and tougher than the Isorropians, who are building a new type of technological society with proven ideas. On the other hand, the ferals are completely reinventing the human race. Talk about starting from scratch. When I was in the BES, the talk about ferals included speculation that a small group of disaffected Isorropians was helping them. After spending two years out here, and seeing those ferals, I think it's possible, but it's just as possible they've learned to eke out a living on nothing but rock and ice.

Sometimes your cover story becomes your story. That's what it feels like out here, that I've gone feral in my own way.

And so here we are, on Isorropia's doorstep. I don't know what's next, though the boss seems to. In the last few weeks, he's been sending me notes that have more than the simple instructions of the early days.

The situation is growing tense here...

Marissa was days away from exposing Galla...

I no longer know Elita. She's a stranger to me now...

It's as if Soares wants to confide in someone, but he has no one to trust. Texting me these random thoughts are like keeping a secret diary, or sharing private thoughts with a pen pal. I've been away from Isorropia so long that I don't understand what he's talking about half the time. The one thing I remember about him was a reputation as a do-gooder.

This came from Soares as the pilgrim train neared Iso: Watch for Galla. He knows about Marissa. Elita can no longer control him.

My sense of danger, even dread, increased. If I see Galla again, I don't know how I'll react. Kill him? Run? Cower in fear, like a rabbit in the mouth of a wolf, waiting for the end?

Here's the last message I got from Soares: The cache is ready. Show them the way. Say nothing about me to Marissa. It occurs to me that's he's saved the refugees' lives, pretty much like he saved mine. Why? Wouldn't he save only his daughter, and the devil take the hindmost? Maybe I don't give him enough credit, but he's always struck me as a patient man. He'll make his final move when he's ready and for reasons that suit his own purposes. He's waiting for something, though I can't imagine what it might be.

CHAPTER 22

THE MASS OF VOTERS, PACKED to the Pynx's capacity, moved in waves to the music of fear. Elita had never seen anything like it in the cavernous hall, named after the hill 15,000 kilometers away where classical Athens gathered to make law 3,000 years before. Friends shouted at one another. Sons waved fists at fathers. Workers poked fingers on boss's chests. Scuffles broke out. The com net slowed with novels' worth of text and images ahead of the emergency session. Factions within factions demanded investigations, demagogues stood on chairs calling for an increase in the defense budget, firebrands preached on moving money from city defense to a relief program.

It was a human maelstrom, compared to Elita's placid memories of accompanying her father as a six-year-old to Ecclesia sessions on his days off from designing low profile wind generators. When he stood to speak, he towered over the people around him, at least from her child's perspective. She adored his calm, clear, and measured voice. Rousing applause followed every comment or speech he made. That was four decades ago.

Today, she was ready to do what she vowed she'd never do: confront her father in public. Everything she'd worked for was at stake.

Suspended over the turbulence was a real-time video feed from the migrant camp, showing the migrants going about their routines in a snowstorm a kilometer from the city. As far as Isorropia was concerned, the barbarians were at the gate.

The eight-meter tall bronze doors in each wall of the Pynx closed with a mournful *clang*. Ceremonial robots guarded the doors. The question before the Ecclesia: Do we let them in or keep them out? For Elita, there was only one answer—keeping the migrants out—but she did not have the power to impose her will. No faction could gain enough leverage to form the majority needed to take action. "You know what makes this doubly scary," she said, monitoring the crowd in the cloakroom, "is that we're all trapped here."

"Trapped?" Lucius sipped a coffee as he deployed extra security bots.

"Like krill in the maw of a whale. It's not like we have any place to run to."

You know what wolves do when they are cornered, don't you, Lita?

Elita didn't respond to Lucius' secure text. She trod lightly around him these days, worried about the consequences of a misinterpreted word. *It's like aiming a loaded revolver at myself every time I say something to him.* She held many cards in this game, but she did not yet know their value as a whole, and she would not show her hand to anyone, not even Lucius, until she decided how to play it. The wild card was her father. *He wanted a constitutional crisis, and he got one.*

The crisis fully manifested in Government Square. Demonstrations and protests, a revered tradition in Isorropia, were common in public spaces. Up until a few days ago, they had the feel of a festival or a party. The shooting of the bull seal changed everything. The media played the image over and over, feeding off the outrage of Isorropians upset over the murder of an endangered animal. Protestors published banners on websites and screeds on com logs denouncing the killing and demanding government action. No amount of apologetic commentary by the humanitarians cooled the public ardor. The shooting disgusted Elita, but she secretly welcomed it, because it bolstered her argument. Until then, the humanitarians led behind the scenes by Ben Soares had slowly gained ground. Elita told journos that the seal's violent death was damning evidence of the migrants' fundamental criminality. *They are showing their true stripes. They do not belong here.* Judging by the daily polls, the humanitarians' rise had stalled.

"The head of the snake has reared up," Lucius announced as Ben Soares arrived by pod car with his entourage. "And the charmer is playing his tune."

From the day Elita was born, she watched her father's machinations and thought of herself as an acolyte, but the way he had managed events in the past days had surprised even her. The listening device planted by Lucius during his faked altercation with Ben had revealed his strategy to help the refugees, despite the Ecclesia's clear message to the contrary. He intended to circumvent the

Legislature's will with back-door means. She didn't care about his rationalizations, and Lucius prepared to arrest him and his cabal of supporters.

However, Elita stopped Lucius. A secret recording was not enough to convict, and the affair might even backfire on her. Instead, she told Lucius to watch her father and gather more evidence. Lucius found the food cache in the dome outside the city, along with the alarming news that elements within the government, including his own security service, were helping Ben. *He must be calling in all his favors, gambling everything on this misguided need to rescue the outsiders. His behavior borders on sedition.*

Elita choked on the unspoken word. *Sedition.* She was doing all she could to protect her beautiful city, and he was doing all he could to undermine her authority and the policies approved by the Ecclesia, the embodiment of the people's will. An archaic word popped into her mind: "Traitor." Kings and presidents called citizens traitors when they helped the state's enemies, but Isorropia had no enemies in that sense of the word. Had her father committed treason against Isorropian values? Did his actions threaten ισορροπία, the balance between her city and Antarctica as its host? If so, is that a hanging offense?

A dream overnight upset her more. Her father, young and strong before he needed medication or an exo to fight his ataxia, stood at the fulcrum of a seesaw in Founders Park while his daughters sat at each end. Both girls were the same age, wore the same clothes, and moved up and down dirge-like as Ben stared into the distance, as if anticipating the silver mask in his future. As the game wore on, Elita grew more frustrated and angry, and pushed harder with her legs. Marissa fought back, but the balance between the two was tilting more and more in Elita's favor, and she laughed, pushing harder and harder until Marissa cried out, scared. The movement stopped. Ben appeared next to Marissa, his foot on her seat, stopping the teeter-totter motion, leaving Elita hanging in the air. Now Ben frightened her, and she looked down through her dangling legs into a black depth with no bottom, and she was slipping.

She woke up sweating, and she knew what the dream meant. *Father will do anything to protect Marissa. That's what he wants the most. He will even protect her over me. He won't balance his love for both of us if she's threatened.* In Elita's family, there would be no ισορροπία of hearts.

As she waited in the cloakroom, her pain turned to defiance tinged with a desire to strike a blow for herself. Her excuse would be the secret she planned to divulge in the Pynx. *We'll see who can rig the scales.* Elita could not throw her father in jail, even if she wanted to, but she had the means to destroy him. *All I have to do is pull the trigger.*

"What's the matter, Lita?" Lucius said. "Are you sick?"

"No, just a little tired. Be good to me and pour me some of that coffee."

Lucius handed her a cup. That morning, she noticed more lines around her eyes and mouth. She feared signaling her internal turmoil about the growing crisis and her father's role in stoking the fires. She applied her usual modest amounts of makeup, but with extra care. She was on the edge of appearing weary, a sign of weakness to the jackals in the Ecclesia.

She also felt her hold on Lucius slipping. After the refugee group led by the man named Enzo split from the main body to return to Nordenskjöld, the media lost interest, preferring to follow the drama approaching Iso. Elita learned that Enzo was one of Lucius' field operatives who happened to be in Nordenskjöld watching the refugee camp when the militia attacked the camp and forced the migrants to leave. Lucius denied it, but Elita guessed he had promised supplies and support if Enzo could persuade the train to turn back. The agent had partially succeeded, and as expected, he contacted Lucius for help. The security chief, however, ignored the request, and Enzo's group disappeared. All this happened behind Elita's back, Lucius claimed, to ensure "plausible deniability" by the government. Not long after the split, a reporter, curious about Enzo's fate, spotted the bodies in a public satellite photo. The images showed two children holding hands in the snow.

For her part, Elita didn't know whether to thank Lucius or fire him. *If he had asked me to send supplies to Enzo, I would've said No. If I had said Yes, how could I defend the Ecclesia's decision to withhold aid from the other migrants?* Elita was not prone to guilt, but she felt regret at the migrant deaths. *If you have no regrets, you have taken no risks.* Lucius, she worried, was becoming too great a risk, and she could not afford any more regrets.

Officially, Enzo's group had over-estimated its chances at surviving the return trip to Nordenskjöld. The public grieved, but it accepted the explanation. It had the opposite reaction to the migrants' arrival at Isorropia's doorstep. Elita called the emergency session to relieve the pressure. The Speaker for the day indicated his readiness to begin, and with Lucius and the other civil servants behind her, she entered the Pynx.

The noise nearly burst her eardrums, but she hid the discomfort behind a smile and a blizzard of handshakes along the carpeted path to the traditional First Citizen's seat. The shoddy, threadbare appearance of the migrants in the video feed reminded Elita of the long-rumored, but never-confirmed ferals. *Wolves in sheep's clothing.*

The randomly chosen Speaker, a pale man of 80 whose bones might snap at the slightest movement, rapped the gavel. Its flat bang and his quiet, but firm call for "Order!" made no dent in the cacophony, and neither did a second, mildly louder rap. Elita wondered if he was up to the task of managing the most raucous session in a generation. It took a moment for her to remember his name: Sill. The Speaker gestured to an aide, who trotted off to a curtained area. The Pynx went black, and in that half-second between surprise and panic, the lights came up again.

"Thank you, ladies and gentlemen." Sill's voice was as papery as his skin. "I apologize for the temporary darkness, but I'm hoping our session today will throw some light on our path forward."

The scattered chuckling showed how few in the crowd were in a joking humor.

"As we all know," Sill continued, "First Citizen Soares—" A smattering of boos echoed in the chamber. "—called this emergency session to determine the next course of action with regard to a group of, er, unexpected visitors outside our defensive perimeter. I'd like to invite the First Citizen to make an opening statement."

Elita bounded up the steps to the speaker's rostrum, careful to show energy, but not imprudence. She didn't look at her father, seated, again modestly, in the second row of chairs. She acknowledged the suffering of the migrants, but repeated in subdued tones the Ecclesia's policy. "However, it appears that events have overtaken that action and we must decide as a city how to handle—"

"Let them in!"

"Don't be stupid. They'll destroy us from the inside."

Voices tumbled over each other like the child gymnasts at the First Harvest ceremony, which seemed a lifetime ago. The Speaker rapped his gavel, and Elita stepped forward to the podium. She was dressed sharply in a newer business style, willing herself to radiate strength and confidence.

"Over the course of the past weeks and months," Elita began, after waiting for the noise in the hall to fall into a murmur, "I've spoken to friends, neighbors, and many others here in this hall today about the migrant problem. We all agree that we must have compassion for their plight."

The First Citizen fleshed out her speech with a patriotic video and tastefully animated text sent over the com net and to a holographic projection above her left shoulder.

"The Warming has devastated the planet, and it shows no sign of easing. The Golden Age of Bounty enjoyed by humanity until a few decades ago will not soon return. Our society is a model for a new balance with nature. Isorropia is carefully built to ensure that Antarctica remains as pristine and pure as the day humans first explored the continent."

An on-the-fly public chart in Elita's minds-eye aggregated individuals' emotional signatures to offer a sense of the mood. "Calm attention with warmth" was the pundits' interpretation. *People love to be reassured that what they know to be true is still true.* On the floor, scattered applause merged into a general approbation.

"As our founders said in our charter, 'The first duty of the city is ισορροπία—'"

"I suppose you'd let them starve to death."

Heads turned. Elita didn't see who called out, either directly or via an avatar. By tradition, anonymity was tolerated on the floor.

Sill rapped his gavel. "Out of order. It is customary not to interrupt the First Citizen when she is speaking."

Here and there, people called out encouragement to Elita. Others booed. "The Ecclesia has created a mechanism for sending aid to the migrants."

A female voice called out. "Crumbs from our overflowing tables. Where's the balance in that?"

Again, Elita couldn't identify who spoke, but she couldn't resist responding. "Nonetheless, we are not ignoring them. We must take care and give them the correct aid at the right time."

"The right time for you is never." The laughter started, and Elita recognized the beginning of the end, if her timing was off. She didn't move a muscle. *The cameras will pick up the slightest tic.* "Our duty—"

"Will the citizen yield the balance of her time?"

The new voice came from deep in the hall, but unlike the other voices, Elita recognized this one instantly. It seemed to come out of the walls.

"I'll be happy to yield to Citizen Soares." Elita guessed what her father had in mind. She was not required to yield time, though it was considered courteous, especially to a citizen as prominent as Ben. His synth-voice was fed directly into the public address system, giving it a supernatural tinge. "As long as the Speaker allows a rebuttal of whatever point the citizen might make?" Elita turned to the Speaker's chair.

Sill was surprised by Elita's question. "Well, it's unusual, but I'll allow it."

Ben edged his way to the rostrum, patted on his back and arms by well-wishers. Even with his exo, he strained to climb the steps. His trouble tore at Elita's heart, despite the temptation to label his behavior an act. *He's pushing himself to his limits.* Elita's eyes widened as a truth stared her in the face: He was failing, and his end was closer than anyone, even she, realized. No shiny technology could mask it. She knew him too well, and he would never admit it. No matter how much the chasm between them widened, he was still her father, the man who had paved the way for the life she led, who had given her everything, at least until Marissa was born. *Why is he trying to take it away from me?* A supporter, trailing Ben, reached out to help him, but the old man waved him off. Elita stepped back from the podium, but remained near, ready to retake her place. Ben eyed her, and she felt a rush of grief. The Pynx was dead silent, waiting for his words.

Ben stood straight, like a gleaming monument. "Good people of our beautiful city, we ought to be proud of our heritage as the first society in human history to enshrine balance with nature as its foremost value. No one can deny the virtue of our founders, including their decision to protect our privacy as we pursue this goal. Our values are unique, and few understand them beyond our virtual walls."

Applause came up from the crowd, along with puzzled looks from citizens Elita recognized as regular supporters of her father. *Not to worry. The leopard cannot change its spots.*

"What our founders did *not* demand of us," Ben said, reducing his volume, "is harming our fellow humans by action or inaction in the name of our values."

Elita and the crowd sensed his direction. Feet shuffled on the marble floor. Some glanced up at the video feed from the camp.

"We've watched these migrants succumb in front of us. How does this square with our Isorropian values? Is our privacy and pride so precious that we will allow children to freeze to death at our gates?"

The catcalls started. Lucius suggested planting a few of Elita's supporters to shout down the humanitarians, but Elita gambled they would do it of their own accord. She was right.

"They're ignorant, contaminated savages, Ben."

"There'll be a flood of them."

"I've heard none of them have ever had a job."

Ben's humanitarians fired back.

"They're human beings, for chrissakes."

"We're not saying let them in, just help them."

"What if they were your kids or grandkids?"

The two sides were so near, physically, that pushing and shoving was inevitable. Elita advised Lucius to wait until the last minute to intervene in altercations. She wanted to be seen as a peacekeeper.

Her father upped the ante. "If we fail to help them, who will take the blame for their deaths? Who will tell their families on the Old Continents? Who will gather the bodies and bury them?"

"The docs would have to grow another heart for you if you tried to dig their graves, Soares."

Smiles and giggles spiced the air. This time, Elita spotted the speaker, a well-known wag.

"You ought to find your heart, sir," Ben retorted. "I believe it's gone missing."

The laughter turned on the wag.

The Speaker interrupted. "If the citizen would come to the point, we could continue the discussion." He was not awed by Ben.

"We cannot ignore suffering." Ben pointed at the feed overhead. The storm had worsened, and blowing snow obscured everything but a vague outline of the dome. "They are our brothers and sisters in humanity. Like our founders, they took a enormous risk by going south. We should respect that, and see our common purpose, to start a new life. No one has evidence they will harm us. Who can say they won't help us achieve our dream, to fix what our species broke? By keeping them out, we may be thwarting our hope to find true ισορροπία."

Elita's stomach hardened. *How did I lose you? What happened to our ισορροπία?*

The crowd applauded politely. The emo-sig chart in Elita's minds-eye showed a shift in disposition toward Ben. The man inhaled. "I propose an emergency appropriation of aid for the refugees, enough to—"

"I believe the citizen's time is expired, Mr Speaker."

Elita steeled herself and stepped up, as if she might nudge Ben out of the way. Her jaw was set for the purpose. Ben twisted around, surprised at the interruption.

Unperturbed, Sill rapped his gavel.

Elita inched forward. "May I respectfully remind the Speaker that I have rebuttal time?"

Ben glared at Elita.

Sill leaned in. "One minute."

Deciding to respect protocol, Ben stepped back, collecting himself.

"Emergency funds are not available," Elita said. "Furthermore, they are not necessary. No one has yet explained how the dome and its supplies happened to be in that valley just as the migrants arrived. The news coms found no public record of strategic food and equipment caches outside the defense perimeter."

Elita kept her eyes on the crowd, resisting the urge to glance at her father to gauge his reaction to the coming revelation.

"However, I have extremely reliable information that points to a group of rogue citizens—" Murmurs rose on the floor. "—who have flaunted the will of the people by financing and placing the cache and leading the migrants to it."

Shouts and cries came up.

"This behavior has placed our beautiful city under direct threat. We know nothing about these migrants. For all we know, they could be armed and wish us harm. Thousands may be following them from the coast."

Elita didn't have to call up the emo-sig chart to see that the crowd's mood had shifted again. The shouts of "Who helped them?" "This is crazy!" and "Why go behind our backs?" told the story.

Elita held her breath a moment. "I regret to report that I have directed the city prosecutor to pursue a complaint that names the conspirators."

"Who's the leader? What's his name?"

The crowd was now a mob, Elita reflected. Instinctively, she turned to Lucius. His eyes were lit with excitement. An expectant silence brought Elita's attention back to the crowd. Her heart pounded, out of fear for her father and of her father. *Now let the knife slip in.* "The leader of the conspiracy is former First Citizen Ben Soares."

Elita exhaled with relief, but the gaping mouths of the crowd demonstrated the level of shock. The most revered living leader of the city, standing before them at the rostrum like a lamb waiting for slaughter, was accused of treason, for lack of a better word. Proof was unnecessary at this point. Emotions ran so high that the accusation was enough. Lynchings were carried out on less evidence. Thousands of pairs of eyes shifted between Elita and Ben. She knew the next question the mob would ask is, "What will the sitting First Citizen do now?"

The problem was, Elita had no specific plan of action once she revealed the truth. Her charge was unprecedented in Isorropian history. The consequences were unpredictable. Arresting her father was out of the question. All she hoped to do was take advantage of the surprise and shock and attempt to sway the Ecclesia finally to her point of view and put the matter to rest. She thought a simple vote to censure her father might neutralize him, but it was impossible to guess how the crowd might react to a call for a humiliating reprimand. For the moment, the mob reeled from a collective punch in the gut. Ben was frozen, but Elita knew his mind was on fire, preparing to strike back. She had to move quickly.

Making note of the watchful security bots along the Pynx's walls, Elita composed the censure motion in her head, following by a motion for a vote to support her position on the migrants. Then, she heard a sob in the crowd, and her own eyes filled with tears. *Father has betrayed me.* She resisted a wave of emotion that might bring tears, but she grasped that the moment had brought the irrevocable break with Ben, whom she loved and respected with all her heart and soul. *He forced me to choose, and I choose my city.*

"Before the First Citizen continues, may I respond?" Before Elita or the Speaker could say yea or nay, the icon stepped to the podium. "Good people, it's true, but it's not a conspiracy, as my child says."

My child? Elita felt the sting of it.

"A small group of us sought to find a limited, legal way to help a group of sick and dying human beings who had made a terrible trek across the continent rivaling the journeys of the Age of Heroes."

"He's a traitor!"

That word again. The utterance was like an unexpected detour in a road, with no arrow pointing right or left. The collective hesitation was painful, and after several seconds ticked off, another shout came from the crowd, and fingers pointed upward to Heaven. Elita followed them to the live feed from the camp. The dome sheltering most of the refugees was ablaze.

Or so it appeared. Elita blinked her watered eyes. The dome glowed orange, but she saw no flames. The camera was too distant to make out faces, especially through the blizzard, but a woman emerged from the entrance, a lit magnesium flare in her hands. Others followed her, trailing smoke and gas from the fire suppression system. The Pynx crowd gasped, as if breathing the same polluted air as the migrants, who shouted at the nearly naked woman with the flare.

Elita texted: Lucius, I don't like this. Cut the feed.

Already trying, but it's on an independent circuit.

As the glow of the fire behind the translucent fabric of the dome faded, Ben seized the initiative. "You see! We have to help them." Ben opened his hands. "What is the First Citizen going to do?"

Elita was now on the defensive, but Lucius rescued her. All the monitors went dark, as well as the minds-eye video feeds. The crowd sent up a sound of disappointment, despite the shocking images. A few demanded the images back.

Not everything, Lucius. I need to see what's going on.

A second later, every screen flickered, as did the minds-eye feeds. The image cleared and for a moment showed nothing but blowing snow and ice. A shadow moved on the edge, and the camera adjusted to find it. The image resolved into the face of a woman, her dark, at-one-time luxurious hair matted and tangled. Inexplicably naked, breasts heavy, and belly flaccid, her eyes and skin were caked with ice. More demon than human, she held out her hand, groping the space in front of her until she ran against the invisible wall of Isorropia's outer defense perimeter. It bent light in all wavelengths and absorbed sound and vibration to avoid the most sophisticated electronic probes. No one, however, made it transparent to human touch, and when the woman bumped into the wall, her wild face changed into an expression of puzzlement, then recognition. The feed didn't carry sound with it, but she mouthed a word: *"Isorropia?"* The Pynx was caught in the refugee woman's drama. *She realized she was wrong.* The woman's eyes fluttered, like the wings of a dying bird, and she sank out of view.

Ben broke the spell. "Mr Speaker, I demand an answer. Will the First Citizen help these people?"

Elita swallowed. Thousands of faces focused on her. For the first time in her life, she felt as exposed as the woman on the screen, not to the physical elements, but to the raw confusion and animal frustration of the crowd, as if, collectively, they would strike at her, if they could, simply to relieve the strain. The woman on the screen was almost certainly dead, but inaction was not an option, and Elita had no idea what to do. To admit as much, however, would be like throwing herself off a cliff into the storm surge of humanity before her. *Father will let me fall into the black beneath my feet.*

Lucius... She sought him out at his place among the other members of her government, but he was gone.

Sill's voice broke through her paralysis. "Madame First Citizen, I must ask you to respond to Citizen Soares' question."

The query offered Elita a point for focus, and she licked her lips. "I'm sorry, Mr Speaker. We've all been shocked by what we've, by what the images show. I've sent Lucius, I mean, BES Security Chief Galla to investigate."

Sill brought himself up and touched the gavel to its sound block. "It's time for a break. We need to wait for what Citizen Galla learns. I'm recessing this session until tomorrow morning at 10:00." He tapped the gavel again.

The crowd filed out, quiet as mourners at a funeral, though the faces were set and firm. What they'd seen only solidified their belief in the correctness of their position, whatever it might be. If anyone had changed their minds, or modified it to suit new circumstances, it wouldn't be clear until the next day, when Elita had to present some kind of way forward. A division would decide the migrants' fate, and Elita's.

Lucius, God help us if you...

Her father came up to her. "I hope you've considered your options carefully, First Citizen."

"In what respect?" Elita found it difficult to meet Ben's gaze. She was six years old again, dwarfed by a man who had outmaneuvered her again.

"Galla is a criminal, a thug, and he abuses power like some people step on insects."

Elita found her courage. "It seems there's more than one criminal in this room, Citizen Soares." She hadn't disagreed with his point about Lucius.

"I'm going to tell you something. Lucius Galla had better do the right thing by those refugees, one in particular."

"Who—?" Elita stopped, understanding whom her father meant. In the midst of the crisis, she had set aside her personal scrutiny of Marissa Sentillius' investigation into the agarwood smuggling and Lucius' potential role. He knew Marissa was there on the ice, but she likely did not know Lucius knew, at least in detail. Whatever had happened between them, Lucius had an interest in eliminating her.

"I don't like what you're suggesting, Father. Lucius Galla may be harsh sometimes, but he always serves the interests of this city. I trust him, else he wouldn't be in my cabinet." *I have to say that. Half-lies are more persuasive than half-truths.*

"I trust him as well, Elita. I trust him to do what's good for Lucius Galla."

With that, Ben turned on his heel, a fluid motion, despite his mass. In her heart of hearts, Elita agreed with her father, but wasn't that the case for anyone who felt threatened? *Of course, Lucius will choose himself. The question is, which of them will I choose?*

CHAPTER 23

Returning to the encampment, Sento crawled into her sleeping bag, set out on the floor of the dome. Sleep took its time coming, and she watched Hosea and Gwen with Awilda's baby boy. The child was quiet as Gwen fed him. She had found formula and bottles in the food supplies. Her face was content, even glowing, despite the tragedy of the mother's death. Some women are meant to be mothers, to raise children and families in an instinctive faith in the future, no matter the odds. Some women have other destinies. The journey to Isorropia had driven Awilda mad, though her pregnancy forestalled the final break with reality, as if Mother Nature knew Awilda's mind was gone, but needed her body a while longer to carry the future forward. After burying Awilda's corpse in a temporary grave, Sento marked its position on the shared map in her minds-eye. It became the last waypoint on the pilgrims' journey.

Sento's feelings toward Hosea were a Gordian knot of sorrow, guilt, sympathy, and jealousy. In that fantastical space between wakefulness and unconsciousness, she wrapped her arms around him as he sobbed over his loss. Like smoke in a wind, the near-dream vanished when he embraced the child. As he absorbed the infant's powerful presence, Hosea's role in the world changed, and Sento understood there was little room for her. The boy would consume all his love. *I'm jealous of a day-old child. I must be going mad, too.*

Her imagination swung again to deeper dreams, and they repeated the same disconnected themes as always, like bricks in a wall held together with weak mortar. Their importance, however, had faded, as measured against her collective feelings for Hosea, Gwen, Bruce, Koi, and the others. If the answer she sought to her identity presented itself, would it mean leaving them behind? The thought pained her. *Will I have to choose between my old self and my new self?*

Sento rose after an hour. It wasn't long enough to restore her, but she felt refreshed. Since Slaughter Inlet, she had fallen off her routine of ranging the camp's perimeter, and she decided to get back into it. According to the clock, most of the camp was asleep. The only missing avatar was Artie's. *Where does he go when he disappears?* Sento splashed fresh water on her face and wrapped herself in the remains of her inner and outer thermals. Happy to be falling into a familiar habit, she checked her pistol and slipped it into her holster. Remembering Artie's warning about protection, she slipped the holster of a bulky staser over her head. The weapon's power pack was fully charged.

She stepped out into sunshine filtered by high clouds. The light was soft, forcing the horizon to blend into the sky at the far edge of the Isorropian Plain. The jagged cliffs of the narrow valley protected the rear and sides of the camp. Walking toward the invisible city wall, she perceived a shimmer, like ripples in a pond. Even in Antarctica, heat waves rose from the ice's surface, like waves off a desert salt pan. She recalled an old technique of hunters. She flicked her eyes to the left and right. Her heart jumped. The movement was broken into a few distinct shapes.

She broadcast an alarm over Bruce's network. Artie, Hosea, everyone. There's people coming.

Kanthaka was the main router for the pilgrims' network before its destruction, but Bruce maintained a backup in his belongings. It was weaker, though, and Sento couldn't be sure everyone heard her call. She sent it again when she saw the group of seven or eight individuals coming toward her, steady and purposeful. They were dressed in all-white Antarctic gear that looked brand-new compared to her rags. *They must come from the city.*

Excited, she walked straight at the emerging group. "Hey!" She waved, unsure what to say or do. "Do you see me?" No one among the pilgrims had time to think about the best way to approach the city or communicate with the people behind the wall. No one had thought a welcoming party might come out first. She continued forward, however, her hands outstretched in an instinctive supplication. "Can you help us?"

Halt. Do not move. Remain still. We will come to you.

The text was accompanied by an audio command in a sexless artificial voice, and Sento obeyed it. The voice was firm, dark, and familiar in a way Sento could not pin down. The figures resolved into seven human shapes and a security robot of an advanced design, taller and bulkier than the humans. It made tiny hissing sounds. Among the humans, Sento could not distinguish male from female, young from mature. They were completely covered with protective gear, including their faces. Insignia on their breasts and shoulders indicated a police force or military. All the humans, except the one in the lead, carried staser rifles. Her heart caught in her throat, but she assured herself that the Isorropians were simply being cautious. The pilgrims were strangers to them.

The squad stopped in front of her. The leader was a couple of centimeters taller than Sento. It was hard to tell with all the gear. The leader paused, as if orienting himself or herself.

Identify yourself.

Sento wanted to cooperate, but she was torn between answering with her real name, which the Isorropians might know, and the name her friends used when they spoke to her. "I'm called Sento."

Who are these people with you?

What was the answer they wanted? The whole story, or something reassuring? "We're refugees. We've come from the coast at Nordenskjöld. We're from all over. Mostly the Americas. We need help. We've lost everything—"

The leader turned to two of the squad members and gestured them forward. Without a word, he strode past Sento as if she had no importance. The two troopers grabbed her by the arms and dragged her with them toward the camp. Surprised, Sento yelped, "Hey, that hurts!" She collected herself and broadcast another text alarm, but an error appeared in her minds-eye complaining about the loss of connectivity. "Why are you blocking our network?"

The leader was deaf to Sento's pleas. Helpless, she struggled to keep pace with the marching troopers, backed up by the mechanical crunch of the heavy robot. "Hosea! Gwen!" Her weak shouts were overwhelmed by the menace of the troopers and the palpable malice of the leader. Hosea emerged from the dome, paused with an impassive glance at Sento, then took deliberate steps toward the leader. Sento wanted to shout another warning, but held back.

"Hello. I'm Hosea Taft. I'm the leader of this group. Are you from Isorropia?" Hosea extended his hand, but the leader did nothing in response.

Halting abruptly, the leader stood face to face with Hosea, hands clasped behind his back. His silence morphed from rude to threatening. He was in control, and he wasn't going to give anything away. With his expression hidden, Sento could only imagine his thinking. *What's wrong? Why doesn't he say anything?*

Hosea pressed forward. "Sir, if you wouldn't mind answering my question—"

Are any more migrants coming? Again, the sexless, synthetic voice chafed Sento.

"No. This is all of us." Hosea hands swept over the crude collection of shelters. "A group of us split off several weeks ago and headed back. I don't know what became of—"

What do you know about her?

Sento stiffened as the leader nodded at her.

"Sento?" Hosea said. "I'm not sure what you mean. She's with us. She joined us at the beach camp."

Sento's not her real name. She's been lying to you.

He already knows me. He knows Marissa Sentillius. How? Sento wanted to ask a million questions, but raw fear and her instincts told her to wait.

Hosea was nonplussed. "I don't understand. She's part of our leadership. She's—" Hosea questioned her with his look, and she shook her head, unsure what to say or do. She had no time to relay what Artie had told her about her true name. She only half-believed it herself. Flanked by the troopers, she felt a prisoner. *As if I were back on the table waiting for the dissing.*

How do I know you're not lying to me?

"She's had some trouble with her memory. I don't see how that's the same as—"

Call everyone in camp outside. I want to see them.

Hosea took a breath. "Of course. You'll want identification and to understand our needs, but do you mind telling us who you are and—" Hosea had no authority here, but he was entitled to basic courtesy and respect, which was not on offer by the troop's commander.

Call everyone out. Every person. Now.

Overhearing the order, Koi ran among the smaller shelters and within a few minutes, a hundred or so individuals milled about, resembling a herd of nervous cattle. Gwen held the new baby. Bruce, delirious with his injury, remained inside.

The troopers positioned themselves in a circle outside the knots of families and groups that had become tribe-like in their affiliations and affections. Sento saw shared anticipation, hope, and anxiety in every eye. For her part, fear took the strongest hold. For more than two years, she was driven by an insatiable need to find Isorropia and move south, always south. She worried the troopers might be a final, insurmountable barrier.

"This is everyone, sir," Hosea said.

The leader unsnapped a flap of his parka's hood to reveal a clean-shaven jaw, full mouth and Roman nose under forehead and eyes that remained hooded and goggled. "I represent the government of the Independent City of Isorropia." At the utterance of the city's name, the crowd and Sento tensed in anticipation and excitement. The main question was answered. They had reached their goal. It wasn't a fantasy.

Every pilgrim gave their full attention to the leader. His unfiltered voice was warm, but rough, as if unused to public speaking, but entirely comfortable giving instructions and getting his way. For Sento, the voice tickled more memories at the edge of her consciousness, maddeningly reluctant to reveal themselves, though they did nothing to assuage her underlying dread about the situation.

"I represent the First Citizen, elected by the Ecclesia. You are attempting to enter a sovereign state without permission. The City of Isorropia has a right to defend its borders and its territorial integrity."

The terms "First Citizen" and "Ecclesia" were as familiar as her own name, as if Sento had used them herself a thousand times, but she had no power to articulate their meaning, like a box with nothing inside.

Hosea spoke up. "Sir, we understand that we are not invited, and we ask your forgiveness, and your forbearance. We've traveled many hundreds of kilometers. Many of us have lost friends and relatives on the journey. I've lost my wife. The places we come from can no longer sustain us. We were attacked in our last refuge. We're all praying your city might offer us another refuge. We only ask for an alley, a corner, a gutter where we can rebuild our lives. We ask that you help us."

The Isorropian leader paced, examining the pilgrims one-by-one at arm's length. Sento hoped he would look past their savage appearance, worn down by travel with little food and warmth, and see the suffering and remaining shreds of dignity. *Maybe he wants to help, but his hands are tied by others.*

Returning to Hosea, the leader lifted his chin and sighed. "I regret to to inform you that it is the policy of the City of Isorropia to deny all requests for asylum or refugee status. You are asked to leave immediately."

After his declaration, the silence was broken only by the whisk of ice crystals blown about the pilgrims' feet. They stood mouths agape, arms limp at their sides. Some smiled, as if waiting for the leader to say he was joking, and they were in fact welcome. After a moment, the truth of his statement hit home. Stunned herself by the cold rebuff, Sento marked the disbelief in all the pilgrims' faces. They hadn't believed in the possibility they would be turned away.

"Sir," Hosea swallowed, "we appreciate that you have application procedures that we have not followed, but surely there must be a way—"

"I'll say this only once more, Mr Taft. You and your group are trespassing. You are not welcome. Isorropia doesn't want you. Go back the way you came. You don't belong here."

The pilgrims murmured to one another, unsure what to do next. At a loss herself, Sento wondered if Artie had somehow brought this about. As Hosea readied to make another plea, Bruce burst out of the dome. "You're the people that tried to kill us before." Wild eyes stared out of an ashen face. "You killed our people back at the Kanthaka River."

The leader, his mouth set, regarded the techie, who had jury-rigged a strap to secure a tablet on the stump of his arm. Even behind the heavy eye protection, Sento sensed the commander's evaluation of Bruce as a potential threat. The leader turned to Hosea. "You said everyone was out of the tents. Who is this?"

Bruce thrust a finger at the leader. "I've been looking at your network, whoever you are. You've got the same network fingerprint as the one that delivered the virus to Kanthaka and the other AIs."

"Sir, he's been badly injured. His painkillers—" Gwen paused for effect as she guided Bruce back into the dome. "Now is not the time, Bruce."

"No. I gave up everything..." He waved his bandaged stump. "...to take a chance at a new life. I say we keep going and ignore whoever he's representing and find a way into the city."

The troopers shifted nervously, recognizing the challenge. The leader took no note of Bruce's call, appearing relaxed and confident.

Hosea regarded the troop leader. "Is this true? Did you insert that malware? If so, it caused the deaths—"

"I'm not concerned with what may or may not have happened to you on your journey here. My role is to turn you back down the trail and away from Isorropia."

Hosea's affect changed from respectful to angry. "You won't even listen to our pleas. What kind of a people are you?"

Grumbling broke out among the pilgrims. "Bruce is right." "Don't listen to him, Hosea." "I'm not going back." Skittish members of the crowd bent heads together, as if making plans. Sento's feeling of alarm nearly burst through, but she grit her teeth. She readied for a coming explosion.

"If you force us to leave," Hosea said, "you'll be killing us as sure as shooting us right here. Is that what your First Citizen wants?"

The leader was unmoved. "I'm giving you a final warning, Mr Taft. If you refuse to cooperate, I won't hesitate to use force to defend my city."

"Won't you let me speak to your First Citizen? Perhaps a small delegation?" Hosea's voiced pitched high. He was losing the argument. "I can't believe a people as advanced as you can be so heartless."

The leader paused, but he had sent a silent command. In a moment, the troopers weapons were at the ready. Sento thought of the staser in her holster and her pistol in her belt. *Why hadn't they searched me or asked about weapons? Overconfidence, or did they assume a fight? Is it a setup?* Her mouth was like cotton, dry from the strain and the lack of moisture in the Antarctic air.

"Trust me, Mr Taft," the leader smirked. "I don't care an ice flea's life for you and your filthy migrants."

Sento calculated the seconds it might take to pull the staser and defend the pilgrims from an assault. No matter how she turned it over in her head, the odds were overwhelmingly against them.

The security robot began a slow perambulation of the rough circle of migrants. Women and children huddled together, whimpering at this unpredicted threat. The leader was using the bot to intimidate the crowd, to keep them in control, much like she'd seen local police do during a bread riot in Punta Arenas. Bruce, however, was behaving strangely, punching on his tablet with one hand like a madman, sweat dripping off his chin despite the chill. Without warning, the bot turned on its heel and took off at a dead run, away from the dome and the camp.

"What's it doing?" The leader was surprised by the bot's behavior. "Stop that man!" He pointed at Bruce.

"Too late, you asshole."

Tearing away at top speed, the bot smashed into the side of a boulder, disintegrating.

"That's what I'm going to do to your dumb-ass defenses, if you don't let us in, and right now."

No, Bruce! That's what he needed. The next minute flew by in a blur. A pilgrim hand reached out for one of the troopers' gun barrels, and it popped, exploding the pilgrim's shoulder in sinew and blood. Sento dropped and rolled to get out of the way of any shots aimed at her. She was surrounded by a forest of running arms and legs. Amid screams, she fumbled to unholster the staser as she heard the distinctive whine of a staser discharge on the other side of the pilgrims' mass. She fired her own staser, and the knee of the nearest trooper blew apart, knocking him into another trooper. Sento crawled behind a jumble of rocks as she fell under aim. Flying bullets knocked off bits of stone above her head. Another staser discharge missed her, though the impact on her stone cover knocked her backwards. Pistol shots signaled that the pilgrims were defending themselves. Out of the corner of her eye, she spied bloody bodies sprawled on the ice. The troopers dragged away a wounded comrade, while another pair fired into the scattering mass of refugees.

The situation changed in an instant when Sento heard automatic weapons fire coming from above the group. She was sprawled on the snow, as flat as she could make herself. The firing was distant, and the effect on the troopers was odd. Sento didn't see the leader, but he was giving orders, judging by the disciplined movements of the troopers. They stopped firing and took cover behind a monolith that stood like a guard at the entrance to the valley. *There's another troop under cover somewhere. They have to be backup, but the tactics are wrong.*

She settled on her own tactics and sought out the leader of the first group of troopers. She was swayed by the belief that she knew him. As she grasped at another vague memory, he ran straight toward her, as if she was a specially reserved target, or trophy. Horrified, she saw his staser pointed directly at her head, and she rolled away as the pressure wave from the shot whizzed past her brow. She raised her staser, but he kicked it away, pain shooting up her arm. He lost his balance in the poor footing, however, and he stumbled face first into the snow. *He's angry and desperate. He'll make stupid mistakes.* He reached for his staser, which had skittered across the ground. She grabbed for his leg, and she pulled herself over his body, hand-over-hand, until she could scratch at his face. His goggles flew off as a punch hit her in the temple. Stunned, she got to her knees, and lifted her eyes to see him, his face fully revealed, angular, attractive in a devilish way, eyes dark, a growing smirk on his face.

"Did you think we'd just let you come home?"

As if a dam burst, the flood of emotions and memories overwhelmed Sento, clouding her mind and freezing her in place. A hurricane of images and thoughts buried her conscious thought, none of it making sense, but all of it belonging to her. *This is me, coming back, all at once.* It forced a cry, though the pain of it was mixed with the pleasure of recognition and an instinctive understanding. *Is this the madness Artie warned me about?* A tiny part of her mind kept its attention on the leader—Galla!—and he raised his staser. She saw his finger squeeze the trigger, and at the same instant, a bullet struck his foot, knocking him off balance. The staser blast threw up chunks of ice at Sento's feet, and a sliver entered her cheek. She fell on her side, stars surrounding the tunnel of her consciousness. A dozen footfalls assaulted her ears, and she blinked as her head turned into the sun. A hooded face blocked the disk, and she lifted her arm, ready to defend herself against Galla.

The face, though wasn't her enemy's. Despite the sun's backlighting, it was bright, reflective, and serene. It fended off her arm gently. "Marissa, it's alright. You're safe. I'm here."

Sento's eyes adjusted, and her mind cleared, though the memories swirled like ice devils. *Galla!* Sento scrambled to her feet. Her staser was empty, and she pulled out her pistol.

"Marissa! Don't shoot. Galla's gone. We're searching for him."

Sento squinted at the new figure before her. The dream face had become real. The man with the silver face was here.

Something else was gone besides Galla. A weight on her psyche, like a yoke on an oxen, lifted. The drive to move south had vanished. She had reached her goal. She had come home.

CHAPTER 24

COFFEE AT SHACKLETON'S?

ELITA READ THE PERPLEXING MINDS-EYE text four or five times before she accepted its meaning: She was in serious physical danger and she needed to meet Lucius at the pre-arranged place immediately. No such cafe called "Shackleton's" existed. It was code for another location. She texted the acknowledgment: Latte with a double shot. It only meant she was on her way.

Her disbelief was overpowering. The text didn't fit the facts as she knew them. No one had threatened her or even spoken a sharp word outside the Ecclesia, where empty threats were routine. Of all the world's chiefs of state, Elita was possibly the safest; she wasn't even assigned a security bot to shadow her after hours. *Has my father attempted a coup? Have the migrants breached our defenses? Has an enemy from the Old Continents taken advantage of our distraction?* She was tempted to call Lucius and confirm, but she held back.

Elita double-checked her "go" bag, the emergency carryall with three days of necessities: high-energy dry foods, medical supplies, and personal items. During security discussions, Lucius harangued her about urgency, but she paused to fill a glass with kitchen tap water to wash away the anxiety drying her mouth. She was nervous about more than Lucius' text. She set the drained glass next to an unlabeled, palm-sized manila envelope on the polished granite. An old contact at the Bureau of Environmental Security handed the envelope to her a few minutes before the Ecclesia session. She already knew every detail about the envelope's contents. The mere fact of its existence confirmed everything she suspected about her security chief, and it frightened her like the diagnosis of a terminal disease. Still, she opened it, and she saw the thumb-sized plastic baggie inside. The value of the dust in the smaller bag could buy the building she lived in, and then some. It was evidence of a heinous crime. She pocketed the baggie, anger and hurt overcoming her anxiety. She shook her head in a vain attempt to banish her fear. *What am I walking in to? What if he knows what I know?*

She had no choice but to trust him.

The elevator whisked Elita to the garage, where she ordered a pod car to take her to the rendezvous. The quiet street ambiance hadn't changed in the hours since she'd come home. *Where is the danger?* A tablet in her lap, Elita swiped through the news chans, and apart from the ongoing protests in Government Square, civil society remained civil.

Shackleton's is closed.

Translation of Lucius' text: *The first meetup location is compromised.*

Meet me at our favorite bench in Founders Park.

He meant: *Go to the BES safe house on Queen Maud Street.*

Elita bit her lip, fighting the urge to call Lucius, but he warned against unnecessary chatter in an emergency. Lucius claimed his cloak-and-dagger practices were standard, but Elita suspected it was a game he liked to play, like a little boy immersed in a VR chase. *Maybe he's seeing something that doesn't exist, but I have to play along.* She scrolled through her messages and noticed an absence of security updates, which Lucius liked to send her every couple of hours, even if the message was a single line: "All is well." The absence of messages was out of character.

The pod car stopped in front of a modest three-story building in one of the oldest parts of town. The area was the closest Isorropia claimed as a poor section, a jumble of close-in structures built on foundations laid by early scientific expeditions to the area. Shadows were deep among the buildings. The summer Antarctic sun felt dimmer. Ordering the pod back to her building's garage, Elita slung the go bag over her shoulder, walked up a short flight of stairs and knocked on the door. No one answered and no invitation came across her minds-eye. The network was active, but she didn't see Lucius' avatar, or anyone else's. She touched the lock pad and the door clicked open to a dark hall.

"Lucius?"

The door closed behind Elita, the latch's click echoing down the hall. Elita knew the house from one previous orientation visit soon after her first election as First Citizen. She was with an entourage, including Lucius, and the house was brightly lit. At the moment, its emptiness unnerved her. She expected Lucius or at least one of his henchmen to greet her or guide her to her lover and security chief. She looked forward to seeing him, despite her mistrust of his motivations. *If he were less of a child, I might fall in love in him.* She missed his presence. He offered a strange comfort, sealed by mutual ambition.

A light caught her eye. The door to a large sitting room was ajar, and dim rays leaked around the jamb. Elita approached the door and laid a knuckle on the painted faux-wood. The door opened a few centimeters, revealing a dark, saucer-sized stain on the carpet. Another streak of maroon pointed toward a man laying prone on a couch.

"You took your time."

"Lucius!"

"I was beginning to think you'd forgotten where to go."

"What happened? You're hurt." Elita resisted an urge to rush to him. "You said I was in danger."

"It never occurred to me that I might need your help."

"You lied to me."

"It was the only way I could think of to get you to come without alerting everyone and his brother."

A blood-soaked towel was loose on his left foot. He wore an unzipped heavy parka that revealed body armor. Lucius pulled himself upright. "My little plan didn't go so well."

"What plan?" Elita stood over her lover, hands out as if wanting to act, but she drew a blank on what she should do.

"You brought the go bag. Good. Does it have the med-kit I gave you?"

Elita nodded. "We need to get you to a hospital."

"No, they'll find me there."

Rummaging through the bag, she found the kit. "Who will find you?"

"Our enemies. Your enemies." Lucius grabbed the kit out of Elita's hands and tore open the package. "Take the towel off my foot."

"What enemies are you talking about? What did you do, Lucius?" Elita lifted the towel off Lucius' foot with the tips of her fingers, and she retched. Lucius had managed to remove the boot, leaving an oozing, transverse laceration visible across the skin.

"Your father, for one. He did this." Lucius winced, and reached for his foot, with the med-kit in his hand. "I can't do it, Elita. You know how."

She'd seen the procedure a dozen times in first-aid training videos, but she'd never actually applied the bio-robotic med-kit. She took the thick bandage roll and unfolded it. "Shouldn't I clean the wound first?"

"Just put it on! It hurts like hell."

Elita lay the bandage on Lucius' foot, roughly covering the laceration. The injured man hissed as it stung. The device smelled of antiseptic and camphor. After a few seconds, its shape changed as the intelligent fabric sought out the form of Lucius' foot and infused the injury with engineered antibodies, white cells, and hormones that promoted cell growth. Lucius leaned back and let out a deep breath, as if he'd held it for an hour.

"Lucius, where have you been? Last time I saw you was during the Ecclesia session."

"Taking care of your problem, just like you asked me too."

"I don't know what you're talking about."

"You wanted to be rid of the migrants, so I tried to oblige."

"And you were shot in the process." Elita glanced down at Lucius' foot. The bandage was hardening into a temporary cast. "You're not making any sense, Lucius. We need to get you to a hospital."

"No! Your father did this to me."

"Ben shot you? How is that even possible?"

"Maybe one of his boys got me. It doesn't matter. He interfered, just like he promised he would. You remember?"

The secret recordings were clear. Ben and his supporters built and supplied the cache outside the defense perimeter in direct opposition to Ecclesia policy. They had an agent shadowing the migrants who would lead them to the cache if necessary. The conspirators said nothing about violence. "That doesn't explain you getting shot, Lucius."

"Christ, Elita. Do I have to spell everything out for you?"

Elita waited.

"We were only going to persuade the migrants to leave. They could take all the supplies with them, if they wanted, but we told them they weren't welcome."

"Shit, Lucius. You threatened them, didn't you?"

"No one was supposed to be hurt. All they had to do was march north. What happened next was their fault, not mine."

"Jesus, what did you do?"

"Your father and his people gave them weapons. Marissa had a staser."

"Marissa! What did you do to her?"

Lucius turned his face away. "Nothing."

Elita thought of the baggie in her pocket. All the information in Marissa's investigation was falling into place. "You tried to kill her, didn't you?"

Lucius' eyes blazed. "Don't accuse me of something you know nothing about."

His falseness infuriated Elita. She could put up with his unauthorized "help" intended to support her political goals, but not his free-lance ass-covering. "I know everything about your extra-curricular activities. Marissa found out, didn't she?"

"Now *you're* not making sense."

Elita removed the baggie and waved it in front of Lucius. "Agarwood incense. Enough to make you richer than Midas. Enough to get you dissed and banished."

Lucius stared wide-eyed at the dust, mind racing. "It's a lie. I never touched it. I'm not that stupid." The security chief found the strength to pull himself to his feet. He limped on the hardened bandage to a window and pulled aside the curtain, as if checking for spies. "How do I even know that's real, that it's not ordinary wood ash?"

"Don't push it, Lucius. It's been tested. I have the report. It's the real thing, enough to send you away forever."

"I tell you I've never touched it."

"You didn't have to, Lucius. The racketeering statutes make you culpable, even if you don't handle the contraband."

Marissa's case file on the agarwood smuggling, with its notes on "LRG," had a folder labeled "Physical Evidence." The folder contained a routine request for spectrographic, DNA, and other analyses. The results were unequivocal: The coarse dust in the baggie was mold-infected heartwood of the genus *Aquilaria* native to Southeast Asia. DNA tests confirmed the tree's genus and the mold species, *Phaeoacremonium parasitica*.

Marissa's file contained a 10-year-old satellite image meta-analysis by the United Nations, commissioned under the Convention on International Trade in Endangered Species of Wild Fauna and Flora, which found only a few tiny, isolated patches of the tree growing in remote valleys on the Malaysian peninsula. Several *Aquilaria* species were biologically extinct, and the genus was threatened with annihilation, another victim of the Warming.

Marissa had discovered a ring smuggling one of the most valuable substances on earth, a natural resin that gave off an exquisite fragrance when burned. The resin came from the wood of a tree that was more or less extinct. The CITES treaty banned nations from importing or exporting the incense, but this crime had special meaning in Isorropia. *We cherish the balance of man and nature, with absolute and total respect for creation.* For an Isorropian to cause, even in part, the loss of a species, especially for personal gain, was a crime akin to genocide. Under city law, a person convicted of contributing to the extinction of a plant or animal species was subject to disidentification and banishment.

The request for the analysis was dated two days before Marissa's disappearance. The conclusion was obvious to Elita. Marissa was close to connecting Lucius to the agarwood ring, and she paid for it with her identity. *That doesn't explain her presence among the refugees.* The case was circumstantial, however. Nothing linked Lucius directly to the ring. Marissa was stopped before she accomplished that goal.

"It's pure speculation," Lucius said. "There's no 'smoking gun,' I think the phrase is."

"There wasn't, until you tried to kill Marissa. Your plan to drive off the migrants was just a cover. You wanted to help yourself, not me."

"Name one person in the world whose motives are pure."

In a flash of insight, Elita saw her lover's true self. "You're a monster, Lucius. You were too much of a coward to kill her two years ago, and you saw an opportunity to make up for your error. You don't give a shit about protecting the city or me."

"None of this would've happened if Marissa hadn't come back. She was supposed to stay away. I admit I toyed with the idea of eliminating her two years ago, but I'm not a murderer, despite what you might think. That's why I sent her away."

"That's one thing I don't get. She disappeared, then showed up with these migrants. Why doesn't she walk up and announce herself?"

"She doesn't know who she is."

"What? Nothing you say adds up." In the next instant, Elita understood. "You had her disidentified off the books. You took away her memories and you dumped her on the street. You bastard. I ought to turn you in right now."

"I doubt you will."

"She's my sister!"

Lucius let out a laugh that shook him down to his injured foot, and he winced. He wiped away a tear, whether from the laughter or the pain, Elita couldn't tell. "Since when have you cared about your *half*-sister? When she went missing, you put on a great show of concern, especially around your father, but you never went beyond the normal missing person procedures. That's how much you cared."

"I did everything I was supposed to do."

"That's my point. That's all you did. Nothing above and beyond." Lucius limped toward Elita, pointing a finger at her chest. "I think I did you a favor. Your father loved his youngest, maybe more than you. She was in your way."

Elita slapped Lucius' hand away. "You're sick. I admit to some jealousy. What sibling wouldn't be jealous of a famous, powerful father? But I would never have dissed her, or done anything to hurt her. I helped her career behind the scenes. I was her friend. To you, she was a threat, so you eliminated her. Or tried to. What I don't understand is why you broke our most cherished laws."

Lucius shrugged. "I saw a need. I filled a need." He returned to the window. "People were willing to buy. I had the connections."

"But the law! Ισορροπία!"

"Oh, come off your high horse. Balance this. Balance that. I tipped the balance a little to my favor, that's all. Anybody who denies trying to game the system once in a while is a hypocrite."

A thumb on the scales, just like Father with Marissa and I.

Here was the greed that had caused the earth so much trouble, the thing the Founders had fought so hard to prevent in Elita's beautiful city. *Lucius was a liability all along, just as Ben warned.* "I have to turn you in, Lucius. It's my duty as an Isorropian and as First Citizen."

"If you do, you won't be First Citizen for long."

"Are you threatening *me* now?"

"Call it a prediction. Forget the 'beautiful city' garbage and think about your situation. I'm your security chief. You hired me. I do your bidding. No, don't shake your head. People will blame you for what I do, whether you ordered it or not. They'll hang what happened outside today on your neck as well as mine."

"What do you mean by 'what happened outside?'" Again, Elita put two-and-two together. "Wait. Let me guess. The migrants fought back, didn't they?"

"They had help," Lucius said. "From your father and his accomplices."

"One of them shot you. Was it Marissa?"

"I don't think so, but it doesn't matter." Lucius' voice dropped to an intense whisper. "It doesn't matter because you're going to protect me."

Lucius was right, and Elita hated him for it. While she might get praise for performing her duty, she'd lose all her credibility as a leader. The Ecclesia teetered on the edge of anarchy, and the slightest whiff of scandal would tip the scales against her and her dreams for the city. *You can't govern if you aren't in office. You can't lead if no one believes in you.* "What do you want me to do?" Her question came out in a hiss.

Lucius lowered himself into a chair. Sweat beaded on his forehead, and his skin's pallor was magnified by the filtered light from the window. "The answer's simple. Arrest your father."

Elita's jaw dropped. "Have you gone completely crazy?"

"Ben Soares has committed a crime. He's interfered with the legal authority of government employees performing their duty. People who answer to him assaulted those employees. At the very least, he's shown contempt for the Ecclesia."

"He's my father!"

"It seems to me you have an opportunity to get rid of an enemy." Lucius grinned. "Use your political smarts, my dear. Get out in front of the problem.

Put him under house arrest while your security chief conducts an investigation. It's the only way you'll survive."

"What about Marissa?"

"Arrest her too. She's obviously in league with her father. Maybe she's been working with him all along to undermine Isorropian society."

"Convenient for you."

"For both of us." Lucius smugness irritated Elita. "Listen to me, lover. You want to serve your beautiful city? You want to protect it from invaders? From people who would corrupt our values? Act quickly. Seize the initiative. You know your father would. Pull the teeth from the tiger's mouth before he bites."

Elita crossed her arms, as if protecting herself from a man she thought she knew. She had never loved him, but at points she was deeply fond of him, and once or twice considered him her closest friend. He stumbled around the room, opening drawers and cabinets, searching for something, until he found them: mist sticks. He chewed on the narcotic nervously, sucking the juice to dull the physical pain not touched by the temporary bandage. He had Elita by the throat, metaphorically. If she turned him in, she would fall, and she might never recover politically. She had to choose him if she wanted to save herself, even if it meant damaging her father's legacy forever. *I've already lost his love.*

"Lucius, if you fail, I will abandon you like the criminal you are."

The security chief tossed the empty mist stick into a recycle bin. "Fair enough."

"Give the arrest order." Elita loomed over him in a weak attempt to reassert her dominance, but Lucius held the trump card, and he was ready to play it. If she didn't shield him, her career was over. She could only rage at him. "I hope you burn in hell."

CHAPTER 25

"RECOVERING YOUR SOUL ISN'T AN everyday occurrence, Sento," said the silver-faced man. He walked close while a woman in heavy outdoor gear much like Galla's helped Sento to the dome. The crimson medical cross on each of the nurse's arms echoed blood stains on the ice.

"I wasn't dead," Sento said. "My soul is still inside. I'm still me." *I'm the me I've constructed.*

"Of course, Marissa. It's a phrase that the few people who've regained their identity after dissing use to describe their experience."

Sento thought the "recovery" was more like another soul awakening inside hers. Or a second version. In the years since her partial disidentification, she had erected a new, albeit fragile, identity, built of the skills, ethics, and values forged by her obsession to move south and find Isorropia. What's more, the pilgrim's journey, which started as a convenience, evolved into a reawakening of ways to connect with others. The dissed were said to forget the meaning of love. Sento remembered because of Hosea, Koi, and the others. They were the family she thought about first when she woke in the mornings. "I prefer you call me 'Sento' for now."

The patch of exposed skin on the man's face was slack and pale, and the faint hisses of the servo motors marked him as exo-assisted. His deep-green eyes were kind and thoughtful. "Do you know who I am?"

The nurse directed Sento to drink a liquid that tasted of citrus. The patient blinked. "Ben Soares." She remembered his title, the same one Galla used before the firefight to give himself authority. "First Citizen of Isorropia." Saying it confused her, because it sounded like a mistake. The answer also dodged the fact of the relationship Sento was not ready to admit.

"Former First Citizen. Retired, you might say." A tinge of disappointment colored his synthetic voice. *He was hoping for the answer that I'm holding back.* He removed the gloves from his hands in the warm dome. Each hand was covered in the exo, which flexed like quicksilver over his fingers. "I know you want to be called 'Sento,' but do you know your, um, previous name, all of it?"

Sento recalled the conversation with Artie Macedon, who told her the name on the scouting trip. "Marissa Sentillius." It felt like the vaguely familiar name of an old school acquaintance she hadn't seen in years. Saying it out loud, however, made it clear and normal. *Of course it's my real name.*

"And you know our connection?" Ben asked the question with a tremor, as if fearful Sento might give the wrong answer, or one that would dissatisfy him. She could no longer resist the inevitable. As she formed the words, the most important emotion was fear of displeasing him, of hurting him. That was the last thing she wanted to do. "You're my father."

"I've been waiting for more than two years to hear those words, Sento."

The artificial voice made the statement sound dull, instead of joyous. Sento anticipated a gush of emotion in herself, but none came. *Am I supposed to feel a surge of filial love? Dissing destroys the heart as well as the mind.* Perhaps it was the exo. Semi-robotic exo-skeletons were not uncommon, but nothing matched Ben's alien appearance, a combination of angel and insect. Despite the coolness of her feelings for her father—a dormant volcano takes time to build to an eruption—his use of her new name relaxed her. *He respects me enough to understand that I'm not the same woman I was two years ago.* "I have a sister."

"Yes. Her name is Elita Soares. She is First Citizen now."

"I don't have your surname, because…" Sento struggled with sorting out the memory. "Elita is my half-sister."

"Elita Soares is the daughter of my wife, who died many years ago. You are the daughter of a woman whom I loved very much, but could not marry."

Since the day she escaped from the warehouse in Valparaíso, Sento's life was a jumble of puzzle pieces that fit some days and not others, as if their edges changed with her moods and the random memories she recovered on her own. In the aftermath of the firefight, her memories began to fall into neat places, but they filled holes among the newer facts of her life, fashioned by the journey of the past months. A picture, though far from complete, was forming. Ben's description of her immediate family links resolved many of her questions and doubts. Her world was coming in to focus. Feeling a swell of energy, she rose from her cot.

"No, Sento, your recovery is only starting." Ben lifted a hand to prevent her from moving.

Sento brushed his hand aside. "Thank you, but I have to take care of my friends." Standing, she saw the others in the dome: Hosea, Bruce, Koi. The nurse that helped Sento tended to Gwen and the baby. Outside, pilgrims waited for care.

"Ben, how many died today?"

"Some bad injuries, but we were very lucky. Everyone survived."

"You weren't part of Galla's sortie."

"I've watched him carefully ever since I began to think that he had hurt you." Ben told her the story of her investigation, hesitating at times to offer too many details, as if fearing to overload his daughter. "When Galla discovered you were among the migrants, he waited for the opportunity to eliminate you as a personal threat, as well as drive the migrants away, which was what your sister wanted."

Why would my sister send us back north? "Galla told you all this?"

"No, but he's predictable in certain ways. I saw today coming, and we were ready."

"We?"

"The story would take too long right now. I'm asking that you trust me, Sento. You and your companions are among friends."

Sento assented. "Where is Galla now?"

"We lost him in the confusion, though he's almost certainly back in the city, possibly with Elita. He'll demand that she protect him."

"From what?"

"He has many enemies."

I'm his worst enemy. The thought troubled Sento. She did not want to make enemies, but Galla had gone beyond simple dislike, beyond active obstruction. He was a devil who first tried to erase her life, then take her life. He would try the latter again. *I have to be ready to kill him to defend myself.* She wondered if she knew how to pull a trigger sending a staser wave or a bullet into his chest.

Sento's minds-eye flickered and requested a re-boot. Bruce often restarted his jury-rigged local network and Sento automatically confirmed the request, but it was quickly apparent the result was unlike any she'd experienced, even in the large South American cities. "I'm seeing the Isorropian network, Ben. My lord, how do you cope with all this?" The subdural electronics updated and Sento was inundated with choices.

"You'll be surprised how fast you get used to it." A goggled man poked his head into the dome. Ben nodded. "My dear, can you call your leadership together?"

"Why?"

"You have a decision to make."

Sento spotted Bruce among the avatars and discovered that a pilgrim group was already set up, along with a subgroup containing Hosea, Gwen, and the others. Responding to a text from Sento, the leaders gathered in the dome. Many had found time to pore through the fresh clothes provided by the Isorropians, but the contrast between them and their new hosts was stark. It was as if people in the poorest *favela* were meeting with the richest capitalists of New York West. Gwen held Hosea's child, though she stood close to Bruce, a fresh dressing on the stump of his arm. The techie reveled in the new world of the Iso network. Koi, fresh-faced and bright-eyed, even after months of hardship, was welcomed as a leader, despite his dozen years. His influence on the pilgrims was stronger than ever. He was the one with the most faith in a god and in reaching the promised land awaiting them.

Sento edged close to Hosea. He stooped with exhaustion, the weight of his wife's suicide, and a massacre's near-miss, weighing on him. She wanted to touch him, but his vulnerability was raw.

Ben addressed the group. "My name is Ben Soares. I want to express my regret for how you were treated on your arrival, but as you've learned, you are not wanted by many Isorropians. My own daughter, the elected leader of our beautiful city, wants you to disappear, or at least return north. That's what led to today's violence. I'm sorry that I was unable to prevent that. I ask your forgiveness and understanding."

The pilgrim leaders listened politely, though Koi was fascinated by the otherworldly mien of Ben. "Do *you* want us to leave?"

The exo-skeleton supported neither a smile nor a frown, but Ben's eyes expressed pleasure in Koi's honest question. "If the people I represent had the power, we would throw open our city's doors to you. As things stand, however, we must be more discreet. This assumes, of course, that you want to come to Isorropia."

"But you say we're not welcome," Hosea said.

"A few weeks ago, I could not have helped you. But things are changing. The people have seen your suffering, and you have many friends in the city besides me."

"I don't think we have a choice," Bruce said to his companions. "We have a newborn baby. The supplies here wouldn't last for a trip back, even if we could carry it all."

"We would help with resupply," Ben said, "but the return journey would be no less arduous."

"My ministry is in Isorropia," Koi said. "Even if they keep the doors closed, I will stay here and live as a hermit."

Sento could no longer resist taking Hosea's hand. "I'll stay with you, no matter what you decide, Hosea."

Ben sat on a camp chair, as if he'd suffered a blow. "Sento—Marissa—I obviously can't force you to come home, but you're a citizen of Isorropia. You belong with your people."

The group turned to Sento. "Marissa?" Hosea's face puzzled. "What does he mean?"

Sento ignored the pilgrims' query. "Ben, you've risked a lot to find me and bring me home. You say that I'm Isorropian, but I don't feel it. I'm not sure what I feel, or where I belong, or who I am. For two years, I lived an isolated life. I only cared about one thing, moving south. Now I've become part of another community. These are my people too. I'm not going to say goodbye to them. It would be as if I'd been dissed all over again."

"Sento, you're scaring us," Gwen said.

"I'm sorry, Gwen, Hosea, all of you. I've never talked much about myself, because I knew so little. Artie Macedon told me a few things, but I wasn't sure if I believed him. I've only just learned about my past from Ben. He's my father, and… It's too much to explain now, but it doesn't matter. You're my friends, my family. I'm not leaving you."

The goggled man caught Ben's attention. The elder stood. "Time is short. You must decide. You can go into the city, but I can't guarantee your safety. Or you can decide to return north. Either way, I will do all I can to help."

Hosea straightened himself, again taking on the mantle of leader. Soon all the pilgrims were debating the choice. Ben and the people he'd brought with him from the city stood apart, listening, but not participating. The discussion did not take long.

"Mr Soares, we've come too far." Hosea spoke with Ben, Sento at his side. "The Warming has left us with nothing to go back to. We'll take our chances in Isorropia."

Sento saw tears in her father's eyes. He stepped to her and brushed her cheek with his exo-assisted hand. "You have my word that I will fight for you, no matter what, even if I have to leave my—my beautiful city. I won't lose you again."

Ben explained the plan and he instructed the pilgrims to take only what they could carry. Despite the loss of people and goods on the journey from Nordenskjöld, each of the tents and places carved out as temporary homes in the dome was heaped with belongings. They left the food and most of the water behind, though Gwen packed extra formula and water for the baby, whose potential name had become the main gossip in camp. It was a welcome distraction.

"It's a boy, but is there a male form of 'Awilda?'" Bruce said.

"Why saddle the child with the name of his mother? He needs his own name." Gwen turned to Hosea. "Is there a family name that gets passed down?"

Hosea shook his head. "I don't remember my parents saying anything."

"Something creative," Sento suggested. "Perseverance. Percy, for short."

"Daniel?" Koi said. "I feel like we're going into the lion's den."

"He survived," Hosea said.

"That's what I mean."

Sento thought of her own survival and perseverance, and realized that she could not have made it on her own to Isorropia. She would've starved or frozen to death on the ice. Every Don Quixote has his Sancho Panza to keep him alive and sane. Sento's companions were her saviors.

The pilgrims moved out under an overcast day, the air crisp and cold, with a light breeze. Each day, the sun dipped lower to the horizon as if reluctant to go into its annual hibernation. They walked in single file, following two of Ben's companions. They left behind four captives from Galla's troop, bound and gagged, not only their physical selves, but their digital selves. Ben apologized to them and promised rescue within a few hours, after the pilgrims were inside the city's defensive perimeters.

The three-hour hike followed a long curve around the city's illusion-generating wall. Sento fell into her old habit of ranging on the pilgrims' flank a few dozen meters distant. *I am my family's protector.* Stopping at an apparently random point, the goggled man concentrated on the wall and stepped forward, disappearing into thin air. The man had passed through a gate, like a sally port in the curtain wall of a medieval castle. Hosea, at his usual place in front, accompanied Ben into the portal, followed one-by-one by the pilgrims. A smiling woman encouraged each refugee, some of whom had second thoughts about their decision. By the time Sento passed through the gate, the hesitation had evaporated, and all the pilgrims were inside.

At first, the interior of the city appeared the same as the exterior. A plain of sunlit ice and wind-blown crystals stretched to the horizon, but when she reversed her view, the wall was a blank white shield that curved upward, letting in full sunlight. The horizon also appeared unnaturally near. It was another wall, as blank as the inside of the outer wall. "We're in a no-man's land," Sento said to herself.

"An outer bailey," Bruce said, taking up Sento's castle analogy. "With a few more defenses." He was the last pilgrim through the portal, and he pointed to an almost invisible shape nestled against the inside of the outer wall. "It reminds me of a pillbox from the early 20th century wars, but probably with computer-managed projectile weapons or a missile battery."

"Actually, a sophisticated robotic defense system," Ben said. "Isorropia is relatively small, as cities go, but we've found some ingenious force-multiplying techniques. For defense only."

"Don't the monitoring systems and personnel know we're here?"

"It's best you don't know the details, Sento, but we have friends who will ensure safe passage." Ben urged Sento and Bruce to join the line of pilgrims snaking towards the inner wall and another of the pillboxes. Filing through another door, the pilgrims gathered in a long, dimly lit corridor that curved along the inner wall. The corridor was wide enough for a phalanx of soldiers or a line of large vehicles. Ben reminded the pilgrims to stay together until they reached their destination, a gymnasium at one of the city's secondary schools. Sento heard the name, and recognized her own high school. "The gym is one of the city's protective public shelters in case of a siege," Ben said. "It's made of hardened concrete, and it's stocked with enough food, water, and supplies for six months. Our strategy assumes you'll be prisoners as the city decides what to do with you."

"Prisoners?" Sento said. *Are we going to be betrayed?*

Ben backtracked. "A poor word choice. You'll be detained, and you won't be able to leave the gym for a time. We believe the city will accept you once it's clear you're not a threat."

"How long will we be prisoners?" Sento said.

"Mr Soares already explained the risks at the dome camp," Hosea interrupted. "We all know what we're getting into. At this point, the worse that can happen is we'll be sent back to the dome."

I can't imagine anything worse, other than being shot.

"Ben, it's time to go," Hosea added.

"Very well."

At an unseen signal, the goggled man led the pilgrims down the corridor to a heavy carbo-steel double-door. Electric motors whined as the doors opened into a second, perpendicular corridor. The pilgrims descended a ramp into a chill, dark, bare-walled tunnel burrowed into the Antarctic ice and rock. Sento imagined a warren of tunnels under the city, highways for moving goods and people in an emergency, or hiding places, like the Underground in London during the German bombing of World War II.

The tunnel curved into an upward ramp, and the pilgrims emerged into a boreal forest. Ten-meter firs and spruces pulled the eye upward to the sky and the one-way transparency of the dome. Office and residential towers soared over the forest. Shafts of sunlight pierced the spaces between the trees, and Sento's feet crunched a thin litter of twigs and conifer needles. The fragrance of sap and mossy decay opened the floodgates of her memory.

Koi ran out in front of the pilgrims, dancing and jumping. "Rejoice! Rejoice! We have reached the new Jerusalem!" Several pilgrims followed him, their eyes drawn upward by the towering trees and buildings.

Sento did not feel the same jubilation as Koi, but a sense of peace seeped into her being. Old information mixed with new, but unlike the severe disorientation of earlier deluges, Sento navigated this new stream easily. She was like a traveler returning to a scene first visited as a child. Beyond the trees was an open space with a playground. It was late evening, and no children crawled over the climbers or chased their parents on the grass by the seesaws.

"Do you remember the park, Sento?" Ben was next to his daughter. "I brought you here a few times."

On her fifth birthday, she was climbing toys that imitated the penguins and seals of the continent, as well as polar bears, never native to Antarctica. Ben was wearing his first, newly acquired exo-skeleton, and he had the awkwardness of a working man in formal clothes. A sensitive child, she knew his limitations, and she didn't push too hard when he turned down her invitations to climb into the miniature castle. She was happy to have him to herself for an afternoon, until his job called him away again. Ben asked after her mother, and Marissa scolded, "You saw her this morning. She's fine."

"I meant, how do you like living with her?"

"Are you going to live with us?" Marissa said.

"I have to take care of your sister. Your mother and I agreed that all four of us living together wouldn't work."

Sento stood beneath a Douglass-fir, puzzled again at Ben's answer all those years ago. As a child, she saw her father so little, and her mother warned her against demanding too much from him. *He loves me, but he loves his city more than any person. That's what Mother said.* As a child, she accepted her mother's word. Now she doubted its truth. She compared the man in her childhood memory to the cyborg before her who had risked his place in Isorropia to save her. He had loved her then, and he loved her now. The thought broke down the final barriers to her feelings for him. He was a father at once distant and loving, who would stake everything on her survival.

"The next part of the trip is the riskiest," Ben said. "There's no direct route through the defense tunnels to the shelter, which means we have to travel above ground."

"We're conspicuous." Sento brushed away a twinge of shame. It wasn't fair to compare the weathered pilgrims to the cleanliness and order of a rich city.

"There's only one way to get a large group to another location in Isorropia quickly," Ben said.

"The rail system."

"You remembered. I'm so pleased."

The details surfaced as easily as the needles falling from the trees. *Artificial wind?* She called up the local map in her minds-eye and found the rail stop. The perspective gave her a view of the surrounding neighborhood. The main landmarks were Government Square, only a block from the park, the city's largest open space, and the Pynx. The minds-eye readout indicated activity in the square, but a text alert warned her to pay attention to Ben and the other guides.

"Ladies and gentlemen, in order to get to the train, we will have to cross about a hundred meters of open ground. Please move quickly and in good order. Our destination is just a few minutes away."

The instruction contained a tension Sento hadn't heard before. Ben's exo and artificial voice concealed more than she realized. He hadn't explained all the risks. The six men and women who accompanied Ben and guided the pilgrims spread out ahead of the group. Their nervousness, well-hidden to this point, was revealed when they lowered the hoods of their parkas and removed goggles and face protection. They scanned the forest, on the lookout for—Sento wasn't sure. She spied no weapons, even during the brief firefight at the dome camp, and whether they still carried guns or stasers wasn't apparent. She'd left her drained staser at the dome, but her pistol was in her holster.

The guides moved toward the rail stop, and Sento found herself again on the edge of the pilgrims, who had given up their single-file habit. Knowing safety was near, or fearing that safety was as distant as the camp at Nordenskjöld, they tramped in bunches. Sento's chest tightened, and she fought the urge to run. The pilgrims looked to her as a leader, and she forced herself to stay calm, despite the viral anxiety. Hosea followed the same rule, walking calmly if purposefully toward the rail stop. Of the adult leaders, Bruce had the least control, licking his lips and rubbing the palm of his one hand on his filthy clothing. Koi was in rapture, though he kept his eyes on the goal across the grassy field.

The mood darkened with the tattoo, almost a rumble, that came from the park's border. Sento felt it first in her feet. The sound competed with her quickening heartbeat, and she stopped to scope the area. The glint of full-faced helmets caught her eye, and she noticed a second troop approaching from the opposite side. A squad of black and green security bots accompanied them. By now, the pilgrims' rising panic boiled over. Starting as a trickle, then as a torrent, the pilgrims rushed toward the rail stop, but the distance was too great. The first troop of disciplined police cut off the lead pilgrims a handful of meters from the entrance, and before the pilgrims could retreat to the tunnel, the second troop blocked the way. They deployed from these positions to surround the pilgrims, as well as Ben and the guides. The pilgrims were bunched in the center. Ben and the guides were outside them. The police surrounded all.

Sento and Hosea, come to me. Though the emotion of text messages was hard to read if the sender didn't bother to attach an emotional signal, Ben's worry was clear. He needed support.

A forest-green uniformed police officer, in helmet and protective armor, stepped forward. Sento recognized the tulip patch of the Bureau of Environmental Security on his shoulder, though it was stylized in a way different from the patches she'd seen in South America. He approached Ben, limping slightly, straining to ignore Sento and Hosea. He halted and waited a few seconds, as if making a decision, or consulting a superior. He unstrapped his helmet and removed it.

"Galla," Ben said. The artificial tones of his voice underscored his contempt.

"First Citizen."

Sento stared at Galla's face. *This man tried to kill me.* Sento itched to draw her weapon, but the troopers, some of whom held staser rifles, persuaded her otherwise. Galla avoided Sento's gaze. *Is he afraid of me, or just avoiding a distraction?*

"What do you want, Galla?" Ben said.

"I'm executing an order."

"From whom?"

"First Citizen Soares."

Sento glanced at Ben. The exo couldn't hide the emotional pain darkening his slack face.

"Show me."

A brief pause signaled the exchange of a message or a shared document between the two men. A notification in Sento's minds-eye contained a link, which Sento opened. It was a sworn warrant.

"I'll give you credit for audacity, Galla. I expected you and Elita to detain these people once I brought them into the city, but arresting me in the open takes balls."

Elita, my sister, ordered this?

"You're a damn fool, Galla." Ben sighed. "You and Elita are not thinking clearly."

"I'd say it's you who aren't thinking clearly, Ben. You're so bent on getting your way with Elita that you defy the entire city. If I were you, I'd go into family therapy, after spending time in custody, of course."

Reacting to the insult, Ben leaned toward Galla, as if ready to spring on him. From Sento's perspective, Galla was almost shrinking. Though many of the details were still fuzzy, the outline of the agarwood smuggling case against the security chief surfaced in her mind. Ben was right to describe him as audacious. Confronting a powerful man in public suggested a desperation that had overcome the discipline that had made it difficult for Marissa Sentillius to build a case. *He's as panicked as the pilgrims.*

"You and Elita misjudged the city's mood, Galla. Look around you."

Except for the police and the pilgrims, the park was empty, but people gathered on the sidewalks and pedestrian thoroughfares that encircled the park. At first, Sento assumed they were like people who stop to stare at a traffic accident. The impression dissipated when she noticed a stream of them coming from Government Square. The crowd was driven by more than curiosity.

The officers in the police cordon faced the surrounded, bunched-up pilgrims, but the men and women in forest green looked over their shoulders at another, disorganized cordon six or seven citizens deep. The police and the crowd were separated by several meters, but the police could not fend off pressure from behind while at the same time detaining the pilgrims. Ben's height and his exo-skeleton made him easy to see from the crowd. All eyes were on him, looking for direction. *Are they his rescuing army?*

Sweat beaded at Galla's temples, but he was determined to carry on. "Where is Taft?"

Hosea stepped forward. "How do you know my name?" *Hosea never saw his face outside.* Sento took up her place next to him.

"I didn't ask for you." Galla finally acknowledged Sento's presence.

Ben growled. "Don't be an idiot, Galla."

"I'm the investigator you tried to diss. I'm the one who found you out." *You tried to kill me.*

Hosea glanced at Sento. *I still haven't explained everything to him.*

Galla hissed, but he ignored Sento's taunt. "Mr Taft, I am Lucius Galla of the BES. You and your party have entered Isorropia illegally. I'm authorized to detain you and immediately return you to the camp location outside the defense perimeter."

Voices among the pilgrims murmured. "Not again." "We won't go back." "Hosea, don't let him."

"My people won't follow your order willingly, Mr Galla," Hosea said.

"You tried that outside and failed. We have a newborn baby," Sento said. "Are you going to send him outside?"

Galla waved his hand, and the ring of troopers inched forward, tightening the noose. Murmuring surged through the Isorropian crowd.

Ben said, "Galla, if you're not careful, there'll be a riot."

"You're the cause of all this, Soares. You defied the Ecclesia and the people. You ignored legal orders from the First Citizen. You're a traitor to our values. Any blood will be on your hands."

Galla inched toward Hosea, who raised himself in a show of pride. Sento wasn't sure how she'd react if Galla touched him. At the last second, Galla switched targets and grabbed Ben's wrist. *He's provoking him.* The security chief underestimated Ben's reaction and his strength. He sent Galla sprawling on the ground. Laughter rippled through the Isorropians from Government Square. Galla got to his feet, and he reached for his staser, though he didn't pull it. "I wanted to avoid violence, Soares."

"Stop! Both of you!" A woman, on the cusp of middle age, pushed through the police cordon.

Galla backed up a step.

Ben whispered, "Lita."

Another puzzle piece fell into place for Sento. Her half-sister, shorter than her father by only a few centimeters, exuded a quiet, business-like charisma. She held herself in a guarded way in front of Ben, as if hiding a feeling of intimidation, while attempting to assert her authority. The younger woman recognized the shape of the face and lips of herself and her father, despite his exo-skeletal mask. The physical resemblance stopped there, but Elita's appearance at the scene sharpened Sento's returning sense of her true self. *My family. Together. Here. My father, my sister, and myself, for the first time in forever.*

"Father," Elita said, "I don't want to do this. No one wants to do this, but your plan has failed."

It's now Ben's time for a decision. Ben considered his older daughter with a mixture of pride and sorrow. In turn, he looked at Hosea, Elita, Lucius, and Sento. He scanned the crowd of pilgrims, police, and ordinary citizens. "Lita, I believe I'm doing the right thing, but I don't want any violence either. I'll go with you, into custody if you like, but you have to promise me."

"Promise what?"

"That you'll take care of these migrants, that you won't turn them out. You know what that would mean for them."

"That's not possible," Galla said, incredulous. "Remember what you've said, Elita. They're a threat to our security and values."

The remark upset Sento. "How can we be a threat? Look at us. We're exhausted, sick. Dozens have died. We've lost family and friends. How are we a threat to Iso?"

"You've changed, Marissa," Elita said. "You were as loyal and strong a citizen of our beautiful city as any, but you've lost your perspective. Our founders set us apart from the rest of the world. We're an exceptional people, living in balance with the earth, in harmony with each other, and we have to be very, very careful about who we allow in our community. Unfortunately, that doesn't include letting any random person into our midst."

"You'd condemn us to death on the ice?" Hosea said.

"I promised them I'd help them if they were turned away," Ben said.

Elita thought a moment. "I will keep that promise, Father, if you surrender peacefully."

"That's not good enough," Sento said. "I have changed, Ms Soares." Sento could not bring herself to say "Elita" or "Sister," especially as it became clear Galla was her ally. Blood is not always the deciding factor for loyalty. "You're morally bankrupt, despite your 'balance with the earth' talk. Maybe we're a threat because you've lost your empathy. Is 'love your neighbor' an alien concept to you? Human decency demands you help us."

"My job is to protect this city, not to debate philosophy with you. In case you don't remember, Isorropia's people govern, and *they've* decided you're a threat, not me." She swept her hand toward the crowd of citizens. "I'm only their instrument, but as I said, I'm willing to compromise: Ben Soares for safe conduct out of the city. I'll also resupply you and help you return to the beach camp in the north. That's a decent offer."

"Otherwise?" Hosea said.

"You'll suffer the consequences." Elita was firm and humorless. "You and your invaders."

Sento could hardly believe the woman standing before her shared half of her DNA with her father. Marissa remembered her half-sister as a distant, but friendly presence, an adult whom her father encouraged her to know. Elita had helped her make the school and job connections that got her a start in life, but the older woman rarely responded to Marissa's attempts to say thank-you. *Was Elita jealous, but loved me anyway?* Marissa was never sure, but Sento concluded that Elita's feelings for her younger sibling were fragile. *We share blood, but that's all.*

"Father," Elita repeated, "the city loves you, but you must make a decision."

"All I want is a chance for these people to start their lives afresh in our beautiful city," Ben said. "Isorropia may not be Utopia, but we can lead the planet into a better day. We start with compassion and openness. Elita, you make it sound as if a barbarian horde is following these people. There's no evidence of any such danger, but you've made up your mind." Ben glanced around. "And you have the guns." He turned to Hosea and Sento. "I'm sorry. The worse thing that could happen is bloodshed. You've suffered enough. I'll do everything I can to see that all your needs are met." Finally, he turned back to Elita. "Do what you need to do."

Elita tried to raise her eyes to her father, but she couldn't manage more than a fleeting look. "Lucius, I'm placing him in your care."

Galla licked his lips, but he controlled himself enough to call for a lieutenant to step forward. "I'm sorry, sir, but standard procedure calls for me to bind your hands."

Ben said nothing, but he extended his arms behind his back, touching his wrists. At this gesture, the citizen crowd beyond the police stirred again. The susurration had an ugly undertone. Sento braced herself. For what, she was unsure. The lieutenant locked the bindings and directed Ben toward a large van. With each step, the crowd's murmur increased, and the police cordon lost some of its military-style discipline.

A second later, a portion of the cordon moved inward, constricting the pilgrims. In her minds-eye, Sento received a text and audio message: This is the police. Remain calm. Officers will follow standard procedure and bind the hands of all adults and children over eight. You will be taken to a place of safety. Galla meant the dome camp, Sento knew, as did the pilgrims, who jostled each other as the police and bots approached. Sento stayed near Hosea and Gwen, who held the baby boy. Koi watched the proceedings, his face a mask of disbelief. Bruce sneered, his bandaged hand weeping again.

The baby starting crying. Even as an infant, he felt the fear and anger of the pilgrims, and perhaps sensed the malevolence of those who wanted to exile him just as he began life. A police officer reached out a hand toward him, and Gwen flinched. Hosea whispered a warning. Sento instinctively inched closer to block the officer, but he persisted. He touched the baby, perhaps accidentally, perhaps deliberately, but the effect was explosive. The child wailed, and as if on signal, the citizen crowd wailed as well. Individuals and small groups pushed on the remaining wall of officers, and the confrontation threatened to devolve into chaos. Some of the pilgrims, prompted by the crowd, pushed from the other direction, trapping the police officers. Themselves frightened, some fought back, pushing both groups of attackers with truncheons.

Ben called out for calm to both sides. Elita stepped back, but Galla took Ben's arm, releasing the lieutenant to reinforce the police line. The noise of shouting and shoving drowned out the audio messages coming into Sento's ears, and anxiety for her own safety was well as her friends made reading the stream of text warnings impossible. A tear gas canister detonated, but the cloud of gas drifted away from Sento. A staser discharged, and when she turned toward the sound, her father dropped to the ground. She yelled in shock and fright at the prospect of her father's killing. Galla stood over her father's inert body, staser in hand, police and pilgrims backing away. When her eyes and Galla's met, he raised the staser again. He was less than a meter away. He pointed it at her chest.

A policeman defending himself against the crowd bumped into Galla, and Sento dropped out of his aim. The line of police broke, and the crowd poured in. Galla was swept away, as were his lieutenant, Hosea, Gwen, the crying baby, Bruce, Koi, and Sento. The torrent flowed first one way than another, like waves bouncing off a sea wall, though Ben's body was as unmoved and immovable as an island of rock. Sento called out first to Ben, then to Hosea, as she avoided collisions with the boiling stew of Isorropians, pilgrims, and police. Elita was missing from the cauldron.

The randomness of the riot brought her face-to-face with Galla. She feared his staser, but his hands were empty, his staser somehow lost. He ran, and Sento ran after him as if she were programmed for it. The security chief pushed through the bodies as if pushing aside jungle underbrush, making a path for Sento to follow even as he tried to escape her. A gap opened in the crush, and Galla climbed over a concrete wall. Following, Sento found herself in the rail station, where the pilgrims planned to board for shelter at the school gym. Like jumping indoors out of a downpour, the sound switched from chaos to the echoes of an open space, save for the pounding of Galla's feet as he ran. His earlier limp vanished. Despite her borderline malnutrition, she stayed within a few meters of the man.

Like a predator on an open plain, she wanted only to bring Galla down. She flashed on the chase for the seal poacher, but like Galla, she had lost her weapon in the melee. She had only her bare hands and her wits to apprehend him, but that was fine with her. *I don't need a gun or a staser. I'll die first before I let him win this time.* Even as she focused on her prey, memories returned of sights and sounds around her. Buildings, corners, benches, road signs, business logos, all returned as landmarks of a familiar place. The final barriers from the failed disidentification fell away, and although she still thought of herself as Sento, her mission as an investigator for the Bureau of Environmental Security took an equal place in her new identity.

Galla kept ahead, but she was gaining ground, and nearly grabbed a handful of his uniform. He twisted through alleys and turned up sidewalks. Sento followed him into a cafe where he collided with a woman carrying drinks, sending her sprawling. Sento leaped over her, and slid into a wall, letting Galla gain a meter or two. He slowed when a cleaning bot failed to avoid him, and Sento came within centimeters of tackling him. During all this, he said nothing, either by voice or text, but Sento heard his labored breathing, even as her heart burst with the effort.

Sento didn't know how far they ran, perhaps a kilometer from the park as the crow flies, but as fast as the chase had started, it stopped. Galla had angled a final time, but his decision led him straight to a locked gate, with a wall to his left and an unclimbable fence to his right. Beyond the gate was a tunnel, but Galla yanked in frustration at the gate's handle. Sento halted, gasping, realizing he had run into a cul-de-sac. He was trapped. Above him was a neon seal's head, glowing blue. It snarled, but in a way to make you laugh. A stylized *Lions* hovered underneath the head. Sento didn't smile.

Everything now made sense to Sento. The inexplicable visions of disembodied, glowing blue heads of seals finally had meaning. Catching her breath, she strode toward Galla, himself gasping for oxygen. With each hand, she grasped his jacket, and he whimpered. She spat, "It was here, wasn't it?"

"Here?" Galla blinked in fear.

"You found me here. You trapped me here. You took me away from everything I was and everyone I loved."

"I don't know what you're—"

"Stop lying. Maybe it wasn't you, but it was people working for you, petty little mobsters you paid or threatened to get rid of me."

"I didn't have a choice."

"You were too much of a coward to kill me outright, maybe because of my father or Elita, but you thought dissing would do the trick. I'd be good as dead, wandering on an Old Continent, socially invisible, a walking ghost."

"I'm sorry." Galla coughed, and Sento saw tears, though whether they were from physical pain or terror, she couldn't tell.

"You won't get any forgiveness from me, especially after I saw what you did to my father."

"I didn't do anything."

"Fucking liar! You killed him. I saw you. Ten minutes ago. You stasered him."

"I don't know if he's dead. You don't know if he's dead."

The possibility pricked at Sento, but she shook if off. "Shut up! I saw him lying there."

"My staser discharged—"

"It doesn't matter, Galla. You thought you got rid of me, but you failed. I remember everything. Every detail, every ounce of evidence against you, every tiny bit of hypocrisy and every lie and *everything*." Sento pushed him against the gate, which rattled like a cage. The comical seal's head glowed above them.

"Lucius Ram Galla, I'm placing you under arrest for contributing to and profiting from the extinction of an endangered species."

Galla slumped to the pavement, tears falling from his sweating face. His bawling wasn't due to his capture, or pain from the run, or from guilt, though Sento doubted he had any feelings of remorse. He cried because of what awaited him, and it satisfied her with its justice.

CHAPTER 26

ELITA HOPED A PEACEFUL, UNEVENTFUL arrest of her father on legitimate grounds might swing the public's mood back to her. *Ben Soares broke the law, and he knew it.* Lucius' handling of the arrest ruined Elita's chances. Wading into the scene herself to negotiate was a desperate tactic, and it worked until Lucius behaved like a bull in a china shop. *To him, subtlety is a 500-kilo bomb instead of a 1,000-kilo bomb.* She had indulged him too much, but until then, he had a hold over her she couldn't explain, like a mother of an impulsive child she can't bring herself to punish for misbehavior. She couldn't, however, watch him every minute. After she withdrew to let Lucius handle the details, and as she spoke one-on-one to citizens gawking at the scene, Lucius had the temerity to shoot Ben.

At the end of the day, it was Lucius behind bars.

Her heels clicked on the concrete floor of the municipal jail, one of the oldest buildings in Isoroppia, and once an Antarctic research facility. Lucius occupied one of the half-dozen cells in a converted sub-basement carved out of Antarctica's granite. The guard shadowing Elita punched in the lock code to a steel door. A backup set of metal keys jangled on his waist.

Isorropia's now-suspended security chief looked up from his tab as he lay on his bunk. "Have you come to gawk at the manacled beast?"

Elita's throat closed on her, preventing an answer. It pained her to see him as a prisoner. For as long as she'd known Lucius Galla, she waffled back and forth between thinking of him as a toy and as a life-partner. That internal debate felt silly and wasteful as he rose to a seated position, his feet on the floor, his powerful arms and shoulders flexing under a jumpsuit. She fought an urge to rush to him and hold him in her arms.

Lucius glanced away, as if sensing her desire. He sighed. "Do you have to keep me here? It's like living in a tomb."

"Aren't they treating you well?" *I'd make you a nice dinner at home, if I could.*

"Like a condemned man." He laughed and nodded at the silent guard. "Good food, stimulating conversation, even a window to the outside world." On the wall, a screen specially made to transmit the same light spectrum as sunlight showed a view of Founders Park, a reminder of his last moments of freedom. "Frankly, I'd rather be in a BES holding cell. The air's better."

"The judge was specific. He wanted you here. Questions about security."

"He means I have too many friends over there who might help me escape." Lucius shrugged. "He's probably right." He yawned, as if bored. "How is your father?"

Elita flashed to the riot after Lucius shot Ben. A cocoon of citizens lifted his unconscious body, stiffened by the exo, to an AI-driven ambulance. Elita accompanied him to the hospital, but his exo-skeleton complicated the ER's resuscitation efforts. After 45 minutes of panic, they revived Ben, but the ordeal had nearly killed him. She was shooed away, and she hadn't seen him since.

"Father is at his apartment now, recuperating. I'm going to visit him later."

"Wish him well for me, will you?" Lucius folded his arms. "For what it's worth, I wasn't aiming at him."

"You were trying to kill Marissa."

"I've got to work on my aim. I missed her twice." He snickered.

How could I have hooked up with this man? The answer was simple: He made her feel good, and his attentions convinced her to ignore his venality. At this point, however, she could not ignore the possibility that he was lying, that he wanted to kill her father, as well as her sister. Feelings, however, cannot be switched off like a light, and a lingering ardor for him remained.

"I wanted to see you, Lucius." *It might be the last time we'll speak in private, more or less.*

"I think you ought to douse that torch you're carrying." The security chief would not meet Elita's gaze. He coughed and swallowed. "I'm not long for this world, though..." His voice trailed off.

"Lucius, you're the closest thing I've had to—"

"What? A mate? Spouse? More than lover? If I was to pick a word, I'd say 'consort.' A man to grace the arm of the queen. I tried to do more for you, out of ambition, and out of love. I do love you, you know. I'd kill your father to get you to love me."

"I can't love you, Lucius, not after what happened."

"I think you do, a little bit. Understandable if I'm wrong, given that you're partly responsible for his near-death experience." Lucius waved a finger at Elita. "I was carrying out your orders, remember? 'Arrest him,' you said." Lucius' tone was accusatory. "You always seem to forget your role in these affairs."

Am I really to blame? "I asked you to arrest him, not shoot him."

"A distinction without a difference, in my world."

"I'm not going to bicker with you, Lucius. I came to tell you that I've made a decision."

"A chance to exact revenge?"

"This is not about my father. That's bad enough, but it's not a capital crime. This is about the agarwood smuggling."

"Judge, jury and executioner, eh?"

"You know that's not how it works." *How do things really work?* Elita considered the truth. The law laid out the procedure for trying capital crimes, which Elita was bound to follow as the chief executive officer of Isorropia. Then there were the unspoken rules, the court of public opinion, the expectations of a public official, the consideration of political consequences, the judgment brought to bear on the consequences of an action on the public good. The two threads—legal and political—didn't always weave well.

What about the personal? A fire still burned in Elita. If she were less ambitious, less concerned with her future, less the daughter of Ben Soares, the greatest First Citizen of Isorropia since its founding, she would take the guard's staser and blow a hole in his chest and rush Lucius Galla out of jail and run away to, where? She had no idea. Isorropia was its own cosmos, existing in a bubble, real and imaginary. She did not know how to live anywhere else. Truth was, while some lovers could not imagine life without one another, she *could* imagine life without Lucius. The realization snuffed the remaining flames, though the ashes were as bitter as the polar winds.

Lucius wove the fingers of his hands behind his neck, like fleshy armor. "Let me summarize my situation. The UN has confirmed that the species of agarwood my business associates and I traded has officially gone extinct. The last sapling was cut five years ago. DNA taken from specimen trees in a natural history museum matched the DNA in incense traced to my activities. I didn't see much point to dissembling, so I confessed to everything. The gang has been rolled up. As this is a capital crime, there will be a trial, but I will almost certainly be convicted and sentenced to disidentification. The public will demand it. Nothing can save me."

"Except me," Elita said quietly.

"And you won't."

As First Citizen, Elita had the power to commute sentences. Every year, the First Citizen's office received appeals for clemency, mostly from petty criminals or juveniles. Her father had once commuted the disidentification of a single mother to 30 years imprisonment. She raised her infant son in prison.

"Let's hear it, then." Lucius stared at the ceiling. "What have you decided to do, or not do?"

Elita straightened her back. Her throat closed again. She could not say the words.

Lucius closed his eyes. He knew the choice she'd made. His affect changed from cynicism to supplication. "I've served Isorropia for 20 years. That must be worth something."

"Ordinarily, I'd agree." Elita's affect shifted as well. "But the stakes are higher than you think." She took refuge in rationalization. "Take a look at your tab." As First Citizen, Elita was one of the few people allowed to communicate with him electronically. "Play the recording, Lucius."

A starving man appeared, his sunken eyes full of desperation. "Why won't you answer my calls? You promised help to get us back to Nordenskjöld. I did what you wanted. I got the migrants to turn back. Not all of them, but I did my best. We're out of food and starving. Where are you?" The recording ended.

Elita said, "Enzo Ticino was a BES agent reporting directly to you. Records show that he sent this and several other messages to you and to me directly. You opened them."

"But you did not," Lucius said. "You ignored his pleas, too."

Elita was forced to the defensive. "I never saw these messages." *I truly did not see this, but no one would believe me if claimed as much in court.*

Lucius' eyes narrowed. "I get it. If this gets out, the official version of the breakaway pilgrims' deaths will be shown to be a lie coordinated by you. Any prosecutor could build a case of manslaughter against you with this evidence, maybe murder." Lucius grinned. "If she wanted to."

Elita willed her emotions for Lucius to heel.

"You've made terrible mistakes, Lucius. You must pay for them."

"Only blood will satisfy the mob. I can hear them: 'Galla must be dissed.'"

The bottom line was clear. No matter her feelings for Lucius, she must ignore the usual petition for clemency and sign his disidentification warrant. Otherwise, she would be lumped into Galla's criminal gang or accused of murdering the agent Ticino and his followers. That would mean giving up her career, her status, her life. The cost was too high.

Her discipline weakening, Elita struggled against tears. She had no option for saving her old lover and her future. One had to go.

I'll pray that the executioner's axe is sharp.

Sento reacted with a disturbing premonition to her father's summons, but she pushed down the awful speculations that crowded her mind like a pestilence. Only a few days had passed since the riot, and her father was sequestered in his home. The doctors allowed no visitors, not even Elita. Approaching his highrise in a pod car, Sento idled over the good wishes sent to Ben on the public com boards. Some asked him to consider running again for First Citizen, a slap at Sento's half-sister. Sento's trepidation had as much to do with Elita as her father; Isorropia's humiliated leader was also invited to his bedside.

As she learned about the political and personal tug-of-war between Elita and Ben, Sento decided her sister was not her friend.

It occurred to Sento that it would be the first time they would be together as a family in many years. Though virtually all of her memory had returned, she couldn't recall the last time the three of them had eaten a meal at the same table or shared a conversation, though the lack of recollection might be a remnant of her failed dissing. *Maybe that's why he wants to see us together. He wants to re-introduce his children to each other.*

The prospect made Sento tense, even irritable. When she told Hosea that Elita would be with her when she saw her father, she complained of her cold shoulder growing up, even when Sento tried to reach out to her. "I liked her when I was a kid, Hosea. I looked up to her, but she was so distant."

"You were a rival, Sen. Why give you a second thought?"

"I guess I shouldn't be surprised at her resistance to letting us into the city. Does she understand that we would've died?"

"It may not be that important. Your father himself might be the issue now."

Whispers swirled about his health, and a blanket of gloom had settled over the city.

Sento breathed out her tension. The municipal police—poor cousins of the BES—manned roadblocks to her father's building, though she couldn't imagine who'd want to harm him. He was nearly a god. Scattered knots of citizens milled about on the street, waiting for word. She flashed her reinstated BES identification at the police via her minds-eye. An officer touched the brim of his cap and waved her through.

The foyer of Ben's building had the atmosphere of a mausoleum. The private elevator's AI recognized Sento, and within a few seconds, she was at the entrance to his suite, the only one on the floor.

Her half-sister Elita opened the door.

This is the woman who nearly sent my friends and I to our deaths.

The milliseconds ticked off as the sisters took the measure of the other. Masking her anxiety, Sento was struck by Elita's practiced confidence, though the edges of her eyes betrayed an inner raggedness. *She's about to lose her lover.* She took no pleasure in Elita's pain. Sento imagined herself in Elita's place, about to lose Hosea, and her heart winced, though they were not lovers in the same sense as the First Citizen and her security chief. When the riot in Founders Park calmed down, and Galla was taken to jail, the refugees, including Sento, were housed in the high school, as they'd planned. Sento and Hosea talked for hours as she recovered more of her memories and he began to accept the loss of Awilda. His tenderness signaled a possible future, but his wounds were raw.

Without a word, Elita stepped aside to let in Sento, like a new servant uncertain of her job. Awkwardness, or humiliation, infused the gesture. "Do you remember Father's apartment, Marissa?"

Hearing her old name begged a negative response, but Sento let it pass. Instead, she took in the at-once familiar and strange apartment, its décor inspired by classic Scandinavian designs, though the front rooms felt more like a display case than a home. The air temperature was normal, but Sento was chilled, as much by Elita as by the sturdy, if faux, maple furniture. "I remember its sparseness."

"Nothing for drunken party guests or klutzy supplicants to knock over and break."

Elita's sarcasm confirmed Sento's disdain. "He was always a practical man."

As if ready to comment or tell an anecdote, Elita inhaled, but she stopped herself. She licked her dry lips. "Marissa, I..." She breathed out.

The elder woman reminded Sento of someone at a religious ceremony unfamiliar with the ritual. "Do you know why Father wanted to see us?" Sento said.

Elita was happy to answer a distracting question. "He's been unusually reticent, but I haven't heard anything alarming."

"He insisted on seeing us together."

"He can be inscrutable sometimes."

"Do you know where he is?"

"In his office, I suppose. It's like an artificial womb, warm and safe."

Sento's eyes climbed the stairs to the office suite.

"He told me he would let us know when he was ready." Elita paused. "Marissa, I'd like to say something to you."

"Okay." Sento tensed again, as if the premonition had returned.

"It may be hard to believe, coming from me, but I'm glad you're back, safe and sound."

Sento let her skepticism wash over her face. "To be honest, I don't believe you. If you included my friends in your statement, I might."

Elita face hardened. "I did what I thought was right for my city."

"Some people are saying you ordered Galla to attack us."

"He overreached his authority."

"Maybe I was the real motivation behind your resistance to letting the pilgrims come. Maybe you hate me because of what Father did to rescue me. Maybe he'd never do the same for you." Sento detected the pain in Elita's gaze. "I'm sorry. That was cruel."

"You don't know me." Elita's eyes blazed. "You don't know anything about how I feel about my father. So you shut the fuck up."

Sento's eyes fell. *It's true. I don't really know her. I never did.*

"Isn't it just possible that Father doesn't care about the refugees either? That it's all about you? Rescuing you at any cost? Even if it means the city dies?"

The idea hit Sento like an ice fall. Would Ben sacrifice a life's work building a city to save one person, even if it was his daughter? "That's not my father." *I'd try to protect Isorropia in the same way Elita did.*

"You think you know him, but you don't." Elita clenched her teeth, but looked away. "I thought I knew him. I thought he was my champion, but he fed me to the wolves. He abandoned me to find you."

In that moment, Sento saw Elita's loneliness. "You hate me."

"I don't hate you, but Father loves you more than what's good for him."

Life is full of fictions. Parents do not love their children equally, but they must say so. Occasionally the truth comes out.

I'm sorry to have kept you waiting. Won't you come upstairs?

Heeding Ben's text, Sento followed Elita up the stairs. Sento admired her sister's athletic figure under her casual, simple outfit. Sento had lost weight during the pilgrims' journey, but she already felt the steady return of her own health.

"Something's wrong," Elita said. Father, I don't see your avatar.

I'm in my bedroom, not my office.

Sento and Elita glanced at each other. His office, apart from the apartment's main room, was his most public space. His bedroom, however, was his most private. Neither sister had spent much time with him there, at least since they were small.

Come quickly.

The room resembled a laboratory more than a comfortable place for sleep and sex. Straightforward furniture hugged the walls under elegant wall-hangings and subdued art. Sunlight struggled to find a way through drapes covering a large window, which looked down on Government Square. The room, however, far from dark, was illuminated by the glowing lights of electronics, backed by a low hum. An auto-nurse attended Ben, though it was parked next to a console.

"Father!" The cry was Elita's, though Sento could've echoed the same disbelief.

In his shining exo-skeleton, Ben appeared to float just above his hospital-style bed, his body bent at the waist, as if propped up. He was surrounded by light that imitated the days-long dawn of an Antarctic sunrise, or the equally stretched twilight of a polar evening.

The women hesitated, like children introduced to a relative for the first time.

"I'm still in here. I won't bite."

Ben's humor broke the tension, and as Sento's eyes adjusted to the low-wattage atmosphere, she saw her father's familiar eyes, full of intelligence and curiosity. Elita touched Ben's hand, partly encased in the exo. Sento placed her hand in her father's as well. He closed his fingers gently over both his daughters', and for a moment, all three people were joined in a tactile embrace.

"Father," Elita said, "why didn't you tell us about this?"

Ben released his grip. "I wasn't certain. The doctors and the roboticists weren't certain, until yesterday. Or maybe I was in denial."

"But you're going to get better, aren't you?" Sento's plea was that of a girl, as much as an adult.

"Not likely. My bio-logics have artificial DNA, customized for me. Turns out they suffer mutations when stressed, the same as natural DNA. Everything fails, eventually."

"How did it happen?" Elita said. "Radiation?" More cosmic rays fell at the earth's poles than at the equator. Rays hitting DNA strands could cause a mutation.

"No one knows. I may have been sick for a long time, but..." His eyes broke contact with Elita.

"Father, what happened?" the First Citizen said.

"The staser blast. At the riot."

"Lucius?"

"The robotics people think the high energy impact might have accelerated the damage. It's only a guess, but the exo failed when I got to the hospital. I nearly died there."

Elita remembered the panic on the doctors' faces. She gripped the bed's low railing until her knuckles were white.

"I swore the docs and techs to secrecy, at least until we knew what happened." A sigh left Ben. "I know my role in this society. I wasn't ready to take responsibility for the consequences of my sudden death at the hands of your security chief."

Sento grasped Ben's meaning. No one in Isorropian history had assassinated a high official, or a former First Citizen. The city believed its form of government protected it from political violence. Ben's violent death would challenge this illusion, and the fact that Lucius killed him might cause chaos.

Horror reigned on Elita's face as she realized her own version of Ben's story. She would be blamed because of her relationships to Lucius. It would be seen as parricide by proxy, eliminating a rival by manipulating a lover.

"You bitch," Sento said, stepping away for her half-sister. "You and your henchman tried to kill me, and then you tried to kill Father."

"Stop, Sen." Ben's voice was hard.

"No, Father. I won't. She's a criminal, the same as Galla."

"Stop!" Ben's voice, despite his illness, broke through Sento's rage. "I don't blame her. This is not her fault."

"How can you say that, Father? Lucius Galla is her right hand. He does her bidding."

"Galla will pay for his crimes. Destroying an entire species is worse than killing one man."

"But you're her father. Our father."

"I'm still only an individual. I don't matter. Galla will suffer the judgment of Isorropia."

Elita had retreated to an upholstered chair, her graceful hands covering her face.

Sento approached her. "I owe Father my life. What do you have to say for yourself?"

Elita rose and pushed Sento aside, as if she were a nothing, and grasped her father's hand and arm. "I'm so sorry, Father. Lucius was out of control. If I'd known something like this would happen, I would've gotten rid of him long ago. He's crazy. Insane!" Tears flowed freely. "I love you, Father. All our little fights were stupid. They don't matter. I'd take back everything I've said and done against you if I could to fix you and everything."

With an effort, Ben brought his other exo'd hand and touched his elder daughter gently. "Lita, I can't be angry at you, at least for very long. I don't blame you. I forgive you."

The statement was nonsensical to Sento. "How can you do that? She's as venal as Galla."

"That's enough, Sen. I won't have you speaking about your sister in that way." Ben's eyes blazed. "I've forgiven her. I expect you to do the same, as far as hurting me is concerned."

"I won't. And I won't forgive her for trying to hurt me."

Elita hissed, "Wake up, little sister. Look at him! He's dying."

Sento knew it, but refused to admit it to herself. She'd seen death again and again on the road to Punta Arenas and the journey to Isorropia, but none who went to their graves were close to her, not even Awilda. The end was coming for her father, but Sento resisted. It flew in the face of the child's belief that a parent would live forever.

Ben's voice croaked, something Sento had never heard before. "I have to say this to both of you. I won't go to my grave with you fighting and hating each other. That's not why I've done what I've done."

Ben raised Elita so that the two women stood side-by-side. "I spent all my capital, everything I have, to find Sento and that meant bringing the refugees to the city. I never lied to you, Elita, about my belief that Isorropia should welcome strangers, but I wouldn't have fought you or undermined you if I hadn't known your sister was alive and well and coming home."

Ben's breath came hard.

"All I wanted was for us to be a family. To be together. That's all."

Sento thought she saw his chest rise and fall underneath the silver plate.

"You must forgive each other, for my sake, and the city's sake. I would never forgive myself knowing I was leaving this life with you at each others' throats."

Elita's tears had stopped. "You're forgetting something, Father." She gestured in Sento's direction. "How could I reconcile with her? You abandoned me for her. On the day she was born and forever after. You love her more!"

"No, my darling. This is what you never understood. I don't love her more. I love her differently."

Elita halted.

"Lita, you are impetuous, intelligent to a fault, and as passionate a protector of this city as any of the Founders. Sento, you are loyal, strong, empathetic, and humble. You are both a joy to me. I'm the luckiest man that has ever lived."

Sento wiped away her own tears.

"If there's any fault here, it's my own. Forgive me for all the mistakes I've made. I loved you both differently, but I didn't love you together as I should have. I've caused all the trouble, created the imbalance that nearly destroyed all three of us." He inhaled. "Help me find what I should've created a long time ago. Be loving sisters. Reconcile. Be a family after I'm gone."

How do you honor a dying man's wishes with someone whom you don't trust? Who may even want you dead? The elder woman crossed her arms and turned away from her father and sister. Sento wondered if Elita struggled with the same questions. Ben had asked forgiveness, and Sento could deny him nothing. That decision was an easy one to make. Could she forgive her sister? She would have to choose to believe that Lucius was the coward who tried to get rid of Sento, not Elita, despite her behavior toward her friends. Lucius would soon disappear, as her Father said. He was no longer a factor in her life, except as a memory, and Elita seemed to repudiate him. Even if she was lying, Lucius would still be gone soon.

Ben lay on his bed, his exo like a husk. For a moment, Sento thought he had already passed, but his color was not yet the gray of the dead. She approached her sister, who stood before the draped window, as if debating whether to open it and see what lay underneath the Antarctic sun. "Elita, Marissa is dead."

The elder sister raised her eyebrows.

"Yes, I'm standing here, but that person no longer exists. Lucius succeeded in part with his plan to make her disappear. I'm back, but as Sento. What I've experienced can't be taken away. I'm not the person I was."

Elita touched a control, and the drapes slid open, revealing the Isorropian skyline in the glow of Antarctic twilight.

"Marissa," Sento said, "might not forgive you, but I can. We're still blood. And when Father passes, the people will still need you. I promise to help however I can."

Elita stepped closer to the window. The panoramic view was framed by ice-capped mountains.

"Let's be friends, or at least not enemies," Sento said, "for Father's sake."

Sento watched her sister's face in profile, so much like her father's, and like her own. Elita struggled with her thoughts, glancing at Sento, Ben, and the city below. The First Citizen, Sento's half-sister, reached out her open hand to the younger woman. Sento took it, and Elita drew her closer, smiling slightly, almost in embarrassment, wrapping her arm in hers, saying nothing, and everything.

EPILOGUE

From the diary of Artemis Macedon

Ben Soares died a week after the riot in Founders Park. The coroner listed the cause of death as a failure of the devices that kept him alive and mobile, but the populace thought different. Lucius Galla killed him, they cried, on the orders of Elita Soares. Ben expected this, and when Elita made his will public, it included a message blaming Galla alone and asking the city to set aside an impulse for revenge. "Focus," he said, "on seeking ισορροπία for the earth, not for me."

I'm contemplating his funeral and his final, private message to me as I sit on this granite ledge in the Transantarctic Mountains—out of the wind, to be sure—looking toward the Pole. I'm struck by the utter peace of the plain stretching before me to the horizon. My mind is settling down, finally, after raging like a cocktail in a blender after I entered the city with the pilgrims. After so long in exile, I found Isorropia with the same sculptural quality to its buildings, the same orderly geometry of its streets, the same obsession with ecological balance, the same backbiting intrigue of its tribal politics, the same abundant hypocrisies. The city was as beautiful as ever, even as I knew its dark underbelly. After Ben's death, for all its pretensions of rationality, Isorropia was a city of rumors, suspicion, and dread.

The great man was interred in the center of the Pynx, the temple to Isorropian democracy he loved so much. Not one citizen stayed away. The procession from his home with his body took five hours to reach his resting place, normally a 20-minute walk. He was buried in his exo-skeleton, as much as part of him as his corrupted flesh. Elita Soares and Marissa Sentillius—though she insists on calling herself Sento—led the train, side by side. At first, the people were subdued, even hostile. After a time, however, applause, polite, then enthusiastic, spread through the crowds. Isorropia was moving on, except for one loose end.

Galla was tried in the Environmental Court, which met in the Pynx to accommodate the clamor for public access. Technically, I was still an officer in the Bureau of Environmental Security, and I provided my share of the evidence to the bessie investigators and the state prosecutor. I was doubly grateful for the greatest invention of western civilization—the hot shower—after meeting with these worthies. The metaphorical dirt on my psyche was centimeters thick.

The irony of the trial literally over Ben Soares' dead body was lost on no one. The proceeding seemed pointless; the frenzied mob had already convicted and sentenced him. If Galla had been released on a technicality, he wouldn't have got ten meters from the jail door before being skinned alive. The news chans covered the investigation and the trial to the point of absurdity without any semblance of fairness or balance. Demagogues claimed Galla was a spy planted by a cabal of carbon-addicted capitalists on the Old Continents. His few defenders said he was a scapegoat for the perpetrators of deeper, ill-defined conspiracies.

Sento testified at the trial as one of the investigators. She held the city spellbound with her story of her attempted disidentification and her journey to Iso. In the three months since her return, her strength, determination, and physical beauty made her a heroine in the public mind, rivaling her father's fame and esteem. I'll never forget one exchange between her and Galla's lawyer. "Do you hate Lucius Galla?" he said.

After a moment, she said, calmly, as if she were meditating. "Yes, I do. He raped my mind."

"And you want revenge?"

"I don't need to want it. The city will take care of that."

Sento knew the trial was not about her, though the illegal attempt at dissing her was among the charges against the disgraced security chief. It was about Galla's utter disregard for Isorropian values, about ισορροπία, about Isorropia's vision of itself.

I admired her pilgrim friends, who were always with her, at least one or two. Taking time off from his job in the hydroponic labs, Hosea Taft was in the gallery every day she was on the witness stand. Sento was always a reserved person, and she didn't show public affection for Hosea, but the way they stood next to each other, and the glances between them, signaled respect and friendship, perhaps love. The gossips predicted a marriage. No one who knew them was surprised. They'd spent several months together on the ice, and understood each other better than many married couples. I was happy for her. Gwen cared for Hosea's boy as if she were his grandmother, with Bruce keeping her company. Koi showed up at one of the trial sessions wearing a costume not unlike the habit worn by mendicant friars. A medieval chronicler might have called his affect "radiant."

The one thing that did surprise me was the relationship between Sento and her half-sister. I'd have thought they'd be mortal enemies, given their recent histories, but the gossip chans and even the serious journos mentioned how the disgraced First Citizen was already rehabilitating herself, often with Sento on her arm. During Galla's trial, Elita was in the gallery behind her sister, not her former lover. Her enemies called her behavior cynical, but the images and vids from parties and charity functions suggested a closeness that couldn't be faked, at least to me. Elita and Sento's effort at peace appeared sincere.

The social death sentence was a formality. Even so, all three thousand or so spectators in the Pnyx held their breath when the jury chair said the word "disidentification" for every capital charge in the indictment. The cameras zoomed into Galla's face as the sentence was read, and he seemed disconnected from what was going on around him. He was one of those few people who wore any clothes well, even an orange jumpsuit, but he looked as if he'd been disidentified already, especially that moment when the last vestiges of identity disappear and the face goes blank. He wouldn't give any interviews after the trial, and he didn't testify, so no one knew what he thought. After all the appeals were exhausted, he had one chance left to avoid dissing: Elita Soares.

The relationship between Galla and the First Citizen was an open secret, but she was not called to testify. The Minister of Justice worried the spectacle would damage the authority of her office. Galla's attorney argued she should recuse herself from ruling on his request for clemency. Afterward, insiders said she never spoke of bowing out. In public, she said her responsibilities overruled any personal considerations. She reveled in dissing her old lover out of spite, or perhaps she'd had enough of him, rumor-mongers declared. Conspiracy theorists speculated someone was blackmailing her into tossing Galla on the ice. Whatever the truth, Galla's request for clemency was denied and the date of his sentence set. Another rumor swept the city that Elita cried for days after her decision.

The actual disidentification procedure is a strange mix of public and secret. The felon is led into a room similar to a hospital operating room, though the law says a human must execute the ultimate sanction, not bots. The felon is asked for last words. Galla had none. Prepped with a sedative, he's strapped onto a table, and a chip is inserted behind the left eye. Chemicals enhance and reinforce the erasure. The procedure lasts an hour.

The streets were empty as people watched the social execution of a human being on all the chans, even the children's chan. At midnight, Lucius Ram Galla ceased to exist in the public and private record. An AI searched through the millions of documents and comments with his name and deleted them or the documents he signed, though legally issued orders remained in effect. His estate was liquidated and his debts paid. His name was never spoken again. For his part, he no longer knew his name.

I neglected to mention the welt. The surgeon injected a set of modified stem cells into his skull, just below the hairline. In a few months, raised bone in the shape of a tulip would mark him as a dissed man.

The next step was secret. A special unit of the BES took the still living and breathing Galla, *sans* identity, to a sally port in the defense perimeter. Disidentification is honed to the point where the man or woman knows how to survive, but has no sense of what they are or who they are. It's such an alien state that the psychiatrists and surgeons who invented the procedure can't describe it to an average individual. The BES unit opened the sally port door, directed Galla through it, and closed the door.

An hour later, I found him sitting on a rock. It was solstice day, and the sun had made its first appearance for the season. He stared at it, as if wondering what the great yellow light was, though he would say "the sun," if you asked. If you asked his name or where he was from, he would look at you as if you were speaking Sanskrit. I introduced myself, and told him to follow me. With no other choices, other than sitting in the same spot forever, he loped behind me like an adolescent puppy.

I was there because Ben Soares asked me. Three days before the disidentification procedure, I received a message notification. It startled me at first, until I learned that the latest fashion among the wealthy was an AI-enhanced post-mortem message to family and friends, a kind of reminder to remember the loved one. With its AI support, the dead could hold a conversation with the living. The image generated by the software was strong and eerie.

"Artie, what are you going to do now?"

"I'm going back outside," I said. "I've been back in the city for almost six months. I don't belong here."

"Are you sure? You saved my daughter's life. You saved all the pilgrims' lives. I'd take care of you, give you a job if you need it. You'd live well."

I didn't understand how an AI might take care of me, but a few things had changed in the two years I was gone. "No, thanks. I've made up my mind."

Ben sighed, a raspy, unnatural sound. "To tell you the truth, I guessed you would go back on the ice. It calls to some people."

He's right.

"Artie, I have one more favor to ask of you."

I was wary. Part of the reason I wanted to go back on the ice was to get away from everything I'd seen in the past year.

"It's a big favor, but I've been thinking. I'm probably going soft, but I dreamed that I had seen Galla's frozen body." He put a finger to his lips, though no sound ever came from that exo-covered mouth. "We're supposed to have evolved our society past the barbarism of execution, but sending him outside even with all the safety gear and food on the continent, is it's own kind of death sentence."

One more hypocrisy. "I'm not sure what I can do about that."

"Artie, I want you to watch over him, at least for a little while."

"Watch over him?"

"Like a guardian angel. Maybe take him up to one of the coastal settlements. Some people ignore the laws against talking or helping the dissed. The ferals ignore the disidentification laws. Maybe he could find a place with them. I want him to have a small chance at living for a while."

"Most dissed people only live a couple of years."

"I'd feel like a hypocrite if he froze to death a day after he was shoved out the door. Wouldn't you?"

Assuming Ben programmed this message before he died, he knew Galla would be convicted and dissed months ahead of the trial and sentence. A vague unease at his prescience muzzled my response to the AI. The conspiracy theorists might have been right all along. I stifled an urge to laugh in hysterics. In light of his foreknowledge, Ben's guilt was absurd, but I still felt as if I owed him. He promised, however, never to ask anything of me again.

It's possible that one or two humans have left footprints on this plain over the centuries. Maybe the ferals have crossed it, but they tend to hug the coast. I've learned to appreciate the solitude of the ice, the simplicity of living day-to-day, and even the freezing cold, which sharpens my senses and hones my attention. Maybe that's why the ferals haven't died off; they enjoy it too much, like an athlete loves the pain of pushing limits. The desert hermits of the early Christian church thought it easier to reach God in a sparse land. Reading about them, I recognized my life, despite the obvious physical differences between Sinai and Antarctica. For all intents and purposes, it's virgin land, as innocent as the driven snow, as my mother used to say. Human corruption, if any infected this place, is long healed, or covered over.

I am human, of course, guilty as any when it comes to error, as is my companion. Each day, the sun rises a little higher in the sky, and Galla watches it like a baby watches a spider. The arrogant, impulsive, self-aggrandizing Galla I knew is no longer there, otherwise I'd shove him off this cliff and cackle as he screamed on the way to his doom. Instead, I feel pity. No one wants to be pitied, but it's my own revenge.

AUTHOR'S NOTE

THANK YOU SO MUCH FOR reading *City of Ice and Dreams*. I sincerely hope you enjoyed it. Writing is a challenging and rewarding experience, and I'd like to hear your feedback. Please take a moment to review my book on Amazon, Goodreads, or your favorite book review site. You can follow me on Facebook (@AuthorJGFollansbee), Twitter (@Joe_Follansbee), and Instagram (@jgfollansbee). You can also follow me on my personal blog. Tell your friends!

City of Ice and Dreams is the second full-length novel in my dystopian thriller series, *Tales From A Warming Planet*. The first novel, *Carbon Run*, is available now on Amazon. Watch for the third full-length novel, *Restoration*, in the spring of 2018. You'll also enjoy the novelette *The Mother Earth Insurgency*, published in 2017. I will also publish a collection of stories under the title *The Mother Earth Insurgency* in 2018.

Thank you!

– Joe Follansbee, Fall 2017

PREVIEW CHAPTER 1 OF *RESTORATION*

People work in this upside-down pie tin?

Junie Wye rolled her eyes. She prepped herself for an about face and a run back to the public car that had dropped her off at the entrance to the derelict, saucer-shaped visitors center. She wanted nothing to do with the place, but the soles of her shoes, despite her raging desire to mount an escape back to San Francisco before it was too late, stuck to the stained sidewalk.

She couldn't disappoint her father. Turning up her classic Greek nose at the brutalist architecture, Junie imagined him directing workers to pry out the letters that once hung on the wall by the glass doors. Reversed shadows of unbleached concrete made the old name easy to read: "Arroyo Grande Reclamation Project." Removing the name was part of taking down the bone-white decommissioned dam looming behind the center. "It's one step toward fixing the planet," her dad said.

Why does Dad need me here? It's hot enough to bake something in the pie tin. I'll end up a cinder.

She knew why. Support. A shoulder to cry on, though he'd never put it that way. Control over a teenager. That was more like it. "Face-time matters," he said. She growled. *Bullshit.*

After two and a half days in the car, Junie was crabby from a rough night's sleep as the car's AI drove the 1,380 kilometers northeast to Utility. She would've arrived sooner, but she had to stop a couple of times to avoid feeling imprisoned in the two-seater. The countryside east of the Cascade Mountains was nothing but a sea of dust and sagebrush. A few orchards of apple and pear trees were an improbable green in this wasteland. She missed the home smell of ocean and cypress.

She'd rather be a million other places, but her father was right about one thing: The cinnamon-red basalt columns that rose in cliffs either side of the arroyo, like old-style bar codes, were breathtaking.

Sweating in the 43-degree heat, she cussed at forgetting her sun hat, and she fought an urge to retrieve it from the car, because she might climb back in and tell the AI to screw this place and take her back to her friends. She and Ed fought about it for days, but she promised him she'd come to Utility. *Dammit.* She had to, because she was 17 and still his responsibility, and he couldn't raise a child from 1,380 kilometers away. *Child? Who made up these stupid rules?* The day she turned 18, she swore to him, she'd steal money from her college fund, buy a plane ticket, and be back in time to entangle herself with Alex and watch the sunset from Golden Gate Park. She secretly hoped Ed would fail again, so she could go home sooner.

Fuck it if I don't love my dad and want him to be happy. And so I'm here.

Her surprise arrival was sweet revenge. Ed budgeted four days for the car and three days in hotels. He assumed Junie preferred to sleep in a bed rather than a public car's uncomfortable cot. Junie was outdoorsy in only a fair-weather way, despite a half-dozen summers at a Girl Scout camp in the Sierra Nevada. Rock climbing, hiking, gossiping, enough to last the rest of the year. *Maybe not gossiping.* It was true she preferred a mattress and sheets to a sleeping bag, but roughing it in the car was worth the chance to get to Utility a day early and see Ed go ape shit.

Pausing on the sidewalk, she shaded her eyes to study dark streaks on the looming dam's—*What's it called? Spillway. Where's the water?* A car with flashing yellow roof lights accelerated out of the nearby "authorized only" parking lot, teasing her curiosity. She watched the car for a few seconds as it raced toward the concrete monster like a police car chasing a robber. After half a kilometer or so, it halted among other vehicles with strobing lights.

Junie stepped through the glass doors into an arena-like open space under the pie tin's roof. The space was empty and deconstructed, as if a parasite had eaten out the interior, leaving a scattering of lonesome cubicles. The contrast between the desert air and the A/C in the building raised goose pimples on her butterscotch skin. She stepped up to a decrepit security bot.

"Excuse me, I'm here to see the project superintendent."

"Junie-girl!" Edward Malcolm Wye's baritone echoed in the cavern of the repurposed building. It seemed to add 10 centimeters to his 188, as well as his open-mouthed smile. Junie's heart melted and she rushed to her father, her tenny-runners silent on the bare concrete floor. Father and daughter hugged, and she took in the smell of his broadcloth shirt tinged with coffee and maple from his breakfast cereal. For a moment, she forgot her resentment of his demand that she move to Utility. For the moment, she let herself be his favorite only child.

She stood on tip-toe to kiss his cheek. "Surprise!"

"You're supposed to be here tomorrow." Ed wasn't angry, just a little nonplussed. "I've been in meetings all day, and I didn't think to check your progress."

"I didn't see any reason to wait, Dad."

"We're in an emerging situation, and I can't break away right now."

Junie had no idea what "emerging" meant, but she took satisfaction from flustering her father. The triumphant feeling faded quickly. He was working, and by the look of the people around him, doing something important. "Sorry, Dad."

"No, I'm glad you're here." He returned the kiss.

Ed made quick introductions for Junie: A well-dressed, if dowdy woman who was mayor of Utility, and a craggy-faced, calloused man who had to be at least 80 years old. *Culchies all.* After a minute of negotiation, the group allowed Junie to come along on a site tour.

God, it's like I'm on a boring field trip. Junie donned a safety vest and a hard-hat labeled "Visitor." Led by the mayor, the group made its way outside to an observation area on the southwest lip of the canyon spanned by the dam. The wooden platform was temporary, unlike the old public platform at the visitors center. Below was the answer to Junie's water question. *There's a brown shitload of it.*

It had been raining like crazy in Canada, the mayor said, and all that water was backed up on the cougher—*What?*—more than was planned for. Junie accessed Wikipedia via her minds-eye to look up the technical terms. The data appeared in her field of vision, though it was an illusion programmed into the implants behind her ear, which fed impulses directly to the occipital lobe of her brain.

Coffer: A watertight enclosure pumped dry to permit construction work below the waterline, as when building bridges or repairing a ship.

The mayor kept going, saying the sheet piling was at its limit and the diversion channel was maxed out. *Speak English, woman.*

Sheet piling: A form of driven piling using thin interlocking sheets of steel to obtain a continuous barrier in the ground.

Junie guessed that "diversion channel" meant the man-made cut in the rock that let off the pressure behind the coffer. Russet water from the upstream flood event surged at the temporary dam, reluctant to bend toward the diversion channel. The only thing between the pilings and the bone-dry, 200-year-old concrete of the Arroyo Grande Dam was the yawning space of the construction pit. The vehicles with the yellow flashing lights raced across the top of the dam.

Junie watched her father talk with the VIPs. He and the mayor were friends from when he grew up in Utility. She was the head of the committee looking at hiring Ed for the job. The old man was on the committee too. Her father was the only finalist who hadn't withdrawn, and he worried that he might not get another job offer for a long time. So much had gone wrong with his work since her mother died, even before. It was part of the reason she came to Utility. Ed needed her near, to know she was safe. *And a shoulder to cry on.*

A vibration shook the ground under Junie's feet. It felt strange, not like earthquakes in California. More like someone dropping a heavy piece of furniture. She texted Ed via her minds-eye: What's going on, Dad?

We're perfectly safe. He didn't attach an emotional signature to the text, but Junie sensed his apprehension.

A notification appeared in Junie's minds-eye. The local network was sending her a video, emblazoned with the tulip logo of the Bureau of Environmental Security. Part of the tour presentation, the moving image was a drone's-eye view of the dam.

No one has built a dam of this size in North America for a century. Most of the economically viable dam sites were used up by the 1960s, and their reservoirs are the source of 20 percent, maybe more, of man-made atmospheric methane. It's 84 times more potent than CO2 as a greenhouse gas.

The information was straight out of Junie's environmental history book.

If you take into account the ecosystem destruction, not to mention the extinct Columbia River salmon runs, and the main justifications for dams—hydropower, irrigation, and flood control—fall apart. The average atmospheric temp is up three degrees since the 20th century. The planet can't handle dams any longer. Arroyo Grande has to come down.

The old man growled and said something about "bessie propaganda."

Another notification interrupted the video. It ordered everyone away from the observation point, but no one in Junie's group moved when they saw the trouble below them. A section of the coffer bowed out like an infected pimple. The welds on the sheet piles had split. Geysers of water under pressure streamed through the broken seams.

Junie gripped the wooden rail as she saw workers on the pit floor tens of meters below scrambling to the single construction elevator. Water from the artificial lake held back by the coffer streamed into the pit. "Dad, those people will drown if they can't get out."

"There's enough time if they hurry." Her father's face was creased with worry.

Human-sized robots jumped off the coffer and scrambled to the dam's face, climbing U-shaped pieces of rebar pounded into the concrete. Junie thought they were good handholds, and some of the workers had the same idea, because they started up the dam face hand-over-hand. They tired quickly, stopping to rest as the bots passed them with little effort. A robot lost its grip and fell at least 50 meters, barely missing a man before it splashed into shallow water at the bottom of the pit. Pumps lifted the seepage water 50 meters, the coffer's height, and dumped the water back into the reservoir, but they were failing one-by-one. About halfway up the dam face, one of those platforms that window washers use on high rises rested against the concrete. Safety lines dangled from the top of the dam to the platform and below it. Workers at the top threw more lines down. Soon the lines draped like spaghetti and Junie worried they'd tangle.

"Dad, some of those lines aren't anchored properly." The climbing instructors at summer camp had drilled her in setting lines and triple-checking knot strength and quality. A poor knot was a prelude to a fall. Her father didn't respond to her observation. Junie was ready to jump down from the platform and fix the problems, but the near panic was like a barricade across a road. *I feel like I should do something.*

Several lines rubbed against the concrete as they swayed under the weight of the terrified workers. Junie watched with horror as one of the lines showed signs of parting. She turned to get her father's attention, but Eddie and the others were distracted by something Junie couldn't see.

Dad, these ropes aren't going to hold all those people.

The silence in reply to her warnings was maddening, as if she didn't exist. Seeing a coming disaster compounded by idiocy, Junie waved at the worker below her, pointing out the fraying lines. They ignored her as well, or they were too far away to hear. She was about to run over to her father to yank on his shirt like a toddler, but he and the others had disappeared, forgetting Junie on the platform. The scene below was chaos, as seams in the coffer opened up and let water gush into the pit. A chain link fence was the only barrier between the platform and the flat top of the dam, and the fabric was rusted and frayed.

To get to the workers on the dam top, she'd have to break the rules, trespassing in an area marked "Danger" and "No admittance" in signage and blinking warnings in her minds-eye. The unfamiliar working landscape was frightening in itself. She'd never visited a construction site before beyond the temporary office at previous projects where her dad worked. But nobody noticed, except her, the concrete cutting through the ropes like a dull saw.

What do I do? I have to help, but no one will listen. She'd seen a climbing accident once. One of the girls at camp didn't belay a line properly and it slipped. The climber fell only two meters, but her left leg shattered into a compound fracture. Junie imagined a worker falling twenty or thirty meters, and she closed her eyes to blot out the carnage.

Junie had to go down there and tell somebody what she saw, or one of those workers climbing the dam face was going to die. She climbed over the platform's makeshift railing and ruined her tenny-runners as she scrambled over the rock. Dust enveloped her as she stopped to push through an opening in the fence. Focused on the rescues, no one on the construction crew stopped her or called to her. She glanced around for robots patrolling the fence, but saw none. She hid the blaring warning in her minds-eye.

On the top of the dam, surrounded by heavy equipment and escaping robots folding themselves into storage, she waved her arms and yelled, again trying to get the attention of a man in a yellow, stained shirt. Junie grabbed his arm. He glanced first at his arm, then her. She didn't belong there, and he didn't expect her. He mouthed *What in h—*.

"Mister, there's a rope over there about to part." Junie pointed at the line that worried her. Robots and autonomous vehicles swerved around the pair. They argued for a minute, but Junie persuaded him to take a closer look. The fibers on the rope's outside layer had already worn to fuzz. The worker cussed and they peered over the edge. They saw a rowboat with a half-dozen people bobbing in the rising water. A few others clung to floating objects, like shipwrecked sailors. The worker shouted, and together, he and Junie pulled the line up.

Junie retied it properly around the base of an old lamp post. She asked for a knife, thinking to cut away the damaged portions of the line. The worker apologized as he handed her a pocket knife. She didn't have time to splice the line, and she wasn't sure how, in any case. She sat crossed-leg and thought back to the advanced climbing demos. She had the videos stored in her minds-eye account, but she didn't want to waste time searching. She gathered up the rope at the frayed point and tied an alpine butterfly, shortening the line, but taking the load off the weakened point. The worker watched in front of her on his haunches, while a drone floated overhead. They tested the knot, let the line back down, and someone grabbed it. The knot held perfectly.

Junie, what the hell are you doing? It was her father.

Putting that rock climbing experience to use. These guys have no idea what they're doing.

Get out of there before you hurt yourself.

You ought to be more worried about this project.

"Don't argue with me." Ed appeared out of nowhere, mad as a cornered cat. "Here hardly ten minutes and you're already making trouble. You!" He pointed at the worker. "Take her to the visitor center."

The worker was about to say something in defense of Junie, but her father stormed away. Meanwhile, the sound of metal scraping and tearing signaled the failure of the coffer, but as Junie watched the water pour through the breach, the last of the construction crew made it to safety, either at the top of the dam or above the water level. Men and women lay on the concrete sweating under a jury-rigged tarp. A few had passed out from the heat. Ambulances and fire trucks with rescue equipment arrived, lights and sirens blaring, but Junie didn't see anyone seriously hurt. Her escort was pulled aside by another supervisor and Junie reached out to a trundling robot carrying water bottles. She opened one and gulped it. She started handing them out to the exhausted.

The pandemonium eased as ambulances carried away the injured. She was exhausted herself and angry at her father and the other adults. At least the hapless worker mouthed an embarrassed "Thanks" as he lifted one end of a stretcher. She made her way to the visitors center parking lot and climbed into the public car, now surrounded by police cars and emergency vehicles, though no humans were in sight. Wiping the sweat and dust off her face and arms with a wet cloth, she darkened the windows of the car and changed into fresh clothes.

I don't want to be here.

She toyed with the idea of telling the car to take her home, back to the Bay Area and her boyfriend and her friends and real family. *If the kids my age are anything like the rubes here, I'll go completely crazy.* Her dad had yelled at her for trying to help after he ignored her warnings. That hurt. She thought her dad needed her, but now she wondered if she was just in the way. *If I hadn't been there, someone might have died, but no one cares.* When she was really pissed off at her father, she thought about her mother, wondering what she might say or do. It was easy to imagine soothing words from her or a sympathetic touch. *You had to die on El Capitan, didn't you? Why couldn't you die of old age, like everyone else?*

Junie told the car to reconfigure the seats to a cot, and she lay down with her arm over her eyes, hoping to keep the tears hidden, even from herself. After dozing a few minutes, she sighed, put the car seat back into normal travel mode, and ordered the windows back to transparency. She punched in a destination to the car's AI, and left the ridiculous pie-tin building behind.

Restoration *is scheduled for release in 2018.*

ALSO IN THE *TALES FROM A WARMING PLANET* SERIES

◆ ◆ ◆

The Mother Earth Insurgency: A Novelette

"Like all gifted sci-fi writers, Joe Follansbee extrapolates from the present to build an imaginative—and in this case action-packed—scenario for the future." – Joyce Yarrow, Pushcart Nominee and author of *Ask the Dead*

Buy now on Amazon!

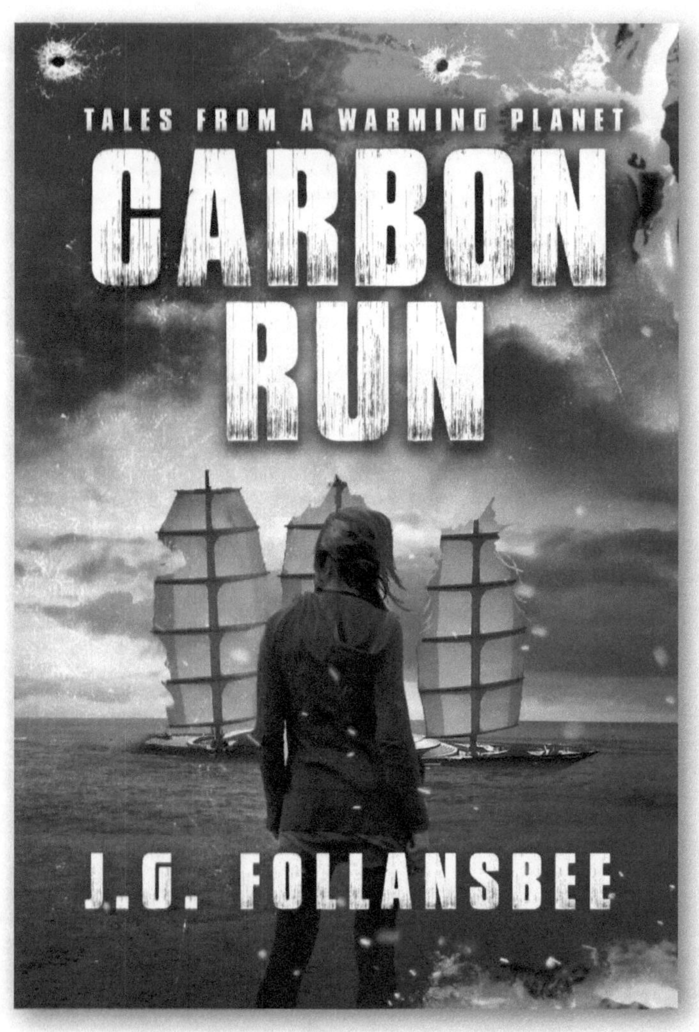

Carbon Run
"A very exciting read" (4.5 stars) — *A Page to Turn*
Buy now on Amazon!

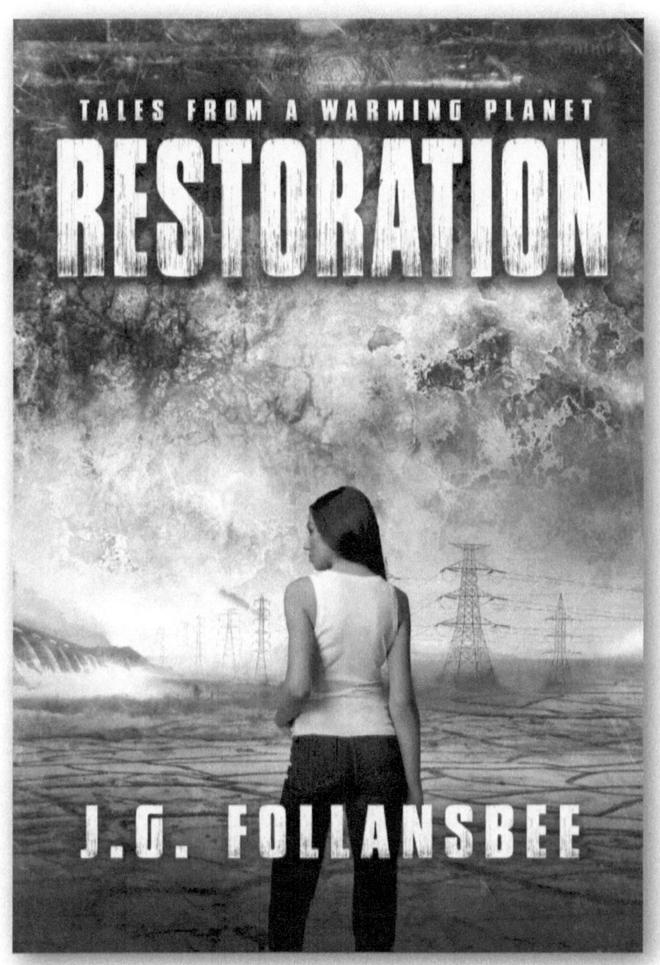

Restoration

Coming Spring 2018

The Mother Earth Insurgency: A Collection of Tales from a Warming Planet

(Spring 2018)

To get early information about release dates, visit my personal blog, http://joefollansbee.com, and sign up for my reader newsletter.

ABOUT THE AUTHOR

J.G. FOLLANSBEE IS THE AUTHOR of science fiction and speculative fiction novels set on an Earth and in a society transformed by climate change. A writer who publishes independently, Follansbee explores themes of survival, justice, and tolerance with strong female protagonists and antagonists. Mr. Follansbee supports meaningful clean energy and transportation policies that combat the damaging effects of climate change. He lives in Seattle.

www.ingramcontent.com/pod-product-compliance
Lightning Source LLC
Chambersburg PA
CBHW031613240626
47153CB00002B/738